a stone in the sea

A *Bleeding Stars* Novel

A.L. Jackson

First Edition

A.L. Jackson
www.aljacksonauthor.com
Cover Design by Mae I Design
Editing by Making Manuscripts
Interior Formatting by Kassi's Kandids Formatting

Print ISBN: 978-1-938404-91-7
eBook ISBN: 978-1-938404-87-0

a stone *in the* sea

dedication

To Amy's Angels and The Jackson Faction. Thank you for inspiring me to continue to do what I love to do! You make waking up each morning and coming to "work" a dream come true.

More from A.L. Jackson

The Regret Series
Lost to You
Take This Regret
If Forever Comes

The Closer to You Series
Come to Me Quietly
Come to Me Softly
Come to Me Recklessly (April 7, 2015)

Stand-Alone Novels
Pulled
When We Collide

Coming in 2015
Drowning to Breathe
Through the Storm

prologue

I DREW IN A THICK, soggy breath, and my boots sank into the damp sand as I met the shoreline. Humidity clung to the dark, endless sky, a dense mist hugging the surface of the ocean that seethed in the night, a toiling mess of beauty and contradiction. I lifted my face to the stars that stretched on forever, an eternal canopy that seemed too low yet impossible to touch.

Sometimes I wished I could reach through it to find all that had been lost.

Lights shone from the huge house on the hill behind me, life stretching its fingers out into the shadows, seeking a way to connect with my spirit, just as the tide raced in as if to embrace me. To wrap me in its arms and pull me under.

It didn't matter what sea I brushed up against.

He was always there.

Waiting for me.

I raised my arms out to my sides and welcomed him because I never wanted to let him go. Didn't ever want to forget. Wind pounded at my face, the taste of salt and sea filling my senses, and I remembered exactly why I was here.

What I was willing to protect, no matter the cost.

one

Sebastian

SAVANNAH. FUCKING. GEORGIA.

How the hell did I end up here?

I propped my hand against the molding encasing the floor-to-ceiling windows overlooking the Atlantic Ocean from the house we were staying on Tybee Island. In the daylight, it appeared peaceful and serene, a gentle rush of the tide as it staked its claim up the bank, then slowly rolled back out to sea.

"You okay?" Anthony asked from behind me.

The rest of the guys were still asleep, but I finally gave up on trying to catch even a wink when the sun came up.

I jerked my attention to where Anthony leaned up against the massive island in the center of the opulent kitchen. My brow got all twisted in an incredulous scowl, all of it directed at him. Anthony Di Pietro.

Sunder's agent, and one of the few people in this world who I actually liked.

Even though I couldn't look at him right now without feeling pissy and annoyed. This was the guy I trusted with the three things in this world that were important to me—my band, the guys in it, and my baby brother.

"No, I'm not okay. There's not one fucking thing okay with this, Anthony. Can they even do this?"

His shoulders lifted to his ears, and he puffed out a heavy breath with a slow shake of his head. "They can do whatever they want. They own you, Baz."

I bit off a bitter laugh. All my life I'd worked to make sure no one owned me. I'd thought it'd be music that would set me free. Then I'd just turned around and sold my soul to the devil.

"You know nothing right now is definitive," he continued. "It might be another warning, but you and I both know we're running out of strings to pull. You all made the right choice, coming here."

Turning around, I raked a hand over my face. "Still can't get my head around this shit."

Guilt got all messed up with the aggression I'd dealt with my entire life. The two combined were enough to strangle me. Yet another fucking disaster I'd gotten myself into. Only this time it affected everyone. But what was I supposed to do? Let that pompous asshole get away with what he'd done?

Hell no.

My chin took on a defiant set when I looked at Anthony. "I won't apologize for what I did."

He was a good guy, mid-forties, three kids he adored, a wife he adored more. Not many people had that kind of integrity in this industry.

Hell, not many people had that kind of integrity at all.

"I'm not asking you to. You think I don't know why you did it?" he asked, his voice coated with empathy, and I knew in my gut the guy completely understood. He tipped his head to the side and narrowed his eyes to prove a point. "But do you really want to broadcast that to the rest of the world?"

I attempted to swallow around the lump wedged at the base of my throat. "No."

He pushed off the island and began to pace, his dress shoes echoing on the marble floor. "You know I'll do everything in my power to put enough pressure on this guy to drop the charges, but in the meantime, you guys need to take advantage of the quiet. Write some music…do some recording. That's why you're here. You don't have to think of it as any other reason."

Looking to the high ceiling, I rubbed under my jaw, trying to keep my shit together. *Right.* Like this was just some kind of awesome retreat. Like we weren't here hiding away at Anthony's seaside mansion when we were supposed to be on our way to France for the start of our European tour.

Scheduling conflicts.

That's what we'd tweeted to the world to announce the cancellation.

And our fans were pissed.

No, we weren't the biggest band in the world. Our style was too dark and gritty and loud for the mainstream airways, but we had a huge-ass following, our shows selling out city after city, our songs downloaded at a rate that blew my mind.

We played and people listened.

But now even that was being threatened.

When I got slapped with assault charges and they yanked the tour sponsorship, Anthony had convinced us to come here. The bottom floor had a state-of-the-art recording studio, plus Anthony figured the place was so secluded and we were so far away from L.A., there was little chance of anyone recognizing us.

The rest of the guys knew why we were here.

Austin didn't.

The last thing he needed was another cross to bear.

Anthony pulled on his suit jacket, straightened his tie. "All of you just need to lie low for the next few weeks. Fitzgerald doesn't want you anywhere in the public eye. Not until Mylton Records decides if they're going to pull the label or not."

"Thought they ate up the punked-out drama." It was all a sneer.

It was good for image. That's what that greedy bastard Fitzgerald had said when he signed us, practically salivating at the mouth when he found out I had a record about ten miles long, and not the music kind.

Anthony curled up his own sarcastic grin. "Oh, you know how the saying goes, Baz…it's all fun and games until someone gets hurt. You start beating on industry execs and the industry is going to take note."

Yeah, and I'd do it again. Without hesitation. I'd always protect my own just like I always had. Scum like Jennings didn't deserve their next breath.

"You know this band has taken on a lot of heat, Baz. First your father, then Mark, and now this."

I tried not to flinch with the impact of hearing Mark's name, but it was there, like a bolt of fiery lightning. I ground my teeth against the pain. Couldn't even begin to go there. Not yet.

It was too raw.

Too fucking raw.

After Julian, I knew that kind of wound didn't heal.

On an exhale, Anthony set an almost pleading expression on his face, like he knew whatever he was getting ready to say was going to be met with resistance. "Just do what I ask for once, Baz. Stay here and pretend like this is exactly where you want to be."

This was the last place I wanted to be.

My voice was hard. "I've never run from shit I have to face."

"You're right, my friend. You just run the opposite direction…head first into it with fists flying. You need to take a step back and rein yourself in. I mean, God, Baz, you beat an executive producer to within in an inch of his life." He took a step forward and set his hand on my shoulder. "I know you, and I know all of this is killing you. But you've always stood up for everyone else in your life. It's time you stood up for yourself and took some time to deal with what's going on inside of you. Because if you don't? You're going to end up losing everything that's important to you and there won't be a damned thing in this world I can do to stop it."

My guts got all tied up in a hundred knots and nausea coiled in my stomach.

He squeezed my shoulder and tossed me a wry smile, doing his best to lighten the mood. "Come on, think of this as a vacation. Just keep your dick in your pants and your fists out of assholes' faces, and everything will turn out fine. I'm heading back to L.A. and I promise you I'll take care of this shit with Jennings, but I can't do it if you're here stirring up more trouble."

Trouble.

I almost snorted.

That shit followed *me* wherever I went. Didn't matter if I was here or in L.A.

Anthony's phone buzzed, and he swiped his finger over it and read the message. "My car's here." He tucked it in his suit jacket pocket. "I've got to get to the airport. I'll keep you posted on everything."

He grabbed his briefcase, adjusted it on his suitcase, and pulled it behind him through the large, open living area toward the double doors leading out front. He paused in the foyer and looked back at me.

"If you can't do this for yourself, then do it for the band. But know they love you, Baz. Don't doubt they understand why you did what you did even better than I do. None of them want to see a repeat of Mark. I'm not sure any one of you would survive it. And since Austin's your family, then he's their family, too."

Feeling like he'd just drop-kicked me in the stomach, I stood there in silence and watched Anthony walk out the door, the thought of losing Austin enough to weaken my knees. That kid was my life. My responsibility.

Sucking in a breath, I forced myself to move, turned around, and plodded up the large curved staircase so I could hit the shower. I froze when I rounded the top and found Austin huddled on the top step, fists gripping handfuls of light brown hair as he rocked with his head buried between his knees.

"Austin." I grabbed the railing to help myself kneel down in front of him. He'd just turned eighteen—was all legs and lanky body—had the same greyish-green eyes as mine, and his hair was shaggy and just as messy as the warped emotions that skewed his enigmatic thoughts. He was good, through and through, but held a heart so full of self-hatred he could see none of it.

He'd taken the blame that was mine and I'd spend the rest of my life erasing it from him.

"Austin," I called again, quieter this time, tugging at one of his hands that ripped at his hair. "Stop."

He shook his head almost violently. "It's my fault."

I grabbed him by the outside of his head, forcing him to look at me. "No. It's not. It's not." I dropped my forehead to his, pleading with him to believe it for once, my voice rough and shallow. "Not your fault."

two
Shea

DIM LIGHTS FILTERED DOWN from the high, exposed rafters of the old historic building, and flameless tabletop lamps flickered from the tall round tables and secluded high-backed booths. The yellowy glow clung to the dingy air, casting everything in a dusky fog. Still, it felt almost as if the night was set on fast motion, a projector beaming blips of indistinct faces and muffled voices through the packed bar, these stolen moments spinning by so quickly as people sought the reprieve found in this special place.

The cavernous room was always dark and seemed to hold a mystery, like a million secrets had been told here and the walls protected them in the safety of their arms.

Never had I imagined I'd come to make this place a piece of my own. The many grueling years spent priming and molding and shaping me for one singular goal, and yet my path had led me straight back here. *Irony.*

But I learned early on some things are much more important than any ambition.

I wound around the tables set up on the hardwood floor and made my way back to the gorgeous antique bar that sat like an island adrift in this sea of revelry. The massive oblong made a full circle, and besides the times when the stage was serving its purpose where it was positioned at the very far end of the colossal building, the bar commanded the focus of *Charlie's*.

I leaned my elbows on top of the dark polished wood. Even though I was tall, I always felt inclined to lift up on my toes, as if to match the lift of my voice. "Hey, Charlie," I shouted over the din of the noisy room, "I need a gin and tonic and two amber ales."

Charlie's back was to me as he hustled behind the bar. He reached up to grab several hurricane glasses from the bar racks suspended on chains from the high ceiling.

Over his shoulder, he shot me a crooked, bearded grin. "You got it, darlin'. Give me a sec to fill your last order. You've been firing 'em at me faster than I can fill 'em."

"That's because the place is packed tonight. I can't keep up, either."

With a short shake of his head, he spun around and began mixing drinks in front of me. "You keep up just fine. This place hasn't run so smooth in years…not until you came back to me." He sent me a wink and slid two drinks my direction, which I quickly arranged on my tray. "I was five minutes from shuttin' this place down until you came and rescued it."

I rolled my eyes at him affectionately.

"Oh, aren't you the charmer."

Always the charmer and always completely full of it. *Charlie's* had been a staple in Savannah for years, and he'd never been anywhere close to shutting it down.

Really, it was Charlie who had done the rescuing.

That charmer who scrambled around the gorgeous antique bar? He was also my uncle, my mother's brother. He was the only one who had been there for me when I didn't have anyone else to turn to, because everyone else had turned me away. He never once told me it was a waste or called it a mistake. He just encouraged me to live my life…on my own terms…terms that everyone else had previously tried to set for me.

Charlie stepped back and wiped his hands on a towel before he ran it over the bar top, eyebrow quirked as he cast me a teasing smile. "That's why you love me, Shea Bear."

The soft spot I'd always held for him glowed with the pet name he'd used for me since I was a little girl.

I balanced my tray in my hands and eyed him over the top of the bar. "I love you because you're the best, Charlie."

It was just a flash, but I saw it there in brown eyes the same as mine, that he cared for me just as much as I cared for him.

In my twenty-three years, I'd come to recognize there were three types of guys.

Maybe it was wrong of me to lump them into categories, but I'd learned to do it for my own self-preservation. As a way to survive in a world that wanted to use me up before it hung me out to dry.

First, there were the assholes. They were easy to spot. They were always after one thing and one thing only.

Pleasure.

It didn't matter if it was sex or money, fame or comfort. It all amounted to the same thing. Every move they made was purposed to bring them self-gratification and they were all too happy to reach out and take whatever they wanted to make it happen. Most of them didn't give a second thought to those they hurt in the process. Hell, they usually took a little more *pleasure* in doing it.

Then there were the nice guys. These guys were a little harder to read because they didn't set out to do people wrong. They were sweet and nice and treated you like a princess right up to the point when they didn't get what they wanted or after they'd had *their* fill of it. These guys would hit you with all kinds of valid excuses, rationalizing their actions to make themselves feel better. Half the time they left you feeling like you were the one who'd done something wrong in the first place.

Last, there were the good guys.

Guys with character. The ones who'd sacrifice for someone else, even if it meant it cost them something, or they had nothing to gain. Even if it meant the end result might not stack in their favor. They just did it because it was the right thing to do.

Charlie Cohns?

He was one of the good guys.

He gave me a little salute before he turned to grin at Tamar, one of the other bartenders, who slipped under the small opening at one end of the bar, arms full of bottles needing restocking. She was older than me by a year or two, had flaming red hair, and pretty much looked like a modern-day pin-up girl, all curves and tattoos and flawlessly applied makeup. Plus the girl took crap from no one. She was the perfect fit beside Charlie who was as casual as they came.

Her full red lips spread into a seductive smile. I was pretty sure she didn't know a different one. "I leave for five minutes and this guy is already slacking off? Get back to work, old man."

"Yeah, yeah, yeah." He cocked his head her direction, eyes on me, and mouthed, "Slave driver."

Laughing, I situated the last of the drinks Charlie had poured onto my tray. "Now Tamar is the real reason this bar is still afloat. You're lucky she headed east when she did."

"Now don't go fillin' this one's head any fuller than it already is. She already thinks she owns the place."

Tamar maneuvered to set the base of all the bottles on the far countertop, arms wrapped around them like she was hugging them. Glasses clanked as they settled, and she straightened up to her full five-foot-one stature. Her five-inch heels still didn't bring her close to Charlie's chin. She tossed her hair off her shoulder. "What do you mean, *think*?"

Charlie laughed and tossed a balled-up towel at her, which she snatched out of the air.

"Oh, I wouldn't dream of thinking *anything*, sugar. Now help me fill these orders. This old man is falling behind."

Somehow that smile turned soft and she went to work.

Without a doubt, it was Charlie who owned all of us.

Both Tamar and I loved him for it.

With my tray balanced, I moved back through the expanding crowd, smiling my most welcoming smile, and saying *excuse me* and *sorry* so I could shoulder through. Music blared from the speakers, all thanks to our sound guy Derrick. A local band was setting up on the stage. They played here often, always a big draw for Saturday nights, both for our regulars and the tourists looking for a good time after they'd spent a lazy day on the beach.

I dodged a few grabby hands from a group of college guys who'd clearly had too much to drink and were in danger of skating from nice guy zone straight into asshole territory, but I'd worked here long enough to know how to deal with them. I just grinned and let it slide right off my bare back.

I stopped at a couple of tables and dropped off drinks, grabbed the order from a group of younger women who had pulled two tables together to accommodate their party, and let my gaze wander to see if I'd missed anyone who needed attention in my section. It got stuck on the lone figure hidden away in the farthest corner booth who hadn't been sitting there the last time I made my rounds.

Weaving through the crowd, I edged toward him. Somehow my footsteps grew slower the closer I got. He wore a black beanie, his head down and his attention trained on his phone lit up in the backdrop of darkness. My eyes were drawn to his hands that held the expensive device, all big and strong, seeming to be just as powerful as this guy's presence. He wore a long-sleeved button-up shirt, the cuffs rolled up his forearms in a careless fashion, revealing intricate ink scrolled along his skin.

A knot of intrigue formed somewhere in my chest.

I was suddenly wishing to be closer, just so I could make out the design.

Even though people came here from all walks of life, young and old, country and rocker, bikers and businessmen, he still seemed to stick out, too vibrant to belong within the confines of these walls. And I hadn't even seen his face.

Inwardly, I rolled my eyes at myself. *Get a grip, Shea.*

Sucking in a breath, I pulled myself together and inched closer to the edge of the horse-shoe booth he was tucked behind. In a voice loud enough to cut through the music and jumble of voices, I gave him my standard greeting. "Hey there, welcome to *Charlie's*."

His hands gripped tighter on the phone when my words hit him, and it seemed to take him an eternity to lift his head, as if he were contemplating whether he really wanted to reveal himself.

And when he did, I kind of wished he hadn't.

For one rapturous second, time stood still as I got lost in a face that had to be the most beautiful I'd ever seen. It wasn't perfect, and maybe that was the problem. His full, full lips were a little crooked on one side, his cheekbones high and defined, his jaw severe—sharp angles—and coated in what had to be three days of scruff. A scar split through his right eyebrow, making it appear lower on that side, and there was a trace of another at the bottom of his chin.

But it was the hardness burning from his strange grey eyes that knocked the breath from my lungs.

No, not perfect.

Just beautiful and dark and a little bit frightening.

My heart thudded and I couldn't stop from taking a startled step back as a slow slide of attraction trickled beneath the surface of my skin—like feathers touching me everywhere—before it gathered to flutter low in my belly. Maybe it'd been far too long since I'd allowed a man to touch me, because all at once I felt the grip slipping on my own little reality. The reality where men didn't cause a reaction like this in me, because I knew better than to go looking for that kind of heartbreak.

No, I didn't have a bunch of priorities or concerns.

I had one.

I couldn't afford to flirt or play—not like normal women my age—couldn't risk the trouble a boy like this would most assuredly bring.

As if he'd want me after he knew, anyway.

The beautiful stranger's frown only deepened, and I felt like a total idiot standing there with my mouth hanging open, tongue-tied.

Blinking away the stupor, I swallowed hard and painted a smile on my face, knowing it probably appeared just as fake as it felt, but this guy had left me staggered, confused, and affected in a way I didn't necessarily like.

"What can I get for you?" I finally managed to say.

Those burning grey eyes narrowed in speculation, and not exactly in a friendly way. Waiting. As if he were waiting on me when I was the one who'd asked the question.

My own head tilted, searching him in the shadows in return, wondering what he was thinking, because he was looking at me as if he were expecting me to call him by name. Suddenly all of those years of self-consciousness came bounding in, and discomfort shifted my feet as I went cold with dread.

Did he recognize me?

It was rare, because I'd grown from a girl to a woman, and my once short, straight blonde hair was now long with wavy curls, woven with streaks of light browns and blondes.

Just when I was about to bolt and send over a different server, he leaned forward and scrubbed a hand over his face. "Uh…yeah…sorry. Gran Patron Platinum or Suprema. Neat."

That voice chased away all my worry. Eclipsing it in song. A rich, velvety sound filling up my ears and tickling my senses.

"Please," he said a little harder than the last, jarring me from the faraway place my mind had just gone. A smirk ticked up at the corner of his pretty, pretty mouth, like he knew precisely where my head had been.

God, this guy was dangerous. And had very expensive taste in tequila.

With one harsh shake of my head, I regained my composure, that feigned smile back in full force. "Sure thing. I'll be right back."

He only nodded, but his eyes softened a fraction.

Just like quicksand.

I wondered what it'd be like if I jumped in.

Tearing myself away before my mind had a chance to entertain any more ridiculous thoughts, I spun around and put some much-needed space between us. I stopped to check on a few other tables on the way back to the bar, all the while pretending I *couldn't* feel the heat of his stare penetrating me, or my spine tingling in awareness where his gaze traced along the skin exposed from the draping, backless fabric of my blouse.

When I returned with his drink, he mumbled a quiet, "Thank you," and I found myself having to force myself not to linger or stare, but couldn't help it when he kept those grey eyes trained on me and tipped the crystal to his pouty mouth, just enough to wet his lips. His tongue peeked out for a taste, and my knees went a little weak.

Good God, he was a sipper.

With shaky fingers, I touched my forehead and felt the heat there. Self-consciously, I tucked a thick lock of my long bangs behind my ear and did my best to clear the lump from my throat. Still, my voice was hoarse. "Let me know if there's anything else I can get for you," I said, fumbling as I backed away.

Every instinct told me I needed to run, that there was something about this beautiful stranger I couldn't resist. What scared me most was the intensity of his stare telling me that he knew exactly what I wouldn't be able to resist and he wouldn't be opposed to using it against me.

I almost breathed a sigh of relief when I found him gone the next time I made my rounds, a hundred-dollar bill trapped beneath the empty glass. However, the overwhelming rush of disappointment distorted the relief.

three
Sebastian

WHAT THE HELL AM I DOING?

I stood on the sidewalk outside the old building. People milled around, laughing as they hopped from bar to bar along the popular river walk, out drinking their cares away.

It was super late, close to two a.m., and the crowds were beginning to thin.

And I knew without a shadow of a doubt that I shouldn't be here.

Night clung to the sky like a blackened drape.

Oppressive and hot.

Like some kind of ominous warning telling me not to step through.

Maybe I was just looking to get laid, which was probably a damned good idea right about now, because maybe it'd undo the knot that'd had me wound up like a fucking kite all day.

But not here.

Because I was curious, and fucking curious and me usually turned out to be a bad combination.

Chewing at my lip, I leaned my shoulders back and craned my head to peer down the street, hoping for something else to catch my attention.

But whatever waited inside these old brick walls seemed way more interesting than anything else within a thousand-mile radius.

I pushed open the heavy doors to *Charlie's*.

Last night I'd come to get away and tonight I found there was nothing I could do to stay away.

It was darker inside than out, country music pumping from the overhead speakers, which was hardly my thing, but it fit right into the vibe that anyone could come here and find something they liked. Last night they were playing some classic rock right before the live band was supposed to come on.

Which was the reason I'd been here in the first place. Anthony had suggested it, told me about this bar on the river that had live music almost every night. He knew the owner, too, said he was a cool guy, and he frequented the place whenever in town. He figured it'd be right up my alley, a place for me to unwind and escape when I got all twitchy and itchy and just needed the one thing that ever brought me peace.

Music.

Whether I was playing it myself, or listening to someone else bring it alive.

So I'd come.

What I wasn't expecting was her.

That fucking gorgeous girl who'd swallowed me whole with just a glimpse. Last night I'd taken off because she'd left me unnerved and out of sorts, which I sure as hell wasn't accustomed to feeling.

Control.

Learned a long time ago that it's the only way to survive in this messed-up world.

And in five seconds flat, that girl had managed to make me feel like I was losing it.

So I'd jumped on my bike and hit the road—rode for hours with nowhere to go—with just the thoughts in my mind and the stirrings of a song fluttering somewhere in my subconscious as company. But even after I'd gone back to the beach house when it was nearing dawn and hashed out all those words on paper, there'd been no getting her off my mind. I had to see her again. Had to know if I'd been fucking hallucinating the strange connection I'd felt with her or if somehow it'd been real.

So here I was.

Curious.

Squinting, I allowed my eyesight to adjust. The place was busier than I expected just an hour before the town shut down for the night, but not packed like last night. My attention bounced around the room, seeking out the one thing I wanted to find.

My chest tightened when I did.

She was at the bar, leaning against it with her arms pressed to the top, talking to the older guy working behind it. Mounds of dark, wavy blonde curls, full and shiny and begging to have my hands wrapped in it, obstructed her face.

She had on a pair of frayed super-short cut-off jeans, which she wore with a pair of red scuffed-up cowgirl boots, showing off miles of long legs that were sleek and tanned, and suddenly had me questioning my control again.

Tonight she'd shed the flowy royal-blue blouse she'd worn yesterday in favor of a red tank top. It was a damned shame because I was dying to catch a glimpse of the creamy expanse of bare skin on her back that her shirt from last night had teased me with.

Everything about her was delicate—her slender arms and the graceful curve of her hips—elegant and soft and supple.

But somehow everything about her felt raw.

Something fierce bristling beneath all that delicious skin.

Her head tipped back and she laughed, too far away for me to hear, close enough to know I wanted to.

God, what was wrong with me? Apparently all the fresh air was fucking with my head.

On a sigh, I pushed away from the door and found the secluded spot in the very back where I'd sat last night. I sank down onto the blood-red velvet cushion, stretched my legs out in front of me, going for the most casual I could muster when I really had no idea what I hoped to gain by being here.

My phone buzzed from my front jeans pocket and I dug it out to read the text.

Zee.

You okay, man? You disappeared.

A small grin formed on my mouth. The Keeper. That's what I called him and he'd earned the title well. He was always checking up, worried about everyone but himself.

Yeah, just went to grab a drink.

His response was almost immediate. *Fine, dickhead, don't invite the rest of us. We're bored as hell over here.*

I chuckled and tapped out a reply. *Maybe I'm sick of all your faces.*

Two seconds later, my phone buzzed again. *Yet you drag our asses clear across the country.*

And just like last night, I felt her before she even spoke.

I froze with my fingers poised on my phone, ready to type out some snarky reply to one of my best friends, when awareness gripped me by the throat.

It was like she held some kind of power to command the hurricane that seemed to hover around her, cover her, protect her. An electric current sparking from her skin, something both dark and alive. Like she was projecting a warning to stay away, all the while sucking me right into the eye of a brewing storm.

Fear.

Whether it was hers or mine, I wasn't sure, but I sensed it, just as strongly as I did when I sat in this very spot last night. At first I'd mistaken it for that fucked-up type of love and admiration ascribed to those who've not earned it. Love of a voice that was never really heard. Love of a face that was never really seen.

You'd think I'd be used to it by now. But with her? When I'd looked up to see that gorgeous face twist up in shock, her hands shaking and some kind of confused desire flaring in her eyes, all it'd done was piss me off. Every inch of me had hardened, most notably my dick and my jaw, because the girl had to be the hottest thing both east *and* west of the Mississippi, and then I'd just been bracing for the downfall. That moment when a girl started squealing when she realized who I was, fawning all over me, trying to get a piece because that's just the way it was.

Everyone wanted a piece of Sebastian Stone.

I would have given her one, too, let her use me up. But I'd have used her up faster. A meaningless night wrapped up in long, long legs, all that golden hair and caramel eyes and a sugar mouth I was dying to taste.

I'd sat there silent, daring her. But she'd seemed lost in her own little daze, like she was really trying to see inside *me* and not the guy everyone else pretended to know.

It'd become clear quickly she had no idea who I was. And I guess that's why I was here. There was something incredibly appealing about her having no clue. It felt good that she wasn't looking at me like some sort of fucked-up prize, something to brag to her girlfriends about after she'd danced all over my dick. Something comforting in her not knowing the gossip and garbage that stewed around my name, that she didn't know the half-truths and straight-up lies.

Best of all, she didn't know the real truth, because that was so much worse than anything else someone could ever make up.

Slowly, my head lifted—like she had some kind of tether attached to it, her tugging soft and slow but greedy at the same time.

I met her eyes.

Caramel.

Sweet.

Kind.

Cautious.

Still they wandered, taking in my face, dropping to trace my arms, lingering on my hands. No. I hadn't been hallucinating. That same tension was palpable, dense and deep. Pulling me deeper.

Finally she focused back on me. "Hi," she said, everything about it self-conscious and adorable. "You're back."

I stretched out further, relaxing into the plush booth. "You remember me?"

Dropping her gaze, she raked her teeth over her bottom lip like she was searching for what she wanted to say, before she looked back at me with an incredulous grin lifted on one side of her mouth. "That was just last night…and you left me a fifty-dollar tip."

The last was almost an accusation.

A short chuckle rumbled from me. "What? Great service."

She rolled her eyes a little, her tone sarcastic. Playful. "Right. On one drink. That's the hardest I've worked in my entire life."

I shrugged. "It was nothing."

She studied me for a second, like she was trying to figure me out, before she softened. "Thank you."

It was honest and sincere and took me completely by surprise. Wasn't used to people thanking me for anything. I was used to them expecting something.

A lump grew in my throat, and that strange feeling was back in full force, a weight I couldn't decipher.

She looked away like she was trying to gather herself. A fake smile was plastered on her face when she returned her attention to me. She'd used it on me last night. A defense, like she wanted to hide. I had the overwhelming urge to reach out and smear it from her mouth with my thumb, smudge out all the counterfeit so she'd again watch me with the blatant curiosity I was watching her with now.

Because when she looked at me like that, I felt real.

"So what can I get for you tonight?"

You.

"Same as last night."

Her feigned smile faltered, replaced with a twitch of something genuine and amused. "Charlie's going to want to come shake your hand. Said he finally had a guy in here with good taste." That genuine smile spread, this time with a flash of white, straight teeth. "Really, I think it's just because he likes guys like you who can run up the bar tab."

She winked, and I squirmed.

God, this girl was something else.

"Charlie?"

"The owner…my uncle." She jerked her head toward the bar to the ratty, bearded guy slinging a drink while he talked to a couple of women tossing them back at the bar. "He's owned this place forever. Feels like I've worked for him for just as long."

"Huh," I said by way of acknowledgment, but really I was taking note of the guy who was Anthony's friend, wondering how much he knew.

Awkwardly, she stepped back and tucked a loose strand of hair behind her ear like she'd sensed my sudden unease. "Let me run and grab that for you. I'll be right back."

"Thanks."

It took her all of two minutes before she returned, sliding the drink my direction. I reached out to meet the action, brushing her hand as the glass came to a stop on the table in front of me.

Dark.

Light.

More.

Confused eyes darted to mine, and her body went rigid.

What the hell are you doing?

I heard her question without her asking it.

Truth was, I didn't fucking know why I was doing what I was doing. All I knew was I couldn't stop. All I knew was the curiosity that had brought me back here had turned to straight up want.

I swallowed hard, tipped the glass her direction. "Thank you."

I could feel her hand shaking as she slowly pulled away. "You're welcome."

She left me there to sip at my drink, the liquid burning as it slid down my throat and pooled like fire in my stomach.

Loved that feeling.

The way it soothed and hurt at the same time.

But tonight I wasn't entirely sure if it was the alcohol or this girl causing the effect, the way my limbs felt a little fumbly and my mouth felt dry. I watched her as she made her way around her tables, laughing lightly. Friendly. Real.

Fucking gorgeous.

Innocent.

Unaware.

Finally she made her way back to me. But she moved differently in my space, all that ease she floated around the room on ripped from beneath her feet, replaced with caution and concern, like she knew exactly what was on my mind and she wasn't sure if she trusted herself to be around me.

Wasn't sure I trusted myself either.

But here I was.

Curious.

Curious.

Curious.

"How are you doing over here?" she asked.

Eyeing her over the top of the glass, I took another sip. My tongue darted out to gather the moisture, the girl watching like she wanted to dip down and get a taste of the tequila coating my tongue.

Every ounce of blood in my body rushed and surged, my cock all too aware of the look on her face.

"Just fine."

She dropped a dishcloth to the table and began wiping it down.

Stalling.

Stalling.

Stalling.

"Long day?" she asked, peeking up at me with warm caramel eyes.

"Too long."

Another long fucking day. Worse than yesterday. Reality was finally setting in.

Caving in, really.

The entire day had been spent fretting about Austin, attempting to engage him in conversation like a normal family would, knowing we weren't anything close to *normal.* Hating what he'd overheard between Anthony and me. Worried he'd slip. All the while I'd worried about the guys who had to adjust to one more piece being knocked out of this busted-up band.

A world tour was huge and having it canceled was a blow none of us knew how to handle. All day, Ash had acted like a pussy bitch, moping and knocking shit around like a disgruntled teenager, while Lyrik stayed locked up in his room, strains of his guitar filtering through the enormous house. Only Zachary remained upbeat, because that was just his style, always trying to lift everyone up when he really should have been the one who was at their lowest.

Zachary, or Zee like he'd picked up when he was a kid, was Mark's little brother and he'd been eager to fill his brother's shoes when we lost him, whether to serve out some kind of penance or as a tribute, I wasn't sure. Either way, he did his best to try and erase the void Mark had left.

But those voids? You couldn't fill them.

I knew better than that.

Her eyes narrowed more. "Where are you from?"

For a second, I hesitated, before I cocked my head and draped my arms out across the back of the booth. "California." A thick lump gathered at the base of my throat, before I forced myself to say it. "I'm Sebastian. But my friends call me Baz."

As casual as could be, while inside I was fucking shaking, thinking saying it would clue her in. There was something desperate inside me that didn't want her to know who I was.

Like maybe for a few hours she could make me forget who I was.

Make me forget.

I waited as my introduction penetrated her, and there was zero recognition behind it. Instead her eyes flashed with a second's disappointment.

"Oh," she said, and there was no missing the lilt of her accent. "Well, it's nice to meet you Sebastian from California. I'm Shea."

This girl was country. Through and through. Pretty damned sure even if I uttered the name *Sunder* she'd have no clue what I was talking about.

Suddenly I was picturing her in a car, top down, blonde hair whipping all around her face while she gripped the steering wheel and belted out a Faith Hill song or some shit.

The thought made me smile.

"What are you grinning at?"

"You."

Heat gathered on her chest, raced up her neck to burn hot on her cheeks, and she was looking at me like she couldn't believe the statement I'd made.

And if it wasn't the cutest fucking thing I'd ever seen.

"Go out with me." The words were out before I could stop them.

And God, it was stupid, because I sure as hell wasn't looking for a *girl.* Didn't need or want that kind of trouble in my life. I had enough of it as it was. Ash and Lyrik fucked around all the time, ate up the girls who threw themselves at us after every show, and I'd be a liar if I said I hadn't taken advantage of that kind of situation on far too many occasions. But somehow about six months ago I'd gone and got stupid, hooked up with one of those Hollywood princesses with a too-bright smile, fake tits, and a starved-out body. Not that she wasn't pretty and fun, because she was, but she'd gone and bailed on me the second things went south. She told me I was a *publicity problem.*

She wanted the look but not the real thing.

Fuck that.

Sad thing was, I really didn't care. I didn't miss her or wonder where we would have ended up had I kept my cool instead of coming unhinged.

But Shea? This girl staring at me with those wide eyes? I wanted to escape into her layers, to skim along the surface, and get lost in the beauty. To feel the shyness. To sink beneath, deeper into that pent-up confusion and dark.

To feel her storm.

Just for a little while.

Make me forget.

Shea startled, before she shook her head, dropping it as she cleared away my spent drink and tossed a couple fresh napkins onto the table. "I don't really date."

I forced some kind of lightness into my voice. "Boyfriend?"

Disbelieving, amused laughter trickled from her. "Nope."

"Married? God, tell me you're not married." It was all flirt and tease, supplied by the relief I wasn't going to have to go around some fucker to get to her, because she wasn't wearing a ring and I was sure I already had the answer to that question.

She bit at her bottom lip, a little hard, the skin blanching beneath the firm hold of her teeth. The redness on her face throbbed. "No," she finally said.

"Then what?"

"I just don't have time for those kinds of distractions."

"It's not a distraction. Everyone has to eat."

With a small laugh, she shook her head a little, her tone sliding back into amusement. "You hardly look like the kind of guy who just wants dinner."

"Just dinner." I flashed her my best grin. "I won't bite."

Her gaze skidded all over me, across the ratted-out old concert tee stretched across my chest, tracing down over my arms covered in ink, slow to travel back to my face. The expression on hers told me she didn't believe me for a second.

"I promise," I said, knowing it was an absolute lie.

She shook her head with a wry smile. "As tempting as it is, I'm going to have to pass. I don't really make it a habit of going out with guys who show up at the bar." She shrugged a delicate bare shoulder, and my mouth watered. The only thing I wanted was a taste of that delicious skin.

"Bad for business, you know."

"Then I won't come back and I won't be your customer. How's that?"

She raised her eyebrows. "See…bad for business."

She was all feisty now, like a fucking cute little kitten swatting at the ball of yarn I kept rolling her way.

And I really, really wanted to play.

"I'll send in replacements…I know three or four guys I could coerce into taking my place. It's a win-win."

"You're ridiculous," she said, this time slanting a sweet smile my direction.

"Not ridiculous. I just know when I want something and I'm willing to put in the work to get it."

She took an almost imperceptible step back, but one I noticed, shuttering and shielding and throwing up all kinds of walls.

Shit. Apparently that was the wrong thing to say.

"Hey, I'm sorry. I didn't mean it that way."

"Didn't you?" she accused.

Damn. Okay. I had no fucking clue what I was doing right now, because I was one hundred percent out of my element. Wasn't lying when I said I never minded the work, but it wasn't usually required when it came to women.

She took another step away. I wanted to reach out and grab her. Stop her. Because I knew she was running away.

Stay.

Stay.

Stay.

She straightened herself out. "Listen, it's just about closing. Anything else I can get you before you go?"

I slumped back.

Fuck.

This was definitely not going like I expected it to.

"No. I'm good."

She turned and walked away from me. For a few minutes I sat there, wondering what in the hell I was doing. Contemplating why when she walked away, it felt like I was losing something. Finally, I climbed to my feet, crossed the now almost empty bar, and plodded down the dimly lit hallway, directed by the sign that read *Restrooms* inside a big pointing index finger.

Apparently drunk assholes needed a little extra help.

I took a piss, washed my hands, and ran my hands over my face as I stared at myself in the dingy mirror.

My eyes didn't even hint toward green. They were a roiling grey. Wild. Unsettled.

Wasn't used to strangers having the power to wind me so tight. Wasn't used to the uncontrolled adrenaline spike that slammed me when she came near, sending all this unfound anticipation firing through my nerves.

Though now it shivered through me like a high gone bad.

Shit.

Exhaling heavily, I stepped outside the restroom and into the long hallway.

Shea stood at the end of it, scribbling something onto a board hanging on the wall.

My lungs squeezed painfully, and that tension grew thick. Solid. Suffocating.

I felt her tense when she sensed me there, that invisible tether stretched taut between us straightening her spine, long hair swishing down her back.

Powerless to stop myself, I edged forward, unable to grasp the draw this girl held over me.

But it was there.

Unmistakable.

Irresistible.

The closer I got, the harder I breathed. Inhale. Exhale. Matching her. Matching me.

Her shoulders lifted and fell, anticipating, and I stopped only inches from my chest meeting her back. For the longest moment we stood there saying nothing, because the silence was too busy shouting a million questions neither of us had the answers to.

God, she smelled delicious, and I had the fundamental urge to get closer.

I lifted my hand, and my fingers grazed across the soft curls that bounced along the small of her back. My cautious touch skimmed up her side, barely brushing over her ribs, up, up, up as it swept under her arm still set to scrawl her pretty script on the whiteboard.

A small gasp shot from her when she realized the hold I had on her, the way my palm came up to rest at the center of her chest, right over her heart that thudded wildly against my touch.

Her body felt so delicate against all my hard—my cock and my heart and the muscles rippling in my arms as my hold tightened.

"Go out with me," I whispered at her ear. But this time it didn't sound so careless or aloof. It was *curious*. Filled with a primal need to figure out what *this* was.

The rush of chills sliding down her back was palpable, slipping into me.

She pressed her hand over mine, holding it closer. "I can't," she whispered just as low, though it sounded like it actually hurt her to force it from her mouth.

"Why?"

"You don't understand."

No, I definitely didn't.

"I like you."

"You don't even know me."

"Maybe I want to."

I hugged her a little closer in an attempt to change her mind—her sweet body tight up against mine—and I was sure

I hadn't felt anything so good in a long time. For the briefest moment, she let me, and God, if holding her didn't feel right. Like she was supposed to be there.

Then she untangled herself and took two steps forward, her shoulders slumped and her head dropped toward the ground.

Defeated.

Pausing, she looked back at me. Warily. With sadness? I wanted to wipe that look from those caramel eyes, eyes whose golden flecks glinted in the light above us.

Maybe that's why I was here, because I could feel her inner turmoil, something deep and dark, just like me, something hard and tainted that was searching for freedom.

I felt my control slip a little further.

I knew it then. What I wanted.

To lose control.

Just for a few hours.

And I wanted to lose it with her.

four

Shea

I SQUINTED THROUGH THE HAZE of light shed by the sagging lamp swinging from the low ceiling, peering over my shoulder deeper into the hallway where I'd left Baz staring back at me. I wanted to make sense of his expression. To make sense of the confusion and hunger smoldering in those strange grey eyes. To make sense of the crazy reaction he'd sent curling through every last one of my nerves.

This wasn't me.

Heart thundering, legs shaking, desire a constant throb right between my thighs.

Yet here I was, my senses on overload, all from a stranger's accosted touch in a dim, dank hallway. It wasn't as if I didn't get hit on all the time. It came with the territory of working at a bar. The alcohol-coated pick-up lines, things guys would never have the guts to say without the courage found in the bottles lined up behind the bar, too friendly hands, and leering eyes.

I'd always remained immune.

Until *him*.

Baz.

This guy who looked at me as if he wanted to sink inside me, searching for a place to drown.

I wanted to let him.

My eyes got stuck on the bob of his thick, strong neck when he swallowed. I knew he'd caught me when his jaw clenched and his hands fisted, before his body took on a confident swagger as he came toward me. He slowed, and his mouth brushed against my jawline that was still twisted his direction as he passed. "Until next time, Shea from Savannah."

His voice was like gravel and scraped across my skin.

God, I liked it.

Ripples of need surged through my veins. I stood there, trying to catch my breath as I slowly unfolded myself and watched him wind his way back to the hidden booth in the very corner of the bar. I was pretty sure I would forevermore think of it as his. Digging his wallet from his back pocket, he tossed another bill onto the table, which I had to assume was only going to be another outrageous example of this guy's oppressive presence.

Too big and strong and mysterious.

Was he trying to impress me?

I shook my head.

No.

Somehow I knew he had nothing to prove.

Exactly the opposite, actually. It was like this stranger was begging me to see beneath all that coarse, harsh beauty.

Guys like him had never been my style, if I even really had a style anymore. I never went for the boy who screamed trouble and heartache and a fast, hard, blinding bliss kind of ride before he ripped apart your little world when he left.

Didn't matter anyway.

Because what I'd told him was the truth. He didn't understand. And he wouldn't. They never did. And I didn't have time for those types of distractions. Because guys like him? That's the only thing they'd ever allow me to be.

On shaky feet, I forced myself to get back to work. I slipped out from the hallway, feeling another shudder roll through me when I caught the way Tamar was eyeing me when I ducked beneath the opening to the bar at the far end. I grabbed a towel and began scrubbing down the gleaming surface, head bowed, and pretending I couldn't feel the intensity radiating from both of Sebastian and Tamar.

But I couldn't help myself, and my gaze got drawn to the movement. In my periphery, I watched the shadowy figure make his way back through the twist of high-top tables toward the entrance. Was it sick that I was hit with the overwhelming urge to drop everything I was doing and follow?

He was tall, but not extremely so, maybe six feet, but it was the way he moved across the floor, the power behind his long stride and the ripple of corded muscles exposed in his arms that made him appear massive. A black tee was stretched across his wide, wide shoulders, snug where it clung to the strength of his back, gripping tight at his narrow waist.

God.

He was beautiful.

Glancing back, he pushed his hand through the longer pieces of brown hair that fell across his eye, and my hands felt shaky, fingers tingly, shattered with the need to be doing that myself.

Tamar stepped into my view, her vivid blue eyes filled with far too much interest. Subtly she cocked her head toward Baz, continuing to dry off the glass she held in her hand. "Who's your friend?"

I tore my gaze from Baz who'd stopped to look back at me and dismissed her with a shake of my head, diving back into wiping down the bar top. "Not my friend."

Even though I wasn't looking at her, I could still feel her judgmental eyes narrow into slits. "You certain about that? He sure seems to think so."

Humorless laughter seeped from me, and I lifted the container that held all the condiments and scrubbed under it before I set it back down. "Lots of guys think we're friends," I said with all the sarcasm I could muster.

"He seems to be the first one you're inclined to agree."

I stopped to look at her. "What?"

Red lips spread into a knowing smirk. "Oh, come on, Shea, you've been a jittery mess since the moment he came waltzing in here last night."

My mouth dropped open.

"What?" She repeated my question with a casual shrug. "I know you better than you think I do."

I wondered if that were possible.

She studied me for a moment, like she was trying to pry the real answer out of me. "So you know who he is?"

I lifted a shoulder, letting it propel my motion as I went to work on a sticky spill that had gathered behind a couple of bottles. "Who knows? Another tourist from California out looking for a good time."

Her dark, perfectly drawn eyebrows drew together in a fierce line. "You've never seen him before?"

"Nope. Not before yesterday."

Almost in disbelief, she shook her head slowly, then pursed her lips when she peeked over at Baz whose entire face turned fiery and hard when her attention landed on him.

I'd thought of him as dangerous. But right then? He looked a little terrifying.

What was with this guy?

She turned back to me. "Just be careful with him, okay?"

Baz's gaze locked on me for the longest moment before he pushed open the door and disappeared into the night.

Warily, I glanced back at Tamar who was staring at me, her expression pointed when I finally snapped out of my stupor. "Because he's going to be back."

And she was right. Over the next week, he came in three different times, each time sitting alone in his secluded corner. Each time he ordered one expensive drink and each time he left me an even larger tip.

Each time he talked with me like our words were the most casual in the world while the intensity brimming between us only seemed to grow.

And each time, he slipped a little deeper into my bones.

five
Sebastian

"ANTHONY, WHAT'S UP, MAN?" I asked with my phone pressed to my ear, standing at the large windows in the kitchen that looked out over the ocean. Even though it was fucking hotter than Hades out there, the humidity thick and suffocating, my gaze landed on the lone figure who sat along the shoreline, legs drawn up to his chest, a black sweatshirt with the hood pulled up over his head.

Austin.

Worry fisted my entire being.

"Baz, thanks for calling me back," Anthony said.

"You have news for me?"

I heard his hesitation through the line, then he blew out a breath. "I do, but I'm afraid it's not the good kind."

My nerves fired, and I began to pace, running my hand over the nape of my neck. "Let's hear it, then."

"Martin Jennings doesn't seem to be willing to flex on this. In fact, it's worse than we expected. He's filing a personal injury suit."

That son of a bitch was suing me?

I should have ended him when I had the chance.

"You've got to be fuckin' kidding me."

"Wish I was."

"What's he claiming?"

"He has the medical files. Broken jaw. Broken ribs. Facial lacerations. Multiple sutures. Extensive bruising. Of course they tacked on emotional trauma to that long list of injuries."

Emotional trauma? I'd show that douchebag *emotional trauma.*

"The good news is I talked with Kenny and he was able to facilitate a mediation with Jennings's attorney. We're still trying to figure all this out without it going to court."

Kenny Lane and I had become really *good* friends in the last couple of years, considering my attorney and my agent spent half their time trying to get my ass out of trouble.

"What's he asking for?"

"Two million."

"Fucking hell."

Figured. Those greedy industry assholes were all the same. Looking to live off someone else's dime. What the hell still didn't make any sense was him dragging my little brother right back into what he'd fought so hard to escape from in the first place. As much as Austin fought to deny it, I didn't question for a second that Jennings had been involved. I had seen him coming out of the trailer.

Saw it.

Knew it.

Felt it deep.

Punk kids like your brother aren't ever going to make it, anyway.

That's what that slimy bastard had said when I confronted him, right before he followed it up with a creepy smirk, and I'd lost my goddamned mind.

"Listen, you and I both know he's not going to squeeze that much out of you. He's starting high and knows he's going to have to settle."

"I don't owe him anything."

Anthony sighed, his own frustration traveling over the phone. "You think I want this guy to win even a cent of your money? Unless you want to come out with the reason for your assault, I don't have a lot of other options to make this go away. You've got to give something if you want to keep this quiet."

I looked out to my baby brother who sat still as a stone, the tide slowly making its way up the bank, like it was stretching toward him. Reaching for him. Begging for him.

And he just waited.

"What do I have to do?" I finally conceded. For Austin, I'd give it all.

"I'm going to need you back in L.A. on the seventeenth of next month. That gives you four weeks to figure out how much you want to give on this…what you want to say, and what you don't want to say. I can't stall them any longer than that, and if we can settle out of court on this, we may just be able to sway him into dropping the criminal charges." His voice got tight. "I'm not willing to let you go to jail for this, Baz. I'm not."

Scrubbing my hand over my face, I drew it down to yank at my chin, agitation tearing through me. This sucked.

No, it didn't just suck.

It was fucking ridiculous.

"Fine. I'll be there."

I could feel Anthony's relief carry all the way from California. "Good. I'm glad to hear you're being smart about this. I know it's not fair."

I grunted, and he was quick to change the subject. "So tell me how the guys are holding up."

"Everyone's…fine."

Antsy. Worried. But here and taking up my back, just like they promised me they always would.

"Are you all staying out of trouble?"

Cynical laughter rolled around in my chest. "Not a whole lot of trouble to be had in these parts, Anthony."

"Right," he countered, calling my bullshit. He knew I could find trouble wherever I went.

Sweet caramel eyes flitted through my mind. Long, long legs. Killer body with a cautious heart.

Dark. Light. Heavy. Soft.

Trouble.

Trouble.

Trouble.

I could feel it, yet I just kept going back for more, sitting in that isolated corner waiting on her to finally change her mind, just for a few hours, to *make me forget.*

Make me forget who I actually was.

"Everyone's hanging tight," I assured him.

"Good to hear. Let me know what else I can do. You know I'm here, whatever you need."

"Yeah, I know. Thanks, man."

He laughed lightly. "All just part of the job."

But we both knew he went far and above any duty he owed to the band. That he wasn't just our agent. A long time ago he started skirting right along the edges of becoming an honorary member of this fucked-up family. His house we'd descended on and taken over proved that.

Had to admit, it was awesome to have someone like him have our backs.

"I'll talk to you soon," he said.

"Yep. Take care." I ended the call and turned back to look out on where my little brother lifted his face to the glaring sun.

Shit.

I stepped through the glass-paned doors and out onto the deck. Rays of light cut through the sky, and I squinted my eyes against its harshness. My heavy boots thudded across the wooden planks as I treaded down the walkway, before they sank into the soft sand. Austin didn't look behind him as I approached, although it was clear he knew I was there. I settled down beside him, mirrored his pose by hugging my knees to my chest.

"How are you doing?" I asked, finally cutting through the silence straining between us.

He shrugged his too-skinny shoulders, his tone way less than enthused. "I'm alive."

I flinched and he dropped his head. "Sorry," he said toward the ground, dangling his hands between his knees.

"Don't do that to me, Austin. I can't lose you. Don't you get that? After everything? It'd kill me."

It was a load to put on his shoulders. But I needed him to know his value. That maybe it felt like this entire world was against him, but that didn't mean he wasn't the center of mine.

"Why? All I do is ruin shit."

"You've made mistakes. Just like the rest of us. It doesn't mean we love you any less."

He scoffed. "Right. Why don't you ask Dad how much he loves me?"

I shut down the growl that clamored around in my chest. That piece of shit didn't deserve to call Austin his son. "Wasn't talking about him. He doesn't love anyone." Not even himself. "I'm talking about me. The guys. None of us blames you for any of this."

He squeezed his hands into fists, puffed a breath out into the humid air. He turned to look at me with tormented grey eyes, dim and drained and full of despair. "I want to live up to that, Baz. I do. But I don't know if I know how."

"This isn't an issue of you living up to it. It's an issue of you accepting it."

His throat wobbled when he swallowed like he was trying to swallow down his emotion. "I'm trying."

"I know, man. I know." I climbed to my feet and clapped him on the shoulder. I faced the house while he stared out toward the sea. I knew he was lost in the same memories that would haunt both of us for the rest of our lives. "You can't live in the past anymore," I murmured quietly, gripping him tightly, like maybe it would help me get through to him.

He watched out over the cresting waves. "No? Then maybe I'll follow you out of it."

A shiver rolled down my spine at his insinuation.

Because it was Austin who didn't deserve to be stuck there.

Not when I was the one who belonged to it.

Ash flicked a bottle cap clear across the kitchen. Dude landed it in the garbage. He proceeded to down half the beer as he turned back to the rest of us who sat around the table, smacking his lips with a big *ah* when he slammed it down on the table, blue eyes filled with mischief. Just like they always were.

Amused, I shook my head at him and took a sip of my beer. "Anthony's gonna cut your balls off if you mess up his house. Better watch yourself."

"Nah…Anthony loves me. Besides, you know me better than to think I'm gonna miss."

"Oh, the skills you have."

Ash laughed. "Add it to my resume…awesome bass player, hot with the ladies, not so bad with words, so-so voice—kickass bottle cap flicker."

"Thinking awful highly of yourself there," I teased, pushing the sole of my shoe to his shin under the table, nudging him back.

He shrugged like the cocky asshole he was, and was doing his best not to bust up laughing. "What? I'm trying to be modest here."

I looked at him over my bottle that was poised at my mouth. "Right."

Lyrik stretched back in his chair, scratching at his bare stomach. "Come on, are we going to play or what? Deal some cards, man," he said, pointing at Ash, before he turned his finger to poke in Zee's direction. "I need to win my money back from this asshole."

"Yeah, man." Zee's entire face lifted with the challenge and he whacked both his hands on the tabletop. "Let's do this."

The guys were always giving each other shit. Constantly. But the four of us? We were family. Brothers. Didn't matter that we didn't have the same blood running through our veins. Loyalty ran thick, and I'd learned a long time ago sometimes that bond mattered more.

The three of them and my baby brother?

They were the only family I needed.

The only family I wanted.

Everyone threw their ante into the center of the table, while Ash shuffled and dealt.

Lyrik groaned when he picked up his cards.

"Looks like you've perfected that poker face." I lifted a brow, taunted him a little, because the guy couldn't win if he cheated.

He tossed his cards facedown on the table. "Damn it. I fold."

Zee cracked up. "God, dude, I'm going to own you in about ten minutes if you keep that up. You might as well pass over the pin to your bank account."

Lyrik leaned over the table and swatted Zee's cards out of his hand. "There…you lose this round, too."

"You're just pissed someone half your age is kicking your ass."

"Half my age?" Lyrik flew out of his chair, knocking it back, and lunged for Zee. "It's your ass that's getting kicked. You're going down, buddy."

Zee howled with laughter as he jumped from his chair and sprang back into the open area of the kitchen, bouncing around on his toes as he gestured with his hands for Lyrik to come and get him. The two of them boxed at each other, not really throwing blows, just messing around the way they always did.

"Come on, old man. You can do better than that," Zee taunted when he ducked and Lyrik's lazy punch landed nothing but air, and Ash and I were stifling our laughter at Zee's over-confidence, because there was no doubt Lyrik could take him down in a second flat. Dude was not one to be fucked with.

But Lyrik would let Zee get away with murder. Hell, he'd probably help him.

Of course Zee was only five years younger than the rest of us. Twenty-one. Sometimes it felt like he was ages younger, still filled with all kinds of wide-eyed innocence, like he hadn't yet come to accept the cold, hard truth of this world. You'd think after Mark, it would have hit him. But no. Here he was, living life to its fullest even when it threatened to suck the life out of the rest of us.

The two of them ended up on the floor, wrestling around like ten year olds, before Zee finally called "uncle".

"That's what I thought." Lyrik shot him a gloating grin and sat back on his haunches, while Zee pushed up to sitting, gasping for breath, then just turned around and dug it in a little more. "Still got all your money, asshole."

Like any of us needed to worry about *money*.

Ash started shuffling for another hand, before he slapped the deck down in frustration. "I'm about to go out of my mind over here. Let's get out of here. I can't stay holed up in this house any longer."

"Not sure that's the best idea." Since when had I become the voice of reason? But we hadn't been out as a group since we got here. Individually? Sure. But it seemed more conspicuous if the four of us went strutting around together, just begging for attention.

It was pretty clear that *voice of reason* was concerned about one person and one person only, the girl who still looked at me as if I was just a regular guy who'd walked in from off the streets.

"Why not? No one has even batted an eye my direction anytime I've run into town. I think we're good to go grab a drink. That's it. No fuckery," Ash reasoned.

Lyrik and Zee both nodded, and Lyrik spoke up. "Yeah, no worries, we'll keep it cool. We just need a breather from these walls before we go *redrum* on your ass."

I scrubbed my palm over my mouth, feeling put on the spot.

Zee looked at me, lifted his chin. "Where have you been sneaking off to every night? Something out there has to be interesting to keep your attention for this long."

Interesting.

That term didn't even come close to describing Shea.

I lifted a casual shoulder, while my blood pressure shot up by about a hundred points. "Nah. It's just a bar where Anthony hangs out at when he's in town. It's cool. There's usually live music."

"Hell, yeah. Let's go check it out. Anything is better than this," Lyrik said, climbing to his feet and flinging back the jet-black hair clinging to his face.

Ash stood and drained his beer. "Let's do it."

Zee grabbed the keys to the Suburban. "I'll drive."

Shit.

"Let me grab a shirt," Lyrik said before he ran upstairs, and I followed him, tapped at Austin's door. I cracked it open. "Hey, man, we're going to run into town and grab a drink. You good?"

Lying on his bed in the dark, he pulled his headphones from his ears and rolled his head back to look at me. "Yep. I'll be here."

I hesitated. "Call me if you need anything, okay?"

He smiled a tight smile. "I'm fine, Baz. Don't worry about me."

Like that would ever happen. But he was an adult and I couldn't go coddling him like a little kid anymore, as much as I wanted to.

"All right. Get some rest."

I clicked his door shut and bounded back downstairs. Excitement and dread were making a play for the win on my feelings. Excitement was rarely an emotion I was familiar with anymore, and it left me feeling all fidgety and on edge, not quite sure what to do with myself.

Everyone was gathered at the front door, ready to head out.

"I'm gonna take my bike. Need to clear my head." More like try to regain my cool. Here I was about to lead my loser friends off to invade my sanctuary. It was bad enough worrying about being discovered night after night.

It was that redheaded bartender that set me off-kilter. The girl screamed L.A. Every exposed inch of her, and I could only assume the sparse bit that she didn't put on display, was covered in tattoos, all leather and high-healed boots, snark painted all over her too-perfect face.

She stuck out in that bar worse than I did.

But it was the way she looked at me that had me betting she knew exactly who I was.

Still, she'd never called me out. She just watched me watching her girl, trying to get a read on me.

Was wondering if that rule would remain true when I paraded through the door with the entire crew in tow.

Zee's brow lifted in concern. "You sure you're fine to ride?"

The Keeper.

"Yeah, man, I've had half a beer. I'm good."

"All right then, we'll follow you out."

I felt a tug of dread, all mixed up with a barrel-load of eager anticipation.

SIX
Shea

I STRUGGLED TO BREAK THROUGH the bottleneck close to the stage, delivering some drinks at a couple of tables and taking the order at a few more. It was Saturday night and *Charlie's* was packed, which was common for a weekend, but especially so when *Carolina George* was playing. Their music was country, but took on a distinct pop edge. Their guitar player, Rick, was something to look at, and the women seemed to flock in just to stare at him all night. The singer, Emily, was completely gorgeous and had a voice that made me get a little lost in my thoughts.

I loved when they played, their songs leaving me feeling bittersweet, a sense of nostalgia locked deep in the center of my chest. It was both beautiful and upbeat, and brought people out in droves on the one night a month they played here.

I made my way back up to where Charlie, Tamar, and our weekend guy, Nathan, worked frantically to keep up with the six waitresses working the floor, plus the slew of people taking up the actual bar. There wasn't a single stool vacant.

I flashed a harried smile at Tamar and slid her the napkin where I'd jotted down my orders. "It's crazy out there."

She grinned, not missing a beat as she filled three chilled mugs from the tap, shaking up a cocktail in her left hand before she poured it over ice. "I love it when it's like this…the energy's so thick you can taste it. And when the band strikes up? It's going to get wild."

Playfully, I rolled my eyes. "I swear, you should be the one up there, the way you get all starry-eyed every time a band takes the stage."

"Why do you think I work here? Love the vibe." She shot me a wink. "But I can't sing to save my life. Believe me, we're all much safer with me slinging the drinks than trying to entertain." She set a drink in front of me and waved her hand dramatically around her. "I've met my calling."

"Thank God for that, because I'm not sure what we'd do without you."

"Hey now," Charlie cut in, knocking her in the shoulder with his as he moved around her and passing a couple beers to another server while looking at me. "What did I tell you about filling up this one's head any more?"

She swatted at him. "Oh, you hush, old man."

"You better watch yourself, Charlie," I warned, arranging drinks on my tray. "One of these days she's going to have enough of you and take off. Then what are you going to do?"

He slapped his hand across his chest. "And break my heart, like that? Tamar wouldn't dream of it."

She bumped him with her hip. "Keep it up, and you'll find out."

I began to tray the rest of my drinks, when the front door swung open for what had to be the millionth time that night. But this time, I took note. Because there was nothing else I could do. I couldn't stop the involuntary shudder that slipped down my spine in that moment when I felt compelled to glance to the right. He stood just inside the door, and his gorgeous face was caught up in a halo of light from the swinging lamp hanging from the rafters, all hard planes and shadows and mystery.

His presence sucked the air from the room and filled it with all his strange intensity, an overwhelming sense that I was shackled to him somehow, every rational part of me knowing I should stay away from him, yet all those silly, absurd, tingly places thrilling whenever he came near.

Something like butterflies scattered in my stomach, a jumble of frantic wings that fluttered hard and fast, taking flight in my veins. Soaring high. Dipping low.

Chemistry.

Is that what this was called?

I hated and loved it all at the same time. The rush of nerves he coaxed from me, the feeling he had control of my emotions, and there wasn't one single thing I could do about it.

Two days had passed since the last time he'd been here. Tonight, his absence had begun to wear on me, and each time the door swung open and it wasn't him, I was hit with a jolt of panic, struck with the fact I might never seeing him again. He didn't live here. That much was clear. Chances were, one day he'd just be *gone.*

As much as I knew it was dangerous thinking, I couldn't help the dread it caused. I'd begun to cling to these nights that had become something special. Something secluded and secret and forbidden that transpired at the very corner booth of this bar.

Something that only belonged to us when we were really nothing at all.

But there he was, staring at me. Usually he headed straight to his booth without acknowledging me, but he just stood there watching me, fully aware I was watching him.

Three guys stepped in behind him. A super tall guy with a shock of ebony hair said something to him. He nodded and said something back.

What the hell?

Funny how I'd come to think of him as his own entity.

A ship in the night that only I could see.

Alone.

Lonely, even. Just like me.

This only served to remind me how little I really knew about him.

"You've got to be shittin' me," Tamar muttered, just loud enough for me to hear. Her attention was trained on Baz and his friends who were gathered at the door, eyes scanning for a place to sit in the chaos abounding in the massive room.

"What?" I asked, almost having to shout.

She was super weird about Baz. Continually telling me to *be careful,* tracking him like she thought I wouldn't notice. But we both knew he'd been coming back for me. And we both knew I *liked* it, even though I refused to do anything about it.

Since the second night he'd been here, he hadn't asked me out again. He'd sit back in the plush booth—vibrant, larger than life, enough to cloud my head and stir up my heart—and talk to me as if it were the most casual thing in the world and he hadn't lit my body on fire in the hallway just days before. But beneath all his ease was a severe intensity, a magnetic force pulling me in.

Tamar looked at me with wide, incredulous eyes, before she shook her head like the four of them were the most shocking thing to ever have walked through *Charlie's* doors. "Nothing," she said with a short, disbelieving laugh and a quick shake of her head. "I'd just come to think your boy there was a loner."

"Not my boy."

"Right." She quirked a sassy grin. "The two of you have *me* feeling sexually frustrated watching you play cat and mouse night after night. I'm about to take matters into my own hands."

"You're gross."

She chuckled. "And you are blind." She grabbed a bottle of tequila and poured it across four shot glasses she had lined up. She glanced back up at me. "What are you waiting for? One of the other girls is going to grab them if you don't get your ass over there. Last thing I need is to deal with you pouting all night because someone stole your man."

I almost corrected her then bit my tongue.

Because when he was here?

Everything about it felt like he was my man.

I weaved my way through all the bodies, focusing on keeping the drinks balanced on my tray from sloshing while I was doing my best to keep my feet from falling out from under me. The way Baz was looking at me as I approached had energy vibrating me all the way to my bones. Like he wanted to devour every inch of me. With each step, my stomach flipped, and those butterflies took off in a mad frenzy.

Butterfly.

The thought gave me pause. A reminder of the one thing in this world that was truly important to me.

I edged forward, and my voice wavered a little when I said, "Hey," not sure if I should act like I knew him or pretend he didn't have my knees knocking.

My wary gaze was pulled to the guys he was with.

If I thought Baz was trouble before, I was sure of it now.

The four of them standing there together looked like they belonged on the cover of some heavy metal magazine, all of them covered in tattoos, wearing tight, tight jeans, torn-up Vans, something like mischief and malice strewn all over their attractive faces. They were all beautiful in their own destructive way. Each stuck out in this bar as if they'd been drawn in with the sole purpose of taking a hit on the ego of every other man in the bar.

But none of the other three were quite like Baz.

Because achieving that would be impossible.

His hands were shoved deep in the pockets of his jeans, the muscles in his forearms twitching with discomfort, and he rocked back on his heels. "Hey," he returned, hoisting up a shoulder without withdrawing his hands. "Brought some friends with me tonight."

Right. I hadn't *noticed.*

I lifted a brow. "Four?"

"Yep." He almost sounded like the fact irritated him.

Looking over my shoulder, I scanned my overflowing section near the stage. I'd just delivered a bill to an older couple who were getting ready to leave. "I should have a table opening up in a second. Let me go save it for you guys. Unless that's too close to the stage and you'd like to wait for something more *private* to open up?"

With that, I turned my attention to Baz, and a little smirk hinted at the corner of his pretty, pretty mouth, because we both knew I was talking about his spot. It was too busy tonight for me to be able to keep it open for him, unsure if he'd even show.

The shorter guy who was all kinds of dimples and wavy blond hair—and just cute enough to delude you into thinking he was less trouble than the rest of the guys—clapped Baz on the back. Blue eyes glinted at me, everything about him confident and cocky in an outright flirty way. "No, darlin', up close will do just fine."

My eyes darted to Baz, who was gnawing on the inside of his bottom lip, like he was debating whether to punch his friend in the throat or laugh at him.

Good Lord. I was going to have my hands full tonight.

"Okay then. Let me get it ready for you." I sucked in a calming breath when I turned away, thankful for the second to clear my head.

I delivered drinks to my tables, then fought to make my way toward the stage to the table the couple was leaving. Quickly I stacked the empties on my tray and wiped down the table. I waved the towel in the air to get Baz's attention, though I knew it was unnecessary. His heated gaze was already locked on me. He signaled his friends to follow and began to make his way through the throng. Though the waters seemed to part for him, not one person in the room exempt to the force of him and his friends.

"Thank you," he said under his breath as he pulled out a stool and took a spot at the high-top table.

"No problem."

He waited until the rest of the guys took their seats then lifted his hand in a casual gesture. "So I was telling my friends here about this cool bar down by the river that I'd come to a couple of times. They wanted to check it out."

"Ah. Well you picked the best night. One of my favorite bands is playing tonight." I let my eyes wander over the four of them. "Although I'm thinking it might not be your style."

The flirty one barked out a laugh. "What, you think we don't fit in?"

I quirked a teasing brow. "And you do?"

"Oh, sweetheart, I fit in anywhere I go. I'm Ash."

He shoved his hand out in front of him and I shook it. "Nice to meet you, Ash. I'm Shea."

Baz pointed at the super-tall black-haired guy. "This is Lyrik."

Lyrik tipped up his chin without saying anything, just scratched at it, flashing the tattoos that covered the back of his hand and bled down his knuckles. Everything about the guy seemed menacing, though he cast me a small smile to say hello.

Baz waved his hand at the guy who had to be a few years younger than the rest of them. His green eyes were bright and almost excited, and his shaggy brown hair seemed to fit his personality perfectly. "And this is Zee," Baz said.

Zee grinned. "It's a pleasure."

Ash tossed a playful glare at Baz. "And just how do you know our Beautiful Shea, here?"

Baz shrugged. "Like I said, I've stopped in a couple of times." He leveled his gaze on me, those strange grey eyes swimming in warmth yet still freezing cold, which seemed to pump me full of the confusion I'd been feeding from for the last two weeks. "This one's hard to forget."

My entire body flamed, red rushing up to grip my face. It was completely unexpected for him to compliment me this way in front of his friends. And Lord, I liked that, too.

Ash winked at me. "Ah. I see the draw of this place now."

I forced the lightness into my tone. "You mean the band that's getting ready to play?"

Laughter ripped from him. "Oh, I like you."

"So what can I get for y'all tonight?"

A wry grin spread across Ash's face. "Why don't you bring four shots of Jager for me and my boy Lyrik here?"

"Not messing around tonight, huh?" I asked, scribbling it down on a napkin.

"Nope. We've been cooped up for the last two weeks and we're ready for a little fun."

Huh.

I wanted to ask him more, but from the scowl that hit Baz's face, I figured it was none of my business.

Lyrik punched at Zee. "And bring this asshole a Coke. He's driving tonight." His eyes narrowed at the younger guy. "Payback, bitch."

Zee just cracked up. "Whatever, dude. If it makes you feel better about losing all your dough, I'll drive."

My gaze traveled over the angles of Baz's strong face. "Your regular?" I asked.

I took a strange pleasure in knowing his regular. I may not know much about him, but I did know that.

"Yep."

Ash poked his tongue into his cheek, a knowing smirk growing as he glanced between Baz and me. Baz's expression got all dark and dangerous. Discomfort rolled through me, and I took a step back. "Give me a second to get these filled and I'll be back."

As I walked a way, I peeked back at Baz. Feeling his weight. That heavy blanket of severity that rolled from him. Stare unyielding. Posture straining in rigid awareness. Like he was trailing me across the room even though he hadn't moved an inch.

God, what was wrong with me? Because the only thing I wanted in that moment was to bury myself in it.

By the time I returned to their table with their drinks, the band had taken the stage. A riot of applause erupted, and the energy Tamar had been talking about burst through the crush who'd vied for a better position up front. A guitar rang out. Rick took his spot in front of his mic, a light giggle slipping from Emily as she glanced at Rick, and then he called out into the crowd, "Good evening."

The entire bar went wild.

"Popular?" Baz asked, shouting to be heard above the noise, waving toward the stage as I set their drinks in front of them.

I leaned toward him so he could hear, and every pore on my skin came alive with his proximity. "Yeah, around here at least."

Like he wasn't all that impressed, he gave an offhanded shrug. "Cool."

"Let me know if you need anything else. I'll be around."

I slipped back into work, filling orders, Emily's sweet voice tickling my ears while the time quickly passed. When she began to sing my favorite song of theirs, I paused at the edge of the dance floor and just took it in, lightly swaying as I got lost in the hypnotic feel of the music. My mouth moved with the words but my tongue remained silent, unwilling to allow my voice to be heard.

The twinge of sadness in my soul reverberated with the lyrics. It was a sad kind of song, and my chest swelled with longing. I squeezed my eyes shut and let myself live there for just a little while.

I stopped back by Baz's table, and Ash and Lyrik ordered another round of drinks, the two of them getting rowdy and unruly. Baz and Zee looked on them with a soft affection that seemed almost out of character for their harsh outward appearance, and again I didn't know how to make sense of Baz. There were so many facets to his personality.

Did I even know him at all?

He cast me a slow smile when I walked by, one that wrapped me up in comfort.

When *Carolina George* finished up, Derrick took over, playing some dance music to keep in step with the carefree atmosphere. Ash and Lyrik took to the dance floor, their moves a little on the goofy side, as if they didn't have a care in the world—completely uninhibited, cutting loose. As I was passing him by, Ash grabbed me and spun me around. I squealed in surprise, enjoying myself far too much when I danced around with him for a few beats, before he released me and turned to take the hand of another girl who'd slid up to grab his attention.

Laughing and trying to catch my breath, I peeked over at Baz who was relaxed back in the high-backed stool, taking me in like it was the most natural thing in the world. Like he was supposed to be looking at me because he couldn't see anything else. Just like my eyes were continually drawn to his gaze.

A shiver of pleasure rolled through me.

It felt amazing to have someone looking at me that way, because it'd been a long, long time since anyone had. And even when they did, it'd never been real.

Now?

I craved it.

Craved it, but only if it was him.

I tore my attention away and focused on the rest of my tables. When I made my way back from the kitchen with an order of appetizers for some women sitting in one of my booths, Baz's table had been vacated. Glasses drained. Stools empty. A short stack of large bills sat like a consolation prize in place of the face I wanted to see.

Disappointment slammed me like a full body blow.

Damn it, Shea. You can't afford to do this.

Couldn't allow myself this type of foolishness.

I knew better.

I forced myself to get back to work, convincing myself it was for the best. Slowly the bar cleared out, and at three a.m. Charlie clicked off the blinking "Open" sign in the front window while the rest of us quickly cleaned up.

Charlie tugged at a lock of my hair while I wiped down my last table. "I'm just about ready, Shea Bear. Let me drop tomorrow's deposit in the safe and we can get out of here."

"Sounds good. I'll meet you out back as I'm going to walk Tamar out. She's antsy to get out of here." Tamar, Charlie, and I were always the last to leave, and Charlie gave me a ride home every night, dropped me safely at my front door, something he'd insisted on doing since I began working here.

"All right, sweetheart."

I grabbed my bag from behind the counter and stuffed the huge wad of money inside. One of the perks of working at this place? The tips always paid my bills. No. It didn't come close to touching the wealth I'd been promised, the goals and aspirations my parents had grilled into my brain from when I was just a little girl.

But I didn't care.

Never would I forget the day I'd been back visiting, in the kitchen baking with my grandma, the woman I'd loved more than anyone else in the world. I could still smell the cinnamon rolls in the oven, the overwhelming comfort I'd felt standing beside her at the counter like it was exactly where I was supposed to be. From the side, she'd smiled at me, softly, almost like she felt sorry for me, and she'd voiced what most would believe to be one the worst clichés that had ever existed.

Money doesn't bring happiness, sweet girl. You remember that, now.

It remained one of the most impactful statements anyone had ever said to me.

Because it'd been the truest.

The most important.

"You ready?" I asked Tamar who slung her purse over her shoulder.

"Absolutely. Let's get the hell out of here."

"Thought you said you loved it here?" I teased.

"Ha. After eight hours? Not so much. My feet are killing me."

"That's what you get for wearing five-inch heels."

Dark blue eyes gleamed back at me as we made our way down the long hall toward the back door. "I wouldn't be able to see over the top of the bar if I didn't wear them."

She pushed open the heavy metal door and stepped into the night, the small parking lot empty except for Tamar's car and Charlie's truck. Her super-high boots crunched against the loose gravel as we walked toward her car. She gave me a quick hug. "Night, Shea. See you Tuesday."

I groaned in contentment. "Two days off. Can't wait." *Charlie's* was closed on Sundays and Mondays, the only days I took off. "Have a good weekend."

"You too." She clicked the locks and slid into the driver's seat, started her car, and backed out. I stepped away, arms over my chest, as I watched her drive off.

With a smile, I turned around, then froze when my sight registered the obscured figure leaning against the wall. A strangled gasp caught in my throat, and my heart took off at a sprint, blood pounding hard in my ears.

Pushing from the wall, he stepped from the shadows, his hands again stuffed deep in his pockets.

My heart rate only increased, the energy radiating from him almost as strong as the disappointment he'd left me with when he'd gone.

I pressed my hand to my chest to try to still the panic thundering against my ribs. "You scared me."

"I'm sorry." The words were soft. "That's the last thing I want to do."

But he did. I was scared of what he was capable of doing to me, the way I knew he held the power to trounce all over this hammering heart, to hold it in his hand and crush it into a million unrecognizable pieces.

"What are you doing here?" I asked on a shaky breath.

He looked to the sky and exhaled heavily, before he leveled his gaze back on me. "The same thing I'm doing every night, Shea. Thinking about you and wondering why the hell I can't stop."

My stomach flipped, and I gulped for air.

"What do you want from me?"

He laughed, lifted his elbows out to his sides in a helpless gesture without pulling his hands free. "Dinner?"

Nonsensical laughter shot from me. "At three in the morning?"

"Breakfast?" he amended, a coy smile pulling at his full, crooked lips.

Tingles spread across my skin, and I ran my hands up my bare arms. "I already told you I don't have time for distractions."

"Come on, Shea. It's just food. Go out with me. Just tonight."

Somehow I knew it was a lie, even though he wanted to believe it was true.

Nervously, I glanced to the back door all the while being inexplicably drawn to this man I didn't even know. I knew I should make a break for it, run for the safety of my little world and give him no opportunity to rip it apart.

"I am hungry," I found myself saying. After a long night of work, it was true. But it had nothing to do with the reason I was giving in.

Because I just wanted to…

I shook my head.

That was it. I just *wanted.* I wanted to be in his space. I wanted to understand why he had this pull on me. I wanted *him.*

Even though I'd never allow myself to have him.

"Let me tell Charlie that you're giving me a ride home. He usually takes me."

A smile spread to take up the whole of his face, and even in the shadows, it was the most brilliant thing I'd ever seen. "Sure. I'll wait right here."

Rushing to the back door, I threw it open. Charlie was just starting down the hallway.

"Hey, you okay?" he asked in concern when he noticed the rattled mess I had to be.

"I think so." I straightened myself and gave him a smile. "I just wanted to let you know I'm going to have Baz give me a ride home."

He scowled. "What? Who's Baz?"

"Suprema guy." I knew that was all it would take to clue him in.

Yep, that did it. His eyes grew wide with shock, then darkened in worry. Concern crested his brow. "You sure that's a good idea, Shea Bear?"

"Yeah, Charlie, I'm sure."

His mouth drew into a grim line, hands on his hips, then he puffed in surrender. "Just be careful."

"I'm not a little girl anymore. You don't need to worry so much."

He chuckled low. "Doesn't mean you're not *my girl*, and I'm gonna worry about you, especially with the likes of him."

Likes of him?

But I wasn't about to get into that with Charlie right now.

"I'll be fine. We're just going to grab something to eat and he'll drop me home."

He gave me a *sure you are* kind of look before he lifted his chin. "All right then."

I turned to walk away when his voice hit me from behind. "And I expect a text from you when you get home, young lady."

I laughed him off with a wave. "Love you, Charlie."

"Love you more."

Stepping back out, the door closed behind me, and I was surrounded by all that energy again, although somehow it'd lightened in the moments I'd been inside. Baz flashed me a genuine smile. "Are you ready?"

"Yeah, just let me text my roommate and tell her I'm going to be late."

He nodded, digging the toe of his shoe into the pavement while I fumbled through my bag and pulled out my phone. I shot out a quick text to my roommate and best friend, April.

Mind if I'm a little late? Going to grab something to eat.

My phone buzzed with her response. *With who?*

Should have known she'd ask questions. I hardly went anywhere and she knew me well enough to know I wouldn't do it alone, especially in the middle of the night.

A guy, will fill you in later, was all I gave her.

Wow, really? No worries here. We're fine. Just be careful.

Seemed a lot of people had been telling me that lately.

I didn't reply, and instead tossed my phone back in my bag, tucked the strap over my shoulder, and smiled at the gorgeous guy whose eyes were tracing my face. The way my skin tingled, I was pretty sure he'd been doing it the entire time.

What was I getting myself into?

"Lead the way," I said, and apparently his idea of leading and mine were entirely different, because he reached for me. He enfolded my hand in his, and his consuming heat gave me a jolt.

He peered over at me with an impish smile, like he felt it too, and he was just as intrigued by it as I was.

He hauled me alongside him to the end of the lot where I hadn't seen the motorcycle that sat gleaming at the edge of the road. "Here we go," he said, swinging our hands between us.

I gaped at him. "You expect me to get on that thing?"

The bike was black and chrome and looked almost as dangerous as the crew he'd rolled in with earlier.

"That thing?" he repeated in horror.

"Yes, that thing." The corner of my mouth quirked up at the wounded expression that took over his entire face.

"Bite your tongue, woman. *That thing* would be the only girl I've ever loved. "

I bit my lip instead, my words becoming playful. "Well, doesn't that answer a lot of questions about you, Sebastian from California?"

Grey eyes danced. "I suppose it does, doesn't it?"

Releasing me, he straddled the heavy machine, legs spread out, feet braced on the ground.

Magnificent.

He handed me the helmet hanging from the handlebars. "Trust me?"

Chuckling, I placed it on my head and fastened it. A surge of excitement engulfed me when I climbed on behind him. "No, not at all."

But tonight that didn't seem to matter in the least. For a few hours, I was letting myself go. Just as long as I didn't let myself go too far.

I wrapped my arms around his waist, and that excitement shifted and transformed, a thrill of desire burning through my blood when he tucked me closer to his back. He drew my thighs around the outside of his legs and secured my hands across the flat, rigid planes of his abdomen.

Oh God, I was in trouble.

He patted my thigh, before he squeezed it tight. "Just for tonight, Shea. Just for tonight."

I tossed a fry at him, cracking up. I might have felt embarrassed at my reaction if it weren't for the fact we were the only two people in the old diner. That and I hadn't had this much fun in a very long time.

"Shut up." I probably sounded like a ditsy girl, but I couldn't find it in myself to care because Baz looked like he hadn't enjoyed himself so much in a long time, either. He looked relaxed, so different from the night when I first met him. Younger. Less intense.

"What?" The most perfect kind of grin was plastered over his face, full, full lips playful, teasing me nonstop over the last hour we'd been sitting here. "You have the cutest drawl I've ever heard."

"I do not."

"You have no idea, do you? I should record you just so you can hear the way you talk."

"It sounds normal to me, crazy boy. Don't you think you have an accent to me?"

"Hell no."

"Yes, you do."

He crossed his arms over his wide chest. "And what do I sound like?"

"You sound like California."

His mouth dropped open. "I take offense to that."

"You should," I shot back, the force of my smile feeling like it might break my face.

He made me feel young again. In reality, I guess I was young, but I didn't have the time to feel like it normally.

"Wow. You're trying to rip my heart out, aren't you?" He dipped a fry in ketchup and popped it in his mouth. "Have you even been to California to warrant such an undeserved hatred?"

"Who hasn't been to California? And eww…all that traffic and smog? No thank you."

He chuckled lightly. "I see your point, but you get used to it."

"Savannah is just fine."

"Not a big city kind of girl, huh?" Pensive eyes studied me, and his words sounded like a true question rather than another jab.

"Definitely. When I came back, I knew I never wanted to leave again."

"Came back?"

I cringed, faked a smile. "Yeah, moved away for a while. But I'm home now."

I was quick to change the subject. "So how long are you going to be in town?" I cringed again because I wasn't sure I wanted to know.

Tension wound through his muscles, and he ran an uneasy hand through his hair. "Don't know, Shea. A little while at least."

My eyes narrowed in speculation, because his tone was all off. "What are you doing in town, anyway?"

Something told me he wasn't here on vacation.

He sighed, an all around frustrated sound when he gave me the vague answer. "Staying at a friend's house until I figure out what the hell I'm doing with my life."

"You don't work?"

Harsh laughter rocked from him. "That's being called into question right now."

"Care to elaborate?" I asked with a lift of my brow, compelled to dig a little further into him, to all that mystery shrouded beneath that blasé, badass posture.

"Care to tell me why a girl like you spends all her time working at a bar?" he countered.

"A girl like me?"

"Smart. Sweet. Seems like an odd place for you to be."

I dropped my gaze to the side. The fiery burn of a blush climbed up my neck and settled on my cheeks, while a flare of guilt licked up my insides. Perhaps I should just tell him. But I didn't want to change the dynamic of tonight, because it was the only one we had.

Just for tonight.

He exhaled. "Why don't we get out of here? If I only have you for tonight, I don't want to waste it on shit we can't change."

I almost laughed because it was like he'd plucked the thoughts right out of my head, and the night would be coming to an end sooner than we knew it.

Baz climbed out, dug into his wallet. Pulling out a large bill, he tossed it on the table.

A smirk tugged at my upper lip. "You have a bad habit of over-tipping, Mr. Guy-Whose-Job-Is-Being-Called-Into-Question."

He barked out a laugh, those grey eyes filling with the sweetest kind of mischief. My body shook of its own accord, unable to stop the reaction he continued to draw right out of me.

"Nah. I know what it's like to work hard and not be appreciated. It's my way of showing that everyone matters, no matter what they do."

Crawling out from the booth, I found myself once again completely confounded by this man, the continual contrast of brash and hard and intimidating up against the gentleness that seemed to seep from him without him even knowing it.

Who is this man?

His big hand closed over mine, his touch ushering in the tension that seemed to act as my own weakness. Enchanted, I followed him out of the diner and into the night. It was deep, the darkest hour that settled over the Earth before the sun shed its light to proclaim a new day.

I wanted to put it on pause. To live in this fantasy, just for a little while.

This time, Baz adjusted the helmet on my head, his eyes locked on mine as he slowly latched the strap, neither of us saying anything when he hooked his leg over the bike, never letting go of my hand as he gently tugged me to follow.

I snuggled up against him, and my body released a contented sigh. I hooked my chin over his shoulder, getting the closest I could get, and Baz kicked it over. The bike rumbled, the engine vibrating beneath us as he took it to the pavement.

He didn't tell me where he was taking me or ask me where I wanted to go. He just rode. And it felt like forever and no time at all as his bike ate up the streets until there was no city behind us, just deserted roads, trees hugging them tight, as tight as Baz and I hugged the corners.

But not nearly as tight as I hugged his waist.

It was exhilarating, liberating. Baz had me feeling like a young girl with dreams again. But this time that young girl wasn't suffocated with elevated dreams that were not her own. Instead she felt the fluttering of dreams that were simple.

A simple girl who wanted a simple boy.

But I knew in my gut Sebastian Stone was anything but simple.

I kind of wanted to panic when he finally turned around and headed back into town. At a stoplight, he turned his face toward me, his nose a fraction from mine, his hand back on my thigh. "Where do you live?"

I gave him a quick rundown on how to get there, back near the bar but a few streets in. I hugged him even tighter as he took the few turns that brought us into my neighborhood, knowing this magical night was coming to an end.

He pulled to a stop in front of the blue two-story historic, white shutters around the windows, the sight of the cute little porch swing hanging from the wooden beams enough to swell my heart in a rush of wistfulness.

"This is you?" he asked as he kicked the stand and cut the engine, and an expectant silence filled the air.

"This is me."

He helped me off then climbed from the bike. His adept fingers worked to remove the helmet and he hooked it on the handlebars.

"There," he said softly, eyes intense as he brushed back some of the hair that could only be a disaster. He let his fingertips trail down my neck. A tremor spread beneath my skin. "Thought I'd take the scenic route to your house. Hope you don't mind."

"I didn't mind," I whispered, hating how much I wanted him to stay when I knew he needed to go.

A few stars clung to the sky as a dim hue of light tugged at the brink of the horizon, a vague threat of the approaching day. The high-pitched drone of bugs hummed from the trees, and the air held still, bottled up, waiting to be breathed across morning's awakening.

Baz and I seemed lost in it. Hovering at the edge.

Releasing me, he stuffed his hands in his pockets, the way he always seemed to do when he didn't know what to do with himself, rocked back on his heels, and squinted at the emerging silhouette of my house.

"You own this place?"

I began to walk toward it, somehow knowing he would follow.

"Yeah." Inhaling deeply, I looked up at my house that wasn't exactly small or modest. "My grandmother left it to me when she passed. This house was always my favorite place in the world." Side by side, we climbed the three steps onto the porch, and I turned to look at him when we stopped in front of the white door. "Every chance I got, this was where I came. It was always my sanctuary, mostly because I wanted to be around my grandma." I gave a tiny, insecure shrug, revealing the most about myself that I ever had. "Now it's my home."

Baz peered into one of the long, horizontal windows that flanked both sides of the door. There were no lights on inside, so it appeared blackened. Blank. Yet he stared at it as if he could see everything inside. "It's perfect for you."

I gave him a soft smile. "I think it is, too."

I hesitated, stuck in the force of his presence that seemed to devour all my sensibilities. "I should go in," I finally said.

He looked to his feet, before he leveled me with all his potency. He gave me a tight nod. "It's late."

I dug in my bag for my keys and slipped the front-door key into the lock, turned the knob, and cracked open the door.

"Goodnight, Baz." I turned away and went to cross the threshold.

I felt him move before I felt the blazing heat of his hand on my neck, beneath my hair, his thumb at my jaw to force me to look back at him.

Indecision swam through his eyes, voice rough. "You're beautiful, Shea. Need you to know that."

Slowly, I shifted, turning to face him, his right hand gliding around to the side of my neck in the same second his left came up to the other side. Holding me. Thumbs ran along the contour of my jaw, strong fingers at my nape tipping back my head.

I felt like I would drown under the intensity of him—my body coming alive—a rapid-fire of sensation licking through my body with the simple touch.

I stopped breathing when he slowly leaned in. His mouth brushed over mine in a feather-light caress.

Once. Twice. Three times.

Testing.

As if he were curious to see what it might feel like.

Like he'd gotten the answer, he gripped my face. There was little movement, just the dizzying sweetness of his lips as they pressed earnestly against my mouth. Baz inhaled, breathing the moment in. I grabbed his wrists to hold him closer as my knees went weak, the man again having the power to evoke the most foolish kind of reaction from me.

He fed from it, I could tell, the way every inch of him hardened and a rumble of pleasure vibrated from his chest.

Spinning us, he pushed me up against the wall. My back hit it with a thud, and his hands were in my hair, yanking me forward in the same second his mouth closed fiercely over mine.

He was no longer gentle, and he swept his tongue along the rim of my bottom lip, teasing at the corner, nipped me once before his tongue slipped inside.

It was an all-out assault.

I moaned with the contact, my body yielding. Welcoming. My hands were suddenly everywhere, touching him, searching him, those stupid little dreams of a simple girl wanting a simple boy tickling my senses, taunting me.

Hard, defined muscles rippled and jerked beneath my greedy touch, and Baz groaned, quick to wedge his knee between my legs and force them apart. He pinned me to the wall, his huge body eclipsing mine, his thigh between my legs.

Pressing.

Pressing.

Pressing.

Pleasure knotted tight and fast.

"Oh, God," I whimpered.

I could feel the plea of his heavy cock begging at my hip. He rubbed himself there, groaned again, and he slipped his hand down and palmed my breast. Through the fabric of my shirt, he dug his thumb into the cup of my bra, flicking at my nipple.

I whimpered more and pulled from his mouth, my head rocking back on the wall as I searched for the air he'd stolen.

He didn't seem to mind, and instead took a path down the side of my neck with his mouth.

"This is feeling a lot like a distraction," I finally managed to say, my fingers sinking into his shoulders when he sucked behind my ear.

"Doesn't everyone deserve to forget?" he mumbled along my skin, his voice hoarse and almost desperate as he kissed his way back up to my mouth, taking more.

But no. I didn't want to forget. I wanted to live. To take in every memory. To make every single one of them count.

"No, I want to remember," I murmured at his mouth.

An unintelligible sound rolled up his throat, something that sounded like pain, like hope. "Let me come inside." He rubbed against me, a friction of jeans and heat and a desperate need to leg go.

And God, I wanted to.

But dawn was beginning to break.

"I can't."

"Why?"

"You wouldn't understand," I whispered.

On a sigh, he dropped his forehead to mine, trying to catch his breath.

He smiled in something that felt like resignation, then playfully nipped at my bottom lip.

"I thought you said you didn't bite?" I teased in an attempt to drag myself out of the moment, fingertips scratching through the thick coat of scruff covering his cheeks.

He chuckled, the sound the thickest kind of molasses. "I think you and I both know that was a lie."

My gaze shifted away, suddenly shy because I was still pinned under this man that I didn't even know. One who knew nothing about me. His body burning. Mine on fire.

I swallowed hard and nudged him away, letting go of the little fantasy I'd allowed myself to live.

Just for tonight.

Because the sun was rising to reveal my reality.

I pushed away from him and took a step toward the door, and Baz grabbed my hand and gave it a gentle squeeze, almost as gentle as the expression on his face.

Again, his understanding was entirely unexpected.

Then he let me go and I shuffled toward my house, feeling a little wobbly and a whole lot aroused.

In the doorway, I turned back to look at him, this beautiful man that my heart ached to know. "Goodnight, Sebastian from California."

He smiled softly. "Goodnight, Shea from Savannah."

seven
Sebastian

THE SHRILL RING FROM MY bedside table jarred me from sleep.

I groaned, clinging to the fringes of sleep, desperate to sink back into its murky depths.

Because she was there. That fucking gorgeous girl, who with one look, swallowed me whole. The one who'd climbed on the back of my bike and held onto me as if her very life depended on it, and it seemed, just for one night, it had.

For a little while, it was just the two of us who existed.

Did it make me pathetic that night two nights ago had been the best time I'd had in as long as I could remember?

Funny, because it didn't come close to ending the way I'd been dying for it to—wrapped up in miles of long legs, buried deep in all her sweet where she just kept pulling me deeper, a few perfect hours to make me *forget.*

Didn't matter.

Because she still *had*, and that fact scared me a little bit because I sure as hell didn't need to go getting messed up on a girl that I was only going to have to leave behind. She was tied here. She had made that much clear.

But that didn't change the fact she made me feel different when I was with her, like maybe not every single thing in this world was bad. As if this girl saw me for who I really was and she actually liked him.

She'd asked me what I wanted from her. The problem was I had no clue. All I knew was it was *more.* That I wanted more of her dark and her light and her heavy and her soft. I wanted more of her sweet breaths and more of her pounding heart.

I wanted more of her kisses.

Fuck.

I wanted more of her kisses.

The phone rang again, vibrating against the wooden tabletop.

Facedown in my pillow, I blindly swatted around for my phone. When I caught hold of it, I flipped onto my back, rubbing at my eye as I answered with a groggy, "Hello?"

"Sebastian."

The spiteful voice punched me in the gut. Anxiety climbed out from it, like ants marching across my skin.

Sucking in a shaky breath, I sat up on the side of the bed. I ground my teeth when the years of resentment came flooding in, washing over all those stupid childhood scars marking up my insides, my heart and spirit and mind.

"What do you want?" I gritted out, crushing the phone in my hand.

He laughed the ugliest sound. "Ah, what, you're not excited to hear from your dear old dad? Have some respect, boy."

I scoffed. He'd lost that a long time ago.

"I think you know the answer to that, so get it over with and let me go back to my life."

"Your life?" he mocked, brutal sarcasm bleeding from his tone. "Glad you have a life to continue on with."

My insides squeezed and bile rose in my throat. "What do you want?" I asked through clenched teeth, refusing to take his bait. "I'm not gonna ask again."

"What do I want? What you owe me."

Fucking money. Always more money.

Taking. Stripping me bare.

Everyone wants a piece of Sebastian Stone.

"Don't owe you anything."

"Yet you take care of that worthless brother of yours." The words sliced through me, a bitter blade. "You might protect him, but I sure as hell won't."

"You mean *your* son?"

"He stopped being my son the day he killed Julian."

A knot formed in the base of my throat, all sharp, crude edges. Heavy. Too heavy. "It wasn't his fault," I grated around it.

"Then why did you lie? Why are we all still lying?"

It was always what he held over my head. The threat to expose Austin and what he had done. To proliferate the lie of what he *had* not. Wouldn't allow him to hurt my little brother any more than he already had.

"How much?"

"Ten."

Bastard.

"Fine. I'll wire the money to you this afternoon."

Satisfied laughter spread maliciously through the phone.

And I hated.

Hated.

Hated.

Hated.

It hadn't always been that way. Once I'd loved my father. Looked up to him and he'd trusted in me. But grief could do ugly things to people, especially ones who already had a propensity toward violence running through their veins. Pair that with bitterness and unrelenting pain? That was the kind of fuel with the power to create a monster.

And a monster he'd become.

Hesitating, I raked a hand through my hair, my head slouched between my shoulders, despising the fact this man held all the cards.

"How's Mom?" I finally asked, wishing I didn't still give a fuck, because she'd stopped caring a long time ago. She'd become just another of his pawns, a hopeless, tormented woman who'd lost herself the day she lost Julian—the day Austin and I had lost everything.

The only thing we had left was each other.

"Don't you worry about her. Just send the money. I expect to see it by the end of the day."

Rage coiled through me, and I threw my phone across the room, every part of me hungering for the satisfaction of him feeling its impact as it smashed against the wall.

Because that same kind of violence ran through me.

Pieces flew, and for the moment, his voice was silenced.

But in my head, his voice was never silent.

Bastard.

My pulse raced, and I pushed to my feet, hands in my hair as I paced, trying to calm the breaths that wheezed in and out of my lungs. I crossed the floor and jerked open the top drawer on the chest against the wall, rummaged around to the bottom until my fingers brushed against the plush fabric.

I wrapped my hand around it, the dingy, stuffed green monkey. I pressed it to my nose, closed my eyes, and saw his smile.

God, I missed him.

That image flickered, the face of the vibrant boy flashing with the silent blips of gray. Lips purple. His lifeless body in my arms as I dragged him to shore.

Austin huddled behind the large rock, shivering and hiding.

Hiding.

Hiding.

Hiding.

I tucked it back inside, underneath all the shit that didn't matter, remembering why it was just Austin and me. The way it always had to be.

Four hours later, I swung my car into one of the parallel parking spots running alongside the quaint streets in the Historic District. Trees lined the sidewalks, branches covered in thick leaves strewing shade over everything, people ambling along the quiet sidewalks in front of the businesses set in old restored buildings.

It was beautiful. Peaceful. And it made me think of Shea.

After my call with my dad this morning, I was left feeling unsettled and itchy, and a part of me knew being with her would take it away. It sucked that *Charlie's* was closed on Sundays and Mondays. I mean, I guess I knew where she lived now, but I wasn't entirely sure of what my reception would be if I just showed up at her door.

Had to admit, I was tempted.

Clicking the lock to my Challenger, I jogged across the street and onto the sidewalk, anger twisting me just a little tighter when I flew into the tiny bank where I transferred ten grand into my father's checking account. I made sure to send about twenty different mental curses with it.

"Thank you, sir," the poor girl behind the counter said with a forced smile, hand shaking as she passed me the receipt. I was sure I looked like a complete freak who'd walked in off the street—all pissy and surly and biting out instructions to her.

Wasn't her fault my dad was an asshole.

"Thank you," I managed with a tight smile as I headed back out into the heated day. The air here was always thick and soggy and like walking into a wall. Just as I was getting ready to cross the street back to my car, I glanced to the right and that was when I saw her.

Or maybe it was the awareness that stopped me in my tracks and drew my gaze her direction.

And God, I couldn't look away as she walked toward me, floating down the sidewalk, insanely gorgeous waves of blonde bouncing around her as she smiled the brightest smile, lighting up the world in the seconds before she encroached on it and took it in the grips of her raging storm.

An enigma.

A hurricane.

Emotion whipped around me, a frenzied stir of energy that crackled through the air.

And for the second time today, I felt as if I'd been punched in the gut, this time my attention locked on who Shea was holding hands with.

Mounds of tight blonde ringlet curls.

Caramel eyes.

A tiny smile big enough to shatter the Earth.

My eyes traveled back to Shea's and she fell to a stop just feet in front of me when she noticed me. I watched the movement of her throat as she slowly swallowed, then protectively squeezed the little girl's hand.

Holy shit.

Shea had a kid.

eight
Shea

SEBASTIAN STOOD THREE FEET away from me with horror etched all over his striking face.

This was the exact reason why I didn't say anything, why I never bothered to try, because their reactions were always the same.

But this time? This time it hurt.

Because it was Sebastian.

Because I wanted him.

Ached for him.

More and more every day.

I gave my daughter's hand a reassuring squeeze, my voice strained when I finally whispered, "Baz."

His Adam's apple grew prominent, and I trailed it as he swallowed hard. I could tell the way he was fighting to continue to look at me, the way he didn't want to look at her, but couldn't resist. His eyes continuously flitted between us, guarded when it landed on her and confused when he turned back to me.

Sadness billowed through me on gentle waves, soft nudges of reality prodding that I should have been more careful.

That I didn't have time for distractions.

Apparently I didn't have the heart for them, either.

My head tipped to the side, telling, reminding, pleading. *I told you.*

Yet he was the one who'd pursued it, the one who couldn't let it go.

Now I'd be the one who paid for it.

"Hey." The word was forced, his attention darting away before he chanced looking back at me. Something regretful flashed in his stormy eyes. "I…uh…" He rubbed his hand over his face, his smile tight when he took two steps back. "I'll see you around, okay?"

Wow.

Okay.

I didn't honor him with an answer.

He probably wouldn't have waited around for one anyway. He ran across the street to a black car parked at the curb that looked just as mean as the bike he'd taken me out on two nights ago.

Dangerous.

I should have heeded all those warning bells that had gone off in every single one of my senses the second I'd seen him.

But I couldn't look away then. And I couldn't look away now. I stood staring while he jerked open the driver's side door. He peered back at me for one fleeting moment before he slipped inside and slammed the door shut, closing himself off behind blackened glass and metal.

Emotion burned at my eyes.

"Mommy?"

My tiny girl looked up at me. *My world.* The reason I lived.

My butterfly.

Swallowing down the glimmers of pain, I smiled at her, squeezing her hand in mine. "Let's go, sweetheart."

Kallie swung her legs from where she sat at the edge of the kitchen counter. A big mixing bowl was at her side, and I stood guard over her while she dumped a measuring cup filled with sugar into the bowl. With wide, brown eyes, she watched as the grains sifted down into the growing mixture of dough.

She giggled when it emptied, little shoulders coming up to touch her chubby cheeks as she shook all over. "There we go, Momma! I did it!"

I kissed her button nose, lightly poked her in the belly. "You did it."

She had to be the cutest thing that had ever graced God's Earth, my sweet girl who sat right in the same spot where my most cherished childhood memories had taken place, the same spot where I'd stood next to my grandmother on the tall step chair, working at her side.

I knew at only four, there was little chance she'd remember these moments, but I hoped they were the foundation of memories, the basis of something beautiful that would forever fill her heart with love and joy.

That's what I wanted for her. For this amazing child to grow up every single day knowing I loved her with every piece of me, that I wanted nothing from her other than to see her become a loving, kind, strong woman. That she chase her dreams, whatever they were. That she learn to respect and demand it in return.

To learn all the things my parents never instilled in me.

My grandmother had left me this place with a letter telling me to find love and to bring it here.

Kallie grinned up at me, a row of tiny, perfect white teeth exposed. With her whole hand, she pushed back the heavy locks of tight curls that had fallen in her face, smearing chunks of dough into her hair.

And there she was.

The love of my life.

So much hair that sometimes I worried she might topple over. So much spunk that she had me laughing every day. So much belief that she made me view the world in a different light.

So much love that she somehow sustained me, and I turned around and poured it right back into her.

But today?

Today had reminded me that my grandmother had meant more of that request. She'd wanted me to find someone to cherish me as much as my grandfather had cherished her.

The crazy thing was, I'd never felt anything was missing from my life.

Not until the day I met Sebastian Stone.

"Okay, we'd better get this mixed up so we can get these cookies in the oven before Auntie April gets home from class. You know she's gonna want one."

"Yay, Auntie April!"

April wasn't really her aunt, but she was my best friend. She had been for years, since she'd stood across the street from my grandmother's house when I was seven years old, looking scared and unsure of her new home that her parents had dragged her to from across the country.

My grandma had nudged me in the back. *Go on, girl. I know you want to talk to her and I can see by the scared look on her face that she needs you to talk to her.*

Fleeing back here when I found out I was pregnant with Kallie, April had moved in and she'd never left. Instead of paying rent, she watched my daughter for me while I worked nights—considering she was the only one I trusted with Kallie—while she finished her master's. It worked perfectly and I thanked God for her every single day.

Kallie picked up the big wooden spoon, and I wrapped my hands around hers, dropping a kiss to her forehead when she peeked up at me, the two of us blending the thick mixture together. We balled them up, set them on the sheet, and I put them in the oven.

"There, all done," I said when I shut the oven door and dialed the timer.

Kallie threw her arms out and wiggled on the counter. "All done!"

"Be careful, Butterfly," I said as I swooped her up into my arms, holding her over the sink while I washed off her hands.

I set her on her feet, and she took off, bouncing around the huge country kitchen.

A soft, satisfied sigh left me as I looked around my favorite room in the house. The appliances had been updated. The chunky granite that was white with silver flecks that made up the countertops was something to die for, accentuating the whitewashed cupboards perfectly. Still, it remained a cohesive mesh of new and old after the restoration. I'd insisted it keep in line with the sanctity of this old home, making it as beautiful today as the day it'd been built.

The side door rattled and April pushed it open.

"Auntie April!" Kallie squeaked, flapping her arms out to her sides. "Look, Imma butterfly."

I covered my mouth, trying not to laugh out loud at the cuteness that continued to come out of my daughter's mouth. April shot me a knowing grin, fighting her own amusement as she pulled Kallie up for a hug. "Yes. There's my Butterfly," April said, giving her a squeeze and nuzzling her nose into Kallie's cheek. "I missed you today."

Butterfly had been Kallie's first word. Charlie had immediately begun calling her that, and it'd stuck. Of course there was no way she was going to shuck the nickname considering that's what she normally demanded people call her.

April set Kallie back on her feet, and dropped her backpack to the floor near the door. She smiled at me. "Smells delicious in here."

April was short and muscular. Strong. And the girl could run faster than anyone on our high school track team. She'd played softball throughout school, and now was studying to be a physical trainer, hoping to get picked up by one of the local teams.

"We get cookies!" Kallie peeped, running circles around us as she continued to dip and soar, her imagination far and fast ahead of her. She suddenly stopped and shoved five fingers toward April's face. "I'm gonna be five…I'm gonna be five!"

Kallie was all knobby knees, chubby belly, and even chubbier cheeks. Even though she only stood to April's knees, she still stole all of her attention. "Oh, you're getting ahead of yourself there, Butterfly. You have to wait a little while until next spring to be five."

"But that's so, so close," Kallie said.

The buzzer dinged, sending Kallie into a flurry of commotion, arms flapping as she hopped around chanting, "Cookies…cookies…cookies."

"I'll grab the ice cream," April offered, digging into the freezer and pulling out the vanilla, while I removed the cookies from the oven. April set out bowls, scooped in ice cream while I placed the hot, oozing chocolate chip cookies on top. And we ate together, grinning, joking around the entire time, while I tried to convince myself that what happened this morning with Sebastian hadn't cut me deep. All the way down in a secret place I didn't even know existed.

I pulled the covers up to Kallie's chin. She wiggled and snuggled into the comfort of her bed. I lightly brushed my nose over hers, and she reached out from the covers and grabbed my head, whispering her eyelashes against mine. "Blutterfly kisses."

"They're my favorite kind," I told her, my heart pressing full.

"Me too!"

I played with one of her ringlets, tugging it straight and letting it bounce back, praying that when I looked at her tonight my smile wasn't sad. Because never had one day passed when I'd regretted my daughter. Nothing would change that. But there was some kind of unknown sadness that had wound itself into my heart.

I set a kiss on her forehead. "Goodnight, my butterfly."

Warm brown eyes smiled up at me. "G'night, my mommy."

Slowly, I stood and crossed her room, paused at the door, and flipped her light switch. It cast shadows around her room. A slice of light from the hallway slanted in to light up her precious cherub face. Her little grin faded, and she scrunched up her nose. "Is dark," she whispered, like it was a secret she could only share with me.

My voice softened and I craned my head, never speaking truer words. "I won't let anything bad happen to you, Kallie.

Not ever. There's nothing to be afraid of." I cast her an encouraging smile. "I'll leave the door open some and Mommy will be right across the hall if you need me, okay?"

Clutching the top of her covers, she nodded emphatically. Trusting me.

And I would. Nothing would hurt her. Not if I had any say about it. I would run. Hide. Fight. Give up my life if that's what it took to keep her safe. I just prayed bringing her here would be enough.

"Goodnight, Kallie-Bug," I murmured again, leaving her door open a crack. Standing outside, I pressed my palm to the wall and blew out a weighted breath, fighting off the nagging sadness that had followed me around all day. I stepped back into the large, open area at the top of the stairs that looked out over the living area below. Downstairs, April was on the couch, her laptop braced on her knees as she typed away.

Even though it was still early, I retreated to my room that was across the landing. I climbed onto my huge, plush bed that I'd never shared with a man, hugged my pillow, and pretended as if the psychological thriller I pulled from my nightstand and squinted at through the muted light from the small lamp could hold my wandering attention.

Ten minutes later, there was a light tapping on the outside of my door. April pushed it partly open and peeked inside. I smiled across at her, a smile that my best friend could see right through.

She pushed it open the rest of the way and propped her shoulder on the doorjamb, head cocked as she crossed her arms over her chest. "Care to tell me what's been going on with you all day?"

I tossed my book aside. "I don't know," I mumbled, rubbing my eyes as I sat up against the headboard.

"You don't know or you don't want to tell me?"

"I'm not sure there's really a whole lot to tell you. It's just…" I looked toward the ceiling as if it held an answer before I turned back to her with a shrug. "Men are all the same, exactly the way I expected them to be."

"I'm going to go out on a limb here and guess this has something to do with the guy you snuck off with the other night? You know, the one you promised to *fill me in* on and then dodged my questions like they were the plague?"

Her brows lifted so high that they disappeared under her blunted dark brown bangs.

I groaned, a sound that was meant to sound bored and uninterested, but it only reflected my pain. April took that as her cue and came to sit at the foot of my bed, her legs criss-crossed.

All in.

The way she always was.

"His name's Sebastian, but everyone calls him Baz."

A dubious frown cut a path across her forehead. "Baz? You went out with a guy named Baz? That was your first mistake," she teased, leering at me. "Just the name *Baz* has player written all over it."

I threw a pillow at her. "Shut up."

Catching it, she laughed and hugged it to her chest. "But seriously…you never go out and then you text me in the middle of the night that you're going out with someone I don't even know…which means *you* don't really even know him. I was worried about you."

I shook my head. "I know. It was stupid. Careless." Still, I knew if I had the choice to go back and erase that night, I wouldn't. I'd willingly do it all over again. "He's been coming into the bar for the last couple of weeks. He's just…"

How did I explain it? The way he made me feel? The desire that seemed impossible to escape. He was both the sun and the darkest night. A promise of heaven and the curse of hell.

Funny how we always want what we shouldn't have.

"The first time he came in, I noticed him, and by the second time he came in, I didn't want him to leave."

"So he's good-looking?"

I rolled my eyes at her.

Good-looking.

"He's…he's…" I struggled for a description sufficient for Sebastian Stone. I looked at her seriously. "He's breathtaking. And I don't mean that in a cliché way. I mean that when I look at him?" I gathered the fingers of my right hand into a tight point, jabbed at the spot at the center of my chest that had been aching for him for the last two weeks, although today it was aching in an entirely different way. "I feel it right here, April. And it hurts and feels amazing all at the same time."

"Oh God, Shea, you really like this guy?"

"Too much." I slanted her a somber smile. "But it doesn't matter anyway." I plucked at a loose thread on my comforter, hoping if I focused on it hard enough it would keep the tears at bay. "I ran into him downtown this afternoon. I had Kallie with me. He took off faster than a dog that'd caught its tail on fire."

"Jerk," she said as if it was going to make me feel any better. My smile just weakened, but hers was just as weak, filled with sympathy and compassion.

I chewed at my bottom lip. Fighting. Fighting the emotion. I sniffled, wiped at a single tear that broke free. "It's fine. I already knew. I already *knew,* April." My voice turned pleading, somewhere inside berating myself for being so foolish. "I shouldn't have let myself get caught up in the moment."

I shouldn't have let those glimmers of a simple girl's dreams invade my mind. Because they'd taken root—each second growing stronger. The impossible idea that someone could love me.

That someone could love *us*.

I should have known it was inevitable I'd end up alone.

April crawled up beside me and pulled me into her arms. "He doesn't deserve you, Shea. Doesn't deserve either of you. Don't let assholes like him bring you down. One of these days, the right guy is going to show up and sweep you right off those pretty feet."

I forced myself to smile at my best friend. She was only trying to help—voicing out loud what I knew was her own secret hope for my daughter and me.

It wasn't her fault I had already been *swept*.

I knew it though, when Baz stood staring at me in shock, a look of terror crossing his perfect features. Hardening them more. Those grey eyes dimming the darkest dark.

I'd already started the fall.

And he wasn't going to be there to catch me.

nine
Sebastian

"WHAT ARE YOU DOING down here?" Lyrik stood on the third step from the bottom, squinting at me. I sat in the virtual dark down in the secluded basement. It was a lounging area outside the recording studio, basically a man cave with couches, TVs, and a pool table. I guess a place to unwind or get sloshed after a gruesome recording session, but I'd been using it as some kind of asylum.

I shrugged at him as I resituated the guitar on my lap. "Nothin'."

He scowled. "Nothin'? What the fuck is up with you, man? Your pissy ass has been even pissier the last few days, and that shit should be damned near impossible."

I grunted. "Love you, too, asshole."

Deep laughter rolled from him, and he drove a hand through the disarray of black hair on top of his head. He sauntered my direction and plopped down on the couch opposite me, a gush of air rushing from his lungs. "Seriously. What's going on with you? You've got the rest of the guys worried. You've basically been down here by yourself for the last three days." A sharp brow lifted in warning. "Zee is about to stage an intervention."

I grabbed the half-empty beer from the coffee table cluttered with papers, empties, and overflowing ashtrays, and gulped down the bitter liquid that had turned warm and tasted like piss. "Just been in the mood to write."

"Huh." Eyes narrowed in speculation, Lyrik scratched his temple with the tip of his index finger. "All right then, let's see what you have."

He reached across the coffee table and snatched up the open notebook with my handwriting scratched all over it, deep lines cutting into all the shit I kept crossing out. The nearby pencil was dulled and blunted with the indecipherable chaos that had bled out on the pages.

That was the problem. I'd been sitting down here for days, searching for the right note. For the right words. For the right feeling.

But all of it remained convoluted. Just contradictions and misapprehensions.

All of it was her.

Dark. Light. Heavy. Soft.

Trouble.

Trouble.

Trouble.

Sitting down here, I'd been fighting through the myriad of conflicting emotions that continued to tear at me, assaulting my insides, squeezing my chest like the girl had some kind of physical control over me.

And God, she wouldn't let me breathe.

Worst part was, I had no clue why I was letting this torture me. Why I was allowing it to eat me alive. But no matter what I did, I couldn't purge that gorgeous face from my mind.

It just kept growing clearer, sinking deeper, coming nearer. Like that sweet, soft spirit was looking for a fracture. A weak spot in my hardened heart where it could slip inside. Where it could cloud and distort and pervert.

Where just for a little while, she would *make me forget.*

Like she was desperate to as well.

Standing outside the bank, realization had rushed in, and all of her warnings became so blatantly clear. I'd felt like an idiot. Shea pushing back wasn't invented to put me off, an easy excuse to shake off unwanted advances. That connection—the overwhelming awareness that gripped me every time I was in her space—the feeling I stood at the cusp of something significant just waiting to transpire. It was real. Undeniable. I could feel the attraction running on a circuit through her, the burn of desire skimming across the surface of her skin.

But below it was something even greater. Something I'd spent the last three days trying to decipher. Something I craved and feared all the same.

The thing about Shea? *Good* was written all over her in bold streaks and colors, and it'd gleamed from her like some kind of halo while she'd stood there holding that little girl's hand…without portraying even an ounce of guilt or shame. I'd been the asshole who'd wanted to scream at her. To demand to know how she couldn't have clued me in on something so important, as if she owed me an explanation. As if she owed me anything at all.

All the while my brain had sped to reorganize every idea I'd had about this girl.

She'd just looked across at me, her expression soft and pleading and filled with every *I told you so* that had come out of her mouth.

She didn't have time for distractions. And she'd meant it.

And I didn't have the capacity for that type of complication.

So I'd walked away.

What I shouldn't have done was look back.

I should have stayed course, hopped in my car, and driven away like every instinct rippling through my body told me to do.

But no.

I'd *looked back*.

Back on beauty.

Back on the source of confusion that had twisted me up for weeks. Back just in time to catch the hurt I'd inflicted darken her storm, cast shadows all over her face, flickers of disappointment, and a spark of anticipated sorrow. Back on a love that my foul intentions didn't have the power to blot out—her intense love for a little girl who looked so much like her mother it had rattled me. Back on a fierce protectiveness as Shea stood unflinchingly at her side.

Back on what for a fleeting moment I wished I could have.

Something good and pure. Something simple and right. Something beautiful and sweet.

Those kinds of thoughts were nothing but stupid and dangerous.

Because I definitely wasn't good and nothing in my life was right, and the last thing Shea needed was someone like me waltzing in to set her world ablaze. God knew I'd burn it right into the ground.

Did it stop me from wishing to take her anyway?

Hell no.

I was pretty sure sitting here stewing in it had only made me want her more. And here I'd been foolish enough to ask her for *one night.* Like somehow that would answer all the questions she'd created in me.

Of course, having that taste of her sweet little body as it was pressed against the wall of her house hadn't helped things one bit. Now I was aching to know every inch, to discover it as I peeled all the clothes from her, to expose her—layer by layer, thought by thought, touch by touch.

More.

More.

More.

Lyrik smirked across at me, glancing up from the notebook he held in his hands. "Since when did you start writing about chicks?"

Since this one decided to invade every last one of my thoughts.

"Not about a chick."

"Really?" he challenged. He turned back to it, reading some of the shit I'd jotted down aloud.

Open telling eyes
Hide them from me
Don't want to see
What's impossible to have
I've lost sight
And I'm losing my way

Ignoring the insinuation, I leaned my head against the back of the couch and closed my eyes, picked lightly at the strings, humming softly as Lyrik read the words again and again.

"Sucks, yeah?" I said toward the ceiling.

"Nah, it's good. Rough, but good. You've got something here. We just need to put some balls into it."

Trust Lyrik to go straight for the *balls*.

He stood and grabbed his guitar from where it was propped on a stand near the wall, plugged it in, and strummed a few heavy chords. And it was always this way, a rhythm we picked up, music flowing free because it was just what we did.

What we'd always done.

It didn't take long for Ash and Zee to make their way down to the basement. Neither of them said anything. They just sat down and joined in to bring this bitter, confused song to life. The progression curved and lifted and bent, an arc that became loud and hard and angry, but filled with longing, all the same.

I felt the presence on the stairs, and I glanced to the side and saw where Austin had folded himself up on a step midway. He hugged his knees to his chest, hoodie pulled up to cover his head, but his heart and mind were present, gravitating along the fringes of our little world.

This place that only belonged to us.

My fucked-up family that consisted of a bunch of guys who were just as messed up as me.

The only family I could afford.

Lyrik nodded across at me, encouraging me to dig in, to feel it in my gut as I belted out the words. Satisfaction spread across his face as he jumped in to sing the chorus, adding in his own words. Making it our own. A sound and style that was indisputably *Sunder*.

But this song?

This song was for her.

And it made me want and wonder and wish for a little *more.*

To feel something different than *this.*

But this?

This was the only thing I had.

I was back.

Didn't mean to be.

Knew I shouldn't be.

But here I was on a Friday night, climbing into the secluded horse-shoe booth with my knee bouncing a million miles a minute, crammed between my asshole friends who'd insisted I had to get out of the house. Where did they bring me? Here.

Lyrik.

Sneaky bastard.

With a lascivious grin, he adjusted his height in the booth. "Ah," he drew out, like he was the most comfortable he'd ever been. "Love this place. So glad Anthony happened to mention it." He elbowed me in the ribs. "Aren't you, Baz?"

A scowl marched across my face.

He thought he had me all figured out—tapping into the source of my ailment—and *he'd* resolved that tossing me right back into the middle of it would be the cure. He was the one who'd suggested we come, citing some band, I knew for a fact he'd never heard of before, was supposed to be playing. He'd rallied the boys, the lot of them all too happy to oblige a repeat trip down to the riverfront where we could slip into the rustic bar and disappear into the shadows, no one paying us any mind.

No one except for the redheaded bartender who always set me off-kilter. She'd caught us the second the door swooped open, the dingy light from above hitting us like a spotlight. Her glare attacked us from behind her post, all those combative daggers shot straight at me as she wiped ferociously at the glossy bar top, like she could wipe the stain of my presence from the bar.

As I watched her sneaking peeks at us now, my gut curled in discomfort. She recognized us. I knew she did and I knew she didn't like it. I knew she liked it even less because I had not a single reason to be here except for Shea.

It was written all over my posture, the way it tensed and bowed as my gaze slithered through the hazed glow of the massive room. Searching. Seeking. Hoping for something I shouldn't have.

Four days ago, I'd had every intention of never seeing Shea again. I'd committed to staying away. Even my warped conscious was honest enough to know I couldn't fuck around with a girl like her, here just long enough to mess with her heart and her head before I left my mess behind.

Yet here I was and it hadn't taken Lyrik all that much effort to convince me to come.

Because somehow Shea had managed to mess with mine.

There was no missing the way *Red's* back went rigid with what I could only presume was staunch protectiveness. It happened in the same moment my lungs tripped over my breath when awareness squeezed all the air from the room. The same moment Shea appeared through the swinging double-doors that led into the kitchen, all smooth honeyed skin and a raging river of long blonde hair.

Fire and light.

I watched as her breath punched from her lungs. For a flash, her knees went weak when her attention was drawn across the room and she found me there. I got the feeling she did it every time she entered the bar, like that same curiosity that had brought me here time and time again compelled her to watch for my return.

Because Shea was hoping for something she shouldn't have, too.

The crumpled expression that slashed lines across that gorgeous face told me she hated herself for being defenseless against it and that she'd never expected me to actually be here.

Hurt.

Hurt.

Hurt.

That emotion zinged through the stifled air like little bolts of lightning.

Hated that I was the one who was responsible for it.

She dropped her eyes to hide the vulnerability of her reaction just about as fast as they'd locked on mine. Rapidly, her shoulders lifted and fell as she studied the floor, like she was calling back her storm, gathering it up, all of that energy condensing to the size of a pinpoint.

It would only be a matter of time before it burst.

Deliberately, she lifted her face and looked at me, the quandary of emotions collected and locked down. Her sweet candied mouth tweaked in a firm set of defiance, every defense mechanism this girl had set to high power as she strutted over to our table, all long legs and slender shoulders and soft seduction.

Anticipation hardened every inch of my body.

Ash grinned at her when she stopped at our table. "Well if it isn't Shea."

"Yep, that's me," she said, clearly trying to blow off his enthusiasm, not at all interested in bar banter.

"What have you been up to, darlin'?" Apparently Ash was too dense to pick up on it or he just didn't care.

Like he didn't expect her to answer, he continued, "Figured there was no better place to be on a Friday night than surrounded by great music and an even prettier face. So here we are."

That pretty face twisted up in some kind of agony, for a second those compressed emotions spilling over.

"That's nice of you to say," she muttered below her breath, seeking relief over her shoulder, scouring for the nearest escape route. Reluctantly, she turned back to us. "What can I get for y'all tonight? It's happy hour and drafts are half off."

She said it as if she hadn't spent a night of flirting and playing just the week before, as if she didn't recognize any of us and she didn't know every single one of us by name.

As if she hadn't climbed on the back of my bike and I hadn't had her pinned against her outside wall.

Of course Zee and Lyrik sensed her discomfort. Lyrik just razzed me with a satisfied grin because the asshole seriously thought he was doing me a favor, while Zee frowned. Concern tipped his head as he studied her, eyes narrowed as he sat back in the booth. Mark had never been like that. Concerned. He didn't give a whole lot of concern about anything but his brother and the band. Didn't even care about himself. Maybe that's why Zee was the complete opposite, making up for his brother's many inadequacies.

Caring.

Caring.

Caring.

"Why don't you just bring us all what we had last week?" Zee offered, and Shea sucked the edge of that plush, pink bottom lip between her teeth, chewed at it as she gave him a tight nod and took a step back, her glance tentative and swift as it passed over me, before she whirled around and went straight for the bar. She returned just a few minutes later, delivered the drinks as if I didn't exist and she wanted me to remain that way.

"Thanks, darlin'," Ash said, laying it on thick because he always did. Dude didn't know any other way.

"Anytime," she whispered.

When she left, Lyrik sprawled his arms out over the back of the booth, his tone all kinds of casual and directed entirely at me. "Do you want to know what I think? I think what we all need is to get laid tonight." He patted me on the back of the head like I was a little kid. "What do you think, Baz Boy?"

My dick was definitely on board, but that was not gonna happen because somehow Shea had become the only thing I wanted, this untouchable girl the only thing I craved. I was itching to get lost in caramel eyes and to swim in honey skin. To be blinded by her light while she drowned me in her sea of dark.

I wanted to fuck and taste and explore. To skim along the fringes of sanity. To slip over the edges of it. To fall and do it without a shred of control.

Somehow I knew it was something I could only experience with her. Getting lost in wide, guileless eyes that still held a million secrets. Feeding off that sweet naivety while she owned me with clever, cunning hands.

No. The simplicity of Shea could never be mistaken for ignorance.

Instead, it was a force I wanted to plug into.

Ash lifted his shot. "I'll drink to that. Seems I've hit a dry spell since I stepped foot into Georgia. We've been cooped up at the beach house too much and it's cramping my style."

Lyrik gestured with his chin toward the mass of carved, ornate wood that seemed to float in the middle of the room. "I call the redhead behind the bar. She's just beggin' to be broken."

Red took that opportune time to glower in our direction as she slid beers to two guys sitting with their backs to us at the bar, her painted red lips drawn in a sneer as she stared at us from between their shoulders.

"Look at her," he said, chuckling under his breath. "All feisty and shit."

Laughter rippled from Ash and he downed his shot, pointed at Lyrik with the small glass still clutched in his hand. "Missin' home and looking for a little L.A., huh?" He waved an indulgent hand around the room. "Look at all this country we have to choose from. Figured we should be taking advantage of it while we have the chance."

Ash's gaze skated over the nameless faces, the girls who'd gathered to watch the band. And there was no doubt about it. There were a ton of girls who screamed country, wearing short shorts and even shorter skirts, pairing them with boots that I'd had no clue I had a thing for until they'd been emblazoned in my mind with the idea of them pressing into my ass while *those* legs were wrapped up tight around my waist.

Lyrik's dark eyes glinted. "Nah. Only thing I'm looking for is something that looks like that. Doesn't matter where she comes from."

One side of Ash's mouth lifted in challenge. "I don't know…I think you might have met your match with that one. Pretty sure she'll chew you up and spit you out."

"Can't chew up what you can't sink your teeth into."

The snicker from Zee was every kind of dubious. "You guys are complete assholes." He pointed between Ash and Lyrik. "The two of you need to come with a warning label."

Ash stretched out his arms, all tattoos and thick muscles. "You'd think this would be enough, but they just keep coming."

Zee shook his head. "See…asshole."

Ash just laughed.

While the guys continued to rib each other, I sat there and sipped at my drink, my gaze trailing Shea as she steadfastly ignored me. But there was nothing stoic about it. The tension that rolled from her golden skin, eyes downcast, face shielded by a tidal wave of blonde.

Every time she passed by, it crashed against me—the turmoil radiating from her.

A building storm.

And I was the cause of it—the heat and the chaos and the driving wind. Passing lawlessness that would only leave a path of destruction in its wake.

Still, I couldn't find it in myself to do the right thing, to stand up and walk out of her life, because every decision I ever made was always the wrong one.

Selfish.

Selfish.

Selfish.

It chanted through me.

But this? This was a primal need.

She breezed by our table, slowing just long enough to ask if we wanted another round. Of course we did. This time it took her a little longer to return. The band had struck up, and the bar had gotten busy, a crush of bodies overflowing and scrambling to get a better view.

I didn't care, because that meant I got to watch her from behind. Leaning up against the bar, braced on her forearms, chatting with the older rough guy who I'd learned was her uncle. His expression when he spoke with her told me he recognized her light, but in a different way— as something to protect and preserve and sustain. Tonight she had on another pair of cut-off jeans, darker this time, and the same red boots that showed off the defined cut of her legs.

My chest squeezed.

The girl had to be the best thing I'd ever seen.

Fucking stunning.

She walked back to our table and divvied out our drinks. She passed mine to me last. This time I didn't think, I just touched. I wrapped my hand around the back of her slim wrist, silently begging her to stay at the exact same time she was pulling away. Soft skin burned against mine, her pulse a thready heave.

Unsettled eyes darted up to me, and she wrenched her hand free. *I don't have time for distractions.* She razed me with the same excuse she'd been giving me for weeks—that shield cutting harsh lines into the contours of her face.

But I wanted one.

I wanted her.

She threw up more of those goddamned walls I wanted to tear down. Her spine straightened in defense as she tore herself away and left me there with my arm stretched across the table in straight-up rejection.

A sarcastic snort rang out from Lyrik as we watched her disappear into the fray. "Oh that was super smooth, dude. Like putty in your hands."

Asshole just had to dig it in.

"Fuck you, man." Yanking my arm back, I cocked my head to the side so I could glare at Lyrik who was having way too much fun at my expense. God, the one drawback of having friends who knew you so well? They picked up on absolutely everything and figured every bit was their business. Weren't a whole lot of secrets between the four of us. Usually that shit didn't matter because I had nothing to hide from them.

But this?

This felt *private*. Like I needed to protect Shea from their prying minds and misplaced assumptions. Just one more thing about her that left me feeling unnerved.

"What was that about, anyway?" Ash asked.

And there we go.

I shrugged. "Wasn't about anything. Don't know what you're talking about."

Incredulous laughter thundered from him. "Right. You should see your face right now. Don't try to tell me it was *nothing*. You hittin' that? Thought there was something going on between you two the last time we were in here."

I almost growled. "Isn't any of your fucking business who I'm *hitting*."

He just laughed harder and jerked his thumb my direction, amused eyes bouncing between Lyrik and Zee. "Holy shit, I think our boy here has a crush. I do believe the sky is falling."

Zee chuckled, but he was watching me, trying to get inside my head the way he always did. "Fucking hot, man. Nothing to be ashamed of there."

I scowled. "I don't have a crush and I'm not hitting anything, so just drop it, all right?"

Motherfucking *crush*. What bullshit. It was time I gave up whatever irrational ideas I had of taking this girl, anyway. Because she belonged to something bigger, needed more than I could ever give her.

Only thing I had to give her was more fucking heartache.

And from the depth of those bottomless eyes, from that protective stance she'd taken when she'd stood next to her little girl, I knew she needed no more of it.

Ash cracked a smile. "Whatever, you just keep telling yourself that."

I'd been telling myself that for weeks. Apparently I wasn't all that convincing.

As the night grew long, I sat and tried to keep my cool while the mood in *Charlie's* escalated.

A furor of energy lit the air as people continued to pack into the bar. The lights were low, casting faces in obscurity, a thick mist of ambiguity. Crammed wall to wall, so many bodies had flooded the cavernous space that I was having a hard time keeping track of Shea. Half of Savannah had to be here tonight. There weren't close to enough seats to go around, so hordes gathered around tables, standing in the walkways, and pushing forward to get closer to the stage. The area where the long row of pool tables taking up part of the opposite side of the bar was completely jammed full of good ol' boys out to shoot a round.

Tonight the country band was loud. Their front man had a deep, raspy voice that reverberated through the speakers, strains of a guitar coming up behind it, the quick beat of drums ushering it along. Voices lifted to be heard above the heavy twang, the din rising to a steady roar as people seemed to grow rowdier and rowdier by the minute.

Shea slipped by, brushing passed me like the tendrils of a midnight breeze. Caramel eyes sought out mine as she passed, her dark calling me home.

She was quick to turn her back.

I stifled a groan when she stopped at a table in front of ours. The sweet sway of her ass nothing but a temptation as she leaned over to try and pass drinks to a couple of women whose table was blocked by a group of guys gathered in a disordered cluster behind it, their voices obnoxious and loud enough I could hear them above the music.

My fists curled when one of them edged forward, pawed at her side and leaned his face in close to her ear, asshole acting like he had something important to say to her when it was as obvious as the tremor that suddenly ripped through my body that he just wanted to cop a feel.

"Down boy," Ash taunted through a chuckle, giving voice to what I'd been trying to deny all night. But it was damned near impossible when the bastard let that hand wander down to grab the swell of her perfect ass.

Knew those types. Saw them everywhere I went. Reaching out to take whatever they wanted whether it belonged to them or not. Assholes who thought the world owed them something. Those who played with people for entertainment.

Guys like Jennings.

A flare of hostility lit up my insides, and I clenched my jaw just as tightly as I pressed my fists into my thighs, trying to snuff out the spike of aggression that jumped through my veins.

Discretely, Shea unraveled herself from his hold. Her face—that had become impossible to purge from my mind—tipped back just enough that I saw that same feigned smile she'd used on me the first time I'd seen her. But when she used it on this guy, it was pained, a forced pleasantry used to ward off attention she most definitely did not want.

It took all the control I had left to force myself to stay still, to sit there instead of lunging from the table to rip this guy's arm clean from his body because he did not get the clue. He spread his hand out, palming her, fingers harassing at the frayed hem of her shorts.

She reared back and swung her shoulders, her body following as she turned on the guy. Anything that had resembled pleasant a few seconds ago had been extinguished. She spat words that I was dying to hear up toward his face, hers twisted in clear insult.

One the asshole clearly deserved but refused to receive.

He grabbed her by the jaw. Squeezed. Fingers he was about to lose indented her skin.

Panic flooded her. I could see it. Feel it. The way those eyes went wide. Her tray clattered to the floor when she let it loose and both her hands flew up to grip at his wrist. Struggling. But he didn't let go. He just mashed his nose up to hers, screaming something at her that got eaten up by the band that played on as if they couldn't sense something intrinsic in me coming apart.

Like a brittle, weakened beam of metal, that one piece that held me together, the control I exerted to make it through this life, bent, bent, bent.

Until it broke.

Shattered.

The way it always did when I was protecting something that meant something to me.

Sharp shards cutting me through.

Red colored my eyes, and black hate throbbed deep in those places I normally did my best to hide.

Shea.

Shea.

Shea.

A harsh breath left Lyrik, the man feeding off my hostility.

Because if there was going to be a brawl? Chances were, he and I were going to be a part of it.

I came out from under the confines of the booth, climbing onto the seat considering I was stuck between my crew. I felt as if I was on fire, incinerating from the inside out, the searing rush of protectiveness surging from my bones. It combusted in terror and rage when he threw her back by the face.

What. The. Fuck?

I lurched when she stumbled back into the table, all that blonde like a whip as it flew, caramel eyes rounding like the pour of espresso. Blackened with fear.

The circle of faces sitting around the table lit up in horror as it wobbled and tipped. All of their stools tumbled back as they rushed to get out of the way when Shea went crashing to the floor.

Glasses rained down. Shattering as amber liquid sloshed and splashed onto the hard wooden planks.

When she hit, her entire body bounced before she slid through the tangled mess.

Lyrik pulled his long, sinewy body to standing in the same second I used the table as a springboard, clearing half the distance before my feet hit the wooden floor.

People screamed and scattered, scrambling to get out of my way while others surged forward, those seeking safety at odds with the mass that were all too eager to see the shedding of blood.

And there would be blood.

He was still leering over her when I came up behind him. It was as if he was two beats from jumping in and debasing her more, when he jerked to look over his shoulder.

The satisfied smirk gleaming in his bombed-out eyes drained when he came to realization, that sobering moment when he understood there would be pain. I grabbed him by the popped-up collar of his preppy-boy shirt and used it as leverage to yank him forward in the same second I cocked my arm back and smashed my fist into his nose.

Blood splattered and he gasped. Squirming in my hold, he flung his arm out wide, the bitch thinking he was going to get a hit in on me. I caught his hand and bent it back. Squeezing. Twisting. Didn't bat an eye that I felt his bones crunching beneath my hold. Pussy dropped to his knees, a plea fumbling from his filthy mouth. "Please."

I landed three quick jabs low to his back, right over his kidney, so hard I was pretty sure he'd be pissing blood for the next week. Just a little present so he'd never forget me. I bent over and leaned in close to his ear, hearing the desperate need for destruction oozing from my own voice. "Next time you want to touch a girl? Remember this. Remember me. And if you ever step foot in this bar again? I will find you." It spilled out in a slow threat. "And I promise you, you don't want that."

I pushed him back, let him fall to a heap in the middle of the floor.

Lyrik, Ash, and Zee surrounded us, keeping the piece of shit's friends at bay. As if any one of them would have the balls to step in and intervene.

I knew my eyes were wide and crazed when I stood up straight and my attention jumped all over the faces staring back at me in shock, could feel the fever as it blistered across my skin. What had to be every occupant in the bar had made a living, thriving ring around us, spectators to the mayhem that had broken loose.

Didn't give two shits about any of that.

I only had one concern.

Shea.

My attention flew to where she was curled up in a ball on her side on the dirty, sticky floor. Her hair was a mess around her, her delicate body rocking slowly as if she were in pain.

I rushed to her side and knelt down, pulled her into my arms, one arm banded around her upper back and the other sliding under her knees. Carefully, I lifted her from the floor, having no clue if this girl was injured or just in shock.

Didn't mean to sigh out in relief when she wrapped those slender arms around my neck, but I did, and I pushed my nose in her hair, pressing kisses to the side of her head and murmuring, "I've got you, Shea. I've got you, baby."

I've got you.

Her chest quaked, and she started to sob.

Charlie suddenly barreled through the crowd, flinging people out of his way, his eyes about as wild as mine had to be as he searched for Shea. Red was right behind him.

"Shea," he wheezed, pausing for a fraction of a second as he took in the sight, before he rushed forward when he saw I held her in my arms. He went to take her, but I deflected, gathering her closer because I was pretty damned sure there was no chance I could let her go.

"I've got her." It sounded like a warning. A promise.

It wasn't until then I realized the band had stopped playing, and a bated silence became palpable in the frantic air—hushed breaths and curious stares—as oglers vied to get a better idea of what had gone down.

A frown cut across Charlie's face, before he stepped back, turned to shout at the male bartender who was standing on top of the bar to see over the crowd. "Get the cops here to get this asshole out of my house." He said it with a sneer as he angled his attention on the little prick who was still writhing on the ground spouting some bullshit about taking me to court and making me pay.

Get in line, motherfucker.

Charlie lifted his head in authority. "Everyone else, go home. This ain't none of your business."

He gestured with his chin. "Come on. This way."

He shoved back through the mass, and I held her close as I followed him, her heart thundering against my chest and her tears seeping into my shirt. He led me through the swinging double doors and through the kitchen. Two cooks stopped what they were doing and looked up in a startled worry as we made our way back toward what looked to be the break room.

Red ran ahead and held open the door.

This time her face wasn't all tweaked with dissatisfaction directed at me, but in its place was a shaky, fumbling concern as she cautiously met my eye as I carried Shea into the room.

Carefully, I laid her down on the worn leather couch pushed up against the wall. I took to a knee at her side and brushed back the hair sticking to her sweet, sweet face, and I knew there wasn't a chance *she* couldn't feel the turmoil trembling through me, the care I shouldn't feel. The adrenaline-infused chaos clouding my head was beginning to clear, leaving me with a foreign feeling snarled like a viper in my gut.

Charlie nudged me aside, and I let him wedge in to get a better spot near the girl who'd undone something inside of me.

"Tamar," he yelled, looking at Red. "Grab me a warm wet cloth and some ice, would you?"

She nodded and shuffled out.

"Shea Bear," he murmured when he turned back to her, his voice hoarse, hands trembling just about as grimly as the panicked fever in my heart. "You hurt, baby girl?"

Groaning, Shea pressed the heel of her hand gingerly to her temple. Her eyes fluttered open. "I hit my head…but I think I'm okay." She blinked and tried to orient herself. "That guy…he…he…"

Flustered, she attempted to sit up and Charlie lightly prodded her back down. "Watch yourself, sweetheart. Let's make sure you're okay before you go out there with claws bared, seeking retaliation." The words cracked on the joke, his own fear patent.

"Baz," she whispered toward the ceiling as if she'd just realized I'd remained there with her. My name falling from her lips had me slipping a little deeper. My pulse was going crazy and I edged farther back to put some much-needed space between us, beginning to pace as I tried to sort out everything I was feeling. I gripped a handful of hair, looked back on the girl who lay on the couch.

At her light and her dark and her peace and her torment.

Lying there in silence, she was clearly trying to come to grips with everything, too.

"I know, Bear, I know," Charlie rumbled low. "We all know. You're okay. We've got you." Charlie issued the soothing promise while peering in my direction, obviously curious about my role in the whole *we got you* bit.

I was pretty damned curious, too.

Because right then I wanted to claim it.

I've got you.

And just for a little while, I didn't want to let go.

ten
Shea

HIS STRANGE INTENSITY FILLED the room. But this time…this time it was different. Elevated and agitated and disturbed. He paced back and forth behind Charlie, a tensed-up bundle of rattled nerves, his attention set on his heavy black boots as he took the room in long, strong strides, then pivoted and took it again. But I could feel the weight of severe grey eyes when he'd cast sly, beseeching looks at me each time he passed. Looks that brimmed with the same turmoil I'd swam in for the last four days. Looks I wasn't entirely sure he knew I was aware he was stealing.

And it *rattled* me.

After the way he'd left me standing with Kallie on the sidewalk at the beginning of the week, I'd been certain I'd never see him again, sure he'd never again grace that secluded spot in the bar that I'd come to know as his own.

The sick thing was I'd actually been mourning him, my movements slowed with sadness, my heart a heavy weight where it beat sluggishly in my chest. Because I was wanting things I couldn't have, simple dreams crushed before they ever had the chance to take flight. But they'd somehow taken root, burrowed deep where the dark, forbidden things in my world were stored like a burden, a closet full of dressed-up skeletons that would forever grieve what was never meant to be.

Still, there was no stopping the way my thoughts were drawn there each time I stepped into the bar, fully expecting to never see him again while equally clinging to the fading hope to catch one last glimpse.

I should have been giving thanks he was gone.

Instead I'd collided with a well of relief when I found him sitting there, the impact of it so strong it had nearly knocked me from my feet. Staring across at me, the expression on his face was as if he'd been suffering from the same affliction—his own skeletons that danced and taunted behind grey, secretive eyes.

The thing was, it'd pissed me off, because I hated feeling so vulnerable amid the overwhelming power of his presence, susceptible to all kinds of foolish things that would only hurt me in the end.

But no. This man—this mysterious, perplexing man—had saved me. He stepped in the line of fire and put himself on *the* line.

Now he raged, scraped-up knuckles clenched into fists in his hair, worry and hurt and fear seeping from his pores.

Tamar hustled back into the room, her expression sympathetic as she settled down on the floor next to Charlie and passed him the washcloth. "Here you go."

"Thanks, sweetheart," he said.

Balling it up, he pressed it to my temple. I winced and moved to hold it to the spot that throbbed and ached. Mentally, I took inventory to find if anything else hurt.

"There you go," Charlie whispered. His gaze tracked down my body, looking for injuries himself. "You sure you're not hurt anywhere else? Can't believe I let that go down in my bar."

Smiling up at him, I attempted a nod, trying to quell some of the outright fear my tough-as-nails uncle was doing his best to hide. Charlie always worried about me and the events of tonight sure weren't going to do anything to allay them. "I'm fine. Just shaken up and a little knot on my head. That's it. I promise."

Charlie huffed. "You just about sent me to an early grave tonight, Shea Bear. Second Tamar here started yelling your name…knowing you were in the middle of it." The shake of his head was bleak. "Wouldn't make it if I let something happen to you," he admitted, a tremble running through the hand he had set on my cheek. "Especially under my roof."

Through a grimace, I pushed up to sitting, ignoring more of Charlie's warnings to sit tight. I combated a rush of dizziness that swirled through my head, straightening myself when it passed. "It wasn't your fault, Charlie. You have to know that… This is a bar. Men are going to get grabby. It's just part of the game."

A snarl ripped from the other side of the room where Sebastian was still pacing. He rubbed the back of his hand over his mouth as if he were wiping off a bitter taste, the sound a clear rebuttal to my statement.

Charlie looked toward him and lifted his chin in some kind of gratitude. "Thanks for being there for her…jumping in when she needed someone. Not a lot of people are willing to risk themselves for someone else."

Baz shrugged through all the tension ringing him tight, the words barely skating through his clenched teeth. "It was nothing."

It was everything.

"Come on, sweetheart, let's get you home." Charlie looked to Tamar. "Can you take care of closing up? Make sure we get shut down early. No one needs to be hanging out tonight. Won't tolerate that kind of garbage going down here."

"Sure," she said.

The bold clash of Baz's voice thundered in the air, striking out her consent. "I've got her. I'll take her home."

A race of palpitations flapped through my chest, and dizziness swooshed again, though this time it had nothing to do with the blow I'd sustained, but completely due to *him*. Stormy, conflicted eyes fell on me as I peeked up at the man—this man I didn't even know and wanted more than anything I'd ever wanted in my life, every risk damned.

Worry furrowed Charlie's brow, and he looked to me, gauging my reaction.

I gave an emphatic nod. "Yeah, that's a good idea. That way you can stay here and help Tamar close up. She doesn't need to be here by herself."

Tamar was quick to protest. "You don't worry about me. I can take care of myself. Let Charlie take care of you. You're going to have a knot the size of a softball come tomorrow. We should really take you to the ER to get you checked out. I mean, God, Shea, you could have a concussion…or…I don't know. You need to take it easy tonight."

I got the feeling a whole lot of her doubt was projected toward Baz who eased up behind them, his big body towering over them as he looked down on me. Restless, he stuffed his hands into his pockets, something I knew he did when he became uneasy.

"I'm fine. Really." I forced a smile. "I just want to go home." I met Sebastian's steely gaze. "Baz can take me."

My answer seemed to penetrate him, before he took a step back. "I'm going to make sure my guys are all set and bring my car around back."

Charlie pushed to his feet. "All right. I'll help her out. You take care of whatever business you need to."

Baz sent a searching gaze my direction as he hesitated at the door, before he pushed it open and disappeared.

Tamar's bright blue eyes fell closed, and she swallowed hard, but she opened them to study me. "You sure you trust him, Shea? You don't know him."

I didn't.

But I wanted to.

"It'll be fine," I promised.

"Hope so." Her tone was soft and sad, and filled with more concern than I thought warranted. But I got it, knew the hurt she'd had at the hands of her ex, the way she'd escaped out east to escape him. Maybe Baz gave her the same vibe—someone so fierce and powerful, an automatic threat.

But it wasn't my body I was concerned about.

"Come on, Shea Bear," Charlie said, stretching out his hand to help me onto unsteady feet. I swayed just a little, my legs still trying to catch up with what had gone down—that jerk of a barely legal kid who thought he had the right to touch me without my permission.

I dealt with grabby hands all the time. Like I told Charlie, it came with the territory. But this had been entirely different, his hands pressing beneath my clothes before he'd pressed them viciously to my face.

I'd been scared, it was true, but the second I'd felt Baz come near, a feeling of safety had captured me.

Charlie wrapped an arm around my shoulders and led me out of the break room, through the kitchen, and down the dimly lit hall. With each step, my heart rate increased. Pushing open the metal back door, he ushered me out into the deep, deep night. Humidity hung thick, and I drew a cleansing breath into the well of my lungs. My nerves were on overdrive listening to the roar of an engine as a car rounded the corner. One I knew could only belong to one man.

Headlights cut into the lot, and that same black car Baz had ducked into four days before rolled to a stop in front of the door. He put it into park and jumped from the driver's seat. He rushed around the front to open the passenger door. It felt as if the heat of his hands seared me when he gripped me by the upper arms and helped me down onto the soft black leather.

He stepped out of the way and Charlie took his place. My burly, softie of an uncle dropped a kiss to my forehead before he pulled back with a smile, touched my chin with his knuckle. "Rest up, Shea Bear. I'll check in tomorrow." Then he turned his attention to Baz and said, "Take care of my girl."

Baz just blinked a long, pained blink, then gave him a short nod.

Charlie headed back inside, and Baz clicked the door shut. Tamar stood near the outside wall, appearing edgy and uptight. The movement of her red lips was vehement, firm, and in no uncertain terms, ripping with warning.

Part of me wanted to roll down the window and hiss at her to mind her own business, assert I knew what I was doing and she didn't need to stand out there and fret over me, and in turn, back Baz into a corner with this unwarranted ambush.

But the rest of me knew she was right. I had no clue what I was getting myself into. All I knew was it was something that lured me, spoke to me, and petrified me all at the same time.

I had already started the fall. Monday I'd thought I'd hit the bottom. But I realized while I was clinging to Baz's neck, held in the safety of his arms, that I'd barely cleared the ledge. Now I felt desperate to find out where I would land.

Saying something sharp and low, Baz backed away from her, shot her a look over his shoulder I couldn't decipher, while he rounded the front and slipped back into his seat. Without sparing me a glance, he put it in drive and flipped us around in the gravel lot, the tires squealing when he took to the street.

Suffocating silence swallowed us while I focused on the way his muscles flexed and bowed as he shifted hard, the ink covering his skin contorting like it ached to tell a story.

A strangled moment passed before I turned to take in the rigid defiance set in his profile. "Thank you," I finally whispered into the stillness. He swallowed hard, and my eyes trailed the bob of his thick, muscular throat. "You saved me tonight. I don't know what would have happened had you not been there."

Dents of conflict slashed all over his gorgeous face when he glanced at me—his voice hard, the words grating up his throat. "I lost it, Shea. That guy touching you?" Disgust deepened those dents. "Couldn't handle it. You don't belong to me, and still, there wasn't one place inside me that could accept the idea of another man touching you. Not one. And I don't fucking know how to make sense of that. But when he *hurt* you?" A curse flew from his mouth. His brow pinched when he spit the word, and he slammed his palm down on the steering wheel, obviously unwilling or unable to finish what was burning to be said, words I knew made him just as vulnerable as the ones boiling inside of me.

He jerked to a stop at the curb in front of my house.

The engine still rumbling, the man stared unseeing into the blaze of lights stretching out into the slumbering night.

Lost in the tension that wound us tight, something that only belonged to us, I stared out into the same nothingness.

My voice was quiet. Unsure. "You think I understand *this*? You think I like feeling this way?" I chanced peeking at him, taking in the sharp curve of his jaw he held taut, and I was sure he wasn't immune to whatever *this* was, either. *This* consuming feeling that came over me every time he was near.

I knew that's why he was here.

"Do you think I like it that you're the only thing I can think about? That when I close my eyes, what I see is your face? That I don't even *know* you, and somehow you feel like one of the most significant people to have ever walked into my life?"

With both hands, he squeezed the steering wheel, still refusing to look my way.

God, maybe this was the most foolish thing I could do, stripping myself bare, laying myself completely at his feet. But I couldn't stop. That unexpected grief from his absence that had followed me through the week pulsed at my insides, those many hidden thoughts and desires seeking a way free.

My voice softened and took on a tone of resignation. "I gave up a long time ago, Baz." Sadly, I turned to consider my house, the windows darkened, the porch swing rocking in a barren sway. "Gave up on dating and men and the idea of love because that little girl has enough love for me. Since the day she was born, she's been the only thing I needed."

I looked back at him, and he was barely breathing—his chest tight and his posture rigid. The air escaping his nose was nothing more than a whispered grunt.

If it were possible, my voice softened more. "And then there was you."

And then there was you.

I figured that's all he needed to know.

Because it was everything. Both an admission and a plea.

I've got you, baby.

It was the only thing I wanted—for Sebastian Stone to have me, even if it was just for a little while.

Without further words, I released my seatbelt and slipped out, quietly latched the door shut behind me, and didn't look back as I headed up the walkway.

Leaving him with the decision.

Because mine had already been made.

A disconcerted thrill sped through me when he finally killed the engine, though I could feel it was done with reluctance and doubt. My nerves lit in a frenzy, with a desire that sang and a fear that stung as my ears tuned into the creak of a door being cranked open then discretely closed. The front running lights flashed and the horn blipped as the car was abandoned on the street. That thick, consuming presence spread over me from behind as I slowly made my way up the three steps onto the porch.

Unsteady and irregular, my heart hammered.

His boots thudded on the freshly stained boards.

I paused at the door and he stopped a fraction away, a heady heat burning into my back. Shakily I dug through my bag to find my key, slid it into the lock, and slowly turned the latch, letting the door drift open to reveal the darkness from within.

A heavy expulsion of air blew strands of my hair. Like a bull before it charged. Filled with lust. Maybe even anger.

"You sure you want me to step through that door?" The words sounded like a threat when he breathed them across my ear.

Because we both knew exactly what would happen if he followed me inside.

"Yes," I promised, knowing it was true, knowing it was wrong, knowing it would ultimately wreck me.

Dropping my head, I stepped over the threshold, almost tiptoeing across the shiny dark hardwood floors.

Find love and bring it here.

My grandmother's words echoed through my mind. Guilt squeezed my ribs. I wasn't foolish enough to believe this man would bring any of it into this house.

Or maybe I was just that much of a fool, wanting him so badly I was willing to take the chance, to take a memory and tuck it away, a reminder of what could be.

Of what I could feel.

Something I've never felt before.

And I felt *it* now, as he followed me in, staying close behind, his footsteps keeping time with mine.

Thud. Thud. Thud.

My pulse beat frantically, and still I couldn't look back as we began to ascend the stairs, my hand gliding up the smooth rail. I couldn't turn to see the expression I knew would be carved on the beautiful, bold lines that amassed his stony expression. The same he'd watched me with all night. With desire and hunger and some kind of unfathomable hate, as if he were just as terrified of me as I was of him.

I mounted the top of the stairs to the second-floor landing.

Normally I would go left and steal into Kallie's room. I'd press gentle kisses to the softness of her cheeks, to her forehead, and brush my fingers through her hair while I watched her sleep and wished for peaceful dreams to enter her mind. Normally I'd pause at April's door and whisper, "I'm home," before I collapsed into bed exhausted and alone.

But tonight. Tonight was anything but normal.

Normally I didn't bring virtual strangers home.

Baz followed me into my shadowy room. The door to the bathroom rested partially ajar and the bright overhead lights bled a faint hue of light in a wedge across the floor. It was messy—clothes strewn across the floor, tossed onto the large chair sitting under the window, the bed unmade.

I stopped in the middle of it, trying to still the thunder pounding through my veins while I listened to the soft click of my bedroom door being closed.

Slowly I turned around. The air just leaving my lungs hitched when I took him in, the captivating force of this man magnified, grey eyes turned to pitch—the most brilliant kind of black.

Savage.

Feral.

I all-out shook beneath the severity, knowing after tonight, I was never going to be the same.

He was going to mark me.

Scar me.

"You see me, Shea?" The gruff question threw me, and he lifted his chin in a challenge I wanted to meet. I knew what he was offering. One last chance to back out. A warning that came with his fierce beauty because we both knew he had the power to lay me to waste.

But where there's beauty, there's also pain.

And I wanted to share in his, because I felt it every time he looked at me. I wanted to immerse myself in it, in him. To be set adrift in all he kept hidden, to slip under, to see and feel and experience what he shored up tight inside.

Slowly, I lifted my own chin. But not in challenge. In surrender. "Show me."

He watched me closely as he pulled a strip of six condoms out of his front pocket.

Correction.

Five.

One was missing.

Jealousy curled through me like a sickness, and I attempted to swallow around it, knowing this wasn't going to end well. My heart was never going to make it.

But in this moment, I didn't care.

Because I was falling.

Falling.

Falling.

Falling.

He tossed them onto the center of my rumpled bed. "Glove box," he said as if he felt the need to explain.

Awareness swelled, perception that belonged only to us, lifting in an arc, barbs of energy prickling at my fevered skin.

Never releasing me from the grip of his gaze, he reached for the collar of his tee and tugged it over his head. Almost defiantly, he stood up straight and stared back at me.

That insane, confusing attraction I'd somehow managed to keep under semi-control, hidden inside, burst—a rapid slide pushing heat through my veins. Gathering fast.

My mouth went dry and I shifted on unsteady feet.

He knelt down and unlaced his boots, rose and toed them off, ticked through the buttons on his fly. Shoving his jeans down his legs, he shrugged out of them, kicked the pile of clothing aside.

Oh. God.

He stood there in nothing but a pair of tight, tight boxer briefs, his thick erection straining against the fabric, pushing at the elastic band in a play to break free.

Just like the first time he lifted his face to me, I was again confronted with more beauty than I could fathom. Again imperfect. And again, I was sure that was part of the problem, because my heart lurched in a bid to meet with his, and my stomach clenched with a flood of desire that sailed straight through me.

My eyes soaked him in.

Dragging across wide, wide shoulders. Tracing his collarbone, and exploring the coarse, rigid muscle that defined his chest. I sucked in a broken breath when I let my eyes wander down to take in how those wide shoulders and chest tapered into the flat planes of his abdomen. Hipbones jutted out from his narrow waist, a deep cut of muscles on his lower stomach that disappeared beneath the waistband of his underwear.

The strength of him was overbearing. Foreboding.

And I was sure I'd never seen a more brutally beautiful man.

But just like his face, scars were etched into his skin, lanced across his chest, one slashed in a long gash across his side. Some deep. Others shallow.

All significant.

Both of his arms were completely covered in ink—colors and swirls and more beauty that spoke of…pain. Bleeding crosses, indecipherable words, and hidden innuendo. One arm depicted a darkened sky, the night infinite. Eternal.

My attention was drawn to the mermaid on his left upper arm. Her face was fierce and evil and somehow angelic. She sat on a rock next to a raging sea swishing her tail. A pocket watch was held gingerly in the scoop of her hands. The watch appeared to be disintegrating, slipping through her fingers, like sands of an hourglass falling through the cracks.

But his torso was bare, except for one tattoo that ran down his side. It was a monkey. A green monkey clearly supposed to be some sort of stuffed animal. A child's toy. The artwork was crafted to appear fluffy, the arms and legs long and lanky. The face was white with plain black dots for the eyes and nose, the smiling mouth a black seam.

But it was turned upside down, bent backward, the arms and legs flailing, as if it were tumbling in a free fall.

It left no illusion of a chance to be saved.

The childlike simplicity of it was gut-wrenching.

And I knew. And I knew. And I knew.

"You see me, Shea?" he asked again, fisted hands at his sides, his voice tight. There was no missing the sharp edge of vulnerability.

"Yes," I whispered, stepping closer, letting my fingertips trail across his collarbone, down the strength of his chest that jumped beneath my touch, to the monkey falling at his side.

Where there's beauty, there's also pain.

A big, callused hand came up to cup the side of my neck, to steal my breath, because it was sweet and completely unexpected. He tilted my chin back with his thumb, his fingernail scratching up and down the hollow of my neck as he stared at me, the brush of it stirring me up more.

Falling.

Falling.

Falling.

"Tried to stay away from you," he murmured, the song of that velvety voice wrapping around me like a full-body embrace. "Tried. But there wasn't one goddamned thing I could do to get you out of my head."

Remorse flashed through his eyes. "Don't wanna hurt you."

We both knew it was already too late.

My face was turned up to his, and he leaned in, slowly, his full, full lips parting just enough to catch my bottom lip between them, tugging softly, letting go.

"Shea," he whispered.

The skin tingled, and a rash of chills skated down my spine. Keeping hold of my neck, Baz followed them with his opposite hand, his palm running flat as it pressed firm into the small of my back, all the way down to my ass where he gripped me tightly, pulled me up close against his cock where it urged against my belly.

A short gasp escaped me.

Like the sound was fuel, heavy hands found my hips, and he spun me fast and pushed me up against the wall next to my door. I hit it with a desirous grunt, and I clung to his shoulders as my knees went weak.

He captured my mouth with a blinding assault of lips and tongue and teeth. His tongue was wet and warm. Demanding. Just as demanding as his fingers that kneaded into my hips, palms sliding down the back of my thighs, trailing back up. As he did, he dragged one of my legs up and then the other until I was tacked against the wall beneath his weight, my legs begging around his waist.

And God, I begged.

He smiled against my mouth as he threaded his fingers with mine and pinned my hands above my head. Rocking against me, he leveled me with darkened eyes. "Say it again."

"Please," I whispered madly, my back arching from the wall, all coherent thoughts slipping away and every kind of irrational, foolish idea rushing in to take their place—all supplied by the euphoric feel of his cock rubbing at the denim between my thighs.

It'd been too, too long. Yet somehow just the right amount of time. This moment for him. This moment for me. For us.

Even though it would crush me, I knew it had to be.

A groan rumbled deep in his chest, and he lifted me from the wall, hiking me farther up his chest. He began to carry me across the room. One hand was tangled in the mass of my hair, bunching it up, the other an iron band around my waist.

He laid me in the center of my bed. My chest took a stuttered heave when he stepped back and looked down at me, my knees rocking with unsettled nerves, my booted feet propped flat on the bed.

Staring down over me, he just stood there, an impenetrable expression hardening his face. Unreadable, yet anything but blank. Like he was processing a million thoughts, while I didn't know much of anything except how I was aching, how each second he wasn't touching me he was driving me closer to going mad.

How it was only one more second I didn't get to be with him. One second lost. One second closer to when he would leave.

He kissed the inside crease of my knee and fire rocketed straight to my core.

I exhaled toward the ceiling. My hands twisted in the sheets and my hips jerked in anticipation. "Please," I said again, because I wasn't sure how much more of this I could take.

He placed another midway at the inside of my thigh, letting a hand glide down the opposite leg, all the way down to brush his fingers along the seam of my shorts.

A little show of fireworks. The promise of more.

His movements were slow and sure when he pulled back to tug the boots from my feet, one by one, peeling off the cushy socks I wore with them. I stretched my toes and dug them into the bed, and he smiled softly as if he liked it, just as he was pressing my knees apart and setting a single knee on the bed. He leaned in far enough to jerk at the button of my shorts, and a trembled breath escaped me when he angled back and dragged them down my legs.

"Goddamn." Baz wet his lips, and he shot me an unfettered glance before looking back at me lying there in my panties and tee. "Got the best legs, baby."

Hot hands splayed wide, riding up the outside of my thighs, scraping over my hips and sides, gathering up the material of my shirt as he went. He slowed as he pulled it over my injured head and tossed it to the floor.

My hair fell around me and my heart beat so hard I could feel it in my ears.

He yanked me closer to him, close enough to the edge that he could snake his hands under my back and unclasp my bra. He slid it off, leaning back to take me in with that covetous hunger he'd been watching me with for weeks. Beneath his severe gaze, my breasts became heavy and tingly. God, I couldn't breathe. His voice dropped low as he reached up to cup them. The brush of his thumbs were like flames as he swept them back and forth across my nipples. "Best tits."

Oh my hell.

He was unraveling me.

He touched the tip of his index finger to the center of my chest.

A palpitation.

He traced it down my belly where he dipped it into my navel, before he inched it low, low, low to snag in the front of the band of my lacy boy-cut underwear. He peeled those off too, leaving me a naked, quivering mess atop my bed, waiting for him, wondering just how deep those scars he'd leave me with were going to go.

"Got the best everything."

I could feel the heat blazing from my skin, increasing with every erotic compliment he cast my way. Beneath them, I'd never felt so beautiful in all my life.

His attention jumped to the scatter of small butterflies that began in a cluster and spread out across my left hip. He darted his eyes to mine.

"Kallie," I whispered, and confusion crowded the creases of his eyes, and a little of that guilt fluttered up. He didn't even know her name. My throat grew thick as I forced it out, both defensive and nervous of his reaction to giving her a name when I knew in mere seconds this man was going to be buried inside of me. "My daughter."

He took me by all kinds of sweet surprise when instead, he drummed his fingers over the tattoo. Soft and slow and reverent, and all those simple dreams tried to crawl up and find safety in my chest. More regret flashed in his eyes when they met with mine, hitting me with some kind of faraway understanding.

Then he seemed to snap and let loose of whatever thread of control he'd been holding onto.

He dragged the tips of his fingers through my wet center.

I jerked. Oh, that felt good.

He hissed a groaned, "Fuck."

He climbed over me, nudging me farther up into the middle of the bed, and twisted out of his underwear all at the same time.

Hit with an overload of sensation, I was suddenly drowning beneath the stunning bulk of this magnificent man.

Because all at once he was everywhere, kissing me on the mouth, the neck, delving down to my chest, soft sucks across the buds of my breasts, harsh lashes at my tongue. Fingers plunged deep inside me, and I panted a strangled, "Yes," because I hadn't been touched in so, so long, and never in a way that made me feel intoxicated like this.

Fingers coated with my wet went sliding back to swirl around the sensitive skin of my ass, and a shocked gasp shot from my mouth. I jumped, before he slipped his fingers back through my sex, dragging up to circle my clit.

Pleasure wound up fast, my head pressed back into the bed and my mouth gaped open, unable to process that he would touch me this way. Everywhere all at once. In places no one else ever had.

How could he know exactly what I needed?

Terror nicked at my belly when I realized I was ready to submit every last one of those places to him.

Baz licked a path up under my jaw, before he edged up onto his knees. All his attention was focused on his fingers that were still sliding deep in my pussy, while he grabbed the pack of condoms with the other hand. He ripped one free with his teeth.

My entire body was alive with energy. With *this* energy, with whatever it was that connected me to this man, whatever it was that made me feel tied to him in an essential way, like nothing in heaven or hell could have stopped this moment from coming to pass.

Staring up at him, he stared down at me. Those eyes brimmed dark and bold. Because maybe we'd been purposed this way, that for tonight I got to touch on heaven before he left me in hell.

He pulled his fingers free, and I couldn't help the cry of frustration that jetted from my mouth at the loss.

A smirk that was pure sex kicked up at the corner of his mouth, his jaw tight with his own anticipation. My legs were shaking, the knot in my throat growing thicker by the second as he grabbed his cock at the base and rolled the condom down his shaft that was every bit as impressive as the rest of him.

Tremors rolled through my limbs. I searched for a breath as he climbed back over me, hands planted on either side of my head. Hovering. Nose to nose. And I could hear the chaotic jaunt of his heart, the pound, pound, pound as he drew closer.

I braced myself on his shoulders, fingers digging in, trying to find purchase on this man I wasn't sure I knew how to reach.

He nudged the thick head of his penis into my opening, just an inch, his breaths going ragged with restraint as his eyes sought mine. "You ready?"

Another threat.

"Yes." The word cracked and I held on.

He filled me with one solid thrust.

I cried out and my legs shook against the outside of his strong thighs. I squirmed and panted, my body struggling to adjust to his size, as he pulled all the way out then plunged back in to the hilt.

A shattered breath.

His name.

Sebastian

Sebastian.

Sebastian.

"Shea," he murmured back. "Feel so good. God, you feel so good."

He picked up a grueling rhythm, like he needed to catch up to the pounding of my hammering heart. His hips slammed into mine.

Again and again.

He wasn't gentle.

Not that I'd expected him to be.

He fucked me. Fucked me and fucked me until we were both drenched with sweat and I was climbing swiftly toward that ledge, sparks of pleasure lighting up, shimmering at the edges of my sight.

The corded muscles on his back twisted in rigid bows as he worked over me, skin bunching beneath my hands as I fought to touch him everywhere. The harsh line of his jaw. Collarbone. The perfect curve of his ass. Skimming back up his sides.

Memorizing.

He dropped to his elbows, holding my head in his hands, fingers twisted up in my hair. Something like anguish passed through his expression, and he forced me to look at him, like he wanted to communicate the words he didn't have the power to say.

Like I could ever look away.

Because I knew.

I knew. I knew. I knew.

He felt it too.

I felt him slipping in, burrowing beneath my skin, sinking into my spirit.

And I couldn't block it or shield it. He was already there.

Energy spiked, tingling in those pleasured places. My clit burned with the threat of bliss and my walls tightened around the full intrusion of him.

"Sebastian," I rasped, pushed right up to the edge.

A precipice.

His mouth came to my ear. "Do you see me?"

Yes. Maybe not all of him. But every piece that was important.

And I fell.

Plunged into his abyss.

Heart first.

Through waves of ecstasy. Deeper. Deeper. To where I touched a sea of stars that blinded my eyes, where I floated in that place that belonged only to us, a place that didn't belong to this world. Where darkness and light reigned and wrong or right had no bearing.

A brutal ecstasy.

I never wanted it to end.

Dropping his forehead to mine, he picked up his pace, hips snapping as his movements became frenzied and uncontrolled.

That intensity billowed between us, wrapping us up, making us one. And I knew he was caught in it too. He pressed his chest to mine, and I could feel the crash of his erratic heart.

He burrowed his face in my neck. "Never," he whispered in what sounded like confusion. On a strangled grunt, he clutched me by the shoulders as he took me whole, the most connected we'd been yet, his body going rigid as he jerked and shook.

Gulping for air, he collapsed on me.

We lay there for the longest time. I didn't think either of us wanted to move. The urge to weep pricked behind my eyes when he finally peeled himself from me and rolled off the edge of the bed.

I tugged the sheet straight up my middle, my legs exposed on both sides, covering up all the important parts. Like he hadn't just ravaged the entirety of them.

My gaze trailed him as he walked to the adjoining bathroom. He didn't bother to shut the door. He stood facing away, all the sublime, imposing curves of his back and bare ass striking up in a golden glow beneath the lights blazing in the bathroom as he dealt with the condom.

My breath went shallow again when he turned to reveal his profile, when he shifted toward the sink, washed his hands, and splashed some water on his face.

He ambled back out, not a lick of self-consciousness slowing him, the man parading *all* that God had given him. With both hands, he raked back the hair from his forehead, his face going coy with a grin at catching me in all my sly, covert gawking.

Right.

Redness flushed up my neck, and I chewed at my lip, dragging the sheet up tighter the closer he came, head tipping farther and farther back into my pillow as he came to stand right over me.

"Hey," Sebastian whispered, sitting down at the edge of the bed.

"Hey."

He splayed his hand across my belly. Through the thinness of the soft, satiny sheet, the heat of him burned me to the core. "You okay?" he asked.

Not even close.

"Yes."

A doubtful, affectionate breath escaped his nose, and he played with a lock of my hair. "You're a terrible liar, you know."

His hand left my stomach, floated toward my face, knuckles tracing down the angle of my jaw.

Contentment left me on a sigh, and my eyes fell closed as I lifted to his touch.

Those knuckles trailed over my chin and down my neck, drifting down the center of my body over the sheet. "This sweet little body of yours tells it all."

I opened my eyes to him where he watched me with concern.

"I'm trying to be okay," I admitted honestly, hopefully. "Not sure I'm ever going to be the same after that."

Okay, definitely sure. Maybe he didn't need to know how vulnerable I was feeling, wondering if it was even possible that it had felt as good to him as it had for me.

An indulgent chuckle spilled from between the full lips of that pretty, pretty mouth. "Amazing, yeah? Haven't felt anything like that in…well…forever. Love your pussy, baby."

Um wow.

Okay.

I was pretty sure I could return the sentiment, of which Sebastian still had proudly on display, but there was no chance I could force something like that from my mouth.

I squirmed under the sheet, and he grabbed hold of the satiny material and tugged it free of my hands. Slowly he pulled it down, inch by excruciating inch, exposing my breasts, then my belly, the erotic tickle mixed with my full-body afterglow making me shiver.

Oh sweet lord. I was in so much trouble.

His voice turned gravelly as he climbed onto all fours, both his knees at my left side, and arms caging at either side of my head. From above, he drenched me in the penetrating intensity of those strange grey eyes. The second's lightness that had seeped into the mood vanished. "You don't need to hide yourself, Shea. Not from me."

Slowly, he shifted to lie down at my side, pulling me to face him. He palmed the curve of my hip. "You are so beautiful. Do you have any idea? The first time I saw you? Thought you had to be the most gorgeous girl I'd ever seen. Now that I've seen all of you, I'm sure of it."

Another flush, and I bit at my lip. "You…you literally stopped me in my tracks." A small, self-conscious laugh tripped from me, and I tickled my fingertips across his strong chest and dared to peek up at him. "I've never been affected by anyone the way I am you."

I tried to clear all the wispy emotion from my throat. It did no good, because it was still there in my voice. "I don't do this," I admitted.

Brows bunched up, Sebastian was touching my face again, trailing fingertips in the hollows under my wide, bewildered eyes, down my nose, a soft caress across my lips. The effect was always the same—a trembling mess of want balling in the pit of my stomach, my heart shooting into a fumbled sprint.

"You think I don't get that?" he asked. His hand brushed at my cheek, and he leaned in, his mouth just below my ear. "I see you, too."

Hope fluttered in the center of my chest—simple, simple dreams.

My thumb sketched along the ridges of the puckered, lifted scar that slanted sideways across his chest.

Caution filled his expression when he looked down at me, eyes narrowed. "Crash."

Shakily I nodded, fingers trailing down to the deep scar over the ribs at his side. "Knife." His voice became hard, like maybe he was sending me a challenge.

Cold dread splintered through my insides.

Sebastian lay there silently, staring at me like he was wondering when I was going to come to my senses and run.

Any sane girl would have done it a long time ago.

But here I was, submitting myself to him and his scars and the mystery hidden in his eyes. Asking for an exclusive invitation into it. Praying they were in his past. Hoping getting to know them would make a difference—that in the long run, it would mean something.

Even if it didn't, it didn't matter.

I wanted to know him in this moment. Every part he'd allow me into.

God, here I'd been warning myself all these weeks that I didn't need this kind of heartbreak.

Now I was begging for it.

I got brave and let my fingers wander down to the monkey pinned between him and my mattress, somehow knowing the simplicity of it was anything but simple.

Sebastian winced, and those full, full lips tipped down on the crooked side, a subtle frown that struck me deep. "Julian."

Another one word answer.

One that wasn't an answer at all. I traced the exposed edges, my silence asking for more.

He trembled at my touch. "My brother. His name was Julian."

Was.

Oh. God.

I could feel the sympathy twist my face just as tight as it twisted my heart. I knew I was in way too deep when this news physically hurt. Focusing on my face, he reached out and pressed his thumb to the lines that had gathered between my eyes, ironing them out, like he needed a distraction for his attention while his thoughts went far away.

"He was eight. Had this monkey he dragged around with him everywhere he went. Didn't matter how many times our mom tried to get rid of it because it was ratty and filthy, or toss it in the garbage because he was getting too old for it, he always managed to dig it back out." The words broke, his pain sinking into my bones. "Fuck…he was a great kid."

"What happened to him?" I asked through a quiet rasp.

Deeper.

Deeper.

Deeper.

Darkness clouded his expression, and he swallowed hard. "Let's not talk about that, yeah? I've been trying to forget it for a long time."

I touched it once more, knowing this scar was so much deeper than any of the others.

Blowing out a pursed breath, I settled closer to his side. Warmth wrapped me tight, just as tight as the arms anchored around me.

"Tell me about your friends," I asked lightly, changing the subject, figuring this one was safer, because I knew the other was closed.

He sighed, though a trace of a smile lifted at his mouth. "Assholes. All of them." It was pure affection beneath overt annoyance.

"I like them," I said, picturing Ash and Lyrik on the dance floor, the easy confidence they exuded. The way they'd all jumped in to protect me tonight.

"Been with them for years. Since we were all just kids trying to figure out a way to make it in this world. Of course we fucked more stuff up than we figured out."

Trouble.

Recognized it when they all showed up at *Charlie's* door.

But there was more to them than that, something better than I'm sure the rest of the world chose to see.

"They're the only family I've got," he continued. "All except for my little brother."

I smiled a small smile. "You have another brother?"

"Yeah, he just turned eighteen. Been taking care of him for the last ten years. Austin." He spoke his name with a quiet reverence, cloaked in a ton of concern. A sad sigh slipped from him and he held me a little closer and admitted quietly, "Julian was his twin."

Whoa. I didn't expect for that admission to hurt so much, but it felt as if my chest was being squeezed, some kind of weight crushing my ribs. I didn't know why. Maybe it was the turmoil I could feel billowing through him just talking about this.

Where were their parents?

"That's good…you taking care of him…Austin," I offered pathetically, because I knew I didn't have the first clue about his life.

But it was the *wanting to* that kept me prodding a little more.

He huffed out a frustrated breath toward the ceiling. "No, Shea. It's not. I tried. I fucking tried, but I led him into all kinds of shit I shouldn't have…just a kid myself, having no clue how it was going to affect him. Both of us have been paying for it ever since."

I lifted up on my elbow, looking down at Sebastian who laid flat on his back. "What does that mean?"

"It means I'm not a good guy."

A flash of fear. I gulped for air.

"I don't believe that," I whispered almost desperately.

He reached up and held my face. "That's because you see all the good in this world, Shea. Don't even know you, but I can see you do. Maybe you see the guy I wished I could be, but I'm not him."

I frowned, and I knew it was sad and confused.

"Took my whole crew down with me. Fighting…drugs…women…taking shit that wasn't ours."

"They look pretty okay to me," I argued.

In the shadows, agony blanketed his eyes. His expression was haunted, hurt and hard and filled with a self-hatred I couldn't understand. "No…there are some things you can't take back."

Asking more got caught on my tongue when he cut me off.

"Who's Kallie's father?" he asked way too out of the blue, making my insides recoil in bitterness.

"He's dead," I shot out just as quickly.

Dead to me, at least.

Baz blanched like the news hit him viciously, before he reached out and caressed gentle fingertips along the angle of my cheek. "God, Shea. I'm so sorry."

Guess I could lie better than he thought I could. But this wasn't something I was willing to share with him, to drag out into the open when this was the way we lived. The way we survived. I couldn't survive Kallie's father, the disparity of what he'd given to me and what he'd robbed me of, any other way.

"Don't be," I urged, wishing to drop it but needing him to understand, wishing with my entire being to reveal it all but refusing to break the promise to myself that I'd never allow another man the power to wreck me the way Kallie's father had.

Not because he'd broken my heart. He hadn't.

He'd simply crushed my world.

"He never would have loved her, and it's better for us both that he's not a part of our lives."

It sounded cruel, I knew.

I could tell he wanted me to explain more, so I cut him off with a kiss, pulled him to me and wrapped my arms around his neck.

Sebastian suddenly reached down and cupped my sex. Startled, I jumped. "My whole life, I've been taking what's not mine to take. Took this, too. Not sure I wanna give it back." Tease was injected into his tone, but this was no joking matter, because honest to God, every last part of me already belonged to him.

Did he know? Could he read it like a playbook in my eyes?

Quickly, he rolled to his back and pulled me on top of him. I giggled, some giddy feeling sweeping through me. "So tell me Sebastian from California, what happens there?"

Who could blame me for digging more?

He sighed, deflected as he looked over my shoulder at the ceiling. "Sex, drugs, and rock and roll happen in California."

Right.

Another warning—as vague as it was vast.

"Why are you here?" I whispered as he rubbed my naked body up and down his, a slow dance that immediately lit me up.

Why are you here in Savannah? Here with me?

I'd seen the way he affected the women in the bar. I knew he could crook his finger and they'd come running.

Squinted eyes met with mine. "I don't have a lot of good in my life, Shea. People would tell me I'm spoiled. That I have everything at my feet. But none of it makes me happy because all of it comes at a cost, one I'm not sure I'm willing to pay any longer. Only thing that matters to me is my brother and the boys."

I frowned. It seemed like everything he said was at odds with the other.

"But you…you got under my skin," he continued. He squeezed me like the idea of it hurt. "Don't know how to get you out from under it."

"Will you stay?" I heard the insecurity wobble through the question, and I knew Baz heard it, too.

"No," he admitted.

Simple. Simple dreams. They were so easy to crush.

"We shouldn't have done this, should we?" he said with more of that remorse as he looked up at me.

"No," I whispered quiet.

He gripped my hips. "But I want to do it again."

"Me too."

In five seconds flat, Sebastian had me on my back, rolling a condom on his dick, and was sinking into me.

And it was every bit as hard and demanding as the first time, but every touch felt more beautiful to me. Every caress pulled me deeper. Every brush of his skin as if he was sinking into mine.

Tamar was right.

I had no idea what I was getting myself into.

eleven

Sebastian

I BARELY CRACKED OPEN an eye. My limbs were sluggish and sated, my dream-addled mind still swimming in a residual sea of lust. A mass of sweet and hair and silky flesh was tucked up close to me. Shea's back burrowed into the den of my body as we lay on our sides. Soft breaths were threatening to lull me right back into the most restful kind of sleep.

Would have, too, if it wasn't for the bustling energy emitted from the source of the mound of tight curls cresting the top of Shea's shoulder that was dragging me out of it.

Pale light filtered in through the large window at my back, and the tiny, tinkling voice to my front had me pressing my eyes shut tighter, wishing that with the simple act I'd disappear.

Three clicks of my heels or some kind of magical shit like that.

Or maybe a *get out of jail free* card.

Because there wasn't a single circumstance in my mind that made this situation okay.

"Momma," the hushed, slight voice continued on in a whisper, all kinds of endearing manners as she lured Shea from sleep. "Wake up, Momma." Excitement infiltrated her tone, and with it, she ticked up the volume, just a notch. "Sunshine is way, way, way up high in the sky. Is pancake time."

Roused, the mattress shifted under Shea as she moved, her bedhead popping up just an inch from her pillow, the perplexity of her movements telling me she was just as disoriented as I'd been thirty seconds ago.

I felt it when the sharpened spikes of coherency caused her to stiffen and stifle whatever freaked-out reaction her good nature made her inclined to have.

Shea slipped discretely out of my hold before she whispered a quiet, "Okay, baby. I'm coming."

Guilt saturated the mote-laden haze stretching through the wedges of morning light, like pillars of salt tossed haphazardly into her room. Shea's guilt. My guilt.

It was suffocating.

I don't have time for distractions.

Never had that sentiment been more glaring than now.

Lying on my side—because really, I was barely allowing myself to breathe, let alone move—I watched Shea awkwardly clutch the sheet to her chest and rummage around on the ground. She did her best to slink into a robe to cover herself, discomfort so thick in the air I couldn't discern if it was hers or mine.

Standing up, she tied the belt around her waist, all that gorgeous hair swishing down her back, teasing me with the memory of just how incredible it'd felt fisted in my hands last night. She leaned down and scooped her daughter into her arms, hitched her onto her hip.

Kallie.

Her daughter's name was Kallie.

Barefoot, Shea shuffled across the carpeted floor, those long legs exposed beneath the short, satiny white robe, her little girl hugging her neck. Contentment gentled across the small, round face when she peered back at me with wide, curious brown eyes.

Caramel.

Just like her mother's.

No fear in them.

Just a soft interest as she met my discomfited gaze.

Shea pressed a kiss to her temple and brushed back the overabundant curls from the child's forehead. Something about it felt apologetic and frantic, like she couldn't believe she let her daughter find her this way.

Kallie just clung tighter, little fingers pulsing in her mother's neck where she held on, her curious stare locked on me.

My chest screamed some unknown emotion. The guilt clotting off the airflow to my lungs was in an outright brawl with the affection that kept trying to find those cracks surrounding my heart, looking for a way in to corrupt and confuse.

Fuck. Couldn't afford feeling this way.

Was feeling it last night under Shea's touch, beneath her eyes, that seemed to see and understand far too much. Like she got me. In a way no one else ever would. Even when she didn't have one fucking inkling who I really was. I felt it strong in the possessiveness that swelled through me with another man having just the audacity to touch her, socked with the protectiveness of it when he made the mistake of hurting her.

Truth was, I'd been feeling it all along. It's what had kept calling me back. What'd gotten me into this fucked-up situation today.

It was hard to resist when you'd experienced little affection in your life. Sure, I loved. My brothers. The guys. But this emotion was something else entirely, something I doubted I even had the capacity to feel. Hailey had come the closest and she had nothing on what I was feeling for Shea. It wasn't even in the same spectrum, just pasty pastels of muted emotion up against the vibrancy of Shea…intense reds and bold blues, blinding white, the deepest black.

Light and dark and simple and profound.

More.

More.

More.

Shea didn't look back at me, while her little girl seemed not to be able to look away. Instead, she quietly latched the door shut behind them when she stepped out, her only acknowledgment she was even considering my presence, like she thought she was leaving me there to sleep away the morning. Thoughtful and kind, the way she always seemed to be.

Or maybe she was just trying to whisk her daughter away from the remnants of our debauchery with as little fanfare as possible.

Didn't blame her a bit.

Groaning, I rolled onto my back and pressed the heels of my hands into my eyes.

Shit.

Shit.

Shit.

Shit.

What did I do?

With a strained sigh, I pushed myself up to sitting at the edge of the bed, scrubbed my face, and forced myself to stand. I stretched my arms over my head, squinted at the muted light seeping in through the early morning fog.

And for the record, the sun was so not way, way, way up high in the sky, and after last night, I could have used about fifty more hours sleep with a little more Shea peppered in between. God, the woman was a fucking masterpiece. I'd have gladly stayed in bed with her all damned day.

But Shea didn't have time for distractions, even though that's exactly what I'd become, quite wittingly, because I knew exactly what was gonna happen when the words shot from my mouth last night.

I've got her.

And I did. Just for a little while, I'd had her.

And for a little while, she'd made me forget.

She'd let me get lost in all her light and dark, let me discover it was far greater than I ever could have imagined. Made me wish for something greater, too.

We both knew that was impossible. This morning had proven that.

I snagged my underwear from the floor and pulled them on as I fumbled toward the adjoining bathroom, stopping long enough to snatch up the three forgotten condom wrappers I'd carelessly tossed onto her floor. Both of us forgetting. Figuring if we had one night, we were going to make it count.

Now both of us were remembering why this was a really fucking bad idea.

I took a piss, hunted through her bottom cabinet for mouthwash that wasn't all that hard to find, swilled a mouthful straight from the bottle. It fucking burned and stung, but somehow that sensation was somewhere down in the cavern of my chest, and I spit it out as if it could rid me of all this shit I didn't want to feel.

Straightening, I stilled when I caught myself in the mirror, something unsettled in my eyes. Regret I knew I'd feel, taking Shea when I knew I shouldn't, knowing it was going to mean more than it should.

I rubbed my palm over my mouth, lifting my chin and dragging my hand down the stubble that was getting way too thick, to my throat that felt way too tight.

The messed up part? I didn't want to feel that regret, didn't ever want to look back on what I'd experienced with her as something stolen, when I was pretty damned sure if I was living a different life she would have been mine.

Didn't want her looking at me like I were sin.

A mistake.

Didn't want it to hurt when I walked away.

But I couldn't have all the other elements without the last.

I plodded back out into her room and quickly dressed. I felt like some creep when I cracked opened the door and peered through the slit to take in the landing of the top floor of Shea's house, wondering just what the protocol was for skipping out with the woman's kid lurking below. Shea had given me no indication of what she wanted me to do, and part of me was wishing that right before we'd finally succumbed to exhaustion at just before dawn, she'd have told me to grab my shit and go.

But that would've meant I'd have been robbed of those two hours of having something I'd never again have—holding Shea while she slept—and fuck it all if I had to give up that.

Outside, it was quiet, zero movement. I sucked in a deep breath and stepped out. Polished hardwood floors creaked beneath my feet, and my attention darted to the large, ornate frames that housed old faded pictures along the wall. Placed at the center was a black and white wedding photo of a couple I could only assume were Shea's grandparents. The man was in a formal military suit, the young woman who was just as striking as Shea, in a simple white-skirted suit, her hair coiled and topped with a little hat with a swath of tulle attached to it.

A bunch of photos were placed around it, growing out.

A single child in a photo that was clearly old, but new enough to be in color. Another with a group of three…three sisters that had to belong to that old couple. A young boy. Another after he'd become a man. Even newer still a group of what had to be grandkids. I stepped closer, searching the faces, picking out Shea right away, all sweet smiles and big curly hair, kind of like her daughter's.

Then there was a large photo. New. But it too had been placed in one of those old frames. A picture of Shea holding a tiny baby, her face in profile as she peered down into the infant's eyes.

My gut clenched tight, and I turned away.

I headed downstairs, unable to keep from taking it in, because studying the decor of Shea's house had been the last thing on my mind when I followed her inside last night. I stepped down into the vacant living room, which had the same dark hardwood floors. It was situated with antique and modern furniture, a blended mesh of old and new that just seemed to work in this house that I guessed had to be at least a hundred fifty years old.

It was gorgeous, too, the intricate crown molding painted a bright white, soft hues of colors on the walls, and the dark brown furniture the perfect contrast. I was no real estate guru, but I was betting the place had to be worth a small fortune.

I mean, I was used to nice shit, but it was always a shallow luxury, cookie-cutter sharp lines in crisp whites, blacks, and grays that drew you into the illusion you had everything you could ever want, when none of it could ever amount to a home.

Home.

No doubt, that's what this was.

And God, it made me happy that Shea had it, the words she'd spoken about her grandmother who she obviously adored running through my mind. There was no mistaking the way Shea felt about her. I wondered if her grandmother had left this house to Shea before or after Kallie, if she'd been around long enough to witness Shea becoming a mom.

The front door stood like a coward's beacon in front of me.

To my left, noises filtered down a short hall.

I looked between them.

Part of me wanted to bolt. Because shit, what the hell else was I supposed to do? But after last night? Couldn't just walk out on Shea without saying goodbye. Sure, I could rack it up to me needing to know if her head was okay, if she was physically hurting after that piece of shit messed with her last night.

But I knew—knew it was more.

I didn't make a sound as I cautiously moved across the super dark hardwood floors, the increasing sounds echoing down the hall serving as a guide toward my destination.

I passed by a black baby grand set up behind the sitting area before I slipped into the short hall. Outside a swinging door, I paused, listening to the sounds coming through.

Voices.

Not just any voice.

Shea's voice.

And she was singing, singing soft and low and throaty. It made me smile. I was right. This girl was country. Through and through. The way she was singing with all that southern soul was proof of that. Her voice pitch perfect. Like she'd been trained to sing that way. She was singing one of those old country songs that everyone knew, even me, about a girl being in love with a boy.

I couldn't resist pushing the door open enough so I could see into the kitchen, the smell of bacon sizzling on the stove enough to overtake every last one of my senses.

All except for the one that couldn't stop listening to Shea sing.

Well, and the one that got caught up in the way she looked standing at the counter in that robe, hair all around her, face so carefree as she sang away while she whipped up pancake batter in a big, yellow ceramic bowl.

And her little girl was singing, too. That tiny voice that knew all the words and had no problem keeping time.

The child was propped up on her knees on a chair where she sat at the small table set up in the breakfast nook, separated from the long row of granite countertop and cabinets where Shea stood by a huge island in the middle.

Shea peered over her shoulder at her daughter, pure adoration on her face.

Light.

Light.

Light.

None of the pangs of dark she let me slip into last night.

Everything here was uncontaminated. Pure. Absolute.

Swiveling her head back to the job at hand, her eye tripped over me and that incredible voice snagged in her throat. The spoon fumbled from her hold and clattered against the bowl.

I felt like an intruder raiding on the tender moment.

Recovering from the surprise, she resituated the bowl in the crook of one elbow, picking back up the spoon with her opposite hand and mixing again, eyeing me with just as many questions as the ones that had been eating at my brain since the second I'd woken up this morning.

Shea'd shared something with me last night I knew she'd shared with few other people. And I was willing to put down bets those people hadn't touched her the way I'd touched her. That the way she'd looked at them hadn't come close to the way she'd looked at me. Like she could see straight through all the bullshit walls I erected around myself, right down to what mattered.

Like somehow what she saw *mattered* to her.

I understood exactly what she meant when she'd told me last night she couldn't make sense of the way I made her feel, because I sure as hell couldn't make sense of the way she made me feel, either.

Physically?

God, the woman had undone me. Time and time again. Hands down the hottest thing I'd ever been given the gift to touch. Perfectly soft in every place she should be, defined muscle everywhere else, a face that made me weak in the knees.

Perfection.

But it was that sweet willing heart that had managed to unravel something fierce inside of me, had me opening up and telling her things I hadn't ever told anyone—even if I'd kept the details as vague as I could. Still hadn't told her who I was, and I guess I planned on keeping it that way.

Red, or Tamar like I'd learned was her name last night, had warned me if I didn't tell her, then she would.

But I couldn't make it form on my tongue. For just one perfect night, I wanted someone to look at me the way Shea had. Knowing I had absolutely nothing to give her and still she wanted it all the same. *Me.*

Knowing we were nothing and everything, captives to that connection she had blistering through me every time we were in the same room.

And it was there.

Still just as strong this morning as she caught me standing there like a voyeur with the door pushed open a mere inch.

A welcoming smile edged one corner of her mouth and she tipped her head to the side.

Inviting me inside.

Inhaling deeply, I wedged myself through the door, thinking if I didn't open it too wide maybe it wouldn't draw so much attention. Then I could get in, tell Shea goodbye, and get out.

No harm, no foul.

My gaze got glued to my feet when Kallie's head poked up in interest, grinning at me with too much sweet and innocence and childhood intrigue.

Curious.

Curious.

Curious.

Look where that had gotten us.

I edged around the other side of Shea, feeling protected by the butcher-block island that took up a good share of the layout of the country kitchen.

A smirk threatened.

Country. Through and through.

But now was not the time to go noticing how fucking adorable Shea was, her pint-sized twin pulling up a close second.

"Hey," I attempted, shifting on my feet as I dragged a shaky hand through the mess on top of my head.

She chewed at that plump pink bottom lip, and a blush crept up her neck.

God, it was way too obvious where her thoughts went traveling, and damn it all if my mind didn't want to go along for the ride.

"Good morning," she murmured low.

I jerked my head up when the swinging door flew open and someone came barreling in. "Hey, Shea, have you seen my—"

The woman's words clipped off and she stopped like she'd slammed into a brick wall. This plain girl with a brown ponytail, and even browner eyes. "What the fu…" Her mouth formed the words without her tongue vocalizing them, and Shea visibly cringed.

The barely contained distress that had taken up residence in my stomach ratcheted up by a thousand notches.

The girl who'd come rushing in looked weakly toward Shea before she turned to Kallie who'd started pounding on the table top. "Hungry…hungry…hungry," she chanted. "Momma's makin' pancakes."

Irritation buzzed through me. This had to be the most awkward moment of my entire life.

"Who are…?" The girl shook her head, looking to Shea for an answer.

I shifted some more.

Shea peeked at me, then turned to the girl who was her…sister?…and said, "This is Baz."

No. There was no resemblance. This had to be a roommate, or more likely a friend with the way she was looking at me in outright horror. A friend I was most definitely not expecting and a friend who I most definitely wasn't prepared for. Not the worry that struck up in her eyes or the little pinpoint daggers that suddenly took them over, like she'd just summed me up and decided I was someone to hate.

She wouldn't be wrong, but it sure as hell didn't make the situation any easier.

Shea ignored her friend gaping at me from the door and cleared her throat.

"Do you want coffee?" she asked me with just as much discomfort as I was drowning in. She gestured with her chin toward the coffee maker that was dribbling the last drops of a full pot into a metal carafe. "I'm making breakfast." She began to ramble, it sounding a whole lot like a plea. "Are you hungry? I don't know what you like…I can throw on some eggs if you'd prefer something different."

I raked a hand through my hair. "I…uh…" Over my shoulder, I looked to the door that I guessed had to lead out to the side of Shea's massive house, to the cute little girl with too wide eyes that spilled over with innocence and joy, back to Shea who was watching me in a way I wished she wouldn't.

With a hope there was no use hoping for.

"I think I'm just gonna…go."

Shea's face crumpled and her jaw locked, as if she was physically trying to master whatever was gripping her inside, this sweet girl struggling to hold back tears that collected fast in her eyes.

Tears I put there.

Shit.

"Shea," I murmured. My hand darted toward her then halted in the air. Honestly, I wasn't sure I could handle touching her. I dropped my voice so only she could hear. "That's not what I meant."

But we both knew that's exactly what I meant. I had every intention of escaping out her door.

And walking away was going to fucking hurt because standing here, we both knew we wouldn't be seeing each other again. I was going back to Anthony's, packing up our shit, and getting the hell out of Savannah. Anthony thought I'd be safe here, but I was in deeper than I'd ever been before.

Trouble.

Told Anthony that shit followed me wherever I went. More like I was a magnet for it, lured right to a girl who I knew without a doubt could turn my life upside down.

She pulled her face out of my reach and her eyes slipped closed, blocking out the sight of me. Her voice was strained and deathly quiet, but I felt the impact of every word. "The last thing I need are lies from you. Please…just go. Don't make me cry in front of my daughter."

Swallowing around the rock scraping up my throat, I nodded. I took a furtive glance at her friend and her daughter, knowing I was nothing but a bastard.

I backed up slowly, then slipped out the door.

Rays of light slanted through the lush leaves on the full trees that surrounded her lot, birds rustled as they chirped and danced through the branches, and the lawn glistened with dew. My boots dented into the earth as I stormed around to the front of the house.

"Shit…shit…shit," I cursed below my breath, gripping two handfuls of hair. I had the intense urge to yank it out because all that discomfort had shifted to anxiety. The thought of never seeing Shea again was completely rejected by every cell in my body.

My car sat on the street where I'd left it. I strode toward it with all the purpose I had left, with every amount of sense I'd shored up and locked away in my twenty-six years.

With all the things I'd learned to survive.

Control.

Control.

Control.

I rounded the front of my car and with each step felt slivers of that control being stripped away.

I pulled my keys from my pocket and clicked the lock. I looked to the sky for some kind of strength. My entire being stalled in front of the car door, my jumbled mind twisted up and focused on the girl.

Or maybe it was my heart.

Just for a while, make me forget.

"Fuck it."

All rational thought escaped me, and I turned and jogged back around the side of her house. I bounded up the three steps. Without a knock, I flung the door open.

Shea gasped out a surprised sound and jumped back from the counter. With her hand pressed to her chest, she stood facing my direction, caramel eyes dulled with sadness.

Hated that I'd put it there.

I didn't hesitate, just strode toward her and buried my hands in her hair and kissed her in a way I was sure was not appropriate for witnesses over breakfast.

She yielded to it. A soft sigh parted her mouth and she opened to me, and I felt myself slipping a little deeper. I pulled back a fraction, our mouths a breath away. Squeezing the sides of her face, I dropped my forehead to hers. "Yes, I want coffee," I whispered. "God yes, I want coffee."

God yes, I want you.

A peal of giggles sounded to my left. Foreheads still pressed together, Shea and I looked over at the source to the tiny blonde-haired girl with a wild mane of tightly wound curls. Little hands were pressed to her mouth as she tried to mask her reaction as if she knew she was witnessing something private, but the way she had her chin popped up, she was doing nothing to cover the full-mouthed smile that showcased a row of bright white baby teeth.

Fucking cute.

"You kissed Momma." She said it like it was the funniest thing she'd ever seen, her tiny shoulders lifted to her ears as if she were being tickled.

Shea pulled away. Embarrassment had her gnawing at that bottom lip, and she glanced up at me from beneath the thick veil of her lashes, before she cast an adoring smile at her daughter who beamed right back.

"He did, didn't he?"

Kallie just giggled more.

Composing herself, Shea took a step back and ran her fingertips down my arm like she was issuing me some kind of thanks. She threaded her fingers through mine.

It felt natural, too, this girl touching me in such a simple way.

Didn't mean things weren't just as awkward as earlier when Shea looked over her shoulder, our hands still twined, to her friend standing there. The girl leaned back and crossed her arms over her chest, outright disgust smeared across her face.

"April," Shea hedged quietly, "this is Sebastian. Baz." She almost corrected the last with a reverence I didn't come close to deserving. Shea tipped her head to the side like she was trying to convey something, and it became apparent this wasn't the first time April had heard my name.

April gave her a succinct nod, like she already knew exactly who I was. Yet she didn't have the first clue who I *really* was, either. "Right. Baz." Her voice was clipped and hard, before she braided it with a dense thread of sarcasm. "So nice of you to drop by so early in the morning."

With a sound clearly shouting *Please don't embarrass me,* Shea cleared her throat. Warily, she looked back at me. "Baz, this is my best friend and roommate, April. April and I have been friends since we were seven. She's…" Her voice lost its edge of apprehension, filled right up with fondness, though she said it like a joke. "She helps take care of Kallie and she thinks she needs to take care of me."

April huffed out a sigh. "Someone has to take care of you." She turned back to me with all kinds of feigned pleasantries, each word oozing a warning. "It's nice to meet you, Sebastian. I hope you stick around longer than to just enjoy the *coffee*."

Shea cringed and I bit back a laugh that came at my own expense, because April's *warm* reception sure as hell didn't do anything to make me feel welcome. But you had to respect someone who didn't hesitate to say exactly what was on their mind.

No doubt, Shea had the same questions running through her own mind. Five minutes ago, I was hightailing it out her door and the next I was running right back through it.

Surely I wasn't the only one who couldn't make sense of it.

"Oh crap!" Shea shouted. The smell of burned pancakes suddenly hit the air, and Shea raced for the burner, yanking the skillet from the flame. "Crap," she said again, then laughed, slanting me an eye. "Guess I was distracted."

Right.

"Ewwww! I don't like burnt pancakes, Momma. They're icky!" This from that same little voice that under April's scrutiny I'd almost forgotten was there.

"It's okay, baby," Shea tossed over her shoulder while she scraped the burnt batter from the pan and into the garbage. "It's only two. Our big ol' bowl is still full of mix. I'll make new. Why don't you set the table? We have a guest this morning, so set it for four. You think you can do that, my big girl?"

"Yep!" Kallie replied, probably a little too enthusiastically for someone who'd just been asked to do a chore.

Shea gestured with her chin toward the table. "Have a seat and I'll get you some coffee."

Awkwardly, I stood there having no idea what to do. Run like I should have in the first place? Intervene on the mess Shea seemed to be making in the kitchen? Or maybe make myself right at home, hunt down a mug, and pour myself some coffee? Shea obviously had her hands full, but April jumped in on the breakfast, so I finally gave up and accepted her direction, heading toward the table.

Caramel eyes went wide as that same curiosity was renewed. My chest got all tight, the little girl setting me on edge.

This had to rank up there with some of the worst ideas I'd ever had, and I'd done some really stupid shit in my life. I knew it was wrong—being here when I knew I couldn't stay—feeding that false hope Shea was watching me with, but I didn't know how to make myself walk away.

I wanted to float in it, just for a little while, in Shea's good and light. Worse yet, I wanted to delve into just a little more of her dark. Wanted her to show me just how deep it went, somehow knowing it would drown me when she did.

I touched the back of the chair to Kallie's right. "Do you mind if I sit here?"

"You can't sit there, silly…that's my mommy's chair." A bell-like laugh rang from her and she pointed to the chair at the opposite side of the table. "You sit in that one. That's our special spot for people who don't live here."

"Um…okay…thank you."

I rubbed a palm over my face. What in the name of God was I doing?

I looked at Shea again, who was stealing a sly glance our way, a grin forming at the corners of her mouth while a whole ton of worry creased the corners of her eyes.

Walking around the table, I pulled out the chair and slipped down onto it, knee bouncing a million miles a minute

"Hi," I said, raking a flustered hand through my hair. "I'm Baz. Your mom's…friend."

So apparently now I thought formal introductions were in order.

Confusion pinched up her nose and she said my name as if I were crazy, her voice lifting my name like a song. "Baz?"

"Well, Sebastian is my real name. But my friends call me Baz."

Her eyes narrowed in speculation. "Am I allowed to call you Baz?"

I drummed my fingers on the table, my nerves out of control. "Sure."

"Okay, Baz." She stuck out her little hand.

I looked at it as if it might burn me, before I hesitantly reached out and took it.

Her head nodded along as she shook my hand and spoke all prim and proper. "It's very nice to meet you, Baz. I'm Kallie Marie Bentley." Her tone turned excited. Words began to fly from her mouth at warp speed. "Did you know I'm four years old? Only for seven months and then I'm gonna be five and then I get to go to big girl school and I get to ride on the bus."

Out of the blue, she flapped her arms. "I'm a butterfly."

Um. Okay.

But my mind went fluttering right back to the kaleidoscope of butterflies gracing Shea's slender hip.

A smile pulled at one side of my mouth.

"You're a butterfly, huh?"

"Yep. Butterflies are so, so pretty and my favorite kind is the Monarch kind. Did you know they fly so, so far?" Her words quieted, like she was sharing a secret with me. "Two thousand whole miles so they can get warm in the winter."

Soft laughter rolled around on my tongue. God, the kid was cute. "Two thousand whole miles? You sure about that?" I whispered back.

She nodded emphatically. "Uh-huh. I know for sure FOR SURE! It says so in my favorite book. You want me to read it to you? I got it right upstairs in my room."

Shea cut in. "How about we read it another time, sweetheart? Breakfast is going to be ready in a couple minutes, and we need the table set if we're going to eat."

From where she stood at the stove, Shea pitched me an apologetic yet graceful smile, because I'd gotten sucked right into the whirlwind that was Kallie Bentley.

"Okay, Momma." Kallie climbed down from the chair she was perched on. I tried to keep my attention trained on Shea wearing that robe and the insane body hidden under it, which wasn't all that safe a subject to concentrate on. It was weird witnessing her here, taken out of the element of the bar, out of the atmosphere of her room last night.

There? Her skin simmered sex, that storm gathering from beneath the surface, like in the shadows it searched for way to be exposed.

But here?

Here she was whimsical and gentle and…and…a mom.

That fact fucked with my head.

My gaze slid right back to the little girl who pushed a step stool up against the counter and climbed to the top step. She carefully pulled down four plates from the cabinet above.

That wasn't such a safe place for my attention, either, because I kept getting that agitated feeling wind up in my chest as I watched her make her way around the kitchen and back to the table. Her little tongue poked out to the side in concentration, her movements controlled as she focused on setting the obviously vintage purple plates safely at each spot.

She slid one in front of me and peeked up at me. "There you go, Baz."

"Thank you," I mumbled.

Shea and April set platters piled high with food on the center of the table. Tender fingers sent chills racing down my spine when Shea fluttered them along the base of my neck, leaning over my shoulder to place a cup filled with steaming coffee down in front of me.

We all sat down and shared a meal together. And it was relaxed and easy and terrifying.

I'd been a fool for wanting to lose control with Shea.

Because I didn't know how I was going to get it back.

Arms crossed over my chest, I had my hip propped up against the counter.

Watching her.

Shea focused on pushing some buttons on the dishwasher, her attention trained away, intensity billowing around us, that invisible tether stretched taut.

Almost reluctantly, she stood to face me. Quiet filled her kitchen, the two of us just looking at each other, the water running through the pipes, and our confused breaths the only sound.

April and Kallie had just left to go to the park, and when they'd gone, it'd stolen all the relative ease. It felt a bit of an olive branch when April had looked at me as if she were making a tough decision, then made a quick glance to Shea, before she'd turned to Kallie and bent her voice in that way women always seemed to do when they talked to little kids.

"How about a trip to the park?" she'd asked, and Kallie had been all over it, flying up the stairs to her room to get changed and bounding back downstairs in less than two minutes. She'd jumped up and down, the ball of pure energy she was, clapping her hands and squealing, "All ready, Auntie April!"

Shea had knelt down and hugged her, murmured, "Have a great time, Butterfly," while she brushed back some of that uncontrolled hair. The kid had gone and flung her arms around my leg, hugging me tight, saying something about me reading to her another time while I'd been completely struck dumb.

April had paused at the door and looked back at us, eyes narrowed. "Three hours," she'd warned, obviously giving the two of us some time alone, because she wasn't immune to the questions swirling between Shea and me, either.

Now Shea cleared her throat, redness on her cheeks. "I'm going to run upstairs for a minute. Why don't you wait for me in the living room? The remote's on the coffee table…it should be easy enough to figure out."

"Sure," I answered, though watching television was the last thing I wanted to do. What I really wanted was to follow her right back up those stairs and go for another round, to see her with the sun shining down around her, lighting up the lush lines of her body while I pounded into the delicious warmth of it.

Don't go there, Stone.

Instead, I trailed her into the living room and watched her jog upstairs and disappear into her room with a quick, unsure glance behind her. I pushed out a strained breath from my lungs, wondering again what in the hell I'd gotten myself into.

My phone buzzed in my pocket. Turning away, I wandered back into the middle of the living room, pulled out my phone to see who'd texted. I swept my finger across the face and couldn't help my grin.

The Keeper.

Should have known he'd be concerned.

Hey, asshole. It's noon and we haven't heard a word from you. Everything good?

Nope. I was completely and utterly fucked.

I tapped out a vague reply to Zee. *Yep. Everything is good.*

Immediately it buzzed again. *You didn't come home last night.*

I resisted rolling my eyes. The kid was a sharp one.

Another text came in right behind the last.

You with Shea?

Yeah, I answered.

Your girl okay?

My girl. What the fuck? Should have known Zee wouldn't leave it alone.

Memories from last night went careening through my head. The way Shea had looked at me when I'd undressed in front of her, seeing beneath all the hard and cold and scarred.

My chest tightened, a painful squeeze of my lungs.

My girl.

Maybe in another lifetime, if I'd chosen another path, if I'd made a million different choices.

She was shaken up, but okay, I returned.

Okay, man, keep us posted.

Will do.

Stuffing my phone back in my pocket, I roamed Shea's living room, looking at the pictures on the walls, the books crammed into the bookshelves, the basket of toys in the corner on the floor.

Home.

And I was invading it, putting a blemish on the safety of this place, but I didn't know how to stop.

I drifted over to the baby grand. With my index finger, I struck one key. The sound rang through the room, and my ear tilted when that hidden place inside me thrashed, pushing from the inside out.

Music had always been my peace.

Drawn, I sat down on the hard bench and my fingers began to move lightly across the keys. Instinctual. I kept my voice barely more than a whisper as I fumbled through the words I'd written for Shea just days before, feeling something bleeding out from within. I got lost in it, in her song and her depth and some kind of fucked-up shame, because I knew I'd done this, was responsible for everything Shea and I were stumbling through. Because I couldn't find the willpower to stay away.

She was my weakness.

I froze when I felt the presence behind me. The song slowly blinked out, the last note lingering in the dense air, before I slowly looked over my shoulder to find Shea. Thoughtful eyes met mine in all their warmth—covering me, pulling me in, dragging me under.

"You play," she said, a statement rather than a question.

"A little," I said with a shrug.

She scoffed. "I would hardly classify that as a little." She shuffled toward me, barefoot, and still wearing that robe. "You have a beautiful voice," she whispered, and again it took on that reverent tone, like she was recognizing something inside me I didn't see.

She ran her fingers up the back of my neck and into my hair, and I lifted my head to it and tried not to moan like a girl when she pressed her hot mouth to my Adam's apple, kissing me there like the temptress she was.

"Such a beautiful, beautiful voice for a beautiful, beautiful man." The words vibrated against my throat.

"Shea." My response was hoarse, uttered toward the ceiling as she kissed up and down my throat. With her daughter's innocent face running like a reel through my mind, I searched inside myself for some kind of resolve. For courage. For a speck of integrity. "I should go. I shouldn't be here. I shouldn't have stayed. Shouldn't have come back."

Never should have come in the first place.

"You're exactly where I want you to be," she coaxed against my skin.

"Shea." It was a plea for one of us to find reason.

"Please," she whispered, hands sinking into my shoulders.

Weak.

Weak.

Weak.

That's what she made me.

Groaning, I gave, because she already had me, and I swiveled a fraction, grabbed her by the hips, and pulled her onto my lap. She was quick to straddle me, a smile taking over her face as I palmed her ass, all those waves of shiny soft hair falling down around us.

"It's hardly fair, you know," she said.

"What's not fair?"

"You…looking the way you do. Then you turn around and have a voice like that? Singing and playing that way?" She pulled back with a grin. "Tell me you don't play guitar. You know what they say, a man with a guitar automatically becomes ten times sexier than any other guy in the room."

I curbed a snort.

Didn't I know it.

And that was exactly the shit I'd come to hate.

"Pair that with this face and this body…" she continued, purely playful.

Any other girl started talking like that and I'd have tossed her from my lap.

Instead, I kneaded my fingers deeper into the flesh of her ass, rocking her into my cock that was at the ready and begging for more.

Shivers rolled through her. "…and I would say you're irresistible, Sebastian Stone."

"Is that all you want me for…my body?" I teased, running my hands up her back, eliciting a pleasured whimper from her.

Fingertips played across my chest, and her expression turned vulnerable, that storm collecting speed. "Yeah. I do want this body." Those fingers fluttered up to my jaw. "And I want this face."

Eyes not leaving mine, she slowly leaned down and kissed me over my heart. "Most of all, I want this," she murmured, hiding nothing, laying herself bare.

Why is she tormenting us both?

My lungs pressed full.

This girl didn't play games. She knew she could send me running, and she just put it out there.

"Don't think I can give you that." The abraded words scraped from my mouth. "I've got so much shit, Shea." I felt the lines pinch my brow, hoping for her to finally see what I tried to show her last night.

But that was the thing.

She'd seen it all, even though she couldn't make out the details.

And still, she wanted me.

"I'm no good for you."

Darkness flashed through her eyes, like lightning striking through dense, gray clouds.

"And I'm no good for you," she contended, wetting her lips, eyes cast downward before she looked back at me. "People might say I come with baggage. But I will *never* consider Kallie anything but the gift she is. The most priceless, precious gift." The confession broke in her throat. "And I have to protect that, Baz. What happened this morning? Her finding us? You make me lose my head."

"I know. I'm sorry. I never should have put you in that position. I should have left."

A pained sound escaped her. "That's the last thing I would have wanted. Being with you? Falling asleep in your arms?" She sucked in a breath. "I needed it, Sebastian…I needed you." She exhaled. "You make me feel like I can breathe."

"Then how does this work?"

"You want it to work?"

"It won't," I bit out, quiet but sharp with implication. "It won't work," I reiterated. "But this morning showed me just how fucking impossible it is to let you go. Not while I'm here, in this city with you. I don't think I can stay away."

Hadn't been able to stay away since the second I saw her. After last night? Wasn't going to be able to start now.

She fisted desperate hands in my shirt, eyes racing across my face.

"I'm going to break you, Shea."

I knew it.

Felt it in my gut.

"You already have."

A growl rumbled in my chest, and I hoisted her up. Piano keys clanked as I propped her up against the shining black.

Fuck, she looked gorgeous there, hair tumbling over her shoulders, the collar of her robe popping open to reveal the curve of just one breast, the outside of her thighs in my needy hands. I ran them under the hem of the satiny material.

"You put on underwear." I faked a pout, and she giggled. That sound was so damned sweet I was sure I'd never grow tired of hearing it, but I knew I'd never get the chance.

"Figured I'd better cover myself up a little. Someone might get the wrong impression that I'm easy or something." It was all a self-conscious tease.

"Nothing easy about you, baby," I countered soft, sliding my fingers under the edges of the lace clinging to her slender hips and pressing my mouth to the skin between her breasts, catching on to the wild beat of her heart. "Every bit of you is complicated. God, you've got me twisted up inside. Every fucking second, thinkin' about you."

If Shea could strip herself bare, then I guessed I owed her a little bit of that, too.

I nudged the robe open wider, exposing those gorgeous round tits and puckered-up pink nipples. "Look at that. So perfect, Shea."

"You see me," she whispered, fingers fluttering up to her neck as she tilted her head back, echoing me from last night. And I knew she wanted me to *see*. To *feel*.

Fuck, I did. I fucking did, and it was reckless and dangerous, every move fraught with peril.

I began to work her panties down her legs. I edged back far enough to drag the lace off one foot, then the other.

I spread her knees wide, perfect pussy on display.

My gaze trailed over her where she was propped up on the piano like an angel, one side of her robe draping off a delicate shoulder, tapering down to where the belt was knotted at her waist.

Or maybe she was the devil with an angel's face, because this girl was going to destroy me.

She reached out and cupped my cheek, her expression soft, surrounded by all her light.

Angel.

Definitely angel.

"Gonna fuck you with my mouth, baby."

She whimpered, and tremors of anticipation rolled through her.

I gripped her by the outside of her thighs, holding her open, dragging my tongue from the root of her ass all the way to her clit.

On a strangled gasp, fingers dove into my hair, yanking hard. "Sebastian."

Fuck, that felt good, 'cause I loved it rough, but I was giving this girl all the gentle I could find.

And I ate her up, tongue lapping between her lips, diving deep.

She just yanked harder. "Shit." That throaty rasp spurred me on.

I teased her opening with a finger, up and down the slick, wet flesh, nipping at that sweet spot that had her writhing with my teeth. I sank two fingers inside and sucked her clit into my mouth.

Like an earthquake I held in the palms of my hands, she shattered, bursting into a billion unrecognizable pieces. Her entire body shook. She cried out, pressing me closer, pushing me away. And she was chanting my name. Again and again. Like it meant something.

And I could feel her storm swarming us, taking us whole. Vapors and whispers of her unknown.

She didn't take the time to come back down. She slid from the piano and right onto her knees, reaching out for my hand to urge me to stand. I fumbled out from under the piano, lust knotted in my stomach and vibrating in my thighs. I hovered over her, looking down at her while she yanked just as fiercely at my fly as she'd yanked at my hair. She didn't take her eyes from me as she freed me from the constraints of my underwear.

I felt trapped by it, by the passion radiating from this mystifying girl.

Her hand was so damned soft when she gripped the base of my cock. She squeezed, and I hissed when she slid her palm up, slowly…deliberately. Her tongue swept along that lush bottom lip as she ran her thumb around the fat ridge of my head. She watched, enraptured, as the shiny bead grew from the slit, sending a fresh rush of anticipation burning through me.

She leaned in and licked it clean.

I jerked and buried my fingers in her hair, just as she drew me deeply into the heat of her mouth.

"Shea…baby…fuck," I mumbled, trying to remain coherent, searching for any threads left of my control as Shea began to stroke me with her mouth. What she couldn't fit, she stroked with her hand. Her tongue was performing all kinds of magic that drove me right out of my damned mind.

I cupped the sides of her head, my pinky fingers sliding along the corners of her mouth, needing to feel where we were connected. She moaned against the sensitive flesh.

Pleasure coiled, that fever tightening my balls and tingling down the inside of my thighs.

I jerked, coming in her mouth, before I stilled with a grunt while Shea swallowed me down.

Never had I seen anything more beautiful than that. Shea's lips wrapped around my cock, her eyes locked on mine.

Caramel.

Honest.

Tainted.

Pure.

My body rolled with the revelry while my head swam in bliss.

She pulled free of me, tongue swiping across her swollen, puffy lips, and tucked me back into my boxers. I dropped to my knees and framed her unforgettable face in my hands.

Floored.

"Don't understand this, Shea. Not for a second. But I'm never going to be the same."

twelve
Shea

GIGGLES RANG IN THE AIR, her head kicked back and her face bursting with happiness as the endearing sound lifted toward the sky. Kallie held onto my hand, her easy trust my comfort, and she shook her head as if what Sebastian had said was completely absurd. She leaned forward so she could see around me to him as he strolled along at my opposite side.

Her words were filled with the same childish laughter. "No, you silly, butterflies don't have noses. They smell with their antennas and taste with their feet." She said it as if it were of the utmost importance, my sweet child thinking it her duty to enlighten him on every single detail she knew about butterflies.

And for the last two weeks, she'd been doing it every chance she got.

Hands stuffed in his pockets, a grin slid across that handsome, handsome face, and my heart beat erratically, a wild crash of foolishness as I watched him interact with my daughter so effortlessly.

"Now that just sounds gross, Kallie. Tasting with your feet?" he said, sparring with her more. He shot me a little wink when I smiled up at him. I loved how he humored my chattering child. Loved how his eyes crinkled at the corners when he did. Loved how he looked with the last of the sun's rays slanting across his face, twilight glinting in those dark grey eyes, and shadows playing along his strong jaw.

Most of all, I loved him here, at my side, as fleeting as I knew it would be, as terrified as I was of having to let him go.

Kallie huffed, my precious child skipping along beside me. "It's not gross!"

"Are you crazy? What if you tasted food with your feet?" he teased.

Kallie's little nose scrunched up at the thought. "No way!" She laughed, grinning widely. "I don't wanna taste nothin' with my feet."

"But I thought you said you were a butterfly?"

Those giggles just kept flowing, and her shoulders lifted up toward her ears, her body twisting up in a little girl's pleasure. Joy radiated from every inch of her.

A breeze rustled through the heavy canopy of trees hugging us from above, the cool evening brushing at our skin. We slowly wove through the crowds and browsed through the seemingly endless rows of vendor tents set up for the craft fair at the park in the center of town. A jazz band played at the end of the park on an elevated stage, and the smell of open barbecue pits and deep fried churros floated on the easy air.

Sebastian hooked his arm casually around my neck.

"Good idea, yeah?" he asked as he leaned down and pressed a kiss to my temple.

I beamed up at him as if I were a little girl, too. One who'd just discovered that knights in shining armor really did exist and this one had come to rescue me from my loneliness.

It had been two weeks since Sebastian had spent that first night irrevocably altering something inside me. Two weeks since he'd shattered me in the best ways possible…then walked out my door and proved he held the power to shatter my heart. But it'd been just as long since he'd turned around and come back to me.

Since he'd *stayed.*

In moments like these, it was easy to pretend that he always would.

We'd spent so much time together, it was becoming hard to remember what it was like before he'd been there, the man making up ideal days full of laughter and ease, perfect nights spent beneath him and above him, our bodies alive, and my heart forming a million memories to sustain me when he was gone.

Because below it all, there always remained the current of the charade we both knew we were playing, that as truthful as our touches and time were, there was a false security in them, a danger that was lurking just beneath the surface. He was still a man I knew so little about, his words always vague but the meaning so transparent. In the cover of darkness, I'd whisper questions to him, desperate to know him more. But he held back, only admitting that he needed me, needed someone who didn't look at him through the past, but instead, lived with him here in the present.

Still, I felt closer to him than I had with anyone else in a very, very long time.

Well, in ever.

He nuzzled his nose behind my ear, and a shiver rolled down my spine, settling in my belly where this bundle of energy thrived, a constant chaos of excitement, a kind of happiness I'd never experienced—as dangerous as I knew it was.

"Tonight's perfect," I whispered, and he pulled me a little closer, the tension that continuously roiled between us mellowed and tempered in the relaxed mood.

"Who's hungry?" he asked, the question directed at Kallie.

"Me! Me! Me!" She jumped on her toes beside me. "I want kettle corn!"

"After dinner," I told her.

Baz mouthed, "You're no fun."

I jostled into him with my shoulder.

He laughed and promised her, "After dinner."

Taking my hand, he led us toward the delicious smell traveling on the wind. We rounded the corner to the food vendors set up along the perimeter of the large square area of lawn in front of the stage, where we ordered plates full of deep-fried chicken and grilled corn-on-the-cob, sat on the grassy, damp ground, and ate together as if we'd done it since the beginning of time. My daughter laughed and Sebastian smiled and played and teased and my heart pressed so full.

"Be right back." Sebastian hopped up and strode across the field. Minutes later, he returned, a huge bag stuffed full of kettle corn crooked in his elbow. "Here you go, sweetheart," he said quietly as he passed the bag to my daughter, and this time it was Kallie's turn to beam up at him. I was praying my daughter wasn't falling for this man as quickly as me, because I couldn't stand to put her heart on the line, not when it was me who had chosen to allow Sebastian into our lives, allowed this distraction to distort our reality.

"Thank you," was uttered with a little contented squeal.

Sebastian stretched out his hand, helped me to stand, tore me up more with the lingering kiss that was far from crude and much too tender. Kallie swayed beside us. Sebastian's hand was at my back, my daughter at my side. We headed back down another row of crafts as we made our way out, the Sunday evening growing late.

Sebastian suddenly stopped at a tent that was crammed with handmade quilted bags and blankets and stuffed animals, a patch-work style of mismatched colors and patterns. "Look at that, Kallie. It's a butterfly."

It was strung up from a top metal beam, hanging down amongst a bevy of birds, the super soft stuffed animal nearly half the size of my dainty daughter.

"It's a Monarch kind," she said quietly in awe, even though this butterfly was bright colors, mismatched prints, and didn't come close to depicting a single one of the butterflies Kallie loved to pretend she was, but neither Sebastian nor I were going to correct her.

"Do you like it?" he asked.

Apparently so by the little happy dance she was doing at my side, her eyes wide and so sweet. My heart was beating wildly because I couldn't stop this man from slipping deeper.

Taking hold.

Sebastian caught the woman's attention who was working the tent. "Can we get that butterfly there, please?"

"Of course." She climbed a ladder and was quick to unhook it while Baz was digging out his wallet from his back pocket and, once again, pulling out a small stack of large bills.

"You don't need to do that, Baz. You already took care of us all day. I'll get it."

He frowned at me. "I want to, Shea. Let me do this."

And I saw that same thing there, the same awareness I felt constantly, that time was stealing away, that he too was rushing to fill up these days with memories, because as hard and rough as he was, I saw the softness, too. Saw that even though I knew he would never admit it, my daughter was impossible not to love.

He knelt down and passed Kallie the butterfly. "There. Right where she belongs."

Excited, thankful noises flew from her mouth as she squeezed and hugged it tight. She sidled up to his side and slipped her hand into his, and something passed through his expression that stole my breath, something dark and hard and sad.

Silently, we traipsed back through the grasses, passing by people still milling around. Many vendors were beginning to tear down their displays as the show wound down and moved onto whatever city called to them next.

We hit the sidewalk that ran along the riverfront. Goosebumps lifted on my skin as a breeze blew across the waters, the air cool and heavy. I pulled in a deep breath, hoping it would push out some of the fear that kept trying to gather in my chest.

We passed by *Charlie's* that was closed down for Sunday night and toward my neighborhood. Kallie began to drag her feet.

Sebastian looked down at her, his voice light. "Are you tired?"

She nodded with a yawn.

"Come here, Little Bug," Sebastian offered quietly into the deepening night, and that murmured sentiment ripped at my spirit, words he'd never called her, something all his own.

Releasing me, he scooped up my daughter and tucked her close to his chest.

Effortlessly.

Kallie clung to him, her head on his shoulder and her butterfly clutched in her arm.

Simple, simple dreams.

They grew bold and unsettled.

He didn't hesitate to carry her up our walkway and through the door. His steps were subdued and quieted as I followed close behind, and he toted her upstairs and into her darkened room. Gently, he laid her down on her bed then stepped aside so I could remove her shoes and tuck her in, my child already drifting to sleep.

I peppered her sweet face with kisses, my precious girl, and she smiled a soft, comfortable smile, and my chest burned with the devotion and love I had for her. Shuffling out, I looked at her once more over my shoulder, before I flipped off her light and left her door open an inch, edging back out to the landing where Sebastian had retreated.

Waiting for me.

He stepped toward my room, his chin lifted like a threat while he held open my door.

My heart beat wildly as I approached him.

He was never gentle, his body always desperate, every touch filled with urgency.

I never minded.

I wanted him raw.

Unbridled.

Because it was the truth he could afford to give me.

Even though I also saw the truth in the gentle way he handled my daughter, in those moments when I was caught in his compassion, in the dedication that slipped from his mouth when he spoke of his brother and friends.

It was Sebastian who didn't know it existed.

He shut the door behind us. Two fumbled moments passed before our clothes were forgotten. Tonight we didn't even make it to the bed. Sebastian was covering himself with a condom as he took me down onto the floor. He hooked my legs up over his shoulders, my breath gone as I became his. My back chafed against the carpet while my spirit was seared by every inch of him.

"Shea," he whispered urgently. Regretfully.

And I was falling.

Falling.

Falling.

Falling.

I could feel him at the ledge, earth crumbling beneath his feet, frantically trying to hold ground.

I clung to him, a selfish part of me wishing for a way to reach up and drag him over the edge with me.

Most of all, I wanted him to jump.

thirteen
Sebastian

CONFUSION SQUEEZED MY CHEST as I neared the doors to *Charlie's,* that constant conflict that raged inside me churning hard, one side pressing at me to keep returning, to go to her, to take her, while the rational side of me—the side that grasped my reality, the side that knew the kind of life I was going to be returning to—kept screaming at me that what I was doing was wrong.

Few things could be more appalling, more selfish, than using up a girl who deserved to be given the world. Not my kind of world. Shea didn't deserve any of that. She didn't need the drama or the depravity, the consequences of the fucked-up nights. Knew in my gut she didn't give two shits about how much money I had in my bank account, either, that she wasn't about sinking greedy claws into some unsuspecting guy, leeching off him until he was bled dry.

The girl could take care of herself.

She was all about *good.* About living right. About her daughter, who had to be the cutest thing I'd ever seen. About spreading her joy and light.

And if that didn't make *me* want to take care of *her.*

But I had nothing to give but more of the debauchery that was my real life. I mean, fuck, in a very short time, I was likely to find my ass behind bars. Again. Shea was so above that, so far above it that I couldn't begin to see it, couldn't even touch on all that light I'd been dying to sink into.

So instead I'd drugged myself on her dark, burying myself in her body every chance I got, feeding from her perfect seduction—the depth she took me to—where I could feel her desperation and burden. I pretended I was half the man she thought I was, keeping all my secrets dirty—hidden and unrevealed.

Pretended I didn't see the way she looked at me.

"Would you two hurry the fuck up?" I glared over my shoulder at Ash and Lyrik who stumbled along behind Zee and me, throwing fake punches, messing around in the middle of the street like a couple of teenagers.

Assholes were already half in the bag.

The afternoon had been spent celebrating. We'd hit that rhythm over the last couple of weeks, when the music just flowed between us, and we'd somehow pieced together the skeleton of our next album. Which seemed like a fucking miracle considering I'd been spending a ton of time with Shea.

Apparently, all that *confusion* had left me feeling inspired.

Ash smirked at me. "You in a hurry or somethin', Baz?"

I gave him a finger and he laughed, shaking his head as they caught up. He clapped me on the shoulder. "Look at you, chomping at the bit. Haven't seen you so worked up about a girl since you were thirteen and Miranda Escobar let you touch her tits." He grinned over at Zee. "Think we're going to have to stage that intervention after all. Our boy's balls have gone missing and someone needs to step in before he becomes a straight-up pussy."

My jaw clenched. Ash was just razzing me, he always did and he always meant nothing by it. But there was something that pricked at my skin with every word he spit out.

Zee caught on. Always did. "Shea's a nice girl, man. Don't be a dick."

And that was precisely it.

Shea was a *nice* girl.

I was fucking around with a nice girl, knowingly messing her up. The only promise I'd given her?

I was going to break her.

And I would.

Shit.

A bolt of anxiety struck me when we stepped inside and my eyes immediately sought out Shea where she was standing at one of the high-top tables, slanting an unassuming smile at a table full of douchebags that looked no different than the one who'd roughed her up—preppy boys out with the belief the world owed them something.

That possessiveness surged like a dam being knocked free.

Like she could feel me there, watching her, she glanced over at me, and her face lit up. She floated toward us, winding through the crowds, but that didn't mean it was empty of the force that lived between us, because it was there. Like from across the room, she was touching me everywhere.

God.

I sucked in a breath, felt myself shaking a little when she came to a stop in front of us. She didn't hesitate, just hiked up on her toes and planted a swift but sweet kiss to my lips.

"Hi," she said.

Couldn't stop the smile flitting at my mouth. "Hey."

"You want your booth?" She craned her head toward the secluded spot that had become like some sort of sanctified altar to the muddled mess she made me.

"Sure."

Of course I did.

"Go on. Let me grab a couple of drinks that are ready at the bar and have Tamar make yours." She eyed the guys, that friendly way she did that made people feel like they were welcome without her saying a word. "Everyone want their regular?"

We'd been here enough that she knew exactly what we'd be ordering.

Ash laughed lightly, scratching at his jaw, as if he were devising a plan. "Sounds good to me, Beautiful Shea. Though make it a double. We're celebrating tonight."

Shea's attention slid my way. "Oh really? And what are we celebrating?"

I had the urge to punch Ash in the throat.

Lyrik stepped in. "Ash finally learned how to wipe his own ass. Dude deserves a gold star."

Shea laughed, the sound jarring through my senses, light and soft and alluring. "Well then, doubles it is."

She turned on her heel, which tonight was about four-inches tall. The girl wore a pair of the sexiest boots I'd ever seen—black leather climbing her calves, ending just below her knees. And a skirt…this black skirt that was way too short, flowing down to brush at the lush flesh at the middle of her thighs. A thin white sweater hugged her waist, loose up top, dripping off one shoulder, a white little tank playing peek-a-boo from underneath.

My mouth was watering and I itched, my gaze refusing to leave her as she strutted away.

Ash poked his head up behind my shoulder, talking near my ear. "Damn, look at those legs. No wonder you keep crawling back here night after night."

I elbowed him in the gut.

Laughing, he doubled over and clutched his stomach. But then he sent me this searching look that was a whole lot more wary than the constant ribbing he usually gave. Zee and Lyrik headed for the booth, and Ash took a couple steps backward, still facing me where I seemed to be rooted to the floor. "Need to tell her, man. You're digging yourself a very deep grave."

Agitation curled through me, and my eyes shifted between him and Shea who was now at the bar, chatting easily with Tamar, while she placed drinks on her tray.

But telling her would mean losing what she and I had. She'd know and she'd no longer look at me the way she did, like she saw beneath all the bullshit to what mattered. I wasn't ready to give up the best thing I'd ever had.

I couldn't.

Not yet.

Drawn, I steered in Shea's direction, some kind of agitation spurring me on. I edged up behind her, hands going to the outside of her thighs, and my nose seeking safety in the full fall of her hair. I breathed her in.

Vanilla.

Sweet.

Sweet.

Sweet.

She jerked in surprise, then released a small giggle and leaned back into my hold.

With my nose, I brushed back some of the hair from her neck and whispered near her ear, "What the hell are you wearing?"

Over her shoulder, she smirked, and she lifted up the delicate cap of her delicious shoulder. "A skirt."

"Really? Doesn't look much like a skirt to me. Looks like a weapon of mass destruction, created with the sole purpose of driving men right out of their goddamned minds. What are you trying to do, make me insane?"

She shrugged a coy little shrug. "There's just this boy I was hoping I might be able to lure home tonight."

"Not much worry in that, baby. I'd follow you anywhere."

"Really?" Vulnerability seeped into her tone. Speared by it, I stilled.

And I could hear her voice coming back to me from that first night. *Will you stay?* The fucked-up thing was, I was so desperate to keep her looking at me *that* way, but in that look was hope for what she shouldn't be hoping for.

I was riding on it.

Biding my time until I crushed it.

Regret flamed at my insides, and softly I nudged her around and edged her up against the bar, sealing my mouth over hers. Her honeyed tongue was so warm and wet and welcoming.

God, I was truly losing my grip on my own fucked-up reality.

A dishtowel hit the side of our faces, and we both jerked back. Charlie flashed an impish grin from behind the bar. "Hey. No making out with the customers, Shea Bear."

A chuckle rolled from me as Shea lit up in embarrassment. Just because I couldn't resist, I leaned in to steal one more quick kiss.

She fisted my shirt in her hands, dragging me to her to steal her own, before she pushed me away by it. "Go on…let me grab your drinks and I'll be right over with them." Her chin lifted in a gesture behind me to the spot tucked in the corner, her voice raspy and low. "I think the guys think they're about to get a show."

I looked back, the lot of them gawking across at us like they were anticipating the most entertainment they'd witnessed to date, which was so backward it wasn't even funny, considering I couldn't count the number of times I'd seen Ash and Lyrik going at it with some girl.

Things weren't exactly private or discreet when you lived lives like ours. We never cared because in the end it just didn't matter.

I eased back, knowing to Shea, it mattered, and it was damned near terrifying realizing how much it mattered to me.

My chest tightened.

She mattered.

Shea smiled, confusion weaving across her brow, and she tilted her head as if she were trying to dig into my thoughts. Quickly, I turned away before I lost a little more of myself, and strode back toward the booth.

Lyrik rubbed at the back of his neck, laughing while his dark eyes met mine, like he was giving me a *you're welcome* for forcing me here and back into this place three weeks ago. What he didn't know was I could never have stayed away.

Then I stopped dead when I heard it.

Dread lifted the hairs at the nape of my neck before it went slithering down my spine. It spread out, closing in on me. Snuffing out the air.

That fucking shrieking, high-pitched squeal.

My name.

My name.

"Oh my God…it is. It's really him. It's Sebastian Stone."

Blood drained from my head, and I could feel it rushing through my ears, siphoning down to pound a frenzied beat at my heart. A cold sweat broke out on my neck.

The shrieking just got louder when I felt this unwanted attention travel to the corner, to that safe place where we'd come to hide. "It's all of them. *Sunder*!"

I could feel my crew come to awareness, feel their own unease, although it was anticipated—something we'd grown used to—as annoying as it was, when we just wanted to be left alone.

I squinted back at the unknown girl who thought she *knew* us, standing out in the front of her small group of friends. A camera flash went off, and I wanted to rush her, rip it from her hands, and smash it into a thousand pieces.

But instead my gaze glided to the bar, drawn to the one. And I knew. I knew I fucking should have just told her, laid it all out, but I hadn't had anything that felt good in so long. For just a few weeks, I wanted that with Shea. A chance to just be *me*. A chance to just *be*.

Hands were suddenly on me, tugging at my shirt, vying for my attention. But my complete attention was trained on Shea where she'd frozen in the spot I'd just left her, head shaking, brown eyes rounded in confusion.

The girl I wanted to knock flat kept repeating my name.

Shea shook and stumbled back against one of the bar stools, something like hurt horror taking hold of her expression as realization set in.

Tamar scrambled for her, ducking under the end of the bar and coming to her side, touching her shoulder as she whispered something frantic and fast at her ear.

She was comforting her, I knew. Tamar wasn't there to call me out. For some reason, she'd kept my secret for all this time. Whole lot of good that did me, considering this bitch pawing at me had just provided the kill shot.

Tears slipped down Shea's face as Tamar gave her whatever explanation she felt she owed her, the lights from above glinting off her cheeks.

Betrayal.

I knew that's what she was seeing when she looked across at me, but I'd been more honest with Shea than I'd been with anyone in my life.

Flinging off the obnoxious hands, I went for her.

But Shea was backing away, shaking her head, the movement quickening with distress the closer I got. Something broke in her expression, her hand pressed to her mouth as if to hold back a sob, and she pulled away from Tamar and ran.

Fled.

Pushing through the crowd, she fumbled on her too-high boots in her bid to escape, almost slipping, but she caught herself before she fell, propelling herself forward and through the swinging doors that led to the kitchen.

I was right behind her, didn't hesitate to barrel through.

Shea slammed the door to the break room where I'd carried her three weeks before.

I grabbed the knob, yanked at it hard.

The thin door rattled but didn't give.

My hand cracked against the wood. "Come on, Shea. Open the door. Let me explain."

Her breaths were heavy and distinct, and I knew she was holding herself up against the other side.

"Shea," I murmured quietly, like an apology, dropping my forehead to the door. "Please."

But what was I gonna say?

Now she knew and she was never going to look at me the same.

And I was left without a reason to keep pretending.

fourteen
Shea

I PRESSED MY HAND TO MY mouth and tried to hold back the sob seeking release. Maybe if I stayed quiet enough, hid myself, I'd disappear. Magically removed from this situation. This painful, painful situation.

God, I was such a fool.

Such a fool, and I felt embarrassed and pathetic and hurt.

The hurt was the worst part.

He banged on the door. Once. Twice. I cringed against the force of it, silently begging him to go away. I squeezed my eyes closed, tears continuing to slip out the sides as I struggled to remain standing under my weakened knees.

"Shea," he said again, his voice muffled and pleading through the door. "Shea, you don't understand."

No, I didn't. Why couldn't he have told me? Because this was too big. Too much. Too *close.*

He pounded once more, before he landed a punch against the wood. A tiny, startled cry escaped me, and I winced at his sudden burst of unmistakable fury. A violent display of frustration. I could feel the energy behind it. The resentment and pain. But there was no chance I could face him right now, not when I didn't know how to make sense of this blow.

Not when I no longer knew if I'd still recognize him.

A heavy, resigned breath reverberated through the slight crack in the jamb. It was as if I could feel that tether of energy snap when he finally gave up and retreated.

Swallowing hard, I pried myself from the door. Every cell in my body shook uncontrollably as I staggered toward the cheap, worn desk that rested in the middle of the near-dark room.

I had to see. Had to know.

Tamar had left me with a vague impression of who he was—what he was—and a bitter ball made up of my own resentment wedged itself somewhere deep in the well of my chest. My chest that quaked and trembled, stinging with the urge to purge this overwhelming emotion.

All I'd wanted was a simple life. Someplace safe and normal, out of reach of the limelight and lies, away from the brutal backbiters and vicious slanderers.

And I'd been foolish enough to allow some piece inside me to cling to the idea that he could become a part of it.

No doubt, he was just like the rest of them.

My heart throbbed painfully and my head involuntarily shook at the thought.

No.

How could I believe that? This man who I'd come to know in the most beautiful of ways. Profound ways I'd never experienced before. In the best of ways.

I slumped down into the office chair. For a few moments, I sat there in the dark, before I lifted an unsteady hand and brushed it against the idle mouse, bringing to life the dated monitor. The bright screen pierced the darkness, at the ready to shatter this childish fantasy I'd been living and shed light on the harsh reality.

My mother would have laughed at me. Reminded me I was nothing but a fool.

Of course, that would mean she'd have to speak to me, and she'd had no desire to do that in years.

I guess I'd had the illusion that Sebastian's secrets belonged to the past and weren't very much in charge of his future.

Sniffling, I wiped my face with my sleeve and did my best to see through the bleariness as I opened the Internet browser and typed *Sebastian Stone* into the Google search bar.

It's something I could have done a million times. Something I should have done. But I felt compelled to respect the privacy of his past, refusing to force him to bring it out into the open. There was always shame when he spoke of it in the ambiguous way he did, and now it all made so much sense.

Sex, drugs, and rock and roll happen in California.

That voice. That incredible voice and the way he played.

The guys who looked as if they'd been plucked right from a magazine.

All the warnings Tamar kept giving me.

"Shit," I choked barely above a breath. She knew. The whole time, she knew.

More embarrassment flooded my veins, my mind spinning and my heart feeling like it might cave in.

And maybe it was foolish to allow it to affect me this way, because there was no doubt harbored in my mind that Sebastian was hiding something from me, and I'd given him that space because he'd so blatantly asked for it.

But *why* remained the question.

My eyes dropped closed as I tried to gather myself. Slowly I opened them and just as slowly pushed the *enter* key.

The page loaded and I was instantly overwhelmed.

On the left was a long list of links, but my eye was immediately drawn to the biography box on the right with the collage of pictures at the very top. His beautiful, rugged face framed in each one.

Hard.

Angry.

Fierce.

I read the bio.

> **Sebastian Stone is an American musician from Los Angeles, California. Stone is a founding member and lead guitarist and vocalist of Sunder.**
>
> **Born: November 21, 1988 (Age 26), Los Angeles, CA**
>
> **Music Groups: Sunder**

God, I'd never even heard of them, secluding myself in my own private world—a world I'd established for my daughter, a bubble to keep us protected and safe.

Sebastian Stone had come crashing right through it.

And I hadn't had the first clue.

I turned to the list of websites and article links running along the left and clicked on the first one—a recent article featured on one of those on-line celebrity sites.

That lump in my throat throbbed as I read through it. It was the kind of article that was snarky and filled with the writer's own insinuations.

Sunder missing in action?

Just weeks after front man, Sebastian Stone, was arrested on assault charges against a producer with Mylton Records, Sunder announced a cancellation days before what was supposed to be the onset of their world tour kicking off in France.

I call foul.

In a Tweet issued to the world, Sunder blamed scheduling conflicts for the cancellation.

Yet Sunder has fallen off the face of the earth, leaving thousands of fans mourning the loss of their beloved band.

Where oh where art thou, Mr. Stone?

I blinked through the tears that wouldn't stop falling, reading and rereading the line that told of his arrest. A ball of dread sank into the pit of my stomach.

I'm not a good guy.

He warned me, and I wouldn't listen.

Shakily, I clicked on the word *Sunder* that stood out in blue, knowing the link would take me deeper, deeper into the man, and deeper into the guys that along with his brother, he claimed as his only family.

The search repopulated. Immediately an article from a little over a year ago caught my eye, and my pulse sped as I scanned the caption, the horrible words growing my torment, my throat locked as I read what was spilled across the page.

> **Mark Kennedy, *Sunder* drummer and founding member, was confirmed dead late Tuesday afternoon of an apparent drug overdose. Kennedy was found in the early morning hours on the band's tour bus while in Dallas, Texas, as part of their *Divided Tour.* Rumors of addiction have swirled around the troubled band since front man Sebastian Stone was arrested and served six months of a two-year sentence on charges of heroin possession and theft more than four years ago.**

And I knew. And I knew. And I knew.

I hadn't been able to look away despite how hard Sebastian had worked to push me away.

Just as intensely as he'd worked to draw me near.

The two of us thriving off something that could never truly be.

I'm no good for you.

Pain took me whole when my gaze locked on the picture tacked on the bottom of the article. It was a brown-haired guy with a hint of curls over his ears who had to be about the same age as Sebastian. What almost looked like a shy smile curved the side of his mouth as he peeked sideways at the camera while walking along a sidewalk. Insecure. Is that what that was? Something about him appeared broken and sad.

In that second, I felt the magnitude of Sebastian's anguish in his murmured words.

Took my whole crew down with me.

Some things you can't take back.

And I hurt for him, ached for him in a way I wished I didn't understand.

Even though it all felt like too much, there was no resisting the incredible longing I felt when I saw the stilled video, the four men who I thought I'd come to know in the secluded booth right outside the door, frozen on the screen. Obviously, it was a live video that had been posted by a fan. I clicked on it and watched *Sunder* come to life.

On stage, Sebastian was something magnificent.

Imposing and fierce.

Never had he looked so *bad*, and my hurting heart fluttered a wayward beat, hitting me with an errant bolt of desire. But it was unstoppable, the undeniable attraction this man held over me like coercion. Like every piece of me was drawn to him—blinded by the lie that *we could somehow fit.*

The video was taken inside a dark, dark music hall by a phone amid a raving crowd, a bedlam of chaos and flinging arms and slamming bodies right up under the elevated stage.

Spotlights flashed and shadows played, Sebastian with a guitar strapped across his chest, fingers sliding in frenzied precision up and down the neck while the other hand strummed a reckless beat, that pretty, pretty mouth pressed up to a microphone, screaming angry, piercing lyrics that I felt more than understood, somehow grasping the meaning of his intensity completely without registering the actual words.

My father would have said this wasn't music.

God. Most of the people in this bar would say this wasn't music.

But it was so Sebastian that it sent another round of tears skidding down my face, my tongue thick and my heart crippled by confusion, as I watched him in what was so clearly his element, a place where he was undeniably free.

Then the song shifted into some kind of harmony, and that beautiful voice he'd graced me with in my living room weeks ago twisted through the aggressive song. Something haunting, silky, and fluid. Lyrik was playing another guitar and stepped up to his mic to sing along to the chorus, Ash on the opposite side, face intense, lost in the bass line. Zee was elevated in the back pounding at a set of drums. Then the song took another turn and slammed back into those thrashing words.

My head jerked up with the light tapping at the door.

"Shea? It's Tamar. You okay?"

Drawing in a breath, I forced myself to stand and cross the room. I hesitated at the door, before I finally unlocked it and cracked it open. Tamar quickly pushed through, shut it, and locked it behind her.

She frowned as she squinted at me through the subdued light of the room. Her face fell. "Not okay."

Humorless laughter rolled from me, and I rubbed both my palms over my puffy, swollen eyes. "No. Not okay."

Turning away, she paced on her blood-red heels and wrung her hands, huffed out a breath before she turned back to me and began to ramble. "I'm sorry, Shea. You have to know how terrible I feel over this. I should have said something a long time ago, but it was the first time I'd ever seen you interested in someone…and…and…" She hiked up her shoulders and dropped them in defeat. "I just wanted you to experience that."

"You recognized him right off?"

Hands on her hips, she dropped her head and gave a quick nod, blazing blue eyes returning to mine. "Yeah. I kept waiting for you to catch on, but then I realized you really had no idea who he was. He made it clear he wanted to keep it that way, too, and as much as it killed me to keep my mouth shut, I decided it wasn't my place to go blabbing to you." She quirked a brow. "And you know how hard it was for me to keep my mouth shut."

"It's not your fault. I just feel stupid that I didn't know."

Hurt that he didn't tell me.

Scared of what he was.

Intrigued by it all the same.

"Don't. Their kind of music is obviously not your thing. I mean, you live in Savannah, Georgia, after all." She winked, doing her best to lighten the mood.

"And it's your thing?"

A grin flitted at the corners of her mouth and she pulled her phone from her back pocket, scrolled through and held it up, showing me her music player catalog that included three *Sunder* albums.

"You're a fan." It sounded like a disappointed statement, although I wasn't entirely sure why I felt that way, like I'd been left out when she'd had a piece of Sebastian long before I ever had.

She rolled her eyes. "Um…I'm no fangirl…but I do like their music."

"Really?" I asked, almost incredulous.

A smirk pulled at her red lips. "What? I like my boys tattooed and screaming."

I laughed a little, but it broke over the emotion still clotted in my chest. I sank back into the office chair, and Tamar stepped over to me, ran her fingers gently through my hair. "Seriously, Shea…are you going to be okay? What happened out there…that couldn't have been easy to take in."

I shook my head. "No, it wasn't."

At first it'd been pure jealousy. I'd been sure Baz had stumbled upon an old lover. Or worse, maybe a not-so-old lover. The one thing I did know was he hadn't been in town all that long, and a flood of insecurity had come barreling in. The fact I really didn't know him or own him or possess him the way he possessed me, and I was hit again with the reality that I was soon going to lose this man.

The only promise he'd ever made me was the one that he was going to break me.

Standing at my side, she hugged my head. "He's still out there, you know. The other guys took off pretty quickly after they'd been discovered."

Slowly I nodded, not knowing what to make of that or what to make of him.

Did this knowledge really make him any different than who he'd been? The person he'd bared to me, the one he'd shown me, the glimpses of his soul he'd given without the benefit of the full picture?

"I'd better get back out there before Charlie comes looking for me."

"Do you mind if I hang out in here for a while?"

"We've got it under control out there. Don't worry about it."

"Thanks."

Tamar locked the door behind her when she left, and I sat in the near darkness while time crept by. Hours dragged, but I found I couldn't make myself stand. At just after three, a key rattled in the lock and Charlie let himself in.

He sighed softly when he found me sitting at the desk with my head propped up in my hand, still feeling small and sad, but somehow resolved.

"We're all finished up out there, Shea Bear."

"Okay."

His lips spread into a grim line, and he crossed his arms over his chest. Since I was a little girl, he'd always been my most staunch protector.

Until Baz.

Funny how after that night when I'd been thrown to the ground, it seemed Sebastian had stepped into that position, like he'd belonged there all along.

"He's still out there," Charlie warned. "I couldn't get him to budge from behind that booth. He's been sitting there all night."

I nodded acceptance. "Go on. I'll have him give me a ride home."

"I don't like it, Shea Bear."

"I don't like it, either."

Regret filled his tone. "Can't believe I didn't see it. Make the connection that he's one of Anthony's boys."

"Not your fault."

"Feels like it is."

My head shook slowly. "I don't think it would have changed anything."

"Yeah, you're probably right." His brow dented with concerned lines. "You scared of him?"

"Terrified," I admitted.

But not in the way he thought. But Charlie just looked at me with sympathy, and I guessed the kind of fear that had me wound tight was exactly what he'd expected. He knew from where it was bred, why it was born.

"Be careful, sweetheart," were the only words he issued before he closed the door behind him and left me to my own decisions, quietly supporting me the way he always had.

Charlie and my grandmother had been the two people to instill a true-kind of confidence in me, the ones who'd taught me to stand tall for what I believed in and to fight for what I wanted. Not the kind of confidence my mother had brainwashed me with. No. They taught me to look for the quiet answers beating in my heart.

I sat there for a couple more minutes, before I finally stood. A tremor rolled through me, and if it were possible, my heart beat faster.

Pound.

Pound.

Pound.

I drew in a shaky breath and opened the door. Darkness shrouded the kitchen that had been closed down for the night. Only a small lamp glowed from the back of the space, and I trailed my hand along the wall to guide me. At the swinging doors, I paused, stuck in the tension that grew thick and suffocating. Slowly I pushed on the door that led out into the main floor.

A tangle of convoluted emotions had me twisted up inside.

But what I ultimately felt had risen to the top.

I stood just inside the empty, dark room. Empty except for the one man who sat as a blackened silhouette, obscured in the shadows, the one who'd managed to strip me of all my defenses.

When I found him sitting there that first time, I thought I'd known better than to go looking for his brand of heartbreak. But Sebastian had revealed in me everything I'd been missing, stamped out my loneliness, and inserted himself in its place. He made me believe in something I'd given up hope on a long time ago because I'd never found it to be real, never believing giving myself wholly to someone was worth the risk.

Now I knew better.

Now I knew it was worth everything.

My movements were cautious and slow as I began to move around the long bar, my gaze locked on him over the top of it, my heels echoing on the hardwood floors. Outside, a lone car roared by, the city on lockdown in the middle of the deep, deep night.

As I approached, Sebastian pushed out from under the booth, the huge bulk of this striking man rising to stand. Energy vibrated through him, hostility and anger and hurt.

And I knew that somewhere along the way I'd gained the power to hurt him, too.

Ten feet away from him, I fell to a stop, my heart beating frantic and wild, desire stampeding out ahead of it.

He lifted his chin, voice like gravel when he spoke. "You see me, Shea?"

His words collided with me, knocking the rest of my reservations free.

And again I lifted my chin in surrender. "Yes."

Yes.

I'd never seen anyone so clearly.

Intensity billowed between us, like a spark before a summer storm. He fisted his hands, grey eyes rife with defensive anger, haunted by his own reality, and I knew he felt it, too. I wasn't alone in all this confusion and doubt.

"Sebast—"

He cut me off by erasing the space. His hungry mouth was suddenly overpowering mine, stealing the words I needed to say. He wrapped the length of my hair up in his hand, forcing my head back as if every element that made him up demanded he get me closer.

His other hand snaked under my skirt and to my ass. Fingers dug in, gripping tight, pulling me flush against the solid mass of everything I wanted for my own.

I whimpered, fighting to form the words.

"Need this…need you," he muttered at my lips, letting his hand slip down between my thighs from behind.

"Sebastian…" I attempted again, then completely gave when his tongue swept into my mouth.

Hot.

Urgent.

Ruthless.

My body came alive with *this* energy. With *this* connection that belonged only to us. Heat spread like wildfire, blistering below my skin, and Sebastian groaned, as if he felt the burn beneath his hands. He urged me back, pinning me up against the high-backed leather at the edge of the horseshoe booth, this secluded spot that had become his.

He broke our kiss and fastened his gaze on me, his throat bobbing heavily as he looked at me in a way I wasn't sure he ever had before, as if he were begging me to hate him, and at the same time, promise I'd never let him go. His fingers curled in the front of my camisole exposed below my scoop-necked sweater, and he tugged it down, baring my breasts.

Thumbs flicked across the buds.

A fever of energy.

A rush of lust.

My head rocked back, and I gasped for a breath.

Feral eyes speared me and I lifted my arms, gripping my hair as I stared back at him, giving him more—showing him that I was offering all of me.

And I could feel his pulse, sense it move, a quickening of severity that pounded through his veins.

I suddenly felt powerful. Beautiful. A requirement for this stunning man.

Something like a growl rumbled in his chest, and he quickly spun me around. In the same second, his arm raked furiously across the booth tabletop, flinging his empties out of the way. One fell to the plush booth seat, another to the floor, the sound of glass crashing on the wooden floors the only noise against our ragged breaths.

He pressed me down with a hand to the back of my neck. Cold polished wood met my bare breasts, and another whimper passed from my tongue as he wedged his knee between my legs, spreading them apart. Air hit my backside as he bunched up my skirt. He yanked at my panties, ripping them free. I heard the rustle of his jeans, the tearing of foil—his body so close I could feel him rolling a condom on his cock.

I sucked in a breath, so turned on I couldn't see.

Fingers glided through my exposed center. "You ready for me?"

That same heady threat, and I shook, bracing myself for the pleasure that only he could bring.

He rocked into me and I cried out, my mouth gaping open and my cheek pressed to the table as I writhed against the perfect intrusion, so big and full and better than anything I'd ever experienced in all my life.

Because he'd somehow become a part of *my everything.*

For a moment, he stilled. Then he withdrew and drove back in.

"Every time," he grunted. "Every fucking time."

Desperate fingers sank into my flesh, gripping my hips as he began to fuck me.

His movements were almost savage.

Sebastian was never gentle. But I could feel something inside him had slipped. Tripped. As if he'd sat out here alone, and during those passing hours he'd wondered if he'd ever get to touch me again and, now that he was, he was taking everything he could while he had the chance.

Frenzied, his thumbs raced along where we were joined.

Something about it felt intimate and raw and honest, and I was falling further, being sucked beneath the surface.

A stone in his sea.

Completely drowning in this man.

Sliding his hands up, he palmed the cheeks of my bottom. Spreading me wider. Taking me deeper.

"Do you feel me?"

Yes.

"Do you feel me, Shea?"

"Yes," I mumbled frantically.

His thumbs ran up and down the crease of my ass, and I gasped out when he swirled a finger around the sensitive flesh, the man touching me in a way that no one else had, and again, my spirit trembled in fear.

In vulnerability.

Defenseless.

Slowly he pushed it inside.

I groaned and dragged a dizzying breath into my lungs, pulling away from him, pressing back, his touch beyond anything I could fathom, eclipsing thought, erasing reason.

Dark, dark pleasure blinded my eyes, indecent and decadent, and I clawed at the wood.

"You're never gonna forget me, Shea." Another threat. "Never."

Every part of me tightened, that thrill swelling full and fast. Lifting me higher.

When in reality, I was falling.

Falling.

Falling.

Falling.

Until I finally hit the bottom.

Shattering.

Splintering.

Breaking completely apart.

Bliss spread far and wide, fragmenting out, saturating every cell in my being.

His name. His name. His name.

On a grunt, he jerked and he cried out mine, gripping me almost painfully, taking me as deeply as he could as his body shook with his release.

I could feel the tremor of his muscles, the power of his being, consuming me.

And there was no stopping them, the words that fought to be said. "I love you." It tumbled from me as a small cry, no longer able to hold it back.

He froze, and my pulse dipped and thudded. So slow. Too loud. A weight bore down on me as I felt every intrinsic part of him detaching.

"Sebastian." It was a plea made up of fear. I told him I didn't have time for distractions. But more than that, I had no time for games. I hadn't played them with him before and I refused to start now.

He needed to know.

Without a response, he pulled out and readjusted my skirt.

Covering me in the moment I was most exposed.

And that emotion was back, pressing firm and fast, squeezing brutally at my chest.

He stepped back, and I could hear him ridding himself of the condom, tossing it in the bin at the wall, wrestling with his jeans.

Tears resurfaced in my eyes, and I struggled to get my camisole up as my mind raced to catch up with the quick, deadly shift in his mood.

I flung around to face him. "Say something," I demanded, though even to me, it sounded weak.

In the dim light, he stared back at me, all of those hard, hard scars evident in his eyes. "What do you want me to say, Shea? You want me to lie to you? Make you promises I can't keep?"

Frantically, I shook my head. "No."

"Then what?"

Wincing, I jerked my head down and to the side, as if it could avert his blows, the harshness behind his words.

"How about the truth?" he continued, taking a looming step forward. "You want that? Did you not get enough of it tonight? Seeing those girls? Do you have any clue about the kind of life I live?"

My attention flew back to him. "Show me," I begged, my voice cracking. I couldn't help bringing us back to that night, when he'd dared me to see him, when I'd already accepted there was no looking away.

Sharp, cutting laughter rocked from him. "You don't want to see that life. Now that's something I can promise you." He pointed to the kitchen door behind him. "Did you look me up while you hid out in there?" It was almost an accusation, and I recoiled at the bitterness he spat from his mouth.

That pretty, pretty mouth that I loved and adored.

I didn't answer. I didn't need to.

"Did you see, Shea? Did you see that in a couple of months I'm probably going back to jail? Did you see I've been there before?" Grief hitched his breath. "Did you know my best friend died because of me?"

I flinched with every spouted reason he gave for me to hate him, for me to take back my admission. I backed farther into the table, shoulders up to my ears as if it could protect me from the agony he seemed intent on bringing us both.

He promised he would wreck me.

When did I stop believing him?

"You want your daughter around someone like me?"

That one hit me hard, and those tears I'd been trying to keep in check fell, uncontrolled. "Someone like you?" I asked, incredulous, pushing back. "Someone who makes her smile and laugh? Someone who listens to her like a four-year-old has the most important things to say? Someone who steps up to protect her mother? Someone like that?"

"You're a fool if you think that's who I really am."

"And you're a coward because you refuse to risk allowing *that* man I see underneath it all to become who you are. A coward because you can't risk being with a woman who has a kid. A coward because you reject the idea of me loving you…the idea of you loving me…just because you haven't experienced that in your life before."

His face screwed up in disbelief. "You think I'm a coward because I can't be with you? That every fucking second I'm not thinking about you? Wishing things were different so maybe I could have a little bit more time? Something good in my life when I've got so much bad? Do you really think I want this life for you, Shea? That I could stand to drag you and Kallie into it?"

I watched the slow roll of his thick neck as he swallowed hard. "Do you have any idea what it's like? Being in the public eye every day of your life? The traveling? The women who throw themselves at me? The shit I see…the shit that I'm a part of?"

Every bit of it I understood.

"You don't have to be with any of those women or be a part of any of that *shit.* It's a choice, Sebastian." Leaning forward, I touched my chest, emphasizing each word. "Be. With. Me."

Pain struck across his expression. "You just don't get it."

"So you're trying to protect me because I'm too stupid and narrow-minded and hick to understand your life?"

"I'm trying to protect you because I don't trust myself with you."

Hurt wove into my tone, just as heavily as it wove with my spirit. "Why didn't you just tell me?"

"Why do you think I didn't tell you? For a million reasons. Because I didn't want you to look at me the way all those other girls look at me…the way that stupid bitch did tonight. I wanted *you* to see *me.* Inside *me.* But the hard truth is *that me* is the same guy I don't want you to know. I told you I was no good. There's so much bad about me and I wish I could erase it all. Be someone different. But I'm not. And just for a little while I wanted to pretend I could be something I'm not."

"You wanted to pretend. With me?" The words broke. "That's all this was? Pretend? Because to me? It was real. I've never felt anything so real." My tone hardened. "And you're a liar if you say you don't feel it, too."

An ugly sound scraped up his throat. "It doesn't matter if it's real, or pretend, or a straight-up lie, it all ends the same. I go back to California tomorrow and I won't be coming back."

Right.

Okay.

I gathered myself, trying not to fall to pieces in front of him. I'd have plenty of time for that later.

I felt as if Sebastian had slapped me across the face. How ironic this blow hurt a million times worse than that jerk-of-a-kid who'd pushed me to the floor. Sebastian had been so inclined to save me then, yet he had no remorse in crushing me now.

With my head down, I crept around him, the heels of my boots much too loud against the wood, the hurt taking hold of me too much to bear.

I ducked under the end of the bar and grabbed my purse where it was stowed on one of the bottom shelves, and tried to keep it together when I slunk back out. My eyes glanced across that striking face, all hard lines and curves and scars, averting just as quickly to my feet. "Take me home," I said through a pained whisper.

He strode across the huge room, eating up the floor like he couldn't wait to escape, didn't pause when he passed me by and headed down the dingy hallway.

Wearily, I glanced back at our booth, at the shards of glass scattered across the floor, at the table where he'd stolen another piece of me.

I'd clean up our mess tomorrow.

He said nothing as I followed him down the hall. Quickly, I locked the back door and got into his car.

Tonight was nothing like the night when he'd rescued me.

That night? My choice had been made.

And tonight, Sebastian had made his.

No words were said as he drove me home. He made no move when he pulled up at the curb. The heavy rumble of the idling engine was the only sound to break up the unbearable silence.

I didn't look back as I wobbled up the walkway on my too-high boots and let myself into the quiet of my house. I climbed the stairs then fell face first into the unmade bed that still smelled like him.

Somehow I'd slipped—tripped—and had been foolish enough to think the dream could become ours. Conflict raged in me. The agony that ate me up with the feeling of being used, at odds with the need to cling to every memory Sebastian and I had made together. To cherish them like I'd promised I would—back when I was fool enough to think it would be enough.

I curled onto my side and hugged a pillow to my aching chest, breathing him in.

And I tried not to succumb to this broken heart.

fifteen
Sebastian

"GOOD TO SEE THE FRESH AIR in Savannah was so good for your sour mood." Anthony Di Pietro was all sarcastic brows and ridicule watching me slouched against the leather in the back seat of the town car.

"Just happy to be home," I said just as hard, this unknown rage boiling in my blood, my anger stony and bristly and damned near out of control. My knee bounced in annoyance and aggression, my focus out the window at what seemed like a never-ending line of houses as we traveled down the narrow, winding road out of Hollywood Hills. The houses were interspersed with tall shrubs, floral trees, and the blurred line of palm trees.

Anthony propped up his elbow on the window seal, index finger at his temple to support his head as he shifted to get a better look at me. "If it's even possible, you seem more bitter than normal."

"Not possible."

In frustration, he shook his head. "The second you stepped off that plane yesterday, I knew something was up. You need to let me in on what's going on with you. You can't go walking into this meeting with a chip on your shoulder. Right now, it's time to play nice and you look like you're ready to rip the face off the next person you see."

I tugged at the tie that felt like a lasso around my neck.

Leading me off to the slaughter.

I'd been dreading this fucking mediation since the moment Anthony had convinced me to take part in it. Up until Tuesday night, I'd had every intention of coming here, then turning right back around and hauling ass straight back to Savannah. It's what'd kept me sane. I'd planned on letting Shea know I had to return to California to take care of some business, no doubt giving her some more of the bullshit answers I'd fed her when she'd asked questions.

And the girl had always just swallowed them. Not because she was naive or half-witted or dumb. But because she respected me, accepted what I would give.

Those quick flashes of truth and touches we'd lived on had been enough to sustain her.

Not anymore.

Because those flickers had caused that sweet girl to fall, and continuing to string her along would be about the most selfish thing I could do.

So I severed it.

Cut her free.

No longer could I handle that storm in her eyes. Couldn't keep ignoring that *feeling* I saw in them every time I looked at her. Every time I touched her. The way *the feeling* swelled—stretching out for me—begging me back with all that hope and beauty and belief.

And I *couldn't* ignore it when Shea had uttered those feelings aloud.

But that girl in the bar had been the reminder that I couldn't forget what was waiting for me back here. That just like Ash had warned me, I'd dug myself a very deep grave.

But that grave had been dug long ago.

Now I was buried in it.

Paying the consequences in the most insufferable way.

But the danger in pretending was it becoming real.

"Baz, look at me. What's going on with you? You need to be prepared when you walk in that room."

"I am prepared."

He scoffed. "You've barely done anything more than grunt at me since my driver picked you up at your house. You're getting ready to walk into a room with *Martin Jennings.* You remember what happened the last time you were with him?"

My chest tightened, anger grating at the raw spot Shea had left behind. Yeah, I remembered. I glared across at Anthony. "And I don't know how sitting in a room full of suits is going to change any of it, because I sure as hell wouldn't take it back. I may not have all the facts, but I fucking know he had something to do with Austin."

Austin had kept his mouth locked tight. Keeping secrets he shouldn't keep. Recognized it the second he woke up in that hospital bed because, just like him, I'd lied and hid and masked for too many years. I knew exactly what that bullshit looked like. Initially I'd gone to Martin to confront him, to get those answers, but the pompous asshole had just laughed, then straightened his fucking suit jacket as if he were shaking me off.

Then he'd given me all the confirmation I'd needed.

Punk kids like your brother aren't ever going to make it, anyway.

Like Austin was trash and him leaving this world would be doing it a favor.

A heavy sigh wheezed from Anthony's lungs. "What you're going to do is sit in there and pretend you're remorseful and you're going to do a damned good job of it."

Pretend.

Laughter erupted from me—cutting and biting—filled with the sheer malice I held deep inside. I wasn't sure if it was directed at Jennings or myself.

"Sick of pretending." The hard edge of my words slipped on the last. God, I sounded like a pussy bitch the way it came out with the blinding regret and shame that had tagged along at my heels since the moment I'd stared Shea down and broke her. Wrecked her just like I promised I would.

"I am on *your* side, Baz. I'm trying to get you out of this. You don't have any chances left. You've used all of them up, both with Mylton Records and the law. You have to suck it up and get through this, as painful as it's going to be. Believe me, I understand it's going to be rough in there. If we could turn the tables and have the threat of jail time hanging over that bastard's head, I'd be all over it, because just like you, I'm positive he had everything to do with what happened with Austin. But we don't have anything on him and he has everything on you."

My mouth opened on a pained breath. "I know you're on my side, Anthony." Slowly I shook my head, lips pursing in a tortured line. "I just don't know how much more of this I can take…if this is worth it any longer."

"What do you mean by *this*?"

I shrugged like it didn't matter, when so much of my life had been spent with it mattering most. "Playing. Writing music. This lifestyle. Just don't know if it's worth the cost anymore."

Surprise pinched his face before it spread out in a slow wave of disbelief. His voice grew quiet. "Damn it, Sebastian. Thought I told you to keep your dick in your pants? This is about some girl?"

Regret that had been lining my insides made a bid to climb right out, clawing at my throat, the sour taste coating my tongue. "Not some girl."

An amazing girl.

An unforgettable girl.

My girl if I wasn't living this life.

Mine if I wasn't getting ready to get my sorry ass hauled off to jail again.

Wouldn't put her through that.

Couldn't.

Cared too much, as foolish as it was.

My jaw clenched, teeth grinding as my hand fisted tight, pressing into the thigh of the black tailored suit pants I'd donned to *pretend* some more, trying not to break apart in the back seat of the town car.

"Shit," he hissed. "What'd you do, Baz?"

"I didn't do anything that wasn't right."

All except for chasing her in the first place.

Should have left well enough alone when she told me she didn't date. That she didn't have time for distractions. But there was something about her that wouldn't let me go, like some piece of her was chasing me, too, hounding me to find out where the curiosity came from, like maybe she'd needed some time for pretending, too.

"Sure looks like you're proud of whatever it was you *didn't* do." A snort filtered from his nose. "When are you going to realize you don't have to be miserable, Sebastian? You spend so much time worrying about your brother. About the band.

Being your agent, I'm going to be the first one to tell you that's important. But as your friend, I'm going to tell you it's about time you understood you don't have to sacrifice one life for the other."

Sarcasm dripped from my soured tongue. "What? You think I can have my cake and eat it too? Maybe you got lucky, man. Got it all. But my life doesn't work out that way. I have too much shit going on…cause too much shit to go *down* in my life." My tone turned incredulous. "And I thought you told me to keep my dick in my pants?"

Now the asshole sounded like he was encouraging me to go for it.

His laughter was hearty, good-natured, and he smiled a wry smile. "Like that was going to happen any more than you staying out of trouble."

This time it was my turn to laugh. "Whatever, man."

Anthony grinned. "And for the record, *I'm* a suit."

The driver pulled to the curb in front of a large building that was probably fourteen or fifteen stories encased in glass. At least ten steps ran along its façade, leading to the smooth glass front doors, the professional building drawing that lump right back to my throat.

"You ready to put this all behind you, Baz?"

Anthony's question was formed with encouragement, with a warning, basically telling me what happened today in the eighth floor conference room was up to me, the end result held in the palm of my hands.

"Ready as I'm ever gonna be."

"Let's do this, then."

Anthony climbed from his side of the car, and I followed, stepping out onto the wide sidewalk that coursed along the front of the building, meshing with the concrete walkway that led to the steps.

High noon. The California sun stood proud, today the sky burning blue, with only a faint hue of the typical hazy gray of smog that forever hugged the city.

I cringed when I heard the voices yelling for me from off to the right, a rapid fire of more bullshit thrown my way.

"Sebastian Stone! Can you tell me where *Sunder* has been hiding?"

"Sebastian…what is the nature of your meeting this afternoon?"

"Is it true *Sunder* is breaking up? Will tonight's show be your last?"

"Mr. Stone, reports say you reconciled with Hailey Marx and have spent the last six weeks at her vacation home in Greece. Can you confirm?"

My mind had been too wrapped up in Shea and this meeting to have been prepared for them—my time in Savannah too easy and peaceful to remember what it was like to have the paparazzi hound you at every turn.

I dropped my head and pushed forward as they swarmed us. Anthony clasped the inside of my upper arm, like he was guiding me, protecting me. "Mr. Stone will not be answering any questions today."

Sebastian.

Sebastian.

Sebastian.

A barb of anger struck me deep.

Everyone wanted a piece of Sebastian Stone.

Their voices cut off when the door fell shut behind us.

"What the fuck are they doing here?" I growled, shaking out my arms like it could rid me of all the vile assumptions they'd thrown my way.

Anthony raised a brow. "What, you think after you've been gone for six weeks there weren't going to be rumors about where you disappeared to? Plus, with the announcement of tonight's show, the media is all over it. This is par for the course. Part of the game. You know that, Baz."

But that was the problem. I didn't know if I still wanted to play.

Anthony had thrown a show together last minute, something to scream *Sunder* was back and we weren't going anywhere. Part of me couldn't wait to wrap my hands around my guitar, to feel the music come alive, to experience the chemistry between the guys and me when we got on stage.

Amid the turbulent chaos roving through a show, somehow I always felt washed in peace.

The other part of me?

I wanted to walk into this meeting, give the bastard whatever he wanted, then walk away. And run straight back to Shea, never turning back.

But that didn't mean the disaster I'd created wouldn't follow me there.

And the guys…they'd stood behind me for my entire life. Supported me when I got thrown in prison the first time, back before we'd ever made it. When we were struggling to get venues to take us, begging everyone and anyone to listen to our demos, and sleeping in the damned van just trying to make a name.

They could have booted me then.

But they'd held out, waited for me because none of them believed in *Sunder* if it didn't mean the four of us made it up.

The second I got out, I'd gone clean, put my all into the band and my brother. When we'd lost Mark, I was sure it was all going to fall to pieces, and with my little brother following down the same path, I'd been sure there'd be no way to mend that kind of break. Until Zee had stepped in and became a balm to all that hurt, even though looking at him still ripped me up inside.

And what? Now I was just going to walk away?

Couldn't do that anymore than I could drag Shea into this life.

Kenny Lane, my attorney, stepped out from where he waited in the foyer, his arm outstretched as he approached. "Sebastian," he greeted, his salt and pepper hair combed in a blunt part on one side, suit tailored and expensive, the man tall and thin and no-nonsense.

I'd liked him the moment I met him.

I shook his hand. "Kenny."

He turned on his heel and started walking, expecting us to follow, and began talking as we did. "Martin Jennings and his team are already upstairs. I've been in preliminary talks with his attorneys. They seem willing to negotiate, but I've sensed some resistance on Mr. Jennings's part. If questions are asked of you, they will be directed to me, and you'll direct your answers back to me. Same as with Jennings and his attorneys. Keep your tone mild and contained. Basically what we're going for here is to agree on a dollar amount to keep the personal injury suit out of court and for Jennings to back away on the criminal charges. If so, I feel confident we can make a plea deal for lesser charges with the state. A fine. Community service. Probation. No jail time."

He'd already gone over all of this with me on the phone yesterday afternoon. Apparently he felt the need to reiterate.

I nodded understanding as he quickly and quietly gave more directions toward my ear, our dress shoes clacking on the marble floors as we rounded into the hall. Kenny pressed the button for the elevator. The doors immediately opened and we stepped into it.

As we ascended, with each floor the dial flicked through, it was like my anxiety ramped up another rung, like I was climbing toward disaster. One step closer to bringing me face-to-face with a man whose life I'd nearly ended.

"Do you have any last questions for me before we go inside?" Kenny asked.

"No. I think I've got it."

Bottom line, I was going to pay.

Just another bitter pill to swallow, more misery added to this insufferable pain.

At the eighth floor, the doors slid open. Kenny walked out ahead of us into the lobby, and Anthony tossed me one last pleading look.

Keep your cool.

He straightened his coat jacket, I knew more out of nerves than anything else. "You can do this, Baz."

Not sure that I really could. I just gave him a succinct nod.

Kenny spoke with the receptionist in the plush office, then led us down a hall to the left, pausing for one moment at the obtrusive double wooden doors. With a short knock, he let himself in. Anthony and I followed him into the large conference room.

And it didn't matter how hard I tried to keep my eyes trained low, to remain neutral and smooth and aloof, my attention jumped right to him. Because I could feel him.

Swimming in all that arrogance, contempt dripping from his pretentious ego.

Martin Jennings sat on the opposite side of the conference table, rocked back in the posh black leather chair, ankle crossed casually over his knee. Probably not any older than thirty, he had his sandy-blond hair slicked back like he was giving tribute to a 1930s mobster. Brown eyes were keen and impatient, but his expression was subtle and interested, like he'd perfected the act of schmoozing—flashing that bright white smile at just the right time to get his way, exploiting what he had to offer up against what he was getting ready to take. Though all I saw? The patronizing glare under all of it.

Of course I couldn't forget the three-inch scar splitting his chin, a little gift I'd left behind to mar that pretty boy face. I was betting he couldn't forget it, either.

Almost panicked, Anthony looked back at me from where he was making pleasantries with Jennings's team and the assigned mediator, like he could feel the ripple of hostility curling like acid in the stagnant air.

"This is Sebastian Stone." Anthony stepped in to introduce me, summoning me forward. And I was doing my all to front all those same kind of pleasantries, giving my best not to glare over their shoulders at the asshole sitting smug in his chair, who seemed to be holding all the cards, when I'd been dealt a bad beat.

"Let's get started, shall we?" Kenny offered, waving his hand out in a gesture for me to take a seat.

Warily, I did.

Directly across from Martin Jennings.

The mediator, Cruz Gonzalez, began. "I believe we all understand the serious nature of the charges brought against your client, Mr. Lane, and this mediation is in no way meant to downplay them, but rather to act as conciliation between the two parties."

Kenny sat forward, hands pressed to the table on either side of the documents spread out in front of him. "Yes, we understand and hope to find a reasonable solution for both parties."

Cruz Gonzalez read through some reports, an outline of what had happened the night I'd completely come unhinged, the injuries incurred, my arrest, and my bail.

Jennings squirmed in indignation and hate as the night was relived. But there was no chance my hate wasn't so much greater. My displeasure steadily grew, that aggressive coil tightening in my gut as Cruz Gonzalez took us on a play-by-play of that night, what had led up to the snap, the break in my mind that had thrown me over the edge.

It made it sound as if I'd rung the doorbell to Martin Jennings's house without an inciting factor.

"There are no disputes on either party that your client, Sebastian Stone, was involved in the incident with Martin Jennings on the night of July 13?" Gonzalez asked.

Kenny gave a slight shake of his head, not needing to look to me for confirmation. I was there. I hadn't denied it then. Wouldn't now.

"And it's agreed that monies are due to Mr. Jennings for his injuries?"

Kenny cast me a furtive glance, and I gave him a tight nod to proceed, as much as it fucking killed me to do it. He looked back at the mediator. "Yes. We agree that Mr. Jennings should be compensated financially for his injuries."

"Currently, Mr. Jennings is seeking two million dollars…"

My mind got lost in a haze as I listened to Jennings's bogus claims, the entitlement behind it. Of course, he was offering zero accountability on his part, unwilling to claim any blame, just an innocent asshole who got in the way of my fit of rage.

What bullshit.

Kenny cleared his throat. "We believe two million dollars is an unreasonable number and would consider a settlement that better reflects actual injuries sustained. Mr. Jennings lost only three days' work, which in no way affected him significantly financially, and he has no lasting injuries. My client is willing to offer one hundred thousand dollars, which more than covers physical and emotional trauma."

Jennings sneered in my direction, bypassing his attorney and the mediator, speaking directly to me. "You really think I'm going to let you get away with a hundred thousand dollars? After you had the nerve to show up at my house? Making demands of me?"

Feathers ruffled in a rustle of pure dismay, all the suits up in arms the second Jennings gave into the outburst that had been building since the second I walked through the door.

As if this could have possibly ended any other way.

Bad blood always boiled.

His attorney leaned in and whispered something severe in his ear.

Jennings just shook him off.

His attention was back on me, that same pompous expression lining every curve of his face. "Do you know who I am?"

Did I know who he was?

Money.

Arrogance.

Ego.

Pride.

I also knew he was one of the reasons *Sunder* was what it was today. He's the one who'd spotted us in that small, dank, musty bar in Tennessee. The one who'd approached us. Fronted the money for our first real studio time. Gained us entrance through all the doors we needed to pass.

Yeah. I knew him.

But none of that counted anymore.

My voice narrowed in challenge. "What I want to know is why you were coming off our bus that night."

"I wasn't anywhere near your bus that night."

I slammed my hand down on the table. "I saw you!"

Everyone had been backstage, hanging out after the show, letting loose the way we always did. I'd skated out back, crossed the darkened lot to the bus, needing to check on my little brother. After what happened to Mark, I'd finally dragged Austin to rehab, bribed my father to sign for him since he was still underage, forced my brother to stay there when all he wanted was to burn himself right into the ground. When he'd been discharged, I wanted to keep him near, but didn't want him too close, because I couldn't stand the thought of me being the reason he was exposed to the things that continued to tear up his life. If he was hanging out backstage, I knew he would.

So I'd told him stay on the bus. That fucking bus where I'd walked in to find Mark months before.

The same bus where I'd seen this asshole stealing out the door.

The same bus where I'd walked inside and found my baby brother just like I'd found Mark, overcome by the same shit I'd been trying to save both of them from. The same shit I'd dragged my best friend into in the first place, then my little brother had just followed suit.

Only this time, I hadn't been too late.

Everyone's eyes darted back and forth between us, trying to catch up.

Only Kenny and Anthony knew what I was talking about. After Mark, we'd made the decision to keep Austin's overdose quiet. I thought I was doing Austin a favor. Protecting him. Keeping the hounds like the ones who were hanging out downstairs from sniffing around in this kid's life who'd suffered more grief than anyone should endure in a lifetime.

Right then, I was pretty sure that had been the wrong decision.

Hindsight's a bitch.

"Excuse me," Jennings's attorney cut in, "but I'm not sure what your client is insinuating here. Let's keep this to the matter at hand."

Matter at hand?

Well this fucking *mattered.*

"Tell me, what did you say to my brother that night? What did you give him?"

Scum like Jennings had their fingers in every pot, and he had his dipped deep, covered in the residue of all that dirty money feeding the addicts in this cursed town, even though he kept the front of a straight-edged businessman.

I knew better.

"You'd be wise to drop this issue, *Mr. Stone.*" Jennings spit my name with a lift of his scarred chin. "You'll notice people who stand in my way don't fair well."

"What the fuck is that supposed to mean?"

"It means don't fuck with me."

I lifted my chin in a mock gesture of his. "Looks to me like I already have."

"Sebastian," Anthony warned, quick and sharp.

A derisive snort puffed from Jennings's nose, anger dying his ears a purpled red. "You're just like Mark and your brother. Pathetic. Desperate."

His statement spun around me on a frantic loop—confusion and dread and alarm.

"What did you just say?" I demanded low, my chest pressing firm, a crush at my ribs.

"All of you. Pathetic."

In a blur of fury and rage, I flew out of my chair. It toppled back as I sprang over the table, because this gleaming wood wasn't about to stand as an obstacle in my way.

Those corrupted brown eyes rounded in shock. Flashed in fear. Then I was on him, dragging him from his chair and slamming him against the wall, my forearm the pin that fastened him to the wall by his throat. I pressed at his lifeline as he struggled at my arm.

"What the fuck do you have to say about Mark?"

I released him for the briefest second, and he wheezed in a sharp breath before I nailed him back to the wall. "Tell me…tell me!" And I realized in that second I *was* that desperate, pathetic person, because I couldn't see, couldn't hear anything but the mania pounding fire into my veins, that same rage that had originally brought me to his door holding me hostage. Demanding I get answers. Only now it was doubled. My teeth ground. "What did you say about Mark? About my brother?"

Hands were all over me, yanking me back, tearing me away.

Voices.

Voices.

Voices.

"Stop…Sebastian. Stop."

Anthony and Kenny hauled me back, and Martin Jennings bent in half, gasping for the air I'd robbed him of.

Hostility vibrated through me, my legs shaking, my heart thrashing in defiance.

Jennings lifted his head, animosity smeared across his face. "You will regret this."

His attorneys and the mediator stood there stunned.

"Come on, Baz…" Words subdued, Anthony pulled at my arm. "This meeting is over."

Silently, Anthony and Kenny led me back downstairs. Cameras set ablaze the second I stepped outside. I didn't even acknowledge them. I went straight for the car sitting at the curb. Two seconds later, Anthony plopped down beside me.

My breaths were ragged. Pained as they dragged in and out of my lungs. "Take me home," I demanded to the driver who glanced at me from the rearview mirror.

Anthony acquiesced with a subtle nod, and the car jerked into traffic, making a couple quick, successive turns to point us in the direction of The Hills.

Rigid, I tried to cool the heat in my brain, to reconcile what Jennings had said with what I knew, to make sense of what had just gone down.

We were heading up the hill before I finally muttered a quiet, "I'm sorry."

Because I was.

Sorry that for once, I couldn't just do what Anthony asked.

But I wasn't sorry enough to wish I could take it back.

Lips spread in a thin line, and Anthony jerked his head once. "Don't be. Wanted to be doing that myself, honestly." He sighed. "I'm going to fix this, Baz. There's no chance you're going to prison and he's not going to see a dime of your money. After that stunt back there? I will do everything and anything I have to do to get you out of this. I promise you. You and I both know what that scum is into, and I'm not about to stand back and allow him to get away with it."

I couldn't answer, because at this point, I didn't care about any of that.

All I cared about was my brother.

The car made a left into our drive, which was basically a short, narrow trail flanked by high shrubs and trees that nearly eclipsed the massive house. Impatiently, I hopped out.

"I'll see you in a couple hours before the show," Anthony called after me as I flung the door shut and ran down the front walk and through the double doors.

Loud music filled the entire house. The guys and some of our friends were standing around, hanging out in the large living area that overlooked the pool and sprawling city below, slamming back beers, prepping for the show, voices elevated and boisterous and carefree.

They all froze with the storm that followed me in, my attention going directly to my guys who I knew were anxious for news.

"How'd it go, man?" Ash asked, dropping the beer he had poised at his mouth to his side. Zee's expression became concerned the second he saw mine. Lyrik chewed at the whole of his bottom lip, like he was biting back whatever he wanted to say, waiting on me to say it first.

I just shook my head and shot for the stairs that led to the upper floor.

I'd fill them in later. Right now, my only concern was my brother.

Austin's room was at the very end of the right hall, tucked away where I thought he'd be most isolated from the impact of this kind of life.

I didn't knock on his door, just threw it open.

Startled, Austin flew up to sitting where he'd been lying on his bed, yanking the headphones from his ears. "What happened? Did you get it dropped?"

Without answering him, I stalked across his floor and gripped him by the face, forcing him to look at me. "Tell me what Martin Jennings was doing on our bus that night. No more bullshit, Austin. I need to know."

Fear clamored through his flinch, and his gaze diverted to the side.

All of this had been weighing heavily on him. Depression had been Austin's life-partner. Somehow I knew his overdose, and me being hit up with assault charges, ushered in the first time my little brother truly understood the consequences of his depression, and that his actions reached out to touch more than just himself, affecting those around him.

Affecting *me.*

Because *he* was what I cared about.

My hands moved to his shoulders, and I shook him. "Goddamn it, Austin, tell me and tell me now. Why the fuck is he spouting shit about both you and Mark? If I'm going to jail for this, at least make it worthwhile," I begged him, even though it sounded harsh and angry. Really, it was my own fear coming through.

Fear for this kid.

This kid who meant the world to me.

I couldn't save Julian. Couldn't save Mark. But if I had to, I'd die saving Austin.

Austin blanched, warily meeting my eyes as he looked up at me where I was towering over him. "I don't know, Baz. All I know was Mark was in deep. He was getting his supply from some of Jennings's guys. The night Mark died…" Austin shook as more grief took him over, "he was acting all sketchy…strung out…but different. Paranoid. He kept saying that he messed up. That's all I know. I swear to you."

Dread curled through me.

"And why was he on the bus with you?"

Shame streaked across Austin's face. "Because I was desperate." The word broke, and his explanation fell from quivering lips. "When you forced me into rehab…I thought…I thought I hated you. Hated that you'd taken from me the one thing that made it feel like I could tolerate this world."

Sorrow belted me. This amazing kid, who had so much to offer…yet he believed he was nothing at all.

"But after a while of being there? I thought maybe…" He shook his head as if he were shaking off the thought. "Thought maybe I could finally be *okay*. That maybe it wasn't going to hurt forever." A tear slid down his face, and his teeth ground in anger. "But when I got out…it was hard…so fucking hard, knowing all I had to do was make a call and I could get lost in it again. And it started to hurt. Started to hurt so bad I couldn't take it anymore, and I knew that the pain was never gonna go away. I'm sorry, Baz. I'm so sorry."

I knew he wasn't talking about the pain of withdrawal, but the pain that'd haunted him since the day he'd lost it all. The day we'd lost it all.

He drew in a shaky breath. "So I dug out a number I knew Mark had stashed in a locked cubby in the bus…one of

Jennings's guys. I texted for some oxies. But it was Martin who showed up. Delivered them to me. I thought it was weird, but he seemed cool enough." He shrugged like it didn't matter. "I swallowed three and that's all I remember."

Anger blistered hot across my skin, but I reined it in, gripped the side of my brother's neck. "It's not gonna hurt forever, Austin. I promise you. I'll find someone to help you…someone who'll help you see you don't have to carry around this guilt." I squeezed tighter. "I promise you…if it's the last thing I do."

Remorse lifted his eyes to meet mine.

Grey.

Sad.

Scared.

Shame leeched into his tone. "That's what I don't get, Baz. Why would you do that? Why would you give up everything for a stupid mistake I made? Since day one, all of this has been my fault."

He was wrong.

It was mine.

"I'd give up everything because I love you, Austin. Because you're *good* and you deserve a *good* life. You gotta get that."

"And what about you?"

Soft, unsatisfied laughter pushed between my pursed lips, and I waved my hand around his room. "Have everything I need, Austin."

But somehow it was no longer enough.

He shook his head. "What about that chick back in Savannah?"

Shea.

Shea.

Shea.

My chest tightened painfully.

"Don't tell me you didn't dig that," he continued, a sly smile working its way onto his mouth, before that smile turned knowing. "I saw you, Baz…I saw that you were happy. You liked her."

Yeah. I fucking did.

I forced a smile. "Believe me, she's better off without me."

Energy vibrated, and that feeling came over me that I'd thrived on for so many years, like a compulsion that drew me forward, swallowing me whole.

Zee stepped out ahead of us, sticks in one hand lifted over his head.

Shouting.

Screams.

That energy flared.

Ash and Lyrik strode out ahead, and I trailed behind them as screams escalated to a riot, the surge of the crowd as they pushed forward to get closer to the stage. Blinding lights shone from above, jutting through the dark, dusky haze that lifted in swells of smoke from the stage floor. Spotlights and colored strobes burst against my eyes, and I grabbed my guitar from the stand, slid the strap over my head.

"How's it going tonight?" I asked into the mic as I played a single chord. More screams. "Heard some of you might've been worried we dipped out on you all." I let a smirk take hold of my face as I wove into the introduction of our first song. "Not going anywhere."

A furor rippled through the rowdy crowd, and the guys and I drove into our first song. That song flowed into the second, the aggressive strains of our music causing me to feel like I'd been welcomed home, like I'd been lifted to a different plane. Like I became someone else when I poured all I had into my songs. Gave it all to those who ate it up. That energy alive as the crowd went completely wild at the foot of the stage.

Heavy heat permeated the dank music theater.

It should have been suffocating.

But it was always on stage where I could breathe.

On stage where I belonged.

On stage where I was *free.*

Without the heavy burdens of this life.

But tonight thoughts of Shea and my baby brother had followed me here, and all of that got mixed up in this. It made me feel off-balance.

Lost in this disorganized contentment.

Pulses of energy crashed into my body on a steady stream of waves.

Adrenaline pitched through my veins, feeding the fans, in turn them feeding me.

I dove into the guitar riff with all the pent-up frustration locked deep inside.

Closer to the mic. Belted out the lyrics.

Bled them, really. Because they were made of me.

I can't touch time
There's no remedy for this space
How long will you hold me under?
Just end it now
End me now

Everyone screamed, and a frenzy of voices sang out the words in a chaotic chorus.

And I felt so alive.

And so completely ruined.

Because I couldn't reconcile *this*, this life I knew, the one we'd strived to attain, created through sweat and blood and unshed tears—through death—with the one my heart told me I wanted.

Lifting my shirt, I wiped the sweat from my face, my body still buzzing and my heart running wild as I headed backstage after the three-song encore.

Ash clapped me on the back as he rushed by, spinning on his heel to look back at me with a huge-ass grin on his face. "Fucking awesome show. Didn't know how bad I was missing it until I got back on that stage."

I raised my chin to him. "Yeah, man. Great show."

He gave me a salute as he spun around again, disappearing into the large reception room with the two attached dressing rooms.

Anthony grabbed my attention from where he was waiting just off stage, gave me a quick hug that was nothing more than a couple quick slaps to my back. "You guys nailed it tonight. Fans were nuts. They needed this."

"It was kind of insane out there," I agreed. "Felt good."

And it did, and I had no clue how to make sense of the mixed emotions, like I was being ripped in two, drawn in separate directions.

Anthony stepped back, expression serious. "Karl Fitzgerald is in the office. He'd like a word."

"All right," I agreed on a clipped nod, my nerves jumping, knowing this could be absolutely nothing, or could forever change the direction of our lives. The guy basically held the future of *Sunder* in the palm of his grubby hand.

Ripping off my sweaty shirt, I snagged the clean one Anthony was offering and threw it over my head.

We headed in the direction of the office, passed by Zee who'd gotten cornered by a group of kids that couldn't have been older than fourteen, the guy all smiles, true attention turned on them as he scrawled out his autograph on anything they shoved at him and gladly answered their questions. Lyrik strolled right on by, all casual but with that never-ceasing threat that seemed to radiate off him, everyone scrambling out of his way. He sent me a questioning eye as I walked along with Anthony. I gave him a lilt of my head, a silent *later*, and he returned the same before he followed Ash's lead and disappeared into the reception room.

Anthony led me into the office. Karl Fitzgerald stood from the old, heavy brown leather rocker office chair, still wearing a suit, always looking completely out of place. "Sebastian Stone," he said, his voice tight and his hand curt.

I shook it. "It's nice to see you, Mr. Fitzgerald."

Actually, I despised the asshole, but I figured *that* kind of greeting wouldn't go over so well.

Apparently he didn't feel the need to fill the space with idle pleasantries, either. "Anthony has filled me in a little on what's going on with your case. He's assured me he's doing everything to ensure this mess is settled out of court."

I resisted the urge to spit out something sarcastic, because after the disaster this afternoon, I was willing to make bets that was not going to happen. But Anthony seemed confident, was standing behind me, so I had to stand behind him. Like family ought, Anthony always had my back.

"We're doing everything we can to make sure that happens," I conceded.

"Good. Then we won't regret that Mylton Records has chosen to keep *Sunder* under its wing and at this point isn't seeking breech of contract. You make sure you get this settled quickly and keep yourself out of jail. We'll get you back out on the road as soon as we're certain an incarceration won't interfere with a tour. We won't be losing money if another is canceled."

My nod was short because he wasn't asking me for an answer. This visit was a warning. *Sunder* was sitting belly up at the last chance saloon. Sad thing was, I had to be grateful for what he clearly considered generosity on his part.

"It seems we have an understanding then." He straightened his tie and was gone, and Anthony was grinning, and I was standing there having no idea how I really felt.

"This is good news, Baz," Anthony said, as if he needed to convince me.

"I know." I rubbed a hand over my face. "I'm going to grab my stuff…head home."

With a speculative eyebrow raised at my subdued response, Anthony simply said, "All right. I'll give you a call tomorrow."

I left the office and went straight to the dressing rooms. Lyrik was on the couch, nursing at a beer while two girls crawled all over him, one on her knees between his rubbing greedy hands up and down his thighs, the other on the couch beside him, fingers preparing to get friendly as she teased under his shirt.

Fucking awesome.

Dude was always such a dog.

I shook my head, grabbed my bag from the floor, and stuffed the couple things I needed inside, doing my best not to be annoyed when I heard the telltale sounds of Ash going at it with some chick in one of the inner dressing rooms.

"So what was that about?" Lyrik asked, referring to the meeting Anthony had whisked me away to.

"Karl Fitzgerald."

Lyrik's dark eyes got intense. "And to what did you owe the pleasure?"

"They're keeping us. Want us back on the road as soon as I clean up some of my shit here."

Staring over at me, he sat silently while he seemed to absorb it, like he was rearranging the fate he'd already accepted and was making it something new. Then he just gave a quick nod. "Thank fuck."

"Thank fuck," I mumbled around an exhaled breath, wondering why there wasn't a whole lot of joy surrounding it.

"You stickin' around tonight?" Lyrik asked, still ignoring the chick who was working on undoing his fly. "We're heading over to Kie's. Looks like you could use a little something to help you unwind."

Fucker had the nerve to smirk at me.

I just shook my head. "Nah, man. Austin's hanging back at the house. I'm going to head home."

The bitch at his side pouted. "You sure you don't want to join in?"

Uh…no, I definitely did not want to join in. Normally after a show, residual energy flowed through me—this strange high filling me with this antsy bliss—and I was usually dying to get my dick wet. And hell, I was. But the last thing I needed was to get anywhere near Lyrik's lanky ass. Getting naked with another dude involved was not ever gonna be my thing.

And the only woman I wanted was Shea.

Goddamn, I'd let that girl take up residence right under my skin.

"You sure you don't want to head over?" This time Lyrik's question was concerned because the asshole knew it, too.

"Nope. I'm good."

Fucking lie, but if it was one I had to tell to make it through this, then I would.

"Give me a buzz if you change your mind."

I slung my bag over my shoulder. "Yep."

His words tripped me up as I pitched open the door. "Gonna have to figure this shit out. You can't go on pretending like everything is just fine and finally coming together for you when it's not. Know you, man."

Pretending.

Pretending.

Pretending.

I didn't honor him with an answer, just let the door slam shut behind me.

I wove through the mass congregating backstage, stopped a couple of times to sign some autographs, faked my way through some smiles for the overanxious girls who wanted pics with me.

"We love you, Sebastian!"

"Sebastian Stone, I love you!"

"Oh my god, I am so in love with you."

All these girls who didn't know me, feeding me all that bullshit they believed, like whatever they felt could possibly be *real.*

I love you. Shea's voice washed through me on a haunted memory, soft and sweet and said as if it were a plea. As if she knew it was going to be rejected. Shunned when it was *real, real, real.*

Remorse nearly overwhelmed me.

Why did she have to be real? Be different? Love me when I didn't have the right to love her back?

I escaped out into the night, hitting the back lot where I hopped in my truck, both my car and bike still back in Savannah waiting to be shipped here in California since we'd packed up and left so fast.

City lights blinked past, my mind straying where it shouldn't as I wound back up the hill toward my house, regret chasing me the whole way home.

I found Austin in one of the big recliner chairs in the theater room, and I plopped down beside him, *pretended* like everything was fine—better than fine—and watched a movie with my baby brother that was already half spent, praying to God that all of this was worth it.

When the movie finished up, rolling through the credits and switching back to the main menu page, Austin stretched. "Good show tonight?"

"Yeah, it was good."

At least that much was honest.

My brow lifted as I looked across at him seriously. "Fitzgerald came by. We get to keep the label."

I knew it'd been eating at Austin since he found out the reason we got sent to Savannah in the first place.

Relief blew across his face, a smile to match. And if that didn't push at my ribs, nudging at my hope. "That's good, right?" he asked.

"It's really good, Austin. Things are good," I promised.

"Awesome." He stood from the recliner and pushed a fist out in front of him. "Going to call it a night."

I bumped him back. "All right. See you in the morning, little brother."

His smile turned shy, like a little boy who just needed the affirmation. "Night, Baz."

He left and I sat in the dark against the stagnant glow of the screen for who knows how long. Finally I gave in and dug my phone from my pocket, wondering why I chose to torture myself. But God, knowing it was there was too much of a temptation to ignore. I clicked into my pictures, scrolled through to the one I wanted. Shea's back was pressed up tight to my chest, those super soft waves all bunched up in my face as she rested her head on my shoulder, her smile sweet and open and telling, my arm holding her close, my phone in my other hand while I snapped the picture of us. Afterward, we'd started making a bunch of goofy faces into the camera, Shea bursting into a fit of laughter. God, I loved that sound.

This was one of those impulsive, normal things I'd done with Shea, taking pictures of us like this girl somehow could belong to me. But this was the only kind of forever I was going to have with her.

Gently, I ran my thumb across the screen, touching that gorgeous face, wishing that forever was real.

Dark. Light. Heavy. Soft.

Trouble.

Trouble.

Trouble.

A smile pulled at just one side of my mouth—sad and adoring—and with every part of me I hoped she was hating me so she wasn't suffering like I was, so she wasn't sitting there missing me the same way I was missing her.

sixteen
Shea

"ONE...TWO...THREE...GO!"

Kallie squealed and took off running. I lumbered along behind her, pretending I couldn't keep up, right at her heels as I chased her through the soft grass in our backyard. She was barefoot, that wild mane of blonde curls flying behind her. A belly full of giggles released into the air as she threw her head back and laughed.

She raised both her hands in the air when she crossed the finish line, which was nothing more than a hose stretched out over the lawn. "I win, Momma! I win!"

She danced around in delightful four-year-old celebration.

From behind, I tackled her, my movements gentle—protective—filled with every ounce of love I held for her as I tumbled with her to the ground.

Nothing ever felt more right than holding my daughter in the safety of my arms.

"No fair," I teased, finding the strength from inside myself to smile down at her adorable face when she grinned up at me, a row of perfect tiny teeth exposed. I ran my knuckle down her chubby cheek. "You're way too fast for me."

She giggled more and lifted her shoulders the way she always did, scrunching up her cute little nose. "You're way, way fast, too, Momma."

God, how much did I love this child? My heart swam full, overflowing with devotion. Though I couldn't stop the way each of those emotions felt heavy, soaked and sodden by those other bits that had come alive with *him*, struck down before they ever had a chance live.

I kissed her forehead. "It's getting late. Mommy needs to get ready for work."

"Oh man," she pouted, then jumped up in the same second that her sweet brown eyes filled with excitement, as if she'd been struck with a sudden realization. She tugged at my hand to help me to stand, jumping around at the same time. "Auntie April said I get to help her make s'ghetti tonight! It's my *favorite.*" She accentuated the word in a relish of country flare.

My mouth dropped open in mock offense. "What? You're having spaghetti for dinner without me? Now that really is no fair."

Pulling impatiently at my hand, she ran ahead of me up the three steps onto the whitewashed back porch, through the large French doors leading into the family room, and down the short hall that made a T at the formal living room and the door to the kitchen. She prattled the entire way. "Don't worry, Momma, I'll make so, so, so much and then I'll put it in your special bowl and put your name on it in the fridge, then you can eat it all gone when you get home."

Kallie swung the kitchen door open, grinning back at me as she ran inside.

"You better! You know how starving I am when I get home from work."

April was at the island butcher block, chopping tomatoes and onions, swaying to the country song playing on the little radio on the counter. Her grin was wide when she caught onto our conversation. "That is if this little one doesn't eat it all first. She's been eating like a monster lately."

Kallie giggled and held her chubby belly. "I not a monster!"

"Are you sure?" April teased her. "It sure seems like you might have turned into a monster to me. I think you just might eat the whole house."

"No way! It's just 'cause I'm getting so, so big. I'm gonna be five, you know."

Affectionate laughter rippled from April, and she smiled across at me, before she directed her attention right back to Kallie. "Why don't you run upstairs and wash your hands and then you can help me get dinner started. Deal?"

"Deal!"

In a flurry, Kallie flung the door open and darted back out, her little feet pounding on the hardwood floors, becoming a distant echo as she barreled up the stairs.

The moment she disappeared, my hand shot out to the counter to steady myself. It felt as if my insides were being contorted by the effort it took to pretend I still remembered how to fully breathe in front of my daughter. My head dropped, and I swallowed down some of the agony trying to work itself up and out, this overwhelming, shocking grief that I'd been completely unprepared for.

It only throbbed in the well of my chest, pressing firm and fast and ferocious, the aftermath of loving too freely and losing too soon.

God, it was the truth.

I wasn't prepared.

Wasn't prepared for how this was actually going to feel.

Something bitter tried to take hold.

Pretending.

I guess Sebastian had me pretending, too. That was the part that hurt the most. He couldn't even admit what we'd shared was real. Even if neither of us had been straightforward about the outside forces affecting our lives, that didn't make it anything *less.*

Footsteps slowly approached, and April eased up behind me and slid her arms around my waist, her concern wrapping me whole. "Are you okay?"

No.

I wasn't okay.

As much as I tried to act like I was, *I was not okay.*

The realization hit me hard. Tears that felt as if they'd spent an entire lifetime being held back broke free. They streaked down my cheeks as a sob burst from that festering well, and I buckled at the middle, pressing my hand to my mouth as if I could push it all back inside.

Eight days had passed since Sebastian had left me. Eight days of sleepless nights. Eight days of pretending to Kallie and April that everything was all right when inside I was completely coming apart. Eight days of skirting Tamar's questions and dodging Charlie's worry. Eight days of quietly succumbing to this broken heart.

Eight days.

Eight days.

Eight days.

Now there was nothing I could do to hide it, no longer anything I could do to avoid it.

He had scarred me. I'd always known he would, but like a fool I'd embraced it, just a simple, silly girl who'd somehow romanticized it, thinking those marks would somehow become a balm. I had foolishly thought the memories would be seared so deep they would last, eradicating my loneliness, those stolen moments enough to preserve and endure and verify.

But no.

Those scars were nothing but a hole, one threatening to cave in and bury me alive.

Chest shaking, I heaved over a sob, and April held me tighter. Her voice was rough. Low. Urgent. "I hate this, Shea. Hate him for doing this to you."

Her words were like fuel to the fire, and I shuddered with the grief that swelled and crested. Rushing over me. Wave after wave after wave. "He's such a coward," I gasped through the tears, angry, hurt, and confused. "Why couldn't he just *love* me?"

All those insecurities came flooding in, and my head was suddenly full of the pictures I'd binged on behind locked doors every single night, my desperate eyes feeding from them as I frantically searched page after page on the Internet.

His face.

His face.

His face.

All those girls.

He'd told me he was no good, and it was evidenced time and time again—the life he led, the one he'd warned me of, paraded in front of me like insult. Like a quick succession of slaps to the face.

"He is a complete fool, Shea," April whispered harshly, as if she could break through to me, make me see. "He will never find a better girl. *Anywhere*," she emphasized. "I don't care who he is or who he knows. He is the one who's missing out."

But that was part of the problem, because I already knew what he was missing. Knew the way Sebastian had looked at me as if he were memorizing, too, like he'd needed me just as desperately as I'd needed him, both of us having no idea what we were lacking, what we needed, until his intensity had called me home.

I was angry that he'd left, that he'd been a coward. But now I was hurting for him, too. I knew I had filled a hole, if only briefly, for *him.* I knew he'd used me to hide from his pain, and I'd been willing to hold him, keep him, love him. Especially if it helped him heal.

Even if it broke me.

Slowly I shook my head, whimpering through the words. "He didn't make me any promises he didn't keep, April. I was the one who let myself go. I was the one who fell in love with him, knowing he was never going to love me back. Knowing he couldn't stay."

I just didn't know what it was he was returning to.

I hated that he'd been so bluntly brutal when he'd again pointed it out, when he'd glared down at me with the intent to crush all those simple, simple dreams that had blossomed too full.

Becoming too bright and vocal and vibrant to ignore.

Until those dreams went spilling over to him.

Hated he'd fucked me like it meant nothing then turned around and walked out.

It made me feel cheap, just a foolish country girl who'd taken up his time while he was hiding away.

April slid around to my front, pushing back the hair matted to my face, her head tipped to the side in understanding.

"You're too good, Shea. And it's my job as your best friend to hate him for you if you can't do it yourself. Someone needs to just because he made you feel this way."

Sympathy filled up the weight of her smile, and I choked over a stuttered laugh. "I hate him a little bit, too."

Hated the decision he'd made, the one that had caused him to walk away.

"You won't feel like this forever," she promised. "You will find someone who's going to love you back. Someone who loves you the way you deserve to be loved. Someone who loves Kallie the way she deserves to be loved."

My spirit thrashed its own dispute, refusing the idea, because the only thing I wanted was him. Wanted him to be the one who loved me. The one who loved Kallie. Because I loved him in that way, in a way that was resolute. Complete. Whole.

Kallie came barreling back in. She stopped short when she saw the scene in the middle of the kitchen. "Momma?" she whispered, fear filling up her tiny voice.

For eight days I'd been protecting her from seeing me this way. Shunning all the dark when I was standing in her light. But I just couldn't fake it anymore.

April nudged me back and murmured, "Go on, you better get ready for work or you're going to be late. I've got her."

Nodding, I turned to look down on my daughter who was staring up at me, confusion and doubt in her eyes. I crossed to her and cupped her cheek, ran my thumb beneath her eye. "It's okay, baby, don't be scared. Mommy's just missing her friend."

"Baz had to go back to work," she said as if it was a suitable explanation for the unbearable ache I'd felt since he'd walked out, because that was the same explanation I'd given her every single time she'd asked for him in the past eight days, which was often, and her asking for him had just worn me down a little more.

"And that's why I'm so sad…because I miss him a whole lot."

Much too innocent to grasp any of this at all, she whispered her reassurance. "It's okay, Momma. He'll get off work soon."

I forced a bright smile, deciding that for now it was best not to correct her because I'd barely just pulled myself together, and telling her he was really gone would suck me right back under. I dropped a tender, lingering kiss to the top of her head. "I have to get ready for work."

A grin took hold of her. "You better hurry or Uncle Charlie's gonna be mad."

Heat permeated the muggy room. My skin sticky. My heart heavy. A haze filtered through the thick air, a tinge of yellow cast from the muted lights hanging from the rafters above. *Carolina George* was back on the stage, and Emily's strong, hypnotizing voice languished from the speakers. It filled me with a yearning unlike anything I'd ever known. Tonight, the familiar nostalgia that wrapped me tight every time she sang was almost suffocating.

People were packed wall-to-wall in the cavernous space, the old walls alive with the secrets they held.

My eyes trailed a path up toward the darkened ceiling that seemed to go on forever, an eternal void that held my own secret, as if this place harbored what had transpired that night forever in its shadows.

Without a doubt, that night had changed me.

Sebastian had changed me.

Altered who I was, what I believed, and what I wanted.

It was somehow liberating and bound me in chains all at the same time.

What a sad, twist of fate it had turned out to be. Sebastian was more afraid of his lifestyle than me.

But I guess when you loved someone, you were willing to accept all the pieces and factors and fragments that made them up, the sum of those adding up to the whole, and you were left with no choice but to *wholly* accept the total of that creation.

And in the end, I'd been completely willing to accept everything that amounted to Sebastian Stone, to face what it may bring, as long as it meant I got to be with him.

Funny how Sebastian had helped me overcome one of my greatest fears without him even knowing it.

The night passed in a blur. Emily's soothing voice was really the only thing I could decipher. The rest of the sounds were just barely acknowledged—words, nods, and forced chitchat, motions meant to get me by.

Whether I felt up to it or not, I had a job to do, and Charlie had stood beside me for so many years, supporting and protecting and encouraging, and I wasn't about to let him down now.

Each time I approached the bar, he watched me with that gentle fatherly concern, and each second I adored him a little more.

Each moment I respected Tamar a little more, too.

Because while they'd been the ones to issue me cautions, telling me to be careful when I'd just turned around and endeavored to be the most reckless I'd ever been in my life, neither of them did anything but continue in that support, as silent as it was, because I couldn't bear to answer their questions.

They really didn't need answers anyway, because they were obvious enough.

Sebastian was gone and I was not okay.

Two days ago when I'd fallen apart in my kitchen, I'd accepted it, but I realized now that in time, that sharp ache would fade and become a permanent part of me, those feelings dulled and blunted, though somehow they would remain just as significant.

I'd also resolved I would never regret loving him. Maybe it was foolish, but that didn't mean it wasn't right, and I'd found myself certain that all those scars he'd left me with might become precious after all. Because I was clinging to every memory as if it were a receding wave, toiling and struggling to stay afloat in the murky waters that threatened to sweep me away in the undertow.

While my face remained just above the surface.

Where I brushed on beauty and light and life.

Refilling my tray with another round of drinks at the bar, I angled back into the crowd where I delivered them, then set my tray on a table that had recently been abandoned, a slew of empties of all different sizes piled on the high-top table. *Carolina George* was playing my favorite song, the one that gripped me with melancholy, the one I always felt compelled to sing along to under my breath.

But tonight…tonight while I cleaned that table with my back to the stage, I felt my mouth moving, the words slipping free. No one could hear me above the riot of noise, anyway, but there was something freeing in the form. Freeing in the fact that I was letting myself go.

That gorgeous song trailed off in its somber finale while I slowly swayed, lost in it, lost in the power that struck like a chord in the dense air.

Emily spoke into the mic. "We're going to take a short break and we'll be right back with you."

Applause lifted around me, and I ducked my head as if it would make me invisible, taking the time to tuck that feeling back deep inside my chest. I tossed a rag to the table, wiping it down while a rush of energy stirred through me.

A clamor took over at the stage, spilling over into the crush of people who gathered at its foot. The high-pitched screech of feedback from a speaker set up on the stage sent my nerves racing, the confused rustle of bodies setting me on edge.

At the mic, a throat was cleared. Deep. Deep. Deep. I realized the sound had hit my ears, but really I *felt* it. Felt all that strange intensity sucking the air from the room, rippling as a billow of curious energy through the crowd before it powered into me.

Chills lifted at the nape of my neck with the light strum of a guitar.

Words came rough where they were muttered into the mic. "Forgive me for stepping in this way, but I have something I've got to say."

My heart stopped dead before it took off at a sprint.

Another light strum of guitar followed by the same voice that'd held me hostage in my living room weeks ago. The same voice that held me hostage in my dreams. The same voice that haunted and comforted and dwelled like a ghost in my mind.

That beautiful, beautiful voice for a beautiful, beautiful man.

Rich and soft, hard as steel, a velvet blade cutting me straight through.

Life… Life passes by. Set in stone, but without direction.
I… I close my eyes. Get lost in a storm, that I never saw coming.

This…this wasn't angry and aggressive like all the songs I'd listened to again and again when I'd been hidden away in my room with buds pressed into my ears, lost to his voice until I'd deciphered every violent word.

No.

Tonight it was sorrowful and filled with the same kind of hurt that had plagued me for days. These words fell over me like a dark cloak of regret, blinding my eyes and trapping me to the spot.

Emotion fisted me everywhere—heart and lungs and soul—and a wave of dizziness rushed me as my legs shook.

Slowly, I turned toward the source of the voice, carefully, worried if I moved too fast it might fracture this fantasy.

My throat throbbed with the sight in front of me.

Sebastian was on stage.

Here.

In Savannah.

At *Charlie's*.

He'd dragged a stool up to the mic and had an acoustic guitar propped on his thigh, one boot hooked on a stool rung and the other bracing himself on the ground.

A single spotlight lit him up, everything else darkened to a near black, because this man was the only thing I could see. His invasive presence struck me with all his severity. His arms corded and taut, the color imprinted on his skin twitching with tension.

My gaze took in his face as if I'd glimpsed beauty for the first time, all sharp angles and defined lines and warped, harsh perfection. And that mouth…that pretty, pretty mouth just kept pouring out words that slammed into me, one after the other.

Regret.

Shame.

Confusion.

Lust.

Those strange grey eyes roved the darkened crowd that couldn't appear to be anything more than silhouettes, but it was as if he felt me, was seeking me out. I whimpered when they locked on me, *finding me*, and the tether that tied us together stretched thin, awareness erupting between us.

Pulling.

Pulling.

Pulling.

A tremor rumbled all the way to my bones, and I pressed my hand to my mouth as he told me things in a song that he'd never had the courage to say before. And they were honest and bold and packed with turmoil.

Please… Please lift me up. Don't have the heart to let you go.

Don't… Don't make me say it. 'Cause I don't know what these feelings mean.

I was in so deep. Drowning in the turbulent waters that were Sebastian Stone.

My face no longer breaking the surface.

And I had no idea if I would make it out alive.

As if he felt my torment, the song broke off in an awkward fumble and his face twisted in regret, sharp and defined.

"Shea." It sounded as a prayer. A petition.

Curiosity rolled through the bar, shoulders swiveling and eyes searching as they tried to interpret what was happening.

Sebastian never looked away when he slowly stood, setting the guitar in a stand, his movements determined as he slid off the front of the riser and dropped to the ground. The sea of bodies parted, his stride long and purposeful—and somehow cautious—as he made his way to me.

And I stood there shaking, moisture gathering in my eyes.

My heart beating wildly.

Madly.

He stopped a foot away.

Swallowing hard, I turned and began to walk, knowing he would follow. I passed by the end of the bar and rounded the corner into the faintly-lit hall. I stopped midway, still facing away. The walls were narrow and the ceiling low, the heat of his presence torrid and red, and if it was possible, that intensity only grew as he slowly advanced from behind.

"Shea," he whispered.

My hands fisted at my sides. "What are you doing here?" I demanded, my voice cracking halfway through.

His answer brushed across the shell of my ear. "It's where you are."

Simple, simple dreams.

They were so easy to crush, but not so easy to kill.

They flickered and flamed and danced and sang, and a shudder hit me with the force of them.

The smallest piece of me wished that they had died because the rest were all-too eager to put all my faith into them.

A big hand wrapped around my wrist. Desire and fear pumped fast through my veins. Slowly he turned me, gaze catching mine before he pulled me into the safety of his chest, his strong arms wrapping me tight. He smelled like warmth and man and mayhem.

A breath left him that fell with the weight of relief.

"Shea," he murmured roughly into my hair.

I clutched his shirt, and I was unsure if I wanted to scream and shout and yell at him, pound out all my pain against his chest, or lock my arms around his waist and beg him to never let me go.

"I missed you," I said, choking over the words. "I missed you so much."

His hands were shaking as he moved to palm my neck, and I could feel the race of my pulse against it, that boom, boom, boom ushered in by his touch. He eased me up against the wall, and I forgot how to breathe all over again when he dipped down to meet my eyes head on.

His hold tightened in emphasis. "I didn't know what it really meant to miss someone until I was missing you."

Imploring eyes traced my face, thumbs creating fire where they skated along my jaw. Shivers rolled through me, head to toe, and again Sebastian Stone held all the power to evoke the most foolish kind of reactions from me.

"You were right, Shea. I fucking walked out on you because I'm a coward. Because I'm terrified of the way you make me feel. Because there is so much about my life that I hate, and I know I care about you enough that I don't want you to get stuck in the middle of it."

He blinked long and hard. "But I can't stay away, either. I fucking tried... Laid awake night after night trying to convince myself that leaving you was the best thing for both of us, that our lives didn't match, but all that did was make me want everything you have to give that much more. By the time a week passed, I was sure I was going out of my mind."

My palms pressed over his hammering heart, my fingers digging into his collarbone, wishing there was a way I could crawl inside.

"You want it to work?" All that vulnerability seeped into my tone.

"God, yes, Shea. No fucking clue how to make that happen, but I want you. Need you in my life, baby. Need to see your smile and hear your voice." He pulled back a fraction, hands cupping my jaw and thumbs moving to caress along my cheeks as he inclined his head. "Want to eat with you, watch TV with you, and make you laugh. Wanna take care of you. Wanna take care of Kallie." He leaned in and whispered in my ear. "Want my cock buried in your sweet little pussy."

Desire quivered low, throbbing sure and strong between my thighs.

"You want me, Shea?"

"Yes," escaped me on a breath. I'd never wanted any man the way I wanted him. "I want it all. But that means *I want it all*, Sebastian. Everything. I can't do this again...hurt this way again. I won't let you come in and out of Kallie's and my life when it's convenient for you."

If there was one thing I'd learned over these last ten days, it was I respected myself too much for that.

I wasn't just protecting my heart. I was protecting Kallie's, too.

"Wouldn't have shown back up here if I wasn't willing to give you both everything, Shea."

Those steely grey eyes hardened, and his hands were back on my neck, as if he were desperate for a way to latch onto me. "I need you to know I might still be going to jail. Tried to fix that while I was gone, but I managed to fuck that up, too. My attorney and manager are doing everything they can to make sure that doesn't happen, but this asshole…this guy was feeding my baby brother pills after he knew he was trying to get clean." He sucked in a breath. "There's a lot of stuff we need to talk about, things you need to know about me, but above it all, I need you to know I will always protect my family, Shea. Won't ever back down from that, no matter what it costs."

Respect and fear and anxiety wound through me, because I completely understood what he was saying. He was asking me to accept the devotion he had for his family, as if I could ever count that a negative. That's something I understood about Baz. His undying devotion. If he was in, he was all in. I knew that counted for me now, too.

Of course the idea of him being locked away was terrifying. Truly. Imagining him behind bars was like a kick straight to the gut. But just like he'd do whatever it took to stand behind and beside and for his family, I would do the same for him.

The same as I would do for my family.

Because that's what you did for the people you loved.

I love you. It burned like bliss on my tongue, but some piece of me was too scared to say it, afraid of the way it'd sent Sebastian running when I'd voiced it the first time.

Instead I let my trembling fingertips run along his full bottom lip. "I hate the thought of you leaving me. But I've known since the first night I was with you how important your brother is to you…how important the guys are. It's one of the things that drew me to you. What makes you who you are. And if you have to go, then I'll be right here waiting for you."

He dropped his forehead to mine, one hand palming the side of my face, fingers gliding into my hair. "Shea…my sweet, sweet girl. Don't wanna hurt you."

This time when he said it, it didn't sound like a promise he would break, but a promise that he'd do anything in his power to keep.

"All week I've felt torn between these two worlds…you and the life I know. But I can't just leave the band behind. I couldn't do that to them." Every muscle in his body tightened, and he sucked in a breath as he rolled his forehead against mine. "And playin'…it's where I'm free, even if I hate the life that goes along with it."

It sounded like an apology.

Under all his sharp scrutiny, I swallowed. Emotion pressed full between us. The words were barely audible, whispered an inch from his mouth. "I would never ask you to give that up."

His nose brushed mine, and I could feel the flicker of his wistful smile, hear the rumble in his chest, then feel his hands cupping my face and sliding down my neck.

"And that's what makes you who you are," he murmured so low, yet I felt the impact of it strike me deep.

My fingers traced his face, nose skimming his, our mouths a fluttered breath away, our bodies giving into a slow sway of attraction.

Feeling.

Feeling.

Feeling.

"Would you kiss the poor boy already?"

Our attention jerked to the side where Charlie was standing at the end of the hall, his forearm bracketed high up on the wall. His grin was wide and somehow sad, filled with worry and concern, but above it all, his hope for my happiness.

"Charlie," I shot out, a little mortified. "What is wrong with you?"

"What? You think I was going to sit out there and not come check on my girl?"

"My girl," Sebastian disputed with a possessive smile tossed over at him.

Charlie chuckled and scratched at his scruffy chin. "So that's how it is, then?"

"Yes, sir."

Charlie slanted an eye my way. "You happy, baby girl?"

"Yeah, Charlie. I'm happy."

So insanely happy.

He just nodded satisfaction and lifted from the wall, turned, then disappeared back out into his bar.

We watched him go, before Sebastian choked out a laugh and looked back at me. "I'm pretty sure your uncle wants to kick my ass."

A small giggle worked its way up. "Yeah, I think he might."

"Good. I deserve it."

Pulling back, I searched his face. "But he let you play?"

Honestly, I was kind of shocked Charlie would concede, that he'd even allow Sebastian the honor of gracing this bar with his presence at all. The last acknowledgment my uncle had made about Baz was a slew of mumbled profanities and something about hunting him down, cutting off his balls, and serving them to him for dinner.

His eyes glinted with amusement. "I might have bribed him."

"And how'd you do that?" I asked, my voice going hoarse when Sebastian tightened his hold, energy growing thick.

"Might have told him I'd do anything…pay anything…to get to you."

My chest squeezed with emotion, but still I teased, "Sounds pretty risky."

"Totally worth the risk."

"Yeah?"

"Yeah."

His nose was back to brushing mine, his kiss hovering a centimeter away as his words turned hard, all coarse and jagged and demanding. "Tell me you're mine."

I pushed up on my toes and wrapped my arm around his head, lifted my chin in brazen challenge. "Not until you tell me you're mine."

A growl rumbled in his chest, and his huge body edged me closer to the wall. He stretched his arms out over my head, hands flat to the wall, stance wide.

Eclipsing me.

Dominating me.

The man possessing complete control.

His mouth skated to my ear. "You own every inch of me."

I was sure my entire existence exhaled the strangled breath it'd been holding since he'd walked out of my life ten days before. "I'm yours."

Then my hands were in his hair, and his were in mine, tongues and hearts and bodies colliding.

My pulse pounded frantically—matching time with his—an extra beat for every second he'd been gone.

Reluctantly, he dragged himself away, panting at my mouth. "Let me take you home."

As difficult as it was, I shook my head and pressed my hand to his chest, knowing I needed some time to catch up to another sudden shift in my life. "No. Not tonight. I need to process this…explain to Kallie that you're back. It's a lot to take in."

Thirty minutes ago I didn't think I'd ever see him again.

And now he was mine.

I watched the jagged roll of his thick neck as he swallowed, and he nodded once. "I get it, baby. Doesn't mean I won't be thinking about you."

"Believe me…the only thing I'll be thinking about is you."

seventeen
Sebastian

NIGHT CLUNG TO THE WALLS. The canvas of moonlight shimmered through the sheer drapes of the floor-to-ceiling windows, and glass balcony doors strewed shadows into the huge room. Outside, the ocean rolled, rushing up the bank before it fell, the soothing calm of the constant ebb and flow of the sea brushing my ears.

Wide awake, I flopped onto my back in the middle of the enormous bed.

Never imagined I'd be back here. Thought when I boarded that plane ten days ago, I'd never return. Thought I'd never be able to handle coming back.

What I didn't know was I wouldn't be able to handle leaving her.

For days, my conscience had struggled and battled and clashed with every convoluted emotion drawing me back here, and I'd done my best to crucify the notion that maybe I could have something more. That maybe with all the shit eating up my life, there was still some room for something greater than all of that.

My chest squeezed tight.

Shea.

That gorgeous girl who swallowed me whole with just one look.

I glanced over at the nightstand clock. *Three thirty-four.*

By now, she should be off work and home. Immediately, I was assaulted with all kinds of visions of that girl laid out across her bed. Where I'd ravaged and explored and fucked. Where I'd tasted and experienced, and got caught up in a storm that I now knew would never free me from its grip.

Unable to resist, I grabbed my phone from the nightstand. A smile tugged at one side of my mouth as I typed out a message. *What are you doing right now?*

I got why she sent me home, demanding some time to think. Our bodies were like tinder. A brush of our skin the match. We would have let the physical devour and distort, silencing words that still needed to be said.

But that didn't mean I wasn't going mad over missing her. Every inch of my body was still drumming with her touches and her kisses and her words.

I lay my phone on my chest, tapping my fingers to the beat of a tune that'd been worming its way into my consciousness.

A few moments passed before my phone vibrated with a call. I lifted it up, and a black background with the message *FaceTime Call from Shea Bentley* lit up the screen.

The grin that had been pulling at my face spread, and I pushed up to sitting, making myself comfortable against the massive leather headboard, all too eager to get a look at my girl.

It was weird feeling…happy. Expectant. Like I was sitting right at the edge of something amazing getting ready to happen. And now it was finally within my reach.

Told her I didn't know what it was like to miss someone until I was missing her. It was true. Different than the consuming pain with missing Julian. With missing Mark. Missing them was resigned because there was nothing I could do to get them back, even though I'd give up my life to do it.

But missing Shea?

Missing Shea was a protest. A riot that just wouldn't sit still.

There was not enough willpower in the world to keep me from coming back to her.

My pulse pounded all around me as I accepted the call.

The image that popped up was a little grainy, the room dusky and illuminated by only a tiny bedside lamp. But the faces? They were unmistakable.

A shock of warm laughter escaped me.

Shea was in Kallie's twin-sized bed, propped up against her headboard with Kallie pulled close to her chest, the camera held out so I could see them both. Kallie was hugging the giant stuffed butterfly we'd picked up at that arts and craft festival the same way her mom was holding her, squeezing tight with that tiny smile that could conquer kingdoms, all her little white teeth exposed with the force of it. The child's hair was an utter disaster, chaotic and twisted curls so fucking cute my heart did a complete flip right in the center of my chest.

Shea was smiling, too. But hers was content and tired around the edges, those compassionate eyes soft, soft, soft, like seeing me soothed her in the same way seeing her soothed me.

God, I was in so deep.

Overpowered and overwhelmed.

Suffocating.

And I didn't ever wanna come up for air.

"Hi, Baz," Kallie said, precious voice filled with sleep.

I rubbed my palm over my eyes, down my face, trying to clear up and sort out what I was feeling. Then I smiled at these girls who were gazing back at me. "Hi, sweetheart. What are you doing up so late?"

Her little shoulders rose to her ears, like she was both embarrassed and excited. "Momma came in my room and woked me up."

Shea smiled, snuggling closer to her little girl, their cheeks pressed together, all that blonde becoming one.

Shea pressed a tender kiss to Kallie's temple, tone light with affection when she spoke. "I snuck in here to give my butterfly kisses when I got home from work, and she thought it was time to wake up." I couldn't see it, but somehow I could feel the blush creeping up Shea's cheeks. "When I told her I saw you tonight, she wanted to call and say goodnight…then she promised she'd go back to sleep. Right, Butterfly?"

"Yep!" Kallie grinned even wider. "You got back from work, Baz?" She said work like wook—pure innocence laced with country—and something significant knotted my gut.

"Yeah, Little Bug, I'm back from work."

And fuck…saying it? Saying it felt like a promise, a promise that wherever I went I'd be coming back.

"I like when you're back from work." She hugged her butterfly, Kallie sweetness and goodness spread across her face. So like her mother.

"I do, too, Kallie."

"All right," Shea said, still holding the phone so I could take in them both. "Let me tuck this little thing back in. I'll call you back in a minute if that's okay?"

Hope infiltrated her tone.

As if I'd ever again turn her away.

"Yeah...definitely...call me back."

"G'night, Baz." A giggle and a grin.

"Night, Little Bug."

Shea swallowed hard, and I could feel it, the rumble of her storm even in the distance. "Goodbye, Baz," she whispered, then the call cut off.

I exhaled heavily toward the ceiling, feeling her weight, knowing all those hopes I'd sent up about Shea not hurting like me had been made in vain. I'd felt the scale of it the second I'd seen that gorgeous, tortured face amid the raving crowd earlier tonight. Felt it with every touch and word she'd given me. Sensed it with every hope and reservation shining so brilliantly in her eyes. But I'd be a liar if I said I didn't take some comfort in it, knowing she needed me just as badly as I needed her.

It took less than five minutes for my phone to vibrate with another FaceTime call. This time when I answered, Shea had her phone in her hand while she was crawling up in that bed that I'd been having fantasies about. The screen jumped around as she moved, jostling across to capture bits of her body, a straight up tease of what was going down in her room. She'd pulled on a fresh white tee, thin fabric gliding down to cover up those slender hips, stopping short to reveal the modest pink panties that were covering up what I was dying to get lost in, miles of long, long legs exposed.

I groaned, and she flopped onto her back, quick to bring the phone up closer so all I could see was that gorgeous face that was blushing right through a sexy grin.

"You trying to kill me, baby?" I asked.

She sucked in her bottom lip, that river of blonde flowing down her pillow.

Want.

Want.

Want.

"I'm about to lose the last shred of my sanity with not being able to touch you."

She grinned some more, but there was something sorrowful behind it. "Wish you were here."

"Tell me what you're thinking, baby. You look sad."

It was weird being this candid with Shea. Because I felt like I knew this girl better than anyone, felt like she knew me better than anyone, too. But I'd never just come right out and said what was on my mind, asked her what was on hers, with straight-up honesty backing it up.

She shook her head. "No, not sad. I'm happy, Baz. So happy I can't put it into words. I can't believe you're here. That you're back." Pausing, she wet her lips. "But there's a part of me that's afraid. Afraid you're going to start questioning us again. That whatever you were scared to expose Kallie and me to in the first place…that it won't just magically go away…and we'll be back to you pushing *me* away. I don't know if I can handle you leaving me like that again."

"I'm not going anywhere."

Relief seemed to settle around her with the reassurance, and that energy lifted, vibrating around her, stretching out to reach me. Shouldn't have been possible with the distance, but it was there, crashing over me, wave after wave meant to incite and lure and alleviate.

Just like she was touching me from across the space.

"Tell me about Mark?" Her voice was soft with the appeal, asking for more.

Wasn't prepared for her to ask something so out of the blue, and her request squeezed at my ribs, because God, that wound was forever raw. I swallowed around it and rolled to lie on my side. Like she was drawn, she did the same, and in that second, the world felt small, like the two of us were side-by-side. Like she was right here with me, and those slender arms were wrapped around me. And there was no sound—nothing vocalized—but I could hear her whisper those same words that terrified me.

I love you.

But she was saying it with her care, with her concern for me. Because she *saw* me. The real me. The girl didn't give a fuck who the world thought I was or the way other people saw me. I'd been so fearful of her knowing, of it changing what we were…how we were.

But no.

Shea reached in to touch beneath it.

"He was my best friend." The admission came on a pained murmur, my mind spinning back to that time.

"My life was so fucked up when I was a teenager, Shea. So much fucking bad that it makes me cringe to start giving you the details, but I don't want to hide any of that from you anymore, either."

I hesitated before I continued. "All of us…me and the guys…" Nostalgia wrapped around me like a dense fog. "We've been friends forever, grew up in the same neighborhood, went to the same school. But Mark? He and I were always closest. Just seemed to get each other. By the time our teenage years hit, his life was as messed up as mine. Maybe there was some kind of solace in that, knowing we both hated it at home, knowing we had little brothers there we had to take care of."

Shea flinched as if me saying it caused her pain. "What was home like?"

Desperation filled her tone, and she leaned in closer, as if she were reaching deeper.

Deeper.

Deeper.

Deeper.

I had nowhere left to hide.

But I found I didn't want to be doing that anymore, anyway. Giving vague explanations and bullshit answers. Even though I'd never directly lied to Shea, I'd always skirted around my truths. Keeping her in the dark. I didn't want any more secrets between us.

"Everything fell apart when Julian died." Grief grabbed me by the throat, and the words came abraded as they ripped from me. God, I wished I was in Shea's bed, in her embrace. "My mom…she was the fucking best. Filled up with so much love. But when she lost him? She never came out of it. She got lost somewhere inside herself and the memories. My dad was always kind of a prick. Drank too much. Said shit he shouldn't say to us when he was pissed off. But without my mom there to intervene…" Too many memories came pressing to the forefront, and I squeezed my eyes shut.

"Baz," she whispered.

I opened them to all that concern staring back at me. Affection. Sorrow. Care.

"Let's just say our house turned into a war zone and I was on the front lines battling our father to keep him away from Austin."

A whimper slipped from her.

Real.

Real.

Real.

"Needing to protect Austin should have been enough to keep me out of trouble," I continued with a shake of my head, "but it was like I was drawn to it. Like it gave me relief from all the bullshit at home. When Austin got a little older, instead of staying at home and protecting him, I started dragging him along with the guys and me. Letting him hang out and witness all the shit a little kid shouldn't see."

A regretful smile tweaked my mouth. "Playing…that's really where all of us connected. We'd hide out in Ash's garage for hours, getting high, writing songs, dreaming of making it big and getting the hell out of our neighborhood."

I realized then I was sharing things with Shea I'd never shared with anyone before. All the guys? They'd been there. Been through it.

Now she was seeing it through my eyes.

"But it got to the point where getting high was no longer enough and over time it got worse and worse. Snorting and shooting anything that was put under our noses, fucking anything that walked, stealing shit to support it all. We had something good—this chemistry between us that made something magical. But we let all the *bad* take over the *good*."

"You do have something good," she disputed quietly, words loaded with encouragement.

"Yeah, but Mark didn't get to see it last. I got out and he didn't. It almost stole my baby brother, too. I'm responsible for all of that."

Shea blinked furiously, head shaking in denial. "We're all responsible for our actions, Baz. You. Mark. Austin. None of you can take back any of the choices you've made. And Mark…he paid the greatest price. And I'm so sorry you went down that road together. I can't even begin to imagine the way you suffer over it. But even before I knew any of this…before I understood where it came from…I saw the way you protect your brother and the rest of the guys. That you'd give up anything to take care of them. Maybe I didn't know *that* guy, who years ago was running from home, getting involved in everything he shouldn't, but I know him now. I know you're a good man, Sebastian. I've seen it. Felt it. I *know* you."

She choked over bewildered laughter. "I spent so much time trying to figure you out. How rough you were…the things you said…all the reasons you were pushing me away. I tried to match it up to this amazing guy who stood up for everyone around him. The one who for the first time in my life made me feel truly alive."

She blinked what seemed a thousand times. "Watching you on stage—"

A sharp pain sliced through me. I hated the thought of her seeing me there, like that, through the eye of a lens—through all the pictures that had been snatched of me through the years. My most vile moments. My most vulnerable moments. The brazen lies and the half-truths, not to mention the cruel reality of who I really was.

"It's incredible, Sebastian." Eyes askew, she chewed at her lip, before she opened up and showed me a little more of her. "What you said the night when you left? About you never wanting me to look at you the way those girls did who came into the bar? Never, Sebastian. I would never see you as *only* that. But when you're on stage? It's the most beautiful thing I've ever seen. It's…it's terrifying and stunning and completely breathtaking."

My head swam with what all those videos must have looked like to her, this girl who was all sweet and country delving into the chaos of my world, the way our music came out sounding like it was us against the world—hate, hard, and hostility.

And here she was.

Embracing it.

"It scares me," she admitted, "who you are. What you do. But I understand it's part of you."

"Shea," I almost pleaded, this girl wringing me tight.

This amazing girl.

My girl.

Didn't think that could ever happen, and I still had no fucking clue how we were going to make this work. Because I was either going back to jail or going back on the road, and neither of those things exactly boded well for the makings of a solid relationship.

Glancing away, she cleared her throat, then settled her gaze back on me. Guilt slid across her features. "I couldn't stop watching you, Baz. I'm sorry I invaded your privacy like that, but anything and everything I could find on you, I read. I watched countless videos of you onstage. Stalked *Sunder's* Facebook page. I'm not proud of it, but it felt like a lifeline. Something tangible to hold onto when I thought I'd never see you again."

"Trust me…if I'd have had a direct tap into your life, I'd have been watching you, too."

She swallowed but didn't look away. Exposed. Refusing to hide anything. "I saw the pictures that were taken at the show last week. Saw the girls flocking all around you." Her voice cracked on the emotion. "That hurt so bad."

I blew out a regretful sigh and roughed a hand over the top of my head. "That's what I tried to warn you about when I left, Shea. That life I live? There's always going to be those girls throwing themselves at me. Girls who'll do anything to get at me."

"I don't care about them." Her tone was hard, forward, and rushed. "What *they* do. As long as it's me who you choose, I can handle all the rest." Her hand fisted against her chest. "Just tell me it's going to be me, Baz. Only me."

The words got choppy. "It's only been you since the first time I saw you at *Charlie's*. You're the only thing I want…the only girl I'm ever gonna take. You hear me, Shea?"

Relief washed through her expression, before it pinched in distress. "This last week…did you…?" She trailed off with the suggestion.

I raked a flustered hand through my hair. "Fuck, Shea, the only pussy I was thinking about was yours. Believe me. You don't have to worry about that. I promise you." I huffed out some of the frustration that'd been boxed up inside, all that anger and anxiety. Dread. "You think it was easy for me? Thinking about you moving on?"

"What?" She shook her head as if she were truly confused, like there'd never even been a chance of it.

Humorlessly, I laughed. "Lyrik…that asshole just wouldn't let it go. Knew I was miserable without you and he rubbed it in every chance he got. Had me convinced that fucker Derrick was over here making his move, sweeping in to take care of you after I trampled all over your heart. I've been plotting that poor guy's murder for the last week."

I said it like a joke, but damn, it was no laughing matter. The idea of Shea with some other guy? Motherfucking torture. Lyrik had goaded me until he knew I was seeing crooked, my sight warped and disfigured, then he went in for the kill just to prove his point. *Wonder what that country drawl sounds like with her screaming his name? Bet it's hot.* I wanted to rip his throat out. When he saw I was about to break, he point blank told me to go and get my girl before he went and got her for me.

"What…the sound guy?" Shea asked with her nose all scrunched up, all sorts of adorable, ruining me a little more.

"Yeah." Dickhead couldn't keep his eyes off her and I knew it was damn near impossible for him to keep his hands off her.

I understood the affliction.

"You're ridiculous. There's nothing going on between me and Derrick."

"He wants there to be."

"No, he doesn't." She giggled this sound that was all light and sweet.

A soft chuckle spilled from me, my mood floating on that honeyed harmony, eyes swimming in that warm caramel. "You're completely blind, Shea. But right now? Let's just say I'm completely fine with you not seein' it."

She smiled a coy smile. "That's because all I can see is you."

And I was probably grinning like a damned fool. But who could blame me? Hadn't had something like this in my life before. Not ever. And it felt fucking amazing.

"I like your bed," she said, tone turning seductive and teasing.

I groaned. "Don't mess with me, woman…I'll be over at your house and dragging you *into* this bed."

"Oh, you will, huh?"

"Ten days without that body? Dying here, baby."

"Can't wait to see you," she whispered, eyes turning intense, all that tangible energy billowing between the distance. Stronger now that we'd busted down some of those walls separating us.

"Tomorrow's Sunday. You still have the day off, right?"

"I do."

"Why don't I pick you and Kallie up tomorrow morning…bring you over here? You haven't ever been here before. We can hang out on the beach and barbecue or something."

"Really? But are all the guys in town?"

A smirk lit on my face. Of course they were. It's just what we did, supported each other, however our lives were going down. "They said if I was coming back, then they were, too."

"Are you sure you want Kallie around all of them? Is that not weird?" Protectiveness rose up in her when Kallie's name was mentioned, like she felt the need to defend her daughter. Truth was, the thought of Kallie hanging around all my hard-ass friends who had not a clue how to act around a little kid was kind of *weird.* But they were going to have to get used to it.

"It'll be cool," I said with a shrug.

Her smile was soft. "I think I'd like that then."

"Good."

A big yawn took her over, the girl all sleepy and sexy and about five seconds from being my complete undoing.

"It's late. I better let you get some rest."

"Yeah…but it's hard to let you go," she admitted shyly.

"Not letting me go. I'll be right here and I'll be there to pick you up at ten, okay?"

"Okay."

A smirk flitted all around my mouth. "Goodnight, Shea from Savannah."

Her expression darkened with her storm, something severe and profound.

Her voice was rough. "Goodnight, Sebastian from California."

At five minutes before ten, I pulled up in the Suburban in front of Shea's house.

This morning I was up with the sun, too anxious to sleep.

I cut the engine and jumped out, running up her walk and onto her porch, something like joy taking over every cell in my body with each pounded step.

The second I rang the doorbell, the front door flew open. Kallie stood there, bouncing on her feet, excitement blazing from her like a full-body halo.

"Baz, you're here! I missed you so, so much!"

She was wearing a blue and white checkered swimsuit and a pair of denim shorts over it, flip-flops on her insanely tiny but chubby feet. Of course she had that butterfly crooked in her elbow.

Jesus help me. I couldn't do anything but pick her up, hug her, because fuck if I hadn't missed her, too. I held her to me and murmured, "I missed you, too," into all that wild hair, my head spinning because I was still having a hard time wrapping it around all of this.

She jerked back, eyes swimming with a thrill. "You're gonna take me to the beach?"

"Yep. Does that sound okay to you?"

"I love the beach!"

"Good thing because we're going to play on it all day."

She formed a fist, her little arm pumping like she was giving me a *cha-ching*. "Yes!"

A chuckle rumbled from me and my attention drifted to Shea who was standing at the bottom of the staircase, one hand on the railing, tender smile trained on us.

Adrenaline spiked, a churn of it rushing through my veins, and I was itching to drive my fingers into all that blonde flowing down around her, that temptation brushing over her bare shoulders and swinging down her back.

She was dressed for a day outside in the sun. A long, printed flowy skirt hugged her waist, draping down to end at her calves. A tight, white tank barely concealed the black bikini top outlined beneath it, thin straps coming up to tie around her neck.

Fucking gorgeous.

Knock the wind right out of me kind of gorgeous.

Sing from the mountaintops kind of gorgeous.

Leave me begging on my knees kind of gorgeous.

Yeah. That kind of gorgeous.

Redness crawled up her neck, and I knew her mind had gone traipsing into thoughts the same, eyes sucking me down like she'd witnessed the sunrise for the first time.

How in the hell was this girl mine?

I strode toward her, Kallie still tucked in the crook of my arm. I didn't hesitate, just drove a hand beneath the river of her hair and gripped her by the back of the neck. I kissed her hard and she kissed me back. Nothing salacious or obscene. But with purpose. Reluctantly, I pulled back, thumb caressing her cheek. "Good morning."

Kallie started giggling and Shea was all smiles and blushes, and every kind of sexy when she swayed in my hold. "Good morning."

"Are you ready to go?"

"Yes!" Kallie supplied.

Shea affectionately rolled her eyes and slung a big beach bag stuffed full of all the girlie shit women thought they needed whenever they went to the beach. Somehow I didn't mind. "Apparently so," she said.

She sidestepped me and headed toward the door. She went to grab the booster seat she'd left sitting just inside the door.

"Here, I've got that." I swung down with Kallie still secured against me, picked it up with my opposite hand.

Laughing hysterically, Kallie hooted like she was on a rollercoaster, clinging to my neck like a safety net. "Don't drop me, Baz! Don't drop me!"

My pulse thudded some strange beat, volatile satisfaction.

"I'm not gonna drop you, silly girl."

We followed her mom down the walk and to the Suburban. I set Kallie down while I fixed her seat in the back right behind Shea. My head spun a little more. Two months ago, had someone told me I'd be concerned with adjusting a car seat so it was level in the back of this Suburban—the one that'd been bought with the sole purpose of rolling around my crew—I would have sneered, told them they had me mistaken for a very different guy.

Leaning down, I picked Kallie up from under her arms. "In you go, Little Bug."

I strapped her in, made sure she was secure, and ran around and hopped in the driver's seat. I leaned over the console to grab a quick kiss from Shea.

Contentment swept through me when I threaded my fingers through hers, and she sighed and sank more comfortably into the leather seats like she felt it, too.

We drove the twenty minutes out of Savannah and into Tybee Island, and cruised around to the end where

Anthony's house butted up against the beach. The whole way, Shea and I chatted casually, Kallie all too willing to chime in and offer her opinion and excitement or confusion on just about everything.

Parking in the circular driveway, I climbed out and was quick to round the front to help Shea out. I dipped in and stole another kiss, because I saw no point in trying to resist.

I was fucking hooked.

Kallie jumped down from her seat and ran up the walkway ahead of us, flapping her arms and jumping around as she scrambled up the seven steps that led to the double doors.

Butterfly.

Couldn't help but smile when I glanced down at Shea. I took her hand and gave it a squeeze.

She let her eyes travel over the massive house. "Nice place."

I shot her a wink. "Think so, huh? Don't get too excited, I don't own it."

With a short laugh, she shook her head. "Don't ever think I'm going to want you for your money, Baz."

I brushed my lips to her temple. "Don't think that. Not for a second."

That fact was liberating. Everyone wanted a piece of Sebastian Stone. But the surface pieces—the fame and the money and the bullshit that amounted to nothing.

Shea? She wanted all the rest.

But fuck, if I didn't want to give all of it to her.

Kallie waited impatiently at the door, and when I slid the key in the lock and the door swung open, she flew right in, not a shy bone in the little girl's body.

All the guys were inside, hanging around the kitchen, appearing antsy and ill at ease. Before I left, I'd hauled their lazy asses out of bed and ordered them to be on their best behavior.

Kallie skidded to a stop when she saw all of them staring back at her.

Okay, so maybe there was a shy bone or two.

And hell, these guys could make a grown man stop dead in his tracks.

Couldn't imagine what they looked like to a four-year-old little girl.

Releasing Shea's hand, I moved to set a calming palm on Kallie's head who was watching the guys with wide, apprehensive eyes. "Hey, Kallie, want to meet some of my friends?"

She glanced up at me like she was asking me for the answer, then turned back to them. "Okay."

Almost awkwardly, I introduced her to Ash, Lyrik, and Zee, fighting a grin as I introduced her the same way as she'd introduced herself to me all those weeks ago. "Guys, this is Kallie Marie Bentley."

Ash and Lyrik were giving me looks that shouted, *What the hell have you gotten yourself into* and *oh dude you are most definitely screwed.* They were the same damn questions and thoughts that'd been swirling through me for weeks. Didn't really know the answer except for that I'd gotten myself into something *good.* Something pure and right.

Of course Zee was always filled with all that *care*, and he dropped down onto a knee and shook her hand. "It's so nice to meet you Kallie Marie."

Little shoulders lifted to her ears, and she swayed, all bashful and timid. "Nice to meet you, too."

"And Kallie, this is my baby brother, Austin."

I gestured to Austin who was standing a little stiffly off to the side, eyes darting between Shea, Kallie, and me, a sly smile hinting at the corner of his mouth, but all kinds of questions in his eyes.

Kallie giggled. "He's not a baby."

Austin actually laughed. Couldn't remember the last time he had. "Ah, yeah." He hooked a thumb toward me. "But this big guy here sure thinks I am."

"No way…he's not a baby, Baz. He's way, way, way big, just like you."

And I realized I was standing there holding this kid's hand like it belonged there while Shea hovered off to the side, taking it in.

When I met that penetrating gaze, I stood up straighter, unable to take my eyes off her as I spoke. "Austin, come meet my girl."

And fuck if everyone's heads didn't about explode just for the fact I said it aloud.

Shea moved forward, watching him with quiet curiosity and uncontained affection. "It's so good to finally meet you," she said.

"Yeah, it's really good to meet you, too," he said, shaking her hand as his gaze slid my direction, like he was assessing if this was what I really wanted, if I'd lost my mind, or if I was just playing around, messing with a girl I shouldn't be messing with.

But this wasn't a game.

And if it was, Shea had me beat.

Everyone headed outside and onto the huge wooden deck that backed the house and overlooked the sea. The entire thing was painted white—railings, floor, and steps. There were a handful of loungers facing the water and a couple round tables with big red umbrellas. A built-in barbecue and bar sat at the very end, and right off to the side were five steps leading to a long boardwalk that hovered just over the thick sand dunes and brush that dumped you right onto the beach.

Today, the blue sky seemed to stretch on forever, the day bright and shimmering, just a few streaks of clouds pulled by the breeze giving it form and depth.

Kallie seemed to warm right up to the guys, and she was busy filling Austin and Zee in on that bounty of information she had about butterflies after one flitted by. Without thought, she grabbed Zee's hand. Jarred by her forwardness, Zee glanced back, clearly asking for guidance. Shea just smiled and he gave a shrug and let Kallie lead him down the walk, nodding away as she skipped along beside him.

So maybe Kallie being here wasn't so weird after all.

Shea leaned that warm body into my side and peeked up at me. "This is perfect, Baz. Thank you for inviting us."

Turning, I framed her face in my hands, whispered close to her mouth. "Don't want you anywhere else, baby."

Okay, so maybe there was one other place I wanted her.

In my bed.

Naked.

Under me.

I skimmed my mouth over hers. Once. Twice. By the third time hunger was pulsing through me, and I was wanting more. Just a brush and this girl lit me up.

"Oh, God, seriously, spare me. Don't tell me we're going to be subject to this mushy bullshit all the time?" Ash shot us both a mocking smirk.

I reached out and smacked him on the back of the head. "Watch your mouth, man."

Asshole just laughed. "Kid isn't even within earshot. You getting protective or somethin'?"

If protective meant willing to skin him alive, then yeah.

He hooked his arm around Shea's neck. "Come on, darlin'. Your boy here woke my ass up at the crack of dawn to hang out on the beach, and we're going to hang out on the beach."

All of us traipsed down the boardwalk, our feet sinking into the warm, coarse sand. Shea unfurled a beach blanket, dumped out a bunch of sand toys for Kallie, and shed her skirt and tee.

Apparently the girl wanted to bring me right to my knees. I knew I was staring, my gaze devouring all that tanned, toned flesh. Really, her black bikini was on the modest side, but it immediately sent my thoughts straying right toward the obscene.

Lyrik patted me on the back of the head just as he clomped down off the steps behind me, voice dropped low and directed toward my ear. "You're completely fucked, my friend."

He scratched at his temple as he eyed me over his shoulder, mumbled, "Lucky bastard," before he shot me a grin filled with a smug *You're welcome,* before he tore off his shirt, tossed it aside, and ran toward and dove into the waves behind Ash.

Yes, lucky bastard was right.

I plopped down next to Shea on the blanket. Kallie dug in the sand in front of us, scooping mounds into a bucket before she dumped them right back out onto the ground, the child chattering nonstop as she played.

Both these girls just had something about them. Light. Sweet. Soft. It compelled and eased and soothed.

For hours, we messed around on the beach like we did it every day, tossing the ball around, chasing after Kallie, the guys wrestling in the crashing waves.

Even Austin hung tight, seeming to be just as enamored by these two as the rest of the guys.

Guess I took some kind of satisfaction in that, knowing they approved. Because I knew by bringing these changes into my life, I was bringing it into theirs, as well.

And they fit.

Waist-deep in water, clowning around with Lyrik and Ash, I looked over to where Shea was watching me. It was like with that one glance, she had me tied, tugging me toward her. Slowly I made my way up the bank and toward her. Coming to a stop in front of her, I stretched out my hand. "Let's go for a walk."

She squinted against the sun glinting in her eyes. "What about Kallie?"

Zee was half buried in the sand by Kallie, grinning like he'd just discovered how to do it.

I angled my head toward Zee. "Looks like Zee has her occupied."

"More like she has *me* occupied," Zee corrected, trying not to laugh and guard himself when Kallie started banging the little red plastic shovel a little lower than any guy would ever be comfortable with to pack down the sand.

"Are you sure you're okay with us leaving her?" Shea asked, observing her daughter with all that affection.

"I have her. No worries. Go on."

Shea let me pull her to stand, and I wove my fingers through hers, strolled along with her at my side. There was hardly a soul on the beach on this end. These houses were privately tucked away from the few resorts and hotels farther up the beach. We walked right at the water's edge, Shea dipping in her toes, lifting her face to the sky, relishing the breeze.

When we finally got out of sight of the guys and Kallie, I stopped her, quick to turn her in my arms. "I've been dying to get you alone." I let my nose wander down her neck, breathing her in. "Missed you so much," I murmured, nibbling at the tender flesh of her earlobe.

Chills tumbled down her spine, all that hair whipping around us as a gust of wind swooped in low to fly over the pounding waves. "You keep saying that."

"That's because it's the truth."

She set both her hands on either side of my waist, pulled back to search my face. "I love that I'm out here with you…that you're letting me into this part of your life that I knew you were keeping hidden away. I spent a lot of time wondering what it was you did in those days you weren't with me."

A low chuckle rumbled from me and I drew her a little closer, her skin warm from the sun where it pressed against my bare chest. "Most of the time I was just thinking about you."

A shy smile pulled at that honeyed mouth, and I leaned in and kissed her.

Soft.

Soft.

Soft.

Shea sighed then our tongues met.

Fire and light.

And I was suddenly kissing her like crazy because I'd been dying to do it all day.

Maybe for all my life.

One hand wound in her hair, and the other hit that sweet spot at the small of her back. I dragged her close, all snug and firm and tight. I knew there was no mistaking how badly I wanted her, my cock aching, my hands greedy, and my mouth seeking what it'd been missing for too long.

She pressed her palms to my chest like she was seeking a way to fall inside.

My hand on her back slid around her narrow waist, traveling up the flat plane of her stomach that jerked and ticked beneath my fingertips.

I swallowed down the little gasps that tumbled from her throat, then let my thumb slip under the bottom of one side of her bikini top. I flicked and teased at her nipple. It pebbled beneath my touch, and Shea whimpered, evoking a throaty groan from me.

"Sebastian," she murmured frantically at my lips, pulling away in the same second she seemed to be begging for more. "Someone might see us."

I grinned against her mouth. "Place is deserted, baby."

My entire hand dipped under that thin piece of fabric, nudging it up, palm full of that perfect round tit. My cock pressed at her stomach, seeking friction, something to alleviate the fucking insane need I had for her.

Lust raged in her expression when she jerked her head back, lips swollen and glistening and parted just enough that I caught a glimpse of that delicious tongue. She leaned back, clinging to my shoulders, her body bowing with the pressure of her own need.

"You can't look at me like that, Shea," I warned. I contemplated ripping off that suit and sinking hard and fast into her tight little body. Right here. Right now. "You gonna let me back into your bed tonight?"

"Yes," she almost begged, fingers burrowing into my skin.

"Are you sure you want me there?" I needed to know. That she was all in. No reservations holding her back.

"Yes. I see you."

My chest tightened with some kind of pride, and both my hands glided down to her bottom. I lifted her a couple inches from the ground, brazenly rubbing her against my dick. I leaned in close to her ear. "Maybe I'll take this ass tonight. You know I've been dying to, don't you?"

Red burst on the skin above her breasts, racing up her neck and hitting those cheeks, heat and flames and a dash of that innocence that clung to this girl.

Dark.

Light.

Heavy.

Soft.

She buried her face in my chest and chanced peeking up at me, her voice coated with panic and desire. "I haven't done that before."

My mouth was at her temple, murmuring low, our bodies moving slowly now as I settled her feet back on the sand. Again I found myself searching inside to find the caution she deserved. "You think I don't know that? You think I don't feel it, Shea, the way your body reacts to me?"

The flashes of fear and the shivers of pleasure.

Wanted to give that to her, but didn't want to send her running, either.

"You think I don't love that about you? How your body screams sex—" I held her closer. "—and your heart's as guiltless as the come."

Caramel eyes blinked up at me, sucking me in, pulling me deeper.

"I'm still trying to make sense of where you came from," I said, getting lost in the depth of those eyes.

Darkness crowded at the creases of them, a billow of her storm, and she gave me a tight smile that I was doing my best to decipher. "I'm just Shea," she whispered, before she shook her head as if she were trying to shake off the thought. She glanced behind her. "We'd better get back."

I dipped my head down, eyes capturing her attention. "Hey, what was that?"

Another shake of her head. "Nothing."

My thumb brushed along the sharp angle of her cheek. "Don't tell me it's nothin' when I know it's something."

She looked up at me, her expression filled with vulnerability. "Later?"

Jealousy rose up in me like it was riding on her storm, because I knew whatever caused that look was brought on by whoever the asshole was who'd fathered Kallie. Didn't matter that he was dead. That I didn't even know his name. Hated him all the same.

"Whatever you need, Shea."

She pressed my hand closer to her face and leaned into it. "I dreamed about this for such a long time…finding someone who looks at me the way you do. Someone who makes me feel the way you do. It still seems impossible."

Anxiety flared inside of me, because it still seemed impossible to me, too.

I didn't answer her, just leaned in and kissed her long.

Slow.

Slow.

Slow.

Savoring her, praying it could last.

I pulled away, cupping her face. "Come on, let's get back before they send out a search team."

Hand-in-hand, we headed back toward the house. By the time we got there, Lyrik had lit the grill and Ash had ducked inside to grab the steaks that'd been marinating in the fridge.

Kallie jumped all around when she saw us. "Momma! Momma! Take me out in the ocean. I wanna play in the waves!"

"Okay!" Shea sang back to her as she approached.

I went in for a quick kiss, gave a quick swat to her awesome ass. "Go on."

Shea jumped and shot me a look over her shoulder that told me, *you're going to pay for that later*, which I was all too anxious to accept my punishment.

Shea took Kallie's hand and led her out into the water. I grabbed a football and gestured to Austin. "Go out."

With a lift of his brow, he shrugged and trotted out away from me, the kid sporting a pair of swim trunks and shedding his hoodie for about the first time in forever, and I found myself taking satisfaction in that, too.

Today was a good fucking day.

I let the ball go, and it went sailing through the air. Austin caught it with an *oomph*. "You throw like a girl," he taunted, throwing it right back.

"Oh really?" This time I tossed it a little harder.

"Really," he said, laughing when it hit him hard in the chest.

Behind me, Kallie squealed, and my attention got caught up in the sound. I looked over my shoulder. Just as I did, a wave splashed into them from behind. Both Shea and Kallie were facing the shore, Shea holding Kallie's hands up over her head so she could jump and splash and kick.

My chest tightened in some kind of foreign pleasure, like a warm blanket wrapped too tight. Like she was drawn, Shea looked over at me, a smile pulling at that gorgeous mouth. God, I loved the way she looked out there with the sun lighting her up, water rushing up and hugging those long legs.

She gazed at me, meeting my eye, all that crazy intensity saturating the air.

So full it knocked the breath from me.

Another wave barreled up and washed into them. Shea shrieked and took a fumbled step forward. She laughed toward the heavens when Kallie tipped her head back, face wet and hair sopping, and begged, "Do it again, Momma! Do it again!"

The next wave built up and lifted behind them. Barreling toward the shore. Bigger than before.

Shea was smiling that unending smile while my world set to pause.

Visions flashed.

Black, dark, and vile.

Vivid.

Panic curled my stomach and my heart stalled out.

"Shea." Her name didn't make it above my breath while the wave gathered strength. It rushed, the white toil of water swelling higher. Surging faster. Like evil had once again reached its fingers up from the pits of hell and stirred the waters. Cast its chaos on the sea.

Unaware, Shea was still smiling when it hit them from behind.

It swallowed them, knocking Shea from her feet.

Shea thrashed wildly when she emerged. She sucked in a surprised, shocked breath, eyes wild as she searched.

Kallie was no longer in her hands.

And Shea was screaming.

Screaming.

Screaming.

Screaming.

I felt it all the way to my soul.

Terror.

Spindles of fear splintered through me, vast and deep and wide.

I scanned the water until my sight caught the little body tumbling in the receding wave off to Shea's right.

Out of reach.

No.

No.

No.

No.

"No… No… No." Suddenly, I was saying it aloud in the same second I was sprinting toward her. Water split under the pounding of my feet, splashing on my thighs, before it got too deep. I dove in, frantic as the salt hit my face, my arms burning with the force of my strokes.

Another wave surged forward, and I propelled myself up and over it, sucking in a breath as I broke the surface, spinning around as I tried to find her.

An arm.

A glimpse of blue.

Blonde awash in the turbulent churning of the sea.

One desperate moment later, Kallie was in my arms and I was dragging her free and carrying her toward the beach.

But there was nothing.

No reaction.

Five seconds of agony that felt like an eternity as I held Shea's daughter in my arms.

Then Kallie was coughing and crying and Shea was there, nearly delirious as she yanked at my arms to get to her while I held Kallie close and stumbled with her onto the shore.

Gently, I laid her on the sand while my world spun. My spirit roared. My head screamed.

Shea dropped to her knees.

Frantically she ran her hands over her daughter's face, trembling fingers through Kallie's drenched hair, pushing it back.

Shaking.

Shaking.

Shaking.

She chanted, "She's okay…she's okay," again and again and again as she touched her all over, reassuring herself.

She's okay.

Lyrik was on his phone, his voice sounding just about as frantic as my mind. He shouted the address and told them to hurry. No doubt he had an ambulance on the way.

"She's okay," Shea said again like the reality had finally taken hold, and she swallowed deep, pulling a crying Kallie into her arms. She was crying, too, as she hugged her and rocked her while she looked toward the sky, like she was sending up a prayer. "She's okay."

Bile burned in my gut when I looked back at Austin. He was still nailed to the same spot. Fists full of hair that he tried to rip from his head. Eyes full of horror and memories and dread.

She's okay.

She's okay.

He wasn't okay.

It felt like an hour passed, but it really was only a few minutes before three paramedics rounded the side of the house. They took the walkway down onto the beach, and I moved to stand beside Shea who refused to let Kallie go while they examined her.

Lyrik, Ash, and Zee gathered behind me. The combined nerves and energy and a thick slick of shock ricocheted between us all.

Austin had disappeared.

"We need to take her in to have her checked out by a doctor and get an X-ray of her lungs to be sure they're clear, but it looks like she was a very lucky girl." One of the younger paramedics gave Shea a reassuring smile. "I think she's going to be just fine."

"Oh my God, thank you." She hugged Kallie closer, still in shock.

"Why don't you get dressed?" he urged. "We have to strap her to the stretcher to move her safely in the ambulance. Does that sound okay?"

Reluctantly, Shea nodded and allowed Kallie to be lifted from her arms.

"Come on, baby," I whispered, helping her to her shaky feet. She seemed to be operating on autopilot as she pulled her clothes over her wet swimsuit while they strapped Kallie onto a little board.

We followed them around to the front of the house, and Shea climbed into the back of the ambulance with Kallie, a blanket around her shoulders, her hair matted, tangled, and littered with sand.

Tremors kept rolling through her and I knew my girl was coming apart.

I gripped her by the face. "I'll be right behind you," I promised.

She squeezed her eyes shut. "Okay."

I turned to the guys. "Watch my brother." My voice was coarse and rough, filled with my own kind a creeping fear.

"We've got him," Lyrik promised with a shake of his head. "Go take care of your girls."

In the Suburban, I followed the ambulance, those twenty minutes it took to get to the hospital almost unbearable.

They unloaded Kallie and took her straight to a curtained-off room. Shea held her on the bed, again refusing to let her go. Awkwardly, I stood at the side, doing my best to keep my cool while they messed with Kallie, checking her, prodding at her, the little girl's face swimming with fear and alarm, but always obedient and respectful.

All I wanted was to take it away. Make it better.

Four hours later, they released Kallie.

She's okay.

Shea picked her up and into her arms, frantically kissed the side of her head, the tremors that held her before still rocking through her body. "I've got you, Butterfly," she whispered to Kallie who appeared almost as exhausted as her mother.

I approached them, pulled both of them to me, and wrapped them in the whole of my arms. "Are you okay?"

I didn't really know who I was asking, but Shea nodded at my chest. "I just need to go home."

"Okay, let's get you both out of here."

I wrapped an arm around Shea's waist and began to steer them back through the corridors, discharge papers in my hand as I led them down the hall and out of the emergency room. The large sliding doors skated open to the early night.

Lights flashed.

Flash.

Flash.

Flash.

I blinked against the surprise of it, and Shea yelped in mortified shock, cringing and burying her face in my chest while hugging Kallie closer to her.

A crowd swarmed around us, and we were bombarded by a cacophony of shouted speculations as the fucking paparazzi stole picture after picture of us. "Sebastian Stone…there are reports there was a near drowning at the home you're staying at nearby. Can you comment?"

"Can you tell us who the child is who was involved?"

"What is your relationship with the child's mother?"

"Does Hailey Marx know you're here?"

I covered the back of Kallie's head with my hand, pressing both of them as close as I could get them.

Guarding.

Hiding.

Protecting.

Refusing to let one of the most traumatic days we'd ever experienced become their entertainment.

"Stay away from us," I warned.

They shouldn't be here, weren't supposed to know where we were. This place was supposed be a sanctuary.

I'd been right when I'd been tempted to give Jennings whatever he wanted and then turn and leave it all behind.

My shit would just follow me back here anyway.

There was no escape.

Anger speared me, and I shoved through the mass, tossing off the assholes encroaching on our space, invading on our lives.

"We don't have anything to say," I growled as they flocked. I wanted to spit as they followed us out to where my SUV was parked in the middle of the lot, a rapid-fire of questions shot at us from every direction.

I rushed to get Shea and Kallie into the back seat, slamming the door shut when they were safely inside.

When I turned, a microphone was thrust in my face. "Who was supposed to be watching the child when she nearly drowned?"

Fury lit, and I surged forward, pushing back. The asshole fell back onto the ground. "I said no fucking comment."

I flung the driver's door open and jumped inside. My heart was hammering so hard it felt like it was going to crack my ribs wide open. I pushed out a breath and gripped the steering wheel.

Anger spiraling.

Despair seeping.

Through the rearview mirror, my eyes darted to Shea and Kallie.

Kallie was clinging to her mother's neck, eyes round and scared, breaths choppy and panted. "Mommy," she cried quietly, her fear and confusion heavy in the air.

Tears streaked down Shea's face, and she refused to meet my eye. "It's okay, Butterfly. I've got you. I've got you."

When Shea finally coaxed Kallie into her booster seat, I put the Suburban into gear.

Part of me wanted to run all these assholes down, the lot of them scattering as I gunned it in reverse, then flung it into drive.

Silence engulfed the cab as I wound around the city, taking a long, twisted route back to Shea's house just in case any of those fuckers made the fatal mistake of trying to follow.

This was the last thing I'd wanted. For my life to affect theirs.

Not after today.

Not after what Kallie had been through.

Not after what Shea had been through.

At just after seven, I pulled up in front of Shea's house and parked at the curb. I went straight for the back passenger side door, pulled Kallie into my arms, and tucked Shea's shivering body into my side.

All our movements were slowed with the trauma of the day.

April had made soup and grilled cheese sandwiches. Kallie inhaled everything, Shea barely touched hers, and I couldn't stomach mine at all.

Shea quietly led Kallie upstairs to give her a bath. Water ran somewhere above, and I paced her kitchen, wishing for a different life. Wondering *again* if it was worth the cost.

April did the dishes and shot me glares that fluctuated between disgust, confusion, and gratefulness.

"You're back," was all she said.

"Yeah," I returned, wishing I could claim it without wondering if it was for the best. Shea had been so eager to accept me for who I was, for what I did, but I didn't think she had the first idea what that was truly going to be like.

An hour passed of giving Shea the space I knew she needed before I couldn't stand it any longer. Slowly I climbed the stairs. I found both of them in Shea's big bed in their pajamas, Shea on her side and wrapped around Kallie, hair wet. No doubt she'd gotten into the bath with her because she couldn't bear the idea of being separated from her.

I stood there watching them in the shadows, Shea's breaths heavy and shallow and pained, Kallie's slowed as she escaped into blissful sleep.

Edging around Shea's bed, I cautiously crawled in bed behind her and tucked her into the well of my chest.

I wondered if she'd come to her senses, realized I wasn't worth this kind of burden, and push me away.

She only pulled my arm tighter around her.

My palm went over Kallie's heart, feeling it beat, the steady rise and fall of her chest as she slept.

My entire body stuttered out a sigh of relief, like the adrenaline that had twisted me tight finally seeped free.

It was as if the same tremor I released rolled straight through Shea.

Voice full of tears, Shea's murmur filled the dark. "I had her, Sebastian. *I had her.*"

I buried my nose in her hair. "I know, baby. I know. The wave was too strong."

She shook her head, like she was discounting what I'd said. "I can't believe I let her go. She should have had on a vest, but I thought…I…" She clung tighter, her mouth whispered against the skin of my forearm. "What would have happened had you not been there? You saved her."

Pain twisted me in two, and my insides quaked, and the words were leaving me before I could stop them. "The sea took Julian."

"No," she whispered so tightly, squeezing me closer, as if she were trying to take the sick reality from me.

Austin drowned him.

The rest of it burned on my tongue, the urge to say it aloud, to lay it all out. The burden that had always seemed too great to bear.

But that was a secret I'd sworn to take to my grave.

"I couldn't allow it to happen again. Not to Kallie. I would have died getting to her if I had to. I won't let anything happen to her." My voice came rough with the promise. "Or to you. I'm going to take care of you."

Wetness seeped into my skin, and Shea sniffled as she allowed herself to cry in my arms.

I swallowed around the lump wedged deep in my throat, pushed the words out around it. "What happened at the hospital—"

"Please." Shea cut me off. "Not tonight. I can't handle anything more tonight. Just…hold me."

Relief poured over me like a balm, giving way to the exhaustion that weighed us down. I didn't allow myself to consider just how terrified I was of her sending me away until she asked me to stay.

I exhaled into the thick silence.

Energy simmered around us. Glowing at the corners of my consciousness. Quiet yet unsettled.

Growing.

Transforming.

Taking on a new life.

eighteen
Shea

MORNING ENCROACHED AT THE window of my bedroom. Slowly, I blinked into the dimness, attempting to orient myself to the promise of a new day after yesterday had threatened a tragedy I would not have survived.

Every inch of me felt as if I'd been run over, like my entire being was raw with open wounds. Driven right into the ground. But I knew all of the pain hinged on the idea of Kallie not being a part of this world.

Sickness clawed at me, dripping slow as it spread through my veins, and I hugged Kallie to me, my precious girl who was still lost in sleep, the horror of the day before leaving her exhausted and weak.

"Thank you, God," I whispered into all her wild, wild hair, pressing my mouth into it as I drew her in.

I knew she was fine, but my head was still filled with a hurricane of *What ifs*.

What if Baz hadn't been there?

What if we'd been alone, the way we'd been so many times before?

What if he hadn't gotten to her in time?

What if.

What if.

What if.

It was enough to leave my soul crushed and my mind on overload.

I'd given up what I'd always believed would be my world so Kallie could become it instead—my joy and my heart and light. My entire life.

But seeing her in Baz's arms? In his care? Suddenly my entire life that had belonged solely to Kallie now also belonged to him, because he'd been sinking into it since the moment I first found him in that secluded corner. Now those simple dreams weren't so simple anymore. I'd always known Sebastian was anything but a simple man and what he made me feel could never be labeled simple.

It was disorder. Every touch fire. Every look a flame.

Last night I could feel it stronger than ever before, emanating from him, the trauma that held him hostage as he whispered his admission into the back of my head.

And I knew.

And I knew.

And I knew.

I had always felt his pain, saw this man more clearly than anyone, yet somehow with every passing moment, he drew me deeper into his darkness and let me glimpse a little more of him.

And I'd wanted to turn to him, to hold him and take it away. Take it on as my own if it would give him solace from his grief. But instead, it was Baz who had held us all night, holding me up when I was sure I was going under. As I'd drifted to sleep, I'd been swept in dreams that had lifted and built, dreams that had flourished into something I never thought they could be, his arms strong and sure, as if he himself were pouring them into me.

Us.

Last night, that's what my heart had proclaimed.

I wanted it.

Forever.

After what happened when we left the hospital, I knew a life with Sebastian would always be complicated. I guess I'd known it all along. And the terrifying thing was, I was all too willing to accept it.

Careful not to disturb her, I unwound myself from Kallie and eased out of bed. I tucked the covers back to her chin, a gentle sweep of her hair as I leaned in and pressed a kiss to her temple, breathing her in again before I silently tiptoed from the room, leaving the door cracked open behind me.

The smell of coffee lifted from below, and I stole down the stairs, the subdued noises echoing from the kitchen urging me on.

Sebastian.

I nudged the swinging doors open to find him facing away in the middle of the room, shirtless, muscles bunched and tensed, the entire room filled with his harsh beauty, the air abrasive and vibrating with his gravity.

A hand gripped his hair and the other had his phone crammed to his ear. "I don't fucking care what you have to do, Anthony…who I have to sue or bribe or pay…get it down. Now."

His voice dripped hostility, his body bristled with anger.

Cautiously, I stepped into the disturbed energy, my stomach twisting tight.

Sebastian froze when he felt me. Each exposed muscle triggered when he finally moved, inch by excruciating inch as he turned to look at me.

Horror stretched across his entire face. He slowly pulled the phone from his ear, cutting the call off without a parting word.

"Shea."

My name was pure remorse.

Sorrow.

Regret.

Fear lifted in my throat, and my hand went there, fingers trembling at my neck as if I could keep this terrible feeling away. "What is it?"

His eyes dropped closed and I knew he wanted to shield me from it. Protect me again. But the terror tumbling through my spirit promised he could not protect me from whatever this was.

"What is it?" I demanded a little louder, and reluctantly he lifted his phone, his jaw clenched as he clicked onto that same celebrity site where I'd read that first article, which had been filled with snide and snark, questioning *Sunder's* whereabouts.

Only this one…

This one was questioning me.

Questioning me as a mother.

Has Stone hit rock bottom?

> ***Sunder* front man, Sebastian Stone, has sunk to an all-time low. Reports have tied him to an unknown single mother in the Savannah, Georgia area where a near drowning took place yesterday at the Tybee Beach vacation home of Anthony De Pietro, *Sunder's* long-time agent. Witnesses say the**

> **child was left unattended in the water while Stone and the mother consorted on the beach. Yet another ugly mark to the tarnished reputation of this infamous bad boy.**

There were pictures…pictures of Sebastian and me playing on the beach, ones of him kissing me, the grainy image blurred out where his hand fondled under my suit, though clear enough that the act was unmistakable.

They made it appear lewd. Trashy and dirty.

A choked cry left me with the ones they had posted of Kallie. Her face was also obscured, paramedics hovering around her where they checked her on the beach after Sebastian had saved her life. There were more of us leaving the hospital, a fearful Kallie shrinking in my arms, Sebastian's expression dangerous as he lashed out at the cameras.

The room spun as this reality struck me. They were accusing me of neglecting my daughter, putting her at risk. As if my daughter's safety came second to my need to have sex with a rock star.

The horror on Sebastian's face had become my own.

Only it took root in every cell of my body.

"I will get this taken down, Shea. I promise you. This is invasion of privacy and, more than that, nothing but lies."

But it was already seen. The insinuations already implied.

And it was only a matter of time before everyone knew my name.

nineteen
Sebastian

NIGHT ENCROACHED, USHERED IN quickly by the storm that grew on the fringe of the horizon, taking possession of the sky. A streak of lightning twisted and tangled through the dense clouds. A jolt to the air, sending a crackle of energy snapping through the darkening heavens.

Another lash of anger singed me as if the lightning had struck against my flesh. I gripped the steering wheel of the Suburban and focused out the windshield as I rolled into Savannah after leaving Anthony's place.

This morning, seeing Shea's reaction had been almost more than I could tolerate, the fear and disgrace that had clouded every feature on that gorgeous face.

I'd been here before. Many times. Not a whole lot could surprise me anymore— the way the stories were slanted, skewed to fit whatever bill they wanted to fill.

But this.

This was appalling. Fucking. Appalling. Those pictures nothing but sickening.

I'd left Shea under the guise of needing to handle it, that I needed to go back to Anthony's office at the house where I'd sit in on Skype calls with my attorney, publicist, and agent throughout the day, seeing to it that this garbage was thrown in the trash bin, exactly where it belonged.

Which was precisely what I'd done.

But it'd been more than that.

I could feel her spirit screaming for a breath, for a chance to come up for air, a reprieve from the constant drama that had eaten up our lives for the past two days.

I knew Shea needed time to process. To grasp what being with me was really going to mean.

Because now she knew firsthand how cruel it could be.

The burdens and the bullshit.

The hurt.

And *this* fucking hurt.

I knew I had to give her the space to decide if someone like me could ever be worth it.

Street lamps blinked past as I drove through town. I resisted another welling of rage. I was about five seconds from coming completely unhinged, turning around, and tracking down the fucker who'd crossed every boundary and line. What I wouldn't give to tear him limb from limb just so he could experience a little of the agony he'd inflicted, the excruciating pain of having someone rip your life apart.

And for what?

Sport?

Financial gain?

Fuck that.

Instead of giving in, I made a turn and inched down Shea's quiet street. I parked at the curb and pushed out a strained breath as I looked over at her darkened house. Trees canted in the harsh gusts of wind, sucked to the side as they lurched and swayed. Something lonely and desperate seeped from the strong, white exterior walls, seeping out across the lawn, stretching out for me.

I cut the engine and climbed from the cab. Nerves hit me as I climbed her steps and slipped the key she'd given me into the lock of the front door.

Sucking in a breath, I pushed it open.

Inside, a heavy darkness crawled along the walls, a quiet so thick I could taste it.

But that energy.

That energy was alive in it.

Her storm.

Pressing and pulling me forward.

I didn't have to call out to her to know she was in Kallie's room.

Silently, I mounted the stairs, wood groaning beneath my feet as I climbed.

April's door was closed, and I figured she would be in her room catching up on studying, the way she seemed to do whenever Shea was home in the evenings.

My chest ached as my mind flipped through every scenario, and that time I'd afforded Shea now felt like a crushing force. Because fuck…if she wanted to send me away? Didn't know if I could do it. Give her up. This girl had become my world.

Resolve settled over me like the slow drizzle of rain, droplets hitting me everywhere until I was completely soaked. I was going to make sure *I was worth it.* Besides, I knew it in my gut that Shea couldn't live without me any more than I could live without her.

Could feel the same damn thing calling out for me from Kallie's room.

More.

More.

More.

Slivers of muted light glowed from the crack in Kallie's door, and I softly nudged it, and it creaked as it fell open to reveal the room.

That energy stirred as the girl stole my breath.

Shea's head was tipped down where she sat in the old, white rocking chair that was tucked in the corner of Kallie's room, my girl's strong, loving arms ensuring comfort within. The chair faced out on the room, and Kallie was curled up on her lap while Shea rocked her, that precious tiny girl lost in the restful abyss of sleep. Shea brushed gentle fingers through Kallie's hair as she peered down at her daughter's face.

Tranquility. Peace and adoration.

Beauty.

What I'd turned away from that day on the street when I'd finally understood how much Shea had to lose. How much she needed to protect. When I *got* why I could never just be a distraction.

Now…now turning away was impossible.

A surge of possessiveness crashed over me, and I struggled to swallow around the rock of emotion that got lodged at the base of my throat.

Shea didn't look up at me, just let her hushed words spill into the room as a soft smile kissed one side of her mouth. "From the time I brought her home from the hospital, I rocked her to sleep in this chair every single night until the day she turned two." Her smile fluttered and flickered, my girl lost to wistfulness. "My grandma used to say a child should never be spoiled rotten, only spoiled until they were sweet. I figured if I rocked her to sleep any longer than that,

I'd be risking crossing over into rotten territory because she was already as sweet as she could be."

My heart pulsed, erratic and wild.

She choked over pensive laughter, and she finally glanced up at me, those warm caramel eyes exposing her vulnerability, that unforgettable face sodden with tears.

Every muscle in my body coiled with reverence.

Gripping me in the tendrils of her storm, the hurricane surrounding her grew fast and fierce.

She turned her attention back to Kallie. "I would sit here and sing to her every night, making up songs about my dreams for her, my dreams for us. How I was going to give her the best life she could possibly wish for. I'd tell her it was just her and me and I was certain that was always going to be enough." Her voice cracked. "And then there was you."

The echoed words from the first night she'd given herself to me raged against the walls of the tiny room.

"Shea," I murmured low, somehow her name coming off like a command, every part of me demanding *this*.

Outside, branches beat at the eaves, and a howl of wind screamed through the cracks of the old house.

Shea dragged her attention up to me. "Do you want to be with me, Sebastian? Really *be* with me?"

On the phone the other night, she'd asked me to promise her that it was only going to be her. I hadn't hesitated. But I knew tonight she was asking for more. That she was asking me if this was going to be worth it.

Slowly, I pushed over the threshold.

Inhale.

Exhale.

Matching her.

Matching me.

Every essential part of her tugged at me. Sucked me in, pulled me deeper.

Deeper.

Deeper.

Deeper.

I stopped a fraction away. Slowly I reached out to touch Shea's face. My thumb traced along the curve of her trembling bottom lip as I set my palm on her cheek. She leaned into it, and something inside me tripped.

Overthrown.

My gaze slid to Kallie, her expression lax and soft, glowing innocence, wild, wild curls.

About as wild as what I was feeling inside.

Watching Shea's face for resistance, I leaned down and gently scooped Kallie into my arms.

The child weighed next to nothing, but God, if she didn't feel like everything.

A sigh expended from her as she snuggled into my hold. Inhaling, I hugged her to me before I carefully nestled her in her bed. She released a jumble of tiny, unintelligible sounds, before she rolled onto her side with her fists pressed to her face. I brushed back her hair and pressed a tender kiss to her temple. One of those little hands came to my cheek as I did, chubby fingers scratching at the rough stubble of my jaw.

"My Baz." The mumble of words distinct. Powerful. Shooting straight through me.

It was staggering—the overwhelming feeling that swept through me—like grief coated in the greatest joy.

I choked back a cry.

Kallie needed a daddy, didn't she?

Someone to protect her. Someone to shelter and defend. Someone to stand for her through every bend and roadblock this life took her through.

Someone to take out any asshole who dared to stand against her.

My mouth went to her forehead, affection pressing full, words like gravel as they ground from my throat. "My Little Bug."

I tugged the covers up to Kallie's chin, dragging in a breath before I turned to Shea who was watching us with the hope I'd always thought she shouldn't be hoping for.

It flamed in the air.

Provoking.

Urging.

God, I was so thankful that hope was still there.

I stretched out my hand, heat clawing up my arm when she touched me. I helped her to stand.

Tears kept up a constant stream down her face as we exited Kallie's room, because I knew Shea wasn't immune to this, either.

We paused just long enough to pull Kallie's door mostly closed, leaving it open just a crack.

Staying a step ahead of Shea, I led her across the landing, my hand firm where it was wrapped around hers.

Sure.

Our breaths filled the air, shallow and labored, our footsteps slowed as we moved toward her bedroom, fire threatening to burn us up.

My body raged with the desire to get lost in her. In the sweetest flesh and caramel and honey. To fuck and taste and adore.

To completely let go.

That was intensified by the anger that had hounded me throughout the day—the fear that my lifestyle might steal them away.

Kallie.

Kallie.

Kallie.

This. Girl.

All of it just added another layer to the insanity Shea yielded over me like power.

More.

Fuck, I wanted more.

My heart slipped into overdrive the second I pulled her into the quiet of her room and clicked the door shut behind us.

Shea stood there in the middle of her room, peeking over at me, timid, yet still simmering sex and lust and everything I thought I could never have.

Thunder rolled in the distance.

That and the rapid fire of our panted breaths were the only sounds.

But my thoughts were deafening. Careening out of control as my gaze traveled over her. She was wearing a long-sleeved button-down satiny sleep shirt, a pair of pale pink shorts to match, those legs and that body and her heart demanding me. Tears still streaked down her cheeks as she struggled to break through the confusion and questions that had always acted as a barrier between us.

And I could feel all of those walls fracturing.

Disintegrating.

She whimpered in anticipation, just as much a prisoner to this as I. "What have you done to me?" she asked into the disorder.

I moved to her, doing my best to keep my composure as my fingertips fluttered along the sharp angle of her jaw, dragging down the delicate slope of her neck.

"Shea," I whispered, drawing nearer. Her mouth parted on a breath, my own mimicking the action just so I could breathe her in.

Intoxicating.

I let my lips graze across the fullness of hers. "Shea," I said again, madness taking me over when she shook, those quivers radiating from her nothing but a fucking match striking across my body. Chills rushed, winding up every cell that made me up, nerve endings coming alive.

My arms were around her waist, tugging her flush, my mouth overtaking hers—the same way she'd overtaken me.

And we spun.

Spun and spun and spun.

Our kisses frantic and touches demanding.

Wouldn't ever get enough.

One arm banded around her waist, I yanked the covers down on her bed. I never let go of that body or that mouth as I crawled with her up into the center of her mattress.

She trembled, and those lush, long legs opened to make room for me, her knees gripping at the outside of my thighs as I sank against her heat, friction and fire and blinding light.

One of my hands went to the mattress to support my weight, the other to the back of her neck, forcing her chin up.

I took possession of her warm, wet mouth.

Devoured what was *always* going to be mine.

I nipped at the plush of her lips. "Do I want to be with you?" I repeated her question on a barely constrained roar, on the fury that there were people out there looking down on this girl in the same way those pictures portrayed.

Like a worthless mother.

Like trash.

When she was nothing less than a treasure.

I kissed along the salty flesh of her cheeks that were soaked with tears, gathering her sorrow, before I kissed right back down to that soft, sexy mouth.

She trembled more and arched into me. "Sebastian."

I edged back onto my knees, my fingers laying siege to the buttons of her pajama top, whispering hoarse as I ate through them. "Do I want to be with you?"

Every inch revealed a little more, the flush on her chest, perfect tits that pebbled as soon as they met with the shock of unsettled air, the flat, delirium-inducing planes of her stomach.

I spread open the sides of her top and shivers lifted across all her silky skin.

Still hovering, I leaned over her, my hands pressing under the fabric so I could push it over the delicate caps of her shoulders and drag it down her back. She lifted just enough for me to twist it free.

I grazed my knuckles over the taut peaks of both breasts, making her jump. Easing back, I pressed a tender kiss to the jut of her hip where the butterflies scattered out from just above the hem of the pajama bottoms. *Butterfly.* My fingers wound in the waistband, dragging both them and her underwear down her legs. I pushed back from the bed so I could peel them off.

My beautiful storm.

A needy sound of protest left her, tightening my chest, sending another wave of overpowering emotion pounding through me.

God, she was a vision.

Lying there—hair strewn out over her pillow, every naked inch of her my own personal perfection—she was seductive and sensual. Teeming with sex and lust, her storm throbbing full, all mixed and muddled with that glow of goodness shining out from around her like her own secret aura.

More.

I undressed in front of her.

The first time I'd done it, it was a warning.

A threat.

Praying this girl would *see* me, understand who I was, and run.

And she did see me.

She fucking saw me and loved me all the same.

This time when I stripped, it was a promise.

I stood there, muscles twitching beneath the irresistible weight of her stare. Bared to her. Completely exposed. My cock straining, my body burning up in the flames of her fire.

Ruined for this girl.

Caramel eyes latched onto me.

That storm fell down around us.

Full force.

Beating.

Beating.

Beating.

A frenzy of light and need and dark, dark, dark.

Tears soaked her face, every line imprinted on my heart and mind.

Words fumbled from her mouth in a desperate confession. "I don't remember how to breathe without you."

And I got it.

Fucking got it.

Because I felt it, too.

This girl had become a necessity.

Fundamental to who I was and who I was always gonna be.

Slowly, I crawled back over her, eyes drifting down to watch that body shake as I did.

I bracketed my forearm above her head, the other hand gathering up both of hers between us. Pulling them to my lips, I kissed across her knuckles, the movement slowed as I dipped down and kissed the moisture gathered in the creases of her eyes.

Inching back just far enough to catch her gaze, my mouth a breath from hers, I asked her again, "Do you see me, Shea?"

This time…this time it was a plea.

Shea pulled one of her hands free, fingertips gentle as they traced across my face, glancing across my lips and over my chin. She pressed them a little harder as she dragged them down my neck, like she was searing them into me, harder still as they moved down my chest.

Like she was again searching for a crack, for a fracture in my worn, scarred heart, for a way to sink inside.

That touch softened, yet somehow gained intensity as she moved it down to where Julian's monkey had been immortalized at my side.

"Yes," she whispered toward my face, that single syllable hitting like an electric charge to the thick air.

And I no longer wanted her to make me forget. I wanted to remember every moment. Cherish each one. Give praise for every second I got to spend with her.

I set my hand on her cheek, words strained as my eyes darted over every inch of her face, memorizing this moment. "I wasn't supposed to fall in love with you."

A small gasp escaped from between those full lips, and a gentle smile tweaked just one side of my mouth as I tilted my head, shifting so I could brush my fingertips along the butterflies taking flight on her hip, my voice growing softer with the power of this admission. "I wasn't supposed to fall in love with her."

Tears streamed ceaselessly from the corners of Shea's eyes, gliding down the side of her face and into her hair as she stared up at me.

"Yes, you were," she said.

Wind pummeled at the outside walls, its power matching the devotion I felt inside. I took her hand and pressed it over my pounding heart.

"You told me you wanted this more than anything, Shea. I'm giving it to you. All of it. Every piece of me…it belongs to you. I have so much shit in my life, and I always thought that was all I was ever going to have. That this life was a trade-off for the band making it, retribution for all the crimes I committed on the road to getting us here. But you changed all that. You gave me hope. Something good to hang onto, and I'm not ever going to let it go."

Awe settled on her face, and she was back to caressing mine. "Find love and bring it here," she murmured just below her breath.

Confusion dented my brow, and a small smile wavered on her mouth as she started to explain. "My grandma…that's what she told me right before she passed." Sorrow clouded her expression, yet somehow all that love still came shining through. "And it was you who found me."

I breathed in her storm, a vibration thundering through my body. "And you found me. Didn't know how lost I was until you did. Until you filled me with everything I'd been missing."

"I love you, Sebastian. More than you could know. More than I can understand."

"Pretty sure I do."

Propped on my left elbow, I let that hand find the back of her neck, lifting her a fraction from the bed, holding all her warmth against me, her nose brushing mine. She exhaled, and I sucked her in.

My right hand trailed down her side, over her slender hip, fingers flicking along the crease at the inside of her thigh. I dipped under the front of her leg so I could grab her by the back of the thigh. I bent her leg up, spreading her wide. Feeling another wave of desperation, that throbbing need, I ran my hand up and down the miles of soft skin, gripping at the flesh of her ass before I skated down the back of her leg and back up again, taking greedy handfuls as I went.

Lightning lit up against the window, illuminating the hunger and need smoldering in Shea.

Wasn't lying when I told her I'd been dying to take that sweet ass.

But not tonight.

Not when violence skimmed beneath my skin. Not when my body burned with the need to protect. Not when I was half mad with lust, half mad with the thirst to ruin anyone who brought harm to this girl. Not when I felt myself standing at the cusp I'd been standing on all along.

Not when I was finally ready to jump.

I pulled back enough to grab the base of my cock, glancing up at her face as I aligned my tip at the heat of her center.

She locked eyes with me, her chest heaving, and her breaths shallow.

I pushed forward, the walls of that perfect pussy gripping my head, begging for more as I held back her thigh and slowly eased in until I was taking her whole.

I stuttered out a strangled groan. "So good. Every time, Shea. Every time and I just want more. Not ever going to stop loving you."

And I fell into her, my body rocking into hers. For the first time, slow and deliberate, that energy consuming us from all sides.

Dark.

Light

Heavy.

Soft.

I blinked erratically, dizzy with *this*, dizzy with *her*.

My cock was bare, burning into her as I claimed her in a way I'd never claimed a girl before. Her body taking all of me, filled up so full she was gasping, writhing below me, sharp, shattered gasps tumbling from her mouth.

I kissed her there, on that innocent mouth, wanting those sounds, too, greedy and desperate to take it all.

Refusing to ever let her go.

"Sebastian," Shea rasped as her fingers sank into the straining, bunched muscles of my shoulders as I worked over her, and I could feel it building, the intensity that bristled through her—her walls clenching, her thighs shaking, before her mouth parted and her head rocked back on her pillow.

Muted moans. A choked sob of pleasure.

My name. My name. My name.

She chanted it again and again, the drum of her song beating into me. Every inch of me tightened, pleasure building strong and fast.

I took her as deep as I could get her as this girl splintered in my arms, seeping into me, sinking fast to where I'd felt her slipping into since the moment I'd met her.

All that beautiful bliss broke, speeding through my cock and my heart and my mind.

Pouring into her, I came in the well of that sweet, tight body.

Some secret part of me was hoping it would take root.

That Shea would be tied to me forever.

She and I creating something *good.*

But I knew without a shadow of a doubt that we already were.

Fingers dug deeper into my shoulders as Shea searched for her breath, our bodies still alight in the passion that swelled between us, a buzz in the air, the energy refusing to let us go.

I pressed a closed-mouthed kiss to her lips before I pulled back to cast her an adoring smile. "I love you."

The one she sent me back reached in to touch me all the way in my scarred heart, this girl fully seated within the cracks.

Right where she always belonged.

"I never needed anyone to love me until I needed you," she said.

I brushed back the hair matted to her forehead, and I felt the frown grow on my face. I hated to go back there, but I knew this had to be resolved before we could move on with our lives. "My attorney got the article pulled."

Swallowing hard, she nodded. "That's good." It sounded like it was hard to say.

I glanced to the side, building up, playing with a lock of her hair before I peered back at her. "Tomorrow I'm going to make a statement. I want the world to know you're with me. No more speculation about you and Kallie. I'm going to tell them you're my family now. They'll hound us for a while with the news, but they'll get bored after a while."

Darkness skated across her features.

"Baby, I know it's scary, but it's the best way. The more we hide, the more they're going to want to know. Let's just get this out of the way so we can move on and put it behind us. We're going to have to face it some time. We might as well do it now."

She shook her head, like she was trying to silence me.

"Sebastian," she whispered, and those tears just wouldn't quit. "I want that, more than anything, for the world to know you're mine. But there's something you need to know about me before you do that."

Dread curled in my stomach and I clung to her a little tighter. "There's nothing you can say that will change the way I feel about you."

Intensity swelled, working right back into a restless frenzy, and I knew…I knew I was now in the eye of her storm.

A counterfeit calm.

"What is it?" I demanded, just needing to know.

Wind battered the window pane, and I jarred with the sound of the doorbell ringing below.

Shea's eyes grew round with worry.

I shook my head. "Leave it. Whoever it is can wait. I need to know what you're talking about, baby."

She hesitated, before the bell rang again, followed by a fist pounding on the door.

"Shit," I muttered. That same anger blistered through me that I'd been subject to throughout the entire day. The sorry fucker who had the audacity to come knocking at Shea's door, shoving microphones and cameras in our faces, was going to pay.

Shea wiggled out from under me and started to roll from the bed. I snatched her by the wrist. "This isn't over, Shea."

She grimaced as she looked back at me from over her shoulder. "No, you're right. This isn't over."

She rushed to pull her pajama shorts back on, fumbled through the buttons of her sleep shirt while I was dragging on my jeans, because I sure as hell wasn't going to allow her to face whatever bullshit was waiting for her outside alone. My bullshit. What I'd dragged into her town and into her life.

Guess maybe that statement I promised to make would be coming tonight rather than in the morning.

Someone pounded again and Shea jogged downstairs. I was right at her heels. I haphazardly raked my hands through my hair, trying to tame what I was sure were the telltale signs that Shea and I had just been going at it. Considering Shea's mussed-up state, there wasn't going to be much denying it anyway.

More fuel for the fire.

Fucking fantastic.

Shea hit the bottom floor and rushed toward the door. She stopped short to peer through the peephole.

A small gasp shot from her and she took a shocked step back, and her head began to shake in clear confusion as she warily inched away from the door.

I moved around her, pushing a hand out toward her as if to tell her to stay.

I peeked through to see what had Shea completely frozen.

Two police officers stood behind a middle-aged woman who was dressed in a cheap suit, her dark hair twisted up in a shrewd bun.

My chest squeezed, and over my shoulder, I glanced at Shea, looking for help, for an indication of what the hell was going on, before my own reality slowly pressed in.

In resignation, I shook my head. "Baby, they're coming for me. I pushed down that asshole at the hospital who was implying we weren't watching Kallie on the beach. He was tossing around the threat of charges today."

Should have known those bastards would never let me get away with defending those I cared about.

"Baz, no." She swallowed hard, like she couldn't fathom it.

"It's going to be okay," I promised.

Reluctantly, I unlocked the door and pulled it open. I stood in the doorframe with arms crossed over my bare chest, almost daring them to come for me, silently calculating how I was going to make that scum's life a living hell.

The woman in the suit reared back, like I'd taken her by surprise, before she cleared her throat and lifted her chin in authority. "I need to speak with Ms. Bentley, please.

Not for me.

What the fuck?

My hackles rose, apprehension shaking me down, and I slowly turned to look back at where Shea's hands trembled where she twisted them out in front of her.

Her voice cracked. "I'm Shea Bentley."

The woman set her hand on the door, as if she were holding it open, keeping us from slamming it in her face.

I suddenly had the overwhelming urge to do exactly that, to run for Shea and wrap her up.

To preserve and defend.

I knew it all the way to my soul.

That was my job now—taking care of Shea, taking care of Kallie.

"I'm Claribel Sanchez with Child Protective Services…"

I felt the bottom drop out of Shea's world.

It dragged mine right along with it.

Shea took a defensive step back as the woman took one forward. Claribel Sanchez produced the folder she had tucked under her arm. "We have an emergency injunction in the care of your daughter, Kallie Bentley. I'm sorry, but we have to remove her from your care pending further investigation of the incident occurring yesterday."

"N-n-no," Shea stuttered over the denial, and she backed up more. Anxiety and desperation scattered through her, defenses turned to full throttle, like she was considering bolting up the stairs and going for her daughter.

I cut in, trying to diffuse the situation. "What is going on here? Kallie was released from the hospital without injuries. She's in no danger."

The woman had the grace of appearing sympathetic as she glanced between Shea and me, who looked like she was about to succumb to the worst kind of anxiety attack. "I'm sorry, but that's for the court to decide. She'll be removed from her mother's care until it's resolved if Ms. Bentley is fit to maintain custody."

"Please," Shea cried, stepping forward as if she were going to take hold of the woman, beseeching, imploring, breaking another piece of my heart. "Please don't do this. My child…she's my life. I would never willingly allow anything bad to happen to her. That article…they lied…I was in the water with her and a wave knocked her from my hold. Please. Don't do this."

Desperation poured from her.

More sympathy from the woman, her eyes traveling around the sanctity and peace of Shea's house, like she was forming her own judgments and maybe they were contrary to the court's.

But I knew well enough that none of that mattered.

This woman was simply doing her job.

How the hell could they determine that from gossip rags? Not interview those who were there? This was fucked.

I dug my phone from my back pocket. Kenny was on speed dial. It went right to voicemail.

Fuck, I silently cursed, ending that call and dialing Anthony. He answered on the second ring. "What now, Sebastian? Please tell me you haven't gone and gotten yourself into more trouble," he asked, resigned, drained from the day.

"CPS is taking Kallie. Get Kenny and now. I want to know who did this and get this reversed. Immediately." Hysteria and anger gushed from me in a steady stream of words. "Tell him to get a team together. Whoever is the best. I want them working on this tonight."

For Shea, I knew even one night was too much.

"Shit," he hissed. "I'm on it."

I clicked off the call.

The two police officers stepped inside with the clear intention to dissuade any untoward opposition on my part, prepared for my counter attack.

"No," Shea begged when the woman began to inch toward her. She stretched her arms across the stairs, a barrier across both railings. "No," she said again.

"Mommy?" That tiny voice drifted from the top of the landing, her fist rubbing the sleep from her eyes as she hugged her butterfly in the bend of her elbow.

"I'm sorry," the woman said again, taking the opportunity to edge around Shea when all of her attention lifted to her daughter.

As she passed, Shea latched a hand onto the woman's arm. "Please don't do this. I will do anything. Please."

"Please don't make this harder than it has to be," the woman returned, slanting her own plea to Shea from over her shoulder as she jerked her arm free and continued the climb to the top of the stairs.

Claribel Sanchez went right for Kallie, picked her up, and dashed right back down.

April appeared at the top of the stairs, confused, obviously trying to decode what was taking place, before she shot me a look that blamed me for all of this.

Pain lanced through the room, and it was like I could feel Shea splintering, completely breaking apart.

"Please, let me at least tell her goodbye."

The woman gave her a reluctant nod, and Shea rushed forward and grasped both sides of Kallie's frightened face. She whispered urgent words to her daughter. "Don't be scared, sweetheart. Mommy is right here and you're going to be home before you know it. Whatever you do, don't forget how much I love you."

Kallie started to cry, finally catching up to the torment rolling from her mother.

Pleading eyes moved to the woman. "Where are you taking her? Tell me she'll be safe."

"She'll be placed with her closest blood relative until the courts decide on the appropriate placement for her."

If Shea was a fit mother.

That's what Claribel Sanchez was saying, and I knew she was just doing what she was paid to do, but fuck, anyone could see this was the safest place for Kallie. That this was where she belonged. That Shea would die before she allowed anything to happen to her daughter.

I would, too.

"Charlie?" Shea begged with a small surge of hope as she began to frantically stumble along behind the woman who headed outside, the two officers leading the way.

The woman just gave a short shake of her head, and swiftly darted out into the dense, hungry night. Clouds billowed thick in the air, suffocating as they sank low to the ground.

Drowning out breath.

Drowning out hope.

Kallie stared back at Shea from over the woman's shoulder, bewildered brown eyes swimming in fear. A little hand stretched for her mother as the woman sped down the steps.

Another stake to my heart.

How could I stand here and allow this to happen? But what was I supposed to do? I hadn't ever felt so tied up in chains in all my life.

Helpless.

Because I'd always fought my way out of every situation.

Fists. Fury. Rage.

They had always been my solution.

But I knew throwing punches would only do more harm.

Shea clamored down behind them, and I followed right behind her. I was doing my best to keep calm, to keep cool, to ignore my temper that was demanding I step in.

Fight.

But that was only going to make it a thousand times worse, and I wasn't about to be responsible for putting Kallie and Shea in a worse predicament than they were already in.

Two cruisers were parked at the curb, a cheap blue import sandwiched between them and my Suburban.

But it was the black Mercedes sitting in front of my SUV that captured my attention. Sleek, low, and foreboding.

Claribel Sanchez jogged toward it, her hand on the back of Kallie's head as if she were protecting her rather than ushering more trauma into this little girl's life.

Scarring purity.

Ruining all that innocence.

Bringing darkness into the light.

My gut twisted into knots with the intense need to intervene, to keep this little girl, my *Little Bug*, from experiencing even a second of this ordeal.

Knew it was my fault. I should have been more aware. Should have known those scavengers would be out there lying in wait.

I hit the walkway at the bottom of Shea's front porch steps when an ominous figure climbed out from the backseat of the Mercedes on the opposite side of the car from us.

Arrogant and contentious.

Most of his body was obscured by the car, his blond hair slicked back. He ducked a fraction as if sheltering himself from the storm rumbling above.

Fierce squalls of wind whipped through the air, diving in low to touch the ground, the world whipped into a frenzy of forewarning.

Awareness slammed me and I skidded to a stop.

Martin Jennings.

What the fuck?

It was the same second Shea saw him there. For the briefest second she stalled, too, like her mind pitched and lurched through shocked confusion as she attempted to catch up to what was happening.

I was lost with her, my senses blurred and cluttered, the hatred I had for this asshole at the forefront as I tried to add it all up, searching for the sum.

Shea seemed to solve it before me.

She cried out—a vicious scream that came from the depths of her in the same second she leapt forward, claws bared, no doubt going in for the attack. She broke into a run behind Claribel just as the woman was reaching the end of the walk.

Both of the officers whirled around with the intent to restrain Shea, but I was quicker, the need to protect her spurring me into action.

I caught her by the waist, my voice straining with the demand, because God knew I wanted to charge every bit as badly as she did. "Shea, no. You're going to make it worse."

She kicked wild legs into the air as I held her back against my chest. She clawed at my arms locked around her, struggling to break free, screaming at Jennings, "You bastard! You bastard! How could you do this? How could you?"

My mind reeled.

Martin Jennings.

Shea knew him.

She *knew* him.

It made no fucking sense.

My hold increased when he smirked across at us from over the top of the car. But it was like he didn't see her at all, like he didn't care he was stealing Shea's daughter, that pretentious pride and arrogance cast fully on me.

"You were warned you'd regret fucking with me."

Dread throbbed through my veins as awareness threatened to take hold.

Claribel Sanchez opened the opposite rear door of the Mercedes, trying to wrangle a thrashing Kallie into the car seat already secured in the back.

Kallie was terrified, crying again and again, "I want my mommy…I want my mommy!"

Shea screamed through the tears bottling up her throat. "You bastard, I will kill you…I will kill you."

Jennings chuckled. "Oh, it's so very nice to see you again, Delaney Rhoads. I can see how much you missed me."

Delaney Rhoads.

Erratic, the world crashed down around me as that name penetrated.

It was only a vague memory from about five years ago.

That rising country star surrounded by scandal and the way the young girl had just dropped out of sight. The uproar and rumors surrounding it, because she'd disappeared in almost the same breath as her first album hit the top of the charts.

I'd had enough scandal in my own life that I'd paid little attention, giving little regard to nonsense that was happening in Tennessee.

Of course, Tennessee was where the bastard had discovered *Sunder* in that shitty bar about six months later.

Oh God.

Kallie's father. He wasn't dead. She was his…he was… Fuck. The man I despised more than anyone else on this earth.

I'd always been terrified I would break Shea.

I was wrong.

It was Shea who was going to break me.

She kicked her legs, still waging her own futile war, the one that demanded she do whatever it took to protect her daughter.

But there was no question the battle fought tonight was lost.

Torment flooded us.

Rising at our feet.

Climbing our bodies.

Waves riding up over our heads.

Drowning.

Drowning.

Drowning.

Claribel Sanchez closed the door, cutting off the sight of Kallie.

Shea wailed, "Kallie…Kallie!"

Martin Jennings tossed a cocky grin my direction before he slipped into the back seat beside the little girl I wanted to call my own.

The little girl who'd breezed through me like the calmest whirlwind, slowly staking claim until she'd taken every inch of me.

The car pulled from the curb and drove into the night.

Shea leaned her head back and released a blood-curdling cry into the air.

A clap of thunder deafened our ears.

Agony.

Agony.

Agony.

And I held her, vowing in her ear, "We will get her back. I promise you, we will get her back."

This girl who'd lied to me. The one I didn't even know.

Sebastian and Shea's story continues in Drowning to Breathe, June 22, 2015

To get the first peek at the entire first chapter of Drowning to Breathe two months early, text "jackson" to 96000 or subscribe to my mailing list http://bit.ly/ALJacksonNewsletter

A note from the author

Thank you so much for reading A Stone in the Sea! I hope you fell in love with Sebastian and Shea's story the same way I did. If you've read anything by me before, you know I don't usually do cliffhangers. Leaving this book off here was a difficult decision for me, but I knew in my gut I couldn't fit their story into the pages of just one book without rushing it, and their full story deserves to be told. You can expect a lot more intensity and sexiness in Drowning to Breathe, but underlying it all, I hope to delve into the deep, emotional bonds of these two characters.

If you'd like to discuss A Stone in the Sea with other A.L. Jackson readers, please consider joining The A.L. Jackson Reader Hangout

http://bit.ly/AmysAngels

To get free books, exclusive excerpts, giveaways, and all the latest news, be sure you subscribe to News from A.L. Jackson

http://bit.ly/ALJacksonNewsletter

For short but sweet updates on releases and sales (no more than 2 texts per month), TEXT "jackson" to 96000

Turn the page to read the first two chapters of Come to Me Recklessly, The Closer to You Series, Book Three, coming from Penguin/Random House April 7, 2015

Come to Me Recklessly

By A.L. Jackson

Prologue

There are few things that hurt so much as a broken heart.

It's physical.

Intense.

Real.

It doesn't matter which way you slice it, analyze it, or add it up, you'll always come up with the exact same sum. The worst part is there is no antidote for this affliction.

They say time mends all things.

I say they are liars.

Maybe it subdues, burying it beneath all the new memories we make, tucked under the burdens and joys and new experiences that life layers on over the years.

But that broken heart?

It's always right there, lying in wait. Ready to crush you when you're slammed with that errant, unexpected thought.

But nothing could have prepared me for this—what it would feel like to look up and find him standing inches from me.

From the moment we met, he always had the power to bring me to my knees. I should have known his control over me would never diminish or dim.

I should have known it only would intensify.

Maybe I should run.

But somewhere inside, I know he'll never let me get far.

Chapter One
Samantha

My phone rang with the special chime, the one reserved just for my brother, Stewart. . I rummaged around for it in my purse while I was browsing through the aisles of Target. The grin taking over my entire face was completely uncontrollable. I just couldn't help it. Talking with him—seeing him—was always the highlight of my day.

Running my thumb across the screen, I clicked the icon where his message waited. I'd never even heard of the app until he'd convinced me I *had* to get it, teasing me I was living in the Stone Ages, which to him I was pretty sure would date all the way back to 2011. I couldn't begin to keep up with all the tech stuff he loved.

I held my finger down on the new unread Snapchat message from *gamelover745*.

An image popped up on the screen, his face all contorted in the goofiest expression, pencils hanging from both his nostrils as he bared his teeth. I choked over a little laugh. The joy I felt every time I saw his face was almost overwhelming as it merged with the twinge of sorrow that tugged at my chest.

Quickly, I shoved the feeling off. He told me he couldn't stand for me to look at him or think of him with pity. I had to respect that. He was so much braver than me, because seeing him sick made me feel so weak.

I forced myself not to fixate on his bald head and pale skin, and instead focused on the antics of this playful boy. The little timer ran down, alerting me I only had five more seconds of the picture, so I quickly read the messy words he scrawled across the image.

I'm sexy and I know it.

On a muted giggle, I shook my head, and I didn't hesitate for a second to lift my phone above my head to snap my own picture. Going for my silliest expression, I crossed my eyes and stuck my tongue out to the side.

So maybe the people milling around me in the middle of the busy store thought I was crazy, or some kind of delusional narcissist, but nothing inside me cared. I'd do anything to see him smile.

I tapped the button so I could write on the picture.

Love you, goofball.

I pushed send.

Seconds later, it chimed again. I clicked to receive his message. This time he was just smiling that unending smile, sitting crossed legged in the middle of his bed, radiating all his beauty and positivity, and that sorrow hit me again, only harder.

Love you back, he'd written on the image.

Letting the timer wind down, I clutched my phone as I cherished his message for the full ten seconds, before our snap expired. The screen went blank. I bit at the inside of my lip, blinking back tears.

Don't, I warned myself, knowing how quickly I could spiral into depression, into a worry I couldn't control, one that would taint the precious time I had with him.

Sucking in a cleansing breath, I tossed my phone back into my purse and wandered over to the cosmetics section, browsing through all the shades and colors of lip gloss. I tossed a shimmery clear one into my cart, then strolled into the shampoo aisle.

Apparently I was in no hurry to get home. It was sad and pathetic, yet here I was, twenty-three years old and passing away my Friday night at a Target.

Ben texted me earlier saying he was going out to grab a beer with the guys and not to wait up for him. All kinds of warning bells went off in my head when I realized him leaving me alone for the night only filled me with an overwhelming relief. That realization hurt my heart, because he'd always been good to me, there for me when I was broken and needed someone to pick up the pieces, making me smile when I thought I never would again.

But with Ben? There had always been something missing. Something significant.

That flame.

The spark that lights you up inside when *the one* walks into the room. You know the one, the one you can't get off your mind, whether you've known him your entire life or he just barreled into it.

Was it wrong I craved someone like that for myself?

Maybe I'd be content with Ben if I'd never felt the flame before. If I'd never known what it was like to need and desire.

But I had. It'd been the kind of fire that had raged and consumed, burning through me until there was nothing left but ashes. I'd thought that love had ruined me, until Ben came in and swept me into his willing arms.

He'd taken care of me, a fact I didn't take lightly. I honored and respected it, the way Ben honored and respected me.

So maybe I never looked the same or felt the same after *he'd* destroyed something inside of me. But I'd survived and I forced myself to find satisfaction in that, willed it to make me stronger instead of feeble and frail.

I tossed a bottle of shampoo I really didn't need into my cart, but it smelled all kinds of good, like vanilla and the sweetest flower, and today I didn't feel like questioning my motives. In fact, I tossed in a body wash for good measure. I rarely treated myself, and I figured I deserved it. The last four years had been spent working my ass off, striving toward my elementary education degree at Arizona State University, and I'd finally landed my first real job a month ago.

Pride shimmered around my consciousness. Not the arrogant kind. I was just…happy. Happy for what I had achieved.

I bit the inside of my lip, doing my best to contain the ridiculous grin I felt pulling at my mouth.

Finally….*finally*…I'd attained something that was all on me.

Ben was always the one who took care of me. But he also had a bad habit of taking all the credit. Like my life would fall apart without him in it.

Slowly, I wound my way up toward the registers. I needed to get out of here before I drained what little I had in my checking account with all my *celebrating*.

I rolled my eyes at myself and squashed the mocking laughter that rolled up my throat.

Yep, livin' large and partying hard.

My life was about as exciting as Friday Night Bingo at the retirement home down the street.

But hey, at least my hair would smell good and my lips would taste even better.

Scanning the registers, I hunted for the shortest line, when my eyes locked on a face that was so familiar, but just out of reach of my recognition. Curiosity consumed me, and I found I couldn't look away.

She was standing at the front of her cart, her attention cast behind her. Obviously, searching for someone.

I stared, unabashed, craning my head to the side as I tried to place the striking green eyes and long black hair. She was gorgeous, enough to make any super model feel self-conscious, but she was wearing the kind of smile that spoke a thousand welcomes.

Two feet in front of her, I came to a standstill, which only caused her warm smile to spread when her gaze landed on me. My attention flitted to the empty infant car seat that was latched onto the basket before it darted back to her face. My stomach twisted into the tightest knot as recognition slammed me somewhere in my subconscious, my throat growing dry when her name formed in my head before it swelled on my tongue. "Aly Moore?" I managed, everything about the question timid and unsure. Well, I wasn't unsure it was her. There was no question, no doubt.

What I wasn't so sure about was if I should actually stop to talk to her. My heart was already beating a million miles a minute, like a stampeding warning crashing through my body, screaming at my limbs to go and go now.

Still, I couldn't move. Short gusts of sorrow were a feeling I was well-accustomed to, dealing with Stewart and all the sadness his illness brought into my life.

But this?

Pain constricted my chest, pressing and pulsing in, and I struggled to find my absent breath.

God, she looked just like *him*. I always did my best to keep him from my thoughts, all the memories of him buried deep, deep enough to pretend they'd forever been forgotten, when in reality, everything I'd ever shared with him was unrelentingly vivid.

Seeing her brought them all flooding back.

His face.

His touch.

I squeezed my eyes, trying to block them out, but they only flashed brighter.

God.

"Samantha Schultz." My name tumbled from her mouth as if it came with some kind of relief. She stretched out her hand, grasping mine. "Oh my gosh, I can't believe it's you. How are you?"

I hadn't seen her in years. Seven, to be exact. She was only two years younger than me, and she'd always been a sweet girl. Sweet *and* smart. Different in a good way, quiet and shy and bold at the same time. I'd always liked her, and some foolish part of me had believed she'd always be a part of my life. I guess I'd taken that for granted, too.

But that's what happens when you're young and naïve and believe in promises that turn out only to be given in vain.

I swallowed over the lump in my throat and forced myself to speak. "I've been good. It's so great to see you." It was all a lie wrapped up in the worst kind of truth.

I dropped my gaze, my eyes landing on the diamonds that glinted from her ring finger where she grasped my hand, and I caught just a peek of the intricate tattoo that was woven below it, like she'd etched a promise of forever into her skin.

A war of emotions spun trough me, and I wanted to fire off a million questions, the most blatant of them jerking my attention between the empty infant carrier and her ring. My mind tumbled through a roller coaster of memories as it did its best to catch up to the years that had passed.

"Oh my God…you're married? And you're a mom." I drew the words out as I finally added up the obvious, and a strange sense of satisfaction at seeing her grown up fell over me. It seemed almost silly, thinking of her that way, considering she was only two years younger than me. Now the years separating our ages didn't seem like such a big deal. Not the way they had then, when I'd thought of her as just a little girl, a hundred years and a thousand miles behind me. It seemed now she'd flown right past me.

With my words, everything about her glowed. She held up her hand to show me the ring I'd just been admiring, her voice soft with a reverent awe. "Can you believe it?" She laughed quietly. "Some days I can't believe it myself."

The joy filling her was so clear, and I chewed at my bottom lip, both welcoming the happiness I felt for her and fighting the jealousy that slipped just under the surface of my skin. Never would I wish any sorrow on her, or desire to steal her happiness away because I didn't have it myself. I wasn't vicious or cruel. But seeing her this way was a stark reminder of what I was missing.

Happiness.

I bit back the bitter feeling, searching for an excuse to get away, because I was finished feeling sorry for myself, when Aly's face transformed into the most radiant smile, her attention locked somewhere behind me. There was nothing I could do but follow her gaze. I looked over my shoulder.

All the surprise at finding Aly Moore amplified, spinning my head with shock when I saw who she was staring at.

Jared Holt strode toward us.

My knees went weak.

The grown man was completely covered in tattoos, every edge of him hard and rough. But none of the surprise I felt was caused by the way he looked, because I'd been there to watch his downward spiral. Part of me was surprised to see he was still alive.

He held an adorable, tiny baby girl protectively against his chest, the child facing out as they approached. She kicked her little legs when she caught sight of her mom.A soft smile pulled at his mouth and warmthflared in his eyes when they landed on Aly.

My heart did crazy, erratic things, and the small sound that worked up my throat was tortured. Someone was trying to pull a sick joke on me, dangling all the bits of my past right in front of my face.

It just had to be Jared.

No, he hadn't been responsible for any of the choices Christopher or I had made. Still, he'd been the catalyst that had driven the confusion.

The overwhelming feeling rushing over me was altogether cruel and welcomed at the same time, because God, how many times had I lain awake at night, unable to sleep because I was thinking of Christopher Moore, wondering where he was and who he'd become? And suddenly here was his world, our world, his sister and his best friend, the people who had been with us and were part of what defined that time—standing in front of me at Target with their little baby girl.

Aly must have sensed my panic. Again she reached out to squeeze my hand. "You remember Jared Holt, don't you?" She obviously knew I did. There was no missing the look that passed between the two of them, a secret conversation transpiring in a glance.

"Of course," I whispered hoarsely.

"Samantha," Jared said as a statement. He handed Aly the little tube of diaper rash ointment he must have gone in search of while she waited at the front of the store. He turned his attention right back to me. "God…it's been years. How are you?"

"Good," I forced out, wondering where in the hell that word even came from because right then, I was definitely not feeling *good.* I was feeling… I blinked and swallowed. I couldn't begin to put my finger on it except to say I was fundamentally disturbed, as if the axis balancing my safe little world had been altered. "How are you?"

The concern that involuntarily laced my tone was probably not needed, because he smiled at Aly as he situated his daughter a little higher up on his chest and kissed her on the top of her head.

"I'm perfect," he said through a rumbled chuckle.

Aly took a step forward and lightly tickled the tiny girl's foot.

The little black-haired, blue-eyed baby kicked more. Her mouth twisted up at just one side, as she was obviously just learning how to control her smile, and she rolled her head back in delight. She suddenly cooed, and her eyes went wide and she jerked as if she'd startled herself with the sound that escaped her.

Aly's voice turned sweet, the kind a mother reserved only for her child. "And this is our Ella…Ella Rose."

Ella Rose.

They'd named their daughter after Jared's mother.

Affection pulsed heavily through my veins as I looked on the three of them, so happy to see their joy. As strong as that emotion was, it wasn't enough to keep my own sadness at bay, and my mind reeled with the questions I wanted to ask about Christopher.

But those questions were dangerous. It wasn't that I didn't want to know. I *couldn't* know.

Instead, I reached out to let their baby girl grip my finger. I shook it a little, and that sweet smile took over her face again, this time directed at me as she tried to shove my finger in her mouth.

I just about melted. I was pretty sure this little girl had the power to single-handedly jumpstart my biological clock. "Well, hello there, Ella Rose. Aren't you the sweetest thing." I glanced up at Aly. "How old is she?"

"She just turned two-months yesterday," she answered. "It feels like she's growing so fast, but I already can't remember what it was like not to have her as a part of our lives. It's such a strange feeling."

My head shook with stunned disbelief. "All of this is crazy." I eyed them happily as some of the shock wore away, as if being in their space was completely natural. "The two of you ending up together."

Aly blushed, and Jared watched her as if she was the anchor that kept him tied to this world. Then he slanted his own mischievous grin my way. "Don't be too surprised, Sam. This girl was always meant for me."

Good God. How Aly wasn't a puddle in the middle of the floor, I didn't know. His words were enough to leave me all swoony and light-headed and they weren't even intended for me. And I wanted to laugh, because he'd always called me Sam, almost like a tease, a dig at his best friend Christopher, who refused to call me anything but Samantha.

It instantly took me back too many years, and I was there, feeling flickers of that flame that had been missing from my life for so long. But those kind of flames had burned me right into the ground. Those kind of flames hurt and scarred.

"So what about you?" Aly asked, stepping back. "What have you been up to? Do you live around here?"

"Yeah, I live with my boyfriend in the neighborhood right behind the shopping center."

"You're kidding me? We do too." She laughed at the coincidence. "We're neighbors."

Here we all were, standing in the same store in this huge city, miles away from where we'd all begun. I almost had the urge to look behind me, fully expecting to see Christopher sauntering toward us, an apparition sent to taunt me in a ruthless twist of fate.

"How is your little brother? I heard he was doing really well after your family moved across town."

After being thrown headfirst into all these tumultuous memories of Christopher, my walls were down, and this time I wasn't prepared for the sadness that sliced straight through me. I attempted to steady my voice. "He was in remission for five years, but the cancer just recently came back."

Aly sobered, and genuine sympathy edged the curve of her mouth. "Oh my God, I'm so sorry," she murmured, and it didn't hurt to hear her say it. Instead, I felt comforted.

"Me too," I agreed, shaking my head as a saddened smile twisted up my mouth. "He's the sweetest kid."Well, he wasn't so much a kid anymore. Really, he was almost a man, but it was hard to look at him that way when he was so frail. "I just keep praying for him, and I spend as much time with him as I can to keep his spirits up. He's been pretty sick with the treatments, so he hasn't been getting out of the house all that much lately. I couldn't imagine having to go through my junior year of high school on-line, but he doesn't complain."

Stewart was now seventeen, the youngest in our family. My brother, Sean, was two years younger than me, in the same grade as Aly had been, and my sister Stephanie was nineteen. My parents had us in quick succession, and had had some kind of overindulgent love fest with our names since theirs' were Sally and Stephen. It used to bother me when I was young.

Not anymore.

We'd been a normal, rambunctious family until Stewart had gotten sick when he was nine. When I met Christopher, Stewart had been at his worst. Well, at his worst...until now.

Ella released a shrill little cry, and squirmed in Jared's hold. Gently, he bounced her, shushing her in a soft whisper against her head. "I think someone is going to need their mommy soon." Soft affection flowed from Jared's laughter. "She goes from completely content to starving in five seconds flat."

"Oh, well I better let you two go," I offered, hating that it sounded almost reluctant. "It was really nice to see you again."

Aly hesitated, glancing at her husband, before she tipped her head and studied me with intent. "Would it be weird if we…I don't know…had coffee or something? I totally understand if you're not comfortable. I get it. But I'd love to really catch up with you if you're up for it. I could use a friend around here."

Maybe that's what I liked about her most. She just came right out and said it, gave voice to that huge elephant that was snuffing out all the air in the room. That and she was genuine and kind.

I refused to allow myself to believe I was agreeing because she was Christopher's sister.

"Yeah, I think I'd like that."

"Good."

She dug around in her huge bag for her phone, while Jared just stood their swaying Ella, his mouth seemingly pressed permanently to the side of her head as he showered her with small kisses.

Aly thumbed across the screen. "What's your number?"

I rattled it off while Aly entered it into her phone. Two seconds later, my phone dinged with a new message.

"There, you have my number, too."

This time, Ella's cry was a demand.

"We'd better get her home so I can feed her. I'll call you soon."

"That would be great."

She hugged me, only glancing back once as she followed Jared into a lane to pay.

I hurried to one of the express registers, all of a sudden feeling guilty, like I'd committed some sort of mortal sin by giving my number to a Moore.

Christopher had broken me, shattered my belief and trust. But more important than that, I had Ben to think about. Ben who had stood by my side. Ben, who even with all his faults, truly cared about me. He was my father's best friend's son, and basically we had grown up together. My parents had raised me with the impression that someone like Ben would be the right kind of guy for me, and with my demolished heart, it hadn't taken him all that much to convince me I belonged with him.

I paid and rushed outside. The blistering Phoenix summer was in full force. Suffocating heat pressed down from above, taking everything hostage, the evening sky heavy with dense clouds building steadily at the edge of the horizon.

My feet pounded on the scorching pavement as I made my way up the aisle to my Ford Escape.

Funny, that suddenly felt like exactly what I needed to do.

Escape.

Take this whole afternoon back.

Leave the classroom of the tiny private school where I'd taken a job as a teacher during their summer program, and instead of coming here gone straight to the small house I shared with Ben –where I was safe and memories of Christopher were buried and hidden in the hope that one day they would finally be forgotten.

I slumped into the driver's seat, my gaze drawn to the little family that came bustling out of the store.

My heart rattled in my chest.

"Shit," I cursed, gripping the wheel. "What am I doing?"

The sick part was I knew the answer to that.

Chapter Two
Christopher

Outside the bedroom door, the party raged on. Timothy's house was splitting at the seams, the way it always was on a Friday night. Music blared, and voices lifted above it, echoing through the thin walls. Distorted sounds pounded heavily against my skin, my eyesight hazy in the deep shadows of the darkened room.

I felt completely weightless and somehow still pinned down by the pungent fog clouding my brain.

Every elemental part of me slowly became detached. Floated away. All of my emotions. All of my thoughts. It was like they hovered somewhere overhead, just out of reach. My entire consciousness faded away, right along with my conscience, leaving me with nothing but the physical.

It's what I craved. Needed. The relief of feeling nothin' but skin on skin.

Even though some part of me hated it at the same time.

Slouched back on the worn out couch in the spare bedroom, I lifted the half-drained bottle of Patron to my lips, idly watching the dull mop of brown hair obstructing the face of the girl who was on her knees, sucking me off.

The only thing I could discern was the pleasure of her hot, needy mouth and the burn of tequila as it roared through my system to settle in a scorching pool in my gut.

She looked up from under her thick veil of hair, brown eyes wide as they searched for a connection, but instead met with the apathy in mine.

That was the fucking problem. I was on disconnect.

That plug had been pulled a long time ago.

Never would I allow someone to have that kind of control over me.

Not like *she* had.

Not ever again.

####

Monday morning, I rolled up in front of Jared and Aly's house at the ass-crack of dawn. I squinted against the bright rays of light burning my eyes as the sun climbed over the horizon, chasing the last of the night from the sky.

I cut the ignition and jumped from the cooled cab of my truck. Heat swallowed me whole. You'd think at 5:30 in the morning we'd get a little reprieve. No such luck. Summers in Phoenix were fucking misery.

That didn't stop the eager smile that tugged at my mouth as I ambled up their walkway.

So what if I had to leave my man card at the door every time I walked through Jared and Aly's door. Call me a pussy, I didn't care.My niece had me wrapped around every single one of her tiny fingers.

I rang the doorbell and rushed my hand through my hair, listening for movement inside. A shadow passed behind the draped window, before metal slid as the lock was unlatched. My sister grinned at me when she opened the door.

"Christopher, aren't you looking chipper this beautiful morning," Aly teased as she lifted a knowing brow, stepping back to let me inside.

So yeah, I'm sure I looked like hell. Both Friday and Saturday nights, I'd been over at Timothy's house, *living* it up. Funny how all that *living* made me feel like death warmed over. Every weekend left me just a little more hollowed out. I was pretty sure I was slowly killing myself, week by week losing just a little more of who I was, carving away more and more of what had been important to me.

Pretty soon there would be nothing left.

But there was no way to get any of it back.

Ancient history bullshit, anyway.

I shoved all the unwelcome thoughts off, rolled my eyes as I ruffled Aly's messy hair. "Yeah, yeah, yeah. You don't have a whole lot of room to talk there, Aly Cat. You look like you got about as much sleep this weekend as I did. Livin' up to your name?"

Dark bags sat heavily under her green eyes, and her near-black hair was all tangled. She was wearing an old stained up t-shirt that had to be Jared's because the girl was swimming in it. Still, my sister was beautiful. Inside and out. No wonder my dumb ass best friend couldn't keep his hands off of her.

She groaned a little, but somehow the sound was filled with pure affection. "Ella decided she was hungry every twenty minutes last night. I have no clue how I even got out of bed this morning. I feel like a walking zombie."

Jared suddenly appeared behind her, wrapping his arms around her waist as he tugged her against his chest. He buried his face somewhere in her neck. "Apparently Ella likes her mommy as much as I do."

I'd just about lost my goddamned mind when I found out these two were hooking up. Not because I didn't like Jared. He'd been my best friend since I was a little kid. Sure, we'd fought like brothers, messed with each other until one of us was crying, but bottom line, we were thicker than blood. Brothers. We were always the first to have the other's back.

Until the day Jared caused that car accident. The one that stole his mother's life. That accident had stolen my best friend, too.

An old kind of pain hit me, and my chest tightened. That car accident had stolen everything. Changed everything. None of us had come out looking the same.

Afterward, the guy had fucked away his life, landed himself in juvie then disappeared for years. I never expected to see him again. When he showed up here last summer, there was no question he was still haunted. I recognized it immediately, because I recognized the same bullshit in myself.

Then he'd gone and taken a liking to my little sister, and all hell broke loose. He and I were too much alike, and I wasn't about to let him bring my sister down. She deserved so much better than that.

Of course the guy had proven me wrong in every way. He loved her. Wholly and completely. Loved her in a way that girls like Aly deserved, with respect and care and devotion.

How could I stand in the way of that?

Didn't mean it didn't make me a little sick to my stomach. I took it upon myself to razz the asshole every chance I got. "Watch yourself, man, no matter which way you cut it, that's still my little sister."

He nuzzled her more, this time lifting his gaze to meet mine, the mischief in his blue eyes meeting the challenge. "And no matter which way you cut it, she's still my wife. This girl belongs to me."

Aly grinned wildly and leaned back into his hold.

My chest tightened more, because it made me happy to see her this way. Happy she got to have this. Not many of us did. Love like that didn't come around often and she'd snatched it up when she saw it, even when it'd seemed dangerous and impossible. But she knew it was worth it.

I'd been the fool who'd let that kind of crazy love go. Didn't matter that I'd been just a stupid punk kid, barely sixteen, or that we were nothing alike and the entire world was against us.

None of it mattered. Not at fucking all. The only thing that mattered was it'd been real.

Cringing, I put a cap on those thoughts, because I wasn't about to go there. Stupid shit that I couldn't deal with. Nor did I want to. All it did was leave me feeling pissy and sorry for myself, scorned by a girl I'd always thought would be mine.

Leaving Aly and Jared all wrapped up in each other, I headed for Ella who was lying on her back on the cushioned play area Aly had set up for her in the family room between their huge ass overstuffed couch and the fireplace.

"There's my girl," I sang as I wound around the couch and knelt down in front of her. Her blue eyes were all bugged-out as she watched the lights flashing on the infant play gym set up over her. Five brightly colored stuffed animals hung down from it, teasing her. She didn't come close to being able to touch them. Yet she had her tiny hands all balled up in fists, her arms flailing and her legs kicking as she stared, fixated, making it clear how badly she wanted to reach out and touch one.

A tiny sound escaped her pursed lips and my heart throbbed a wayward beat.

Yep, man card at the door.

This little girl owned me.

"Don't worry, angel…give it a few weeks, and that monkey is yours," I promised as I bent down and maneuvered her from under the play gym and into my arms.

"Come give Uncle kisses before your daddy drags me off to a grueling day of work."

"Grueling my ass," Jared shot from the other side of the room. "You're in the air conditioned office while me and the guys are out doing the grunt work. I'd say you have it pretty easy there, my friend."

Laughing it off because what he said was nothing but true, I brought Ella's face close to mine. She offered me one of those little grins that I felt right in the center of my chest. She reached out, her nails digging into my bottom lip as she grabbed for me. I kissed them. "You take care of your mommy while we're gone."

"She always does," Aly said, watching us with a soft smile on her face. Something shifted in her expression, and she bit at her lip and quickly turned her face to the floor.

I felt the frown crease my forehead. I knew my sister pretty damned well, and that meant I was pretty damned sure she was holding something back. "What?" I asked, my eyes narrowing as I pinned her with a stare.

She lifted her head, blinked, looked away. "Nothing."

At the same second, Jared tensed up a little, like he knew exactly what was running through Aly's mind.

Nothing my ass.

My frown deepened. "Nothing?" I challenged, my brow rising.

Aly shook her head and looked almost repentant. Unease slowly snaked its way through my senses. My gaze darted between the two of them. Something was up. Something they didn't want me to know. A silent tension filled the room.

"Nothing," she reaffirmed in what I knew was a lie. "I just…" She shrugged. "Seeing you with Ella like that makes me happy."

"Come on, man, we need to get a move on," Jared cut in, obviously putting an end to my questioning. He walked to the kitchen island and grabbed the small cooler he kept stocked with food, water, and sodas. "It's going to be a busy day and an even busier week. You may just find yourself on the job. Then I'll let you complain about work being grueling." He tossed me a mocking wink, then sauntered up behind Aly, hugging her as he whispered something in her ear.

Below her breath, she laughed and nodded her head.

Three months ago, my brother-in-law aka best friend who bagged my little sister, had somehow managed to persuade me into starting a new venture with him. I went straight from a lazy college student, one who gave little thought to what he was going to do with his life after he graduated—because the truth was, he really didn't give a shit—to business owner in the matter of weeks.

I mean, fuck, me being part-owner in the remodeling business with Jared and our other partner, Kenny? All signs pointed at a no-go. I wasn't exactly what most would consider the ambitious type. But somehow Jared convinced me to team up with him, said he didn't want to do it without me. Jared and Kenny had fronted the money, and now I was doing my all to live up to it. Turned out I was pretty damned good at, too, basically running all the business shit that didn't deal with the hard labor, all of the accounting and paperwork that needed to be dealt with in the office, although the company was growing so fast there'd been a couple of times Jared had hauled me out on a job when he was short-handed. It was crazy going from scrimping every month to having more money in my bank account than I knew what to do with. I wasn't loaded by any means, but it sure felt nice not to have to check my bank balance any time I wanted to buy something.

Truth was, I liked having a reason to drag my ass out of bed in the morning. And I had two. The other one cooed, grabbing my attention. I kissed Ella at the corner of her mouth. "Stay sweet, little one."

I passed her off to Aly and followed Jared out the door and into the approaching day. Jared climbed into the passenger seat of my truck.

Each week, we traded off driving. We figured after I moved into my new place a couple miles away, there was no reason for both of us to hike it across town separately since Jared checked in at the office every morning before he headed out to the job sites in a work truck.

After Aly moved out, the apartment we had shared near the U of A campus had felt all wrong. Lonely. I knew it was time to make a change. Plus being so near to them gave me an excuse to stop by all the time so I could hang out with Ella.

I glanced across at Jared as I hopped into the driver's seat of my brand new truck, the leather already heating up with the rising sun that blazed through the window. He smirked at me, lifted his chin. Guess it wasn't so bad hanging out with him, either. Honestly, it'd been good watching him come back to life, overcoming the darkness that had plagued him since his mother's death.

A flash of resentment twisted through me, and I quickly tamped it down. I didn't blame him. Couldn't. He'd been through more than I could ever imagine. What had happened wasn't his fault. I'd made those mistakes all on my own.

I started the truck and shifted into gear. "So what was that back there?" I asked.

His face lifted in a clueless expression. "Don't know what you're talking about."

I cut my eye toward him, watching the little twitch of his jaw when he gritted his teeth. He averted his gaze to his tablet and clicked into his schedule, asshole acting like he was all too busy to look my way.

Right.

He knew exactly what I was talking about.

And whatever it was, I wasn't really sure I wanted to know.

about the author

A.L. Jackson is the New York Times Bestselling Author of *Take This Regret* and *Lost to You*, as well as other contemporary romance titles, including *Pulled, When We Collide, If Forever Comes, Come to Me Quietly, and Come to Me Softly.*

She first found a love for writing during her days as a young mother and college student. She filled the journals she carried with short stories and poems used as an emotional outlet for the difficulties and joys she found in day-to-day life.

Years later, she shared a short story she'd been working on with her two closest friends and, with their encouragement, this story became her first full length novel. A.L. now spends her days writing in Southern Arizona where she lives with her husband and three children.

Connect with A.L. Jackson online:

www.aljacksonauthor.com
www.facebook.com/aljacksonauthor
www.twitter.com/aljacksonauthor
Instagram: @aljacksonauthor
Newsletter http://bit.ly/ALJacksonNewsletter
For quick mobile updates, text "jackson" to 96000

Made in the USA
Lexington, KY
17 May 2015